DEFENDER CHIMERA

DEFENDER CHIMERA

PROTECTION, INC: DEFENDERS #4

ZOE CHANT

CHAPTER 1

Fen lay handcuffed and seething on the floor, face to face with her business rival and enemy, the brilliant and arrogant Carter Howe.

When she'd been ambushed, given some knockout drug, and tossed into the cargo bay of an airplane bound for who knows where, she'd been frightened but not panicked. It had been obvious what was going on, given that she owned one of the three top tech companies in America: she was being held for ransom. It was horrible and scary and she could lose a whole lot of money if the cops weren't on their game, but it wasn't as if her life was in danger. The criminals would get nothing if they killed her.

Then a handcuffed man had been tossed in with her. When he'd woken up and she'd seen his face, her fear had transmuted into incandescent rage.

"You!" Carter Howe exclaimed, like he was genuinely surprised. The *nerve* of him!

"You!" Fen snarled. She would have liked to add some choice insults, but she was so furious that it rendered her speechless.

"Fenella Kim!" Carter spoke if he was uttering the name of some famous villainess, like Cruella De Vil or Maleficent.

"Carter Howe!" Fen was thinking of Voldemort and Darth Vader.

It was the first time she'd encountered him in person, but he'd been a thorn in her side for years. It wasn't just that he owned one of the other three top tech companies in America, and so was her natural rival; it was *him*, specifically.

Her mind skipped and skittered over flashes of the Carter Howe Experience, like the world's most annoying highlights (or rather low-lights) video. Carter's arrogant emails when he'd attempted a hostile takeover of her company. Carter's famous face smirking from the cover of *Wired* magazine. Carter's famous face smirking all over the news when he'd mysteriously disappeared. Carter's famous face smirking all over the news *again* when he'd mysteriously reappeared a year later. Carter's hypocritically outraged emails when she'd attempted a hostile takeover of his company in revenge.

And here was Carter's famous face, in the actual flesh, mere inches away from her after he'd had her *kidnapped!*

"You!" Fen repeated, summing it all up. "I might've known it would be *you!*"

"Me?" Carter protested. "What did I do?"

"Don't pretend you don't know what I'm talking about when I'm lying here handcuffed. This is some plot of yours!"

"Not unless I'm plotting against myself too," Carter pointed out. "In case you haven't noticed, I'm also handcuffed. Not to mention footcuffed. And lying on a cold hard floor with a splitting headache and my coat getting all creased."

"I noticed," Fen snarled. "You do look a mess."

She'd been so shocked and furious at the sight of him that she hadn't processed the implications. She needed to take a step back—a metaphorical step, given that she was tied up on the floor—and get her brain into gear.

Focus, she told herself.

It was so annoying that after all these years and all her practice, she still hadn't focused on the relevant details automatically, or even automatically reminded herself to do it. That was probably why she'd gotten kidnapped in the first place. If she'd been paying attention when she'd run out to grab a quick coffee—

She was losing track of things again.

Focus.

She took a deep breath, concentrating on her lungs and chest expanding. Though her chest couldn't fully expand in the cramped position she was in, and the cold floor was so uncomfortable and the footcuffs (was that a real word?) were especially cold and—

Focus, she reminded herself. *What can you touch?*

That was unusually difficult. She could only touch her own hands, and it was weird to try to focus on touching when she was also being touched.

Good enough, she decided. *Now, observe.*

She'd already observed her surroundings to death. She was in a big empty cargo space with glaring white lights, she felt a vibration and heard a low thrum that meant she was on an airplane, and she smelled harsh chemicals and metal. Now it was time to observe the thorn in her side, the pebble in her shoe, the oh so famous and brilliant Carter Howe.

She'd seen him so often in photos and video, it was strange to observe him in person. And even if she'd seen him in person before, it would presumably have been standing up or sitting down, not lying on the floor with his ankles cuffed together and his hands cuffed behind his back and his black hair mussed and dusty.

He was taller than she'd realized. Her practiced eye, used to measuring lengths and widths, estimated that he'd be 6'2" straightened out and without shoes, give or take a half inch or so. Broad shoulders. His white shirt was pulled tight by the handcuffs, showing a more muscular chest than she'd noticed in pictures. He must have a personal trainer and high-tech workout gear, which also explained his shoulders. And his forearms. And (his pants were pulled very tight too, that had to be uncomfortable) his thighs and a distinctly impressive—

Fen yanked her observation away from that. She did not want to be thinking about her enemy's dick. Gross. At least, it ought to be gross.

Ugh, she told herself firmly. *Gross.*

Desperately trying to drag her attention away from his body, she decided to focus on his clothes. Carter was always immaculately dressed, which was something Fen noticed because she was too. She'd spent some time before he'd arrived seething over the wreck the kidnappers had made of her suit and shoes by dumping her on a dirty floor. His clothes and shoes were as expensive and well-chosen as hers, and in just as much of a mess. His shoes, of fine Italian leather, were scuffed. His white linen shirt was rumpled and stained with engine oil. His signature long black coat was dusty and scrunched beneath him.

He was a mess. The kidnappers must have hit him over the head rather than drugging him. Dried blood was smeared over one side of his face and had glued some of his hair together. A bruise spread across his temple. None of that looked fake.

Fen ruthlessly crushed the sympathy that had flickered up at the sight of his injuries. Instead, she focused on his face. His features were more rugged than really worked with his image: his chin too strong, his mouth too wide, his eyes too deep-set. He was supposed to be a billionaire genius playboy, but his face suggested something tough and strong beneath the glamour.

She kept coming back to his eyes. She'd never been able to identify their color in photos and video. Close up and in real life, she could see that they were hazel, which never photographs well. His were a particularly attractive shade, a blend of deep green and rich brown, like a pool of clear water in an ancient forest. His lashes were thick and black, as were his eyebrows. She'd always suspected him of wearing very subtle mascara and eyeliner based on how amazing his eyes looked in photos and video, but now she realized with annoyance that he just had the world's greatest eyelashes.

He *definitely* manicured his eyebrows, though. No one's were that perfect without help.

She took a deep breath, and that one wasn't to force herself to focus. Her arrogant enemy Carter Howe was the best-smelling thing on the plane. Of course he was, he could afford the absolute best cologne and soap, but he also seemed to naturally smell good, or else he'd invented an incredibly realistic cologne named something like *Eau de Sexy…*

Focus.

He had the strangest expression on his face. He'd looked annoyed before, but now he looked like he too was deeply focused, intent, almost enraptured…

With a start, she realized that he was observing her right back. She wondered what information he'd gleaned from her.

"Well?" Carter demanded. "Satisfied that I didn't kidnap myself?"

Reluctantly, she came to the conclusion that he hadn't. She couldn't imagine him deliberately damaging his carefully maintained body, let alone his expensive clothes. Nor did she think he'd allow himself to appear in such an unflattering position next to her. Or that he was a good enough actor to fake that level of irritation.

But she couldn't resist saying, "Maybe you set it up so I'd trauma-bond with you and tell you business secrets."

He gave a disgusted snort. "If I wanted your business secrets, I'd take over your company, not kidnap us both and cross my fingers you'd draw me some blueprints with your hands cuffed."

"You already tried to take over Little Bit," she retorted. "And you failed. Maybe this is your desperate last resort to destroy me."

"Why would I do something as ridiculous as stage a kidnapping when I could destroy you the traditional way, by making sure Howe Enterprises has better products?"

"Because you can't. I make sure Little Bit has better products," she retorted. "Maybe you wanted me to disappear for a while and then return with a wild story, so my company looks unstable and our stock prices plunge and our investors drop us and invest with you."

"Right." He sounded almost… hurt. "A disappearance followed by a wild story followed by people investing elsewhere. Definitely sounds like something I'd do to you. Oh wait, *I* was the one who disappeared and returned a year later with a wild story, and *your* company was the one that benefited. Maybe I should suspect you of staging that. God knows everyone thought I faked it for publicity."

She felt abashed, though there was no reason for her to. It was true that she and her company Little Bit, along with the third big tech company, TicTech and its CEO Eldon McManus, had profited from Howe Enterprises nearly imploding in chaos and legal trouble after Carter had vanished. But she'd had nothing to do with Howe Enterprises' misfortunes.

And Carter's explanation of what had happened, when he'd finally reappeared, had been absolutely ridiculous. *Sure* he'd been flying alone and crashed his small plane in the ocean and had been stranded on a tiny island for a year, living on fish and coconuts without even a volleyball for company. No one had believed it.

But the photos and video after he'd come back hadn't suggested a publicity stunt. The smirk was gone. He'd lost weight, which made sense if you believed in the fish and coconuts, and he'd looked haggard. Even haunted. She hadn't believed the tropical island story, but it was obvious that it was a cover for something real. She'd assumed he'd either been in rehab for some kind of addiction or in treatment for a serious illness that he hadn't wanted to make public.

Even now, he looked haunted just talking about it.

"I never thought you faked it for publicity," she said. "I know *something* bad happened."

His face seemed to freeze over, leaving him completely expressionless. In an equally guarded voice, he said, "Roll over so your back is to me."

"You can say, 'I don't want to talk about it.' You don't need to order me to do random things to change the subject."

"I wasn't changing the subject," he snapped. "Seriously, roll over."

"Why? What don't you want me to see?"

"Do you always jump to the worst possible conclusion?" he demanded.

Forbearing to point out that she'd *just said* she didn't believe that he'd vanished as a publicity stunt, she retorted, "When it comes to you."

Carter heaved a put-upon sigh, then rolled over himself, showing her his back and cuffed hands. A very nice back, she couldn't help noticing. Very muscular. The back was an underrated part of the body. So many sexy parts to it. The narrow groove of the spine, for instance. If it hadn't belonged to Carter Howe, she'd have wanted to run her finger along it. If she hadn't been handcuffed, it would have been a temptation she'd have struggled to resist.

"See what I'm holding?" he asked.

She yanked her attention to his hands. He held something shiny and delicate and metallic.

"Hairpins?" she asked.

He lowered his voice, even though they were alone in the chilly cargo hold and the roar of the engine would make it impossible for anyone outside to hear them. "Lockpicks. I had them concealed in a hidden seam in my pants."

Her voice rose in exasperation. "You've had lockpicks this entire time, and you lay here chit-chatting instead of using them?"

Aggravated, he said, "I've been trying to get them out this entire time. My hands are cuffed behind my back, remember? Now roll over so your hands are next to mine, and I'll get your cuffs off."

"Can you really do that?"

He snorted. "No, I carry them solely as a treasured keepsake."

"I really hope you're being sarcastic."

"Of course I can use them," he snapped. "Now roll over, unless you like lying on a freezing cold floor with your shoulders pulled halfway out of their sockets."

She did not. Fen rolled over, which was not at all comfortable while handcuffed, wriggled closer to him, then writhed down until their hands were level. At least his back was turned too, so he wouldn't see her squirming on the floor like an earthworm.

She stopped when their hands touched. It was remarkable how much you could observe by feel alone. His hands were big, with his nails cut short and nicely buffed. She could feel the shapes of calluses and a few little scars, but like his nails, his hands were well cared-for. No rough edges. His movements felt practiced and competent as he manipulated the tiny lockpicks.

"How'd you learn to do this?" she asked.

"My teammate—I mean, an associate of mine—taught me. Merlin said to think of it as playing Jenga with a stack of very fragile, very expensive, blown glass vases."

The image of Carter doing exactly that leaped into her mind. The vases in her mental image had big bright flowers on them, like a stained glass window, and he handled them with almost sensual delicacy.

Her mind bounced away from that image, jumping to the luxuriant sensation of the heat of his hands. The airplane was cold, and her hands especially had been freezing. Carter's hands were deliciously warm. *Carter* was deliciously warm. They were close enough that she could bask in his body heat even without directly touching. If his clothes were off, it would be even better…

Stop it, she scolded herself. *He's your enemy. Imagining him naked is gross.*

Her treacherous mind responded with a detailed and vivid image of Carter naked. It was annoyingly not gross.

"Does it distract you to talk?" she asked, though it was obvious that unlike her, he had no trouble focusing. But it was the first thing that came to her mind to get it off the Carter-feels-so-good and Carter-would-look-so-good track.

"No, it's fine," he said.

Of course it's fine. Everything comes easily to the great Carter Howe.

She gritted her teeth, torn between bitterness at that thought, general aggravation with him, guilt for being aggravated with him when he was trying to rescue her, hope that they really would be rescued, and frustration with her own uncooperative mind. Why did she have to work so hard to do normal things like paying attention?

"How did you get here?" Carter asked.

As if he didn't know! Her fists clenched involuntarily, making the cuffs jerk. His hands twitched, clutching at the picks.

"I got a call from your office," she said. "Y
with me to discuss my hostile takeover of How
you didn't get one, the next call would be from

"*I* didn't say anything," he retorted. "You got
claiming to be from my office. For the record,
from your office, saying the exact same thing. A
Little Bit isn't going to get its little paws on my

"Just you wait," she said automatically, but th
as her hands relaxed. Begrudgingly, she said, "I
Given that you're handcuffed too. I went to get so
call, and someone jumped me. They stuck a clot
smelled like chemicals. It was some knockout dru
What about you?"

"Very similar. I left a—" He broke off abruptly.

"Yes?" Fen inquired when he didn't continue. "Yo
ant meeting? A bomb threat? Six naked supermodels

She couldn't see his face, but she could *feel* him ro
barbecue with my team— I left a barbecue. After get
from your office. I got jumped too. And here I am."

"Here we are," she corrected him. "Well, it's obvious v

"Yes," he said grimly. "It is."

She was relieved that they were finally on the same
we have something in common after all: we're both wor
for ransom. Maybe you shouldn't break us loose. We're
not dead. But they're probably armed. If we surprise ther
shoot us by accident."

Her handcuffs hit the floor with a clink. Fen sat up, flexi
and torn between relief and dismay. "Guess that ship has s

"You can put your cuffs back on, if you like." He was alrea
away at his own. It was fascinating to watch him pick t
his own cuffs entirely by feel. His movements were even
surer than when he'd worked on hers, as if he'd practiced for
situation.

ht, even discussing being cautious isn't manly. But getting our-
killed for no reason is a great idea."

handcuffs came open. Carter sat up and rotated his shoulders
eck. They popped audibly. He scowled at her. "That's not what
ook, there's more going on than you know."

ke what?"

ignored her and bent over his footcuffs. Ankle cuffs? They should
ther handcuffs and footcuffs, or wrist cuffs and ankle cuffs. It
e no sense for one set to be named for the body parts they covered,
the other set to be named for the body parts they were restraining.
lish was such a weird language. Not that Korean was any less weird,
r as she could tell. She wondered what cuffs were called in Korean.
could ask her father. If she wanted to speak to her father, which
didn't.

en dragged her attention back to the conversation, hoping she
dn't missed Carter saying something. "What's going on that I don't
ow about?"

From his response, either she had missed something or he was being
structive and unhelpful on purpose. He glanced up, glared at her,
d said, "Fine, have it your way. You sit here and I'll go deal with the
dnappers."

She ground her teeth. "You're talking as if I decided to get myself
idnapped. It's not stupid to want to think before we act."

As soon as the words were out of her mouth, her father's voice echoed
n her mind, as loud and clear as if he was in the cargo bay with her:
"Do you ever *think before you act, Fenella?"* And then her mother's, less
oud but equally clear: *"Dear, don't expect* thought *from Fenella. She's
like a feather in the wind."*

Fen fixed her gaze on Carter, summoning the *look* that made men
quail, daring him to scorn and sneer. But he didn't. His jaw was
clenched as if he was grinding his teeth too. But she had the oddest
sense that he wasn't frustrated with her, but rather with himself.

"I am thinking. I think..." He paused, then spoke as if the words

were dragged out of him by force. "...you have a point. Confronting an unknown number of kidnappers with unknown weapons is dangerous. But I wouldn't worry about guns specifically. We're on an airplane. They won't risk depressurizing it."

"Great. I'd only worried about getting shot. Now I'm worried about getting depressurized, too."

Now she could actually hear him grinding his teeth. She wondered if he slept with a mouthguard, like she did. Her dentist had said lots of people in high-pressure jobs used them.

He rapidly unlocked his footcuffs or ankle cuffs or whatever was trapping his feet, then stood up, stretched, and dusted off his long black coat. There were stains and greasy streaks on it; he looked pained when his fingers encountered them. Along with a lot of dust, bright blue hairs drifted to the floor.

"Got a blue cat?" Fen inquired.

Carter seemed bizarrely unnerved by her silly joke. "No! No cat, blue or otherwise. I don't have pets. I'm too busy for pets. I have a job, you know."

"Okay." She barely stopped herself from adding, *you weirdo.*

"The kidnappers must've dumped me on a blue carpet at some point. They're not hairs. They're fiber strands." He stared deeply into her eyes, as if willing her to believe. What was *up* with him?

And then she realized, and felt stupid for not getting it sooner. He was scared. He was determined to confront the kidnappers because he was afraid of what might happen if he didn't. And he was fixating on random stuff like carpet fibers because, unlike their actual reality, that was safe and comforting.

For the second time since seeing his injuries, she sympathized with him. She was afraid of startling their kidnappers into accidentally harming them, and he was afraid of leaving them alone in case harm was their plan. They didn't agree on what the danger was or how to face it, but they felt the same fear.

"Okay." This time she didn't say it sarcastically.

Carter didn't seem to register that she'd said anything at all. He was patting down his coat and pants in very specific places and muttering to himself. "Took my gun, took my cell phone, took my beacon, took my wallet, took my flashlight. Didn't find my lockpicks, didn't find my mini-wrench, didn't find my spare credit card."

"They took my purse too. Hey, you carry a gun?"

"This sort of thing is always a possibility, in our position," he pointed out.

She hated to admit that he was right. She had security at her company and an alarm system at her house, but she'd never carried a weapon or used a bodyguard. When was the last time anyone famous had been kidnapped for ransom in America? It wasn't a thing that happened here.

Except, of course, it had.

He looked down at her. "Do you want me to take off your footcuffs or replace your handcuffs?"

In other words, did she want to sit here like a lump while he launched into his probably futile and possibly suicidal attack, or did she want to join in and probably get hurt at the very least but possibly help it succeed? She wanted to trash his expensive signature coat some more for making her make that decision.

"Do you have an actual plan?" Fen asked.

To her surprise, he gave a confident nod. Indicating the door, he said, "I'll pick that lock, jump the kidnappers, tie them up, fly the plane, use its radio to figure out where the hell we are, and land at the nearest airport."

"Something goes between 'jump the kidnappers' and 'tie them up,' doesn't it? What are you, a one-man army?"

Loftily, he said, "I'll have you know that I've studied the practical type of fighting arts for years."

"Great," she sighed. "You do think you're a one-man army. Okay, fine. Uncuff me. I'll… shove them or something."

Carter had knelt beside her ankles, lockpicks at the ready, the instant she'd given him the go-ahead. But when she finished speaking, he looked up, startled. "What? No, you're not coming with me."

"Then why are you unlocking me?"

"To give you a chance to escape if my plan doesn't work out? So your feet won't get cramped?" Her whatever-they-were-called cuffs fell to the floor.

She scrambled up, wincing at the pins-and-needles stinging that made her wobble on her stiletto heels. "Look, we don't know how many of them there are. I don't know kung fu, but I'm willing to hit them with any loose object I see."

"Absolutely not. You'll get in the way. And be a distraction. What if one of them holds a gun to your head and tells me to surrender? We'll all be better off if you stay here."

"Like a piece of luggage," Fen muttered, but couldn't argue with his reasoning. "Okay, fine. I'll wait by the door to catch you if they toss you back in."

"You do that."

Carter strode to the door, his long coat flaring dramatically behind him. It swirled around his ankles when he stopped, making him look like some dashing action hero. She had to admit, her enemy knew how to dress.

She hoped he also knew how to fight.

CHAPTER 2

Fenella Kim stood beside Carter at the cargo bay door, staring at him like he was a lunatic. She'd been doing a lot of that ever since they'd woken up and seen each other, and he couldn't exactly blame her.

He'd often imagined his first in-person meeting with her. Sometimes he'd pictured it in a courtroom where they were suing each other. Occasionally he'd envisioned them accidentally running into each other on the street. Mostly he'd figured they'd eventually be forced to have an in-person meeting in some huge boardroom, with a phalanx of lawyers and business associates on each side. Given that she was in process of attempting a hostile takeover of his company, he'd expected that meeting to happen sometime soon.

Clearly, his imagination had been insufficient. It had never once occurred to him that he'd get hit over the head and wake up on an airplane, hands cuffed behind his back and getting flown to God knows where, and discover that the woman handcuffed on the floor beside him was an angry and disheveled Fenella Kim.

And yet, there they were.

He probably could have averted some of the "you lunatic" stares if he could have explained what was really going on. But it wasn't as if he could have said, "I'm a shifter, born with the ability to turn into a snow leopard. When I disappeared and then reappeared and said I'd been stuck on a desert island, I'd actually been kidnapped and experimented on by a black ops agency called Apex. They killed my snow leopard and turned me into a monster. There's some very bad people out there who'd love to use me or experiment on me. This kidnapping isn't about ransom. In fact, it isn't about you at all. I'm the target and you somehow got swept up with me."

He could have said that. He even could have proved it—the shifter part, anyway.

But he'd never let anyone see him shift once he'd escaped from Apex. As far as he was concerned, no one ever would. And if he ever was forced to reveal his new and very much unimproved shift form, it sure as hell wouldn't be to that thorn in his side, that Lego under his bare foot, the gorgeous genius businesswoman Fenella Kim.

"Are you sure you don't want me to go with you?" she whispered.

She was standing very close to him, and he could once again breathe in her scent. With her stiletto heels and black-and-white business suit and razor-edged, asymmetrical haircut, he'd have expected her to wear an expensive modern perfume with some jarring note like asphalt or sea brine. But it was light and ethereal and floral: old-fashioned water of violets.

Like so much about her, it was unexpected. Her voice was surprisingly easy on the ears when it wasn't echoing across phone lines, sharp with hostility or icy politeness. Photographs and video emphasized her delicate bone structure, so he'd always thought she was tiny, but though she was slim, she wasn't short. She had no idea what had really happened to him, but she'd never thought he'd rigged his own disappearance as a publicity stunt.

"You don't have to do this by yourself," she said.

And there was more unexpectedness. She had no idea how to fight and believed that it was safer not to, not to mention that she hated him, but she'd twice now offered to put herself in danger so he wouldn't have to go alone.

Fenella lifted one hand. Her hands were beautifully formed, with slim fingers and nails that provided the only color in her black-and-white aesthetic. No cliché blood-red or feminine pink or 2edgy4U blue for Fenella Kim: her fingernails were glossy pewter, unexpected and striking. Like everything else about her, her nail polish was precisely calculated, cleverly chosen, and designed to impress.

"Carter?" She laid her hand on his arm.

Her touch sent a jolt of cold fear through him. He was a valuable prize, but their kidnappers had no interest in her. She was disposable. He couldn't risk it.

Still, he hesitated. Though he knew what he had to do, he couldn't stop looking at her. Her expertly applied makeup was smudged, but that didn't make her any less beautiful. There was a bruise along her cheekbone where one of their captors must have roughly tossed her to the floor. She was a shark in heels in the boardroom, but she would have been unconscious then. Totally helpless. And they'd hurt her.

The ravening horde of his inner monsters didn't like that any better than Carter did, and started ranting and howling inside his head.

Kill them, growled one of his monsters.

Rip out their throats with our teeth, came a snarl that reminded Carter achingly of his lost snow leopard.

Kill, kill, kill, screeched a monster.

Blood-red pulsed across his inner eye as the monster who communicated only in colors conveyed its fury.

Carter's heart agreed with them, but his mind warned him to be cautious. He was unarmed. He was undoubtedly outnumbered. Unlike the other people Apex had experimented on, he didn't have any special powers. He could shift, but…

Yes shift!

Rip them to bits with our claws!

Our fangs!

Our talons!

[eager electric blue]

[bloodthirsty scarlet]

Shut up! Carter silently screamed at them. *I'd rather die than have Fenella Kim find out that I'm a monster!*

His inner monsters raged and howled and shrieked their defiance. Fenella was again staring at him like he was a lunatic. If he couldn't get the monsters to lay off, he wouldn't even be able to hear her if she said something.

Want to cooperate and let one *of you out, so I have a shot at turning into an actual animal instead of a grotesque horror?* Carter inquired.

Yes, me, screeched a monster.

No, me, howled a monster.

Me!

Me!

Me!

[arrogant gold]

Carter gave an inward sigh. He had never been able convince only one of them to emerge at a time, and he suspected it wouldn't help even if he could. They weren't normal animals anymore; they were monsters, like him. He didn't know why he kept trying. The triumph of hope over experience, he supposed.

We're not shifting, Carter silently informed the monsters. *We're in a plane, remember? And you know what sort of horrifying* things *we turn into when we shift, remember? We'd probably blow out a window and kill us all!*

The monsters backed off, recognizing that as a real possibility. Carter had gotten better at forcing them into shapes that looked ghastly but were at least functional, but even now, it took a while. He didn't have time for that now.

He turned away from Fenella and listened at the door, trying to bring his once-keen shifter hearing to bear. Most shifters had enhanced senses even in their human forms, related to the animal they became; like his lost snow leopard, Carter's hearing and vision had been exceptional. But now he could sometimes access enhanced senses, including some that hadn't been enhanced before, and sometimes not, with no pattern that he'd ever been able to discern.

He didn't hear anything through the door but the roar of the engine. Mentally crossing his fingers that it was because there was nothing to hear, he rapidly picked the lock.

Carter eased the door open the tiniest crack. Peering through, he saw that the plane was just big enough to have cargo space at all. Duffel bags and other gear that presumably was normally stored in cargo was piled around. Three men he didn't recognize were playing cards. No one else was in view. He didn't see any weapons, but that didn't mean there weren't any.

The size of the plane meant he was dealing with five enemies, maximum: the three he could see, a pilot, and possibly a co-pilot. But the pilot wouldn't be likely to leave to join the fight, so he could have as few as three people he actually had to fight.

He could handle this without shifting. Probably. He hoped.

Turning to Fenella, he said in her ear, "Whatever you do, don't open this door."

In a single smooth motion, Carter stepped out of the door and shut it behind him. As the three men started to leap up, he grabbed a fire extinguisher and slammed it into one kidnapper's jaw. The man he struck went down, flopping ungracefully over a duffel bag.

As the other kidnappers rushed him, Carter dropped and rolled, then rose with a heavy duffel bag in his hands. He used it like a battering ram, shoving both the men backward. One scrambled out of the way, but the other tripped over a tool bag on the floor and fell over backward. Carter dropped down on top of him and pinned him with one hand on his chest. He raised his other fist, intending to knock the kidnapper out with a punch to the jaw.

Something exploded under his hand with a loud bang. Carter jerked back with a yell of surprise and pain, echoed by that of the kidnapper. The man's jacket pocket was smoking and blackened, making unsettling popping noises. Sparks shot from ruined cloth.

Things went south very fast after that.

Fenella Kim flung open the cargo hold door and charged out, screaming at ear-splitting volume, "CARTER!"

"Fenella!" Carter yelled. "Get back in there!"

The kidnapper with the mini-bomb or whatever had exploded in his pocket took advantage of his distraction, flinging himself forward and knocking Carter over backward. The back of Carter's head slammed into the floor, exactly where the kidnappers had hit him before, leaving him dazed. A lump of smoking, sparking, popping plastic and metal fell out of the kidnapper's jacket pocket and onto Carter's chest. As if in a dream, he recognized a half-melted cell phone.

Now the explosion made sense. Ever since he'd been experimented on, electronics had a tendency to explode or catch fire or short out when he was around.

The third kidnapper pinned Carter's arms behind his head.

A man came out of the cockpit with a wet cloth in his hand. The co-pilot, presumably. He ignored Fenella and headed straight for Carter. The sharp chemical smell of ether was unmistakable.

Carter struggled to get up, but he was being held down by two people and the knock on the head made him feel like he was moving in slow motion.

Fenella picked up a rolling soda can and hurled it at the man with the ether cloth. It bounced off his head, making him stagger.

"Bill!" called the man who'd been beaned by a Sprite. "Get her!"

Bill, whose jacket was still smoking, lunged and grabbed Fenella, pinning her arms in a bear hug. She stomped on his foot with a stiletto heel. He let out a yell of rage and pain, but didn't let go. Instead, he jerked her off her feet and held her in the air.

The man with the ether cloth dropped down beside Carter, his hand driving toward Carter's face.

His only chance now was to shift. Whatever hideous shape he assumed, it was very likely not to have its breathing apparatus near the ether.

Fenella was struggling furiously, kicking and thrashing and screaming loud enough to wake the dead. If Carter shifted now, she'd see him for the monster that he was.

He hesitated.

The ether cloth came down across his face. The last thing Carter heard before everything went black was another anguished cry from Bill as Fenella bit him.

CHAPTER 3

There is nothing more unpleasant than waking up lying in something wet and sticky, other than waking up with a headache while lying in something wet and sticky. When Fen woke up, she realized that the worst awakening of all was that plus opening her eyes and seeing the giant face of her business rival and enemy hovering over her from six inches away.

She recoiled. "Get away from me!"

"Sorry I checked to make sure you were alive," Carter said grumpily, moving back.

Her memories returned in a rush. Apparently she really had gotten kidnapped with Carter Howe, because there he was, lying beside her and propped up on his elbows. But where were they?

"Sorry," she muttered. "You were… close."

"I woke up beside you about thirty seconds ago," he said, scowling. "I haven't even had a chance to sit up yet."

They sat up, wincing. Carter obviously had a headache too, and her recoil had jammed the back of her head into a mud puddle. They looked around.

"What the actual fuck," she said.

"My thought exactly," he remarked.

They were no longer on an airplane. Nor were there any kidnappers in sight. They appeared to be alone in a hot, humid, muddy swamp. It was day, which told her absolutely nothing about how much time had passed. She could hear nothing but chirps and croaks and other animal noises, along with an occasional, ominous plop. The ground was soft with mud and weeds, not far from a stretch of dark water. The water was dotted with lily pads and little islands. Beyond it she could see gnarled trees and reeds and more swamp. The air had a very distinctive muddy smell that no one would ever use in a perfume, not even as a bottom note.

"Did they dump us here?" Fen asked.

"Apparently." Carter sounded like he didn't believe the evidence of his own senses. "I guess they drugged you too, huh?"

"Yeah, right after they got you. I knew there'd be too many of them for you to fight."

He looked stung. "I got distracted. Why'd you charge out, anyway? I told you to stay in the cargo hold."

"I heard a gunshot, and I thought the plane might depressurize." She folded her arms across her muddy chest, clipping her words off with what she hoped was enough finality that he wouldn't think to ask her what she had intended to do about the depressurized plane. The truth was, she'd heard the shot and rushed out thinking that Carter had been hit. For some reason, at the time that had upset her.

"There was no gunshot."

"I heard it," she said, annoyed. Why did he always have to contradict her?

"Remember the kidnapper who grabbed you, the one they called Bill?" Carter asked. "Did you notice his jacket?"

"Yeah. He'd been shot, but he was wearing a bulletproof vest or something."

He shook his head. "He wasn't shot. He had a cell phone in his pocket, and it exploded."

She stared at him. "What? Really? Did you have a… a tiny bomb or something on you?"

"I wish. No..." His gaze shifted away as if he was hiding something. "No, it just exploded." He shrugged, as if cell phones spontaneously exploding was totally normal.

"Well, that's bizarre." But then, so was everything else. "Look, when I said I knew there'd be too many of them to fight, I didn't mean it as a put-down. So you couldn't fight five kidnappers all by yourself, so what? It was brave of you to try."

Not smart, she thought. *But brave.*

He gave her a deeply suspicious look, as if he'd heard her thought. Then he said, "Thanks for helping out. That was brave of you, too. Also, excellent aim with the soda can. You've got a hell of a throwing arm."

"I pitch in a softball league of women entrepreneurs," she said with pride. Then she added gloomily, "It didn't make a difference, though."

"I didn't make a difference either," said Carter. "And I should have. You did everything you possibly could have."

"So did you."

"No... I mean..." He trailed off, looking deeply, genuinely ashamed and guilty.

"I know the Man Code of Manliness says all men should be able to take out an infinite number of bad guys unarmed and singlehanded," said Fen. "But come on! You're an inventor and a businessman, not John McClane. And also, ho ho ho, you don't have a machine gun."

He managed a laugh. "True. Well, let's get out of here before they come back."

"You think they'll come back?"

"I'm sure of it." But he looked more guilty than worried.

He was probably thinking he needed to defeat them all to prove his manly, manly worth. It was one of the times when Fen was glad she hadn't been born a man. Trying to live up to impossible expectations was bad enough for a woman, but at least she didn't feel guilty for failing to defeat five kidnappers with a soda can. She grinned to herself.

"What's so funny about thinking they'll come back?" Carter

demanded.

"Nothing. I wasn't laughing at you. In fact, I wasn't thinking about you at all."

"Oh." He looked deflated rather than relieved.

"I was remembering how I nailed that guy with the Sprite, and then I stomped the other guy with my high heel and then I bit him and then I kicked him in the balls."

She smiled again. Despite her fear and fury, it had been a deeply satisfying moment to watch him fold over.

"You kicked him in the nuts?" Carter asked.

"Yes, right after you got drugged. Then the guy who drugged you drugged me."

"Good job. Wish I'd seen it."

She was unexpectedly gratified by his praise. A silence fell, broken only by the sounds of birds and bugs and frogs.

They looked at each other. Both of them were smeared with mud, and Carter was additionally smeared with blood. Fen remembered his story about getting marooned on a desert island. She still didn't believe it. But if it had been true, this was what he might have looked like, cut and bruised and dirty and disheveled, his expensive clothes ruined. But based on how he looked now, he wouldn't have panicked. He'd have been supremely put out.

"I only got these last week," he sighed, gazing at his shoes. "They're direct from Ferragamo's workshop in Florence. Custom-made."

They were covered in sticky mud and absolutely ruined. Fen glumly eyed her Jimmy Choo stilettos, wondering if they were salvageable. She could at least rinse the mud off them.

She stood up to give it a try, and the heels sank all the way down through the ground.

It was an unsettling feeling, as if the earth itself wasn't quite solid beneath her feet. She took another cautious step toward the water. Not only did her heels immediately sink again, but she realized that the unsteady feeling hadn't been an illusion. When she took a step, the ground itself quivered.

"Carter...?" Like the earth she stood on, her voice quavered.

He jumped to his feet, then crouched slightly for balance. "What the hell...?"

Her mind flew from one unlikely possibility to the next. A swarm of tiny earthquakes that coincidentally were timed with their feet. They were standing on quicksand. They were in a virtual reality simulation. It was all a dream. They were on a gigantic float mattress dressed up to look like swampland.

And then she knew what it was. "This is a floating island."

"What?"

"It has to be. Some swamps have them. They're giant masses of plant matter stuck together with more plants growing on top of them, thick enough to support the weight of a person. You can only tell what they are because they quiver when you walk on them."

"Huh." Carter prodded the ground suspiciously with the toe of his muddy shoe. "Did you grow up in a swamp?"

"I grew up in Washington, DC. I remember this from..." She gave him *the look,* daring him to laugh. "Girl Scouts."

He didn't laugh. Instead, he looked excited. "Do you remember what places have floating islands? Could that tell you where we are?"

Regretfully, she shook her head. "No. All I remember is they're mostly in the south. Florida? Georgia? Mississippi? Somewhere around there."

It was clear from his expression that the American south was also foreign territory to him. "Well, that's an improvement on 'somewhere with a swamp.' Let's walk around the island. Maybe we'll see dry land."

As they approached the water's edge, what she had thought were lumps of mud opened bulgy eyes, let out loud shrieks, and leaped into the water.

Fen and Carter both jumped, which was an unnerving thing to do when the ground under your feet wasn't quite steady.

"What the hell are those?" Carter exclaimed.

Goggle eyes and wide mouths now floated above the surface of the black water.

"Bullfrogs," said Fen.

"Ugh!" He shuddered. "They're disgusting. Are you sure you didn't grow up in a swamp?"

"I read books," she informed him. "They're big frogs, that's all."

He gazed in horror at the bullfrogs. The bullfrogs gulped and croaked and stared back at him.

"Those are not big frogs," he said. "Those are small eldritch horrors. They're all swollen and lumpy and slimy."

"I think they're cute," she said.

He gave her an unexpectedly mischievous glance. "I dare you to pet one."

"I will if you catch one for me."

Their eyes met. In natural light, his eyes looked more green than brown, and they had a sparkle in them she hadn't seen before. Despite the mud and blood and sweat, she could see that there might be reasons he turned up on Most Eligible Bachelor lists other than being rich, famous, brilliant, and not completely hideous.

With a shriek and a plop, a bullfrog leaped out from under his feet and into the water.

"Ugh!" He backed away from the shore. "I don't know what sort of books you've read, but if you ever read H. P. Lovecraft, you'd know those were clearly the inspiration for Cthulhu."

As they continued their walk around the island, this time farther from the shore, she said, "I read Lovecraft when I was a kid. He's boring and racist and it's his fault I spent years thinking 'gibbous' meant 'spooky.' Every time something creepy appeared, the moon was gibbous. I only found out it actually meant 'three-quarters full' when I wrote an essay that said Halloween is the only gibbous holiday."

He laughed. "I was reading Lovecraft right about the same time I learned that Bactrian camels have two humps. So I assumed 'batrachian' meant 'like a two-humped camel.'"

Then it was her turn to laugh. "He called all his eldritch horrors batrachian, didn't he? Kind of cuts down on the scare factor if you're picturing a camel... What *does* batrachian mean?"

"Frog-like," he said triumphantly. "I only found out when I went to college and it was in a biology textbook. So yeah, Lovecraft has a lot to answer for, but he was completely right about bullfrogs."

"They're cute," she said. "He was prejudiced."

Funny, she thought. *I'd never have imagined that Carter Howe and I would have read the same weird, outdated author when we were kids.*

"Why were you reading Lovecraft?" Carter asked. "He's so old-school."

"My parents are old-school." That was one way of phrasing it, and it wasn't as if she was going to tell the truth about her family to Carter Howe of all people. "We only had classics in the house when I was growing up. What about you?"

"I loved pulp fiction when I was a kid. If it had a tentacle monster on the cover, I'd buy it." He sounded bitter and self-loathing, as if he'd confessed to something both illegal and disgusting.

Fen had an unexpected moment of sympathy with him. Someone must have shamed him for his tastes too—his parents, probably—and he still carried that with him. "When I was a kid, I was obsessed with *The Babysitters Club*. I used to buy them with my allowance and hide them under my bed."

"Why'd you hide them?"

"Because my parents disapproved of trash books, as they called them."

"That's too bad," said Carter. "People should let kids be kids. My parents never judged the books I read, no matter how trashy they were. I always appreciated that about them."

As they walked on, she puzzled over that exchange. Had she spaced out and missed something he'd said that would make sense of why he'd seemed ashamed of reading pulp fiction one second and approving of it the next? Had she completely misread his tone? Either of those seemed completely plausible.

And so, she thought grimly, *is the possibility that Carter Howe is inexplicable and weird. Reading trashy horror is deeply shameful! Reading trashy horror is absolutely fine! Cell phones just randomly explode! Bullfrogs are terrifying!*

Because of the tall shrubs and small trees growing on the floating island, it was impossible to see from any given point how big it was. But when they pushed through a clump of bushes (Carter gave a moan of dismay as thorns ripped his coat, and Fen ground her teeth as berries squished against her jacket), they found an open, beach-like area that curved gently into the water.

And there, floating in the dark water and tied securely to a tree, was a boat.

Carter's hand dropped to his hip as he jumped in front of her. "Get down!"

She ducked behind the nearest shrub and crouched on the quivering muddy ground, waiting for shouts and fighting and gunfire. But nothing happened. She peered through the bushes, and saw Carter prowling around, his muddy coat slapping at his ankles, scowling. No one else was in sight.

She stood up. "I don't think it's the kidnappers' boat. I think we've found civilization!"

His scowl lifted. "God, I hope so."

They hurried to the boat. It was small and brown, with paddles and no outboard motor. Fen, whose only boat experience had been with the Girl Scouts, couldn't tell anything more about it. Presumably it was a fishing boat, and if they searched or waited long enough, the fishers would return and take them away from this godforsaken muddy—

And then she saw what was inside the boat. "What the actual fuck."

"I knew this was too good to be true."

The boat contained her purse. She'd had it with her when she'd been kidnapped, but it had been gone when she'd woken up on the plane. It also contained an open wallet showing Carter's ID, a bag crammed with assorted gadgets and miniature tools, several plastic water containers, and a printed-out note.

He picked up the bag. "This is most of what I keep in my coat. Not my gun, of course."

Fen rummaged through her purse. "Looks like everything's here but my cell phone."

"Yeah, mine's gone too."

Moving in perfect synchronicity, they both grabbed for the note. She got the left side, he got the right, and they read it together.

Have you ever hunted? Some hunters say the lion is the most dangerous game to hunt.

"Leopard," Carter muttered. "It's the snow leopard."

Some say the tiger. Some say the Cape Buffalo. Some say the moose. But a true hunter knows that MAN is the most dangerous game!

"Seriously?" Fen burst out.

"I don't believe this," said Carter.

They returned their attention to the note, reading incredulously.

We are hunters who wish to challenge ourselves by hunting the most dangerous game. But for you, it will BE the most dangerous game!

"Wasn't this a movie?" asked Fen.

"At least two movies," said Carter. "They were based on a short story."

"Let me guess: 'The Most Dangerous Game.'"

"You got it."

The water is on us—we wouldn't want you to get sick! That wouldn't be fair. But you'll have to forage for food. Nature will provide a feast… if you can identify it!

"Fair?!" burst out Fen.

"Swamp foraging," moaned Carter.

Can your little tech toys stand up to real hunters who know the way of the jungle? We'll find out! We're giving you a boat and one day's start, so it won't be over too quickly. And then… the hunt is on!

"My little tech toys?!" Carter exclaimed, his tone full of outrage.

"What absolute bollocks!" Fen said.

"Bollocks? Let me guess, your favorite show is *Downton Abbey*."

"No, my mother is English." She stared at the note. "They can't be serious!"

"They were serious enough to kidnap us," Carter said.

As Fen spoke, she knew she was repeating herself, but the situation seemed to call for it. "What the actual fuck."

CHAPTER 4

Carter was fascinated to see that Fenella Kim seemed more outraged and astonished than terrified by the idea of being hunted. True, that was also how he felt, but he'd had prior experience with dangerous situations. He'd even been kidnapped before. As far as he knew, the most dangerous situation Fenella had ever faced was when he'd attempted a hostile takeover of her company.

All the same, he intended to get her to safety as fast as he could.

He rapidly sorted through the tools and parts in the bag. Some of the more obviously useful items had been taken, but he could do a lot with what he had left. And they hadn't taken his meds, which was a relief. Best of all, he had everything he needed to build—

"Come on," said Fenella crisply. "We'd better get going before these lunatics show up with rifles and a human taxidermy kit."

She startled a laugh out of him. "No, wait. I can build a radio."

"With what, three twigs and a mini screwdriver?"

He held the bag open, letting her peek into it. "I have a lot more than that."

"I don't see a transformer."

"I can build it."

"An oscillator?" she asked.

"I can build that too," he replied.

"Seriously?"

"Sure. Have you ever built a radio?"

"I'm not stupid!" The yell abruptly burst from her. Fenella's fists were clenched, her face bright red.

He was baffled by her sudden anger. "Not knowing how to build a radio doesn't make you stupid."

"Well, I do know how to build one! I don't see all the parts you need, that's all."

"Okay." Still confused, Carter fished through the bag, showing her everything he needed. "See, here's an inductor… and I can use these to make capacitors…"

"Okay, okay." She still seemed irritated, but had cooled down considerably from her first outburst. Glancing around, she said, "Why don't we start paddling, and you can work on it on the way?"

"We need to stay in one place once we signal, and building it won't take me long." Now he was getting annoyed. Why didn't she believe him? He was literally famous for building things.

"How long?"

"Twenty minutes. Thirty, max. I'll send an SOS, and we'll be airlifted out of here within the hour."

"Okay, fine. Let's give it a try."

She watched him intently as he worked. Normally he didn't mind that. In fact, when it was someone like Fenella who understood what he was doing, he even enjoyed it. But a nagging voice muttered at him as he made the components and put them together, a voice that was not a monster's but his own, speaking doubts he'd never had before he'd disappeared.

He wasn't worried that it wouldn't work; he knew it would. He didn't doubt his own skill; that hadn't changed. But ever since his snow leopard had been murdered and a mob of monsters had been crammed inside him, sometimes when he worked on electronics or even went near them, things went wrong.

It's one of you, isn't it? Carter accused his inner monsters. *One of you is an electric eel or a platypus or something like that, and you zap things.*

The monsters hissed and snarled and screeched and flashed their angry denial. He didn't believe a word—or color—of it.

Well, don't do it now, he told them. *You can keep on trashing my life because God knows I can't stop you, but Fenella Kim is innocent. Grouchy and touchy and vengeful, but innocent. Let me get her out of here, and then you can blow up my refrigerator on your own time.*

He was so absorbed in his work that he barely noticed time passing until he had finished. He stretched and looked up, right into the dark and beautiful eyes of Fenella Kim.

"It looks good," she said, a touch grudgingly. "And I think you're within thirty minutes."

Her praise was unexpectedly pleasing. Of course he'd made it well and on time. He was Carter Howe, wasn't he?

"Time to get out of here." With a proud smile, he turned it on.

There was a muffled *whump* and a flash of light as the radio exploded.

He instinctively lunged to shield Fenella just as she flung up her arms to cover her face. Her elbow hit his cheekbone with a sharp crack, adding yet another bruise to his growing collection. Both of them went down into the squishy ground.

"Are you hurt?" he asked urgently.

"Carter!" she exclaimed. "Are you all right?"

They picked themselves up and inspected each other for injuries. The back of his left hand was slightly burned, and she plucked a few metal fragments from her forearms. Their injuries were minor, but the radio's were fatal. There was nothing left to salvage.

"How on earth do you make a radio explode?" Fenella demanded. "I thought the worst that could happen is we'd waste time and it wouldn't work!"

For lack of an actual explanation, he said, "Me too."

She gave him a blistering glare, then turned to the boat. "I don't suppose you carry a compass in case you get kidnapped and dumped in a swamp?"

It was unnerving how close she kept getting to the truth. He *had* kept one on his person ever since he'd gotten kidnapped. "I do, actually, but they took it. You're right, it'd be good to have one so we don't go in circles. I can build one."

"So can I." She glared at him. "And mine won't explode."

"Girl Scouts again?"

Icily, she said, "Little Bit isn't all marketing and design, you know. I may not be an inventor, but I understand the science behind our products quite well."

Carter blew out an exasperated breath. "That wasn't what I meant. I learned how to build my own compass in sixth grade science class."

She eyed him suspiciously, then admitted, "Me too. Have you got all the stuff for it?"

He found a magnet and a roll of wire, and used his mini wire cutter to clip off a short length. He handed it to Fenella, who rubbed it against the magnet while he used his mini-welder to melt a sheet of plastic into a cup shape. Once it had cooled, he filled it with swamp water.

"Got anything that floats in your purse?" he asked.

She shook her head and picked up a leaf from the ground. "I did learn this in Girl Scouts."

Fenella placed the magnetized wire on the leaf, and floated the leaf in the cup. They watched as it gently turned, orienting itself in a north-south direction.

"Compass accomplished!" Fenella cried.

They gave each other a high-five. Her dainty hand smacked sharply into his.

Glancing at the shadows, he said, "That way's north. I don't know which way we ought to go, though."

"If most swamps are in the south, then shouldn't we go north?" Fenella suggested. "It might give us a better chance of getting to the edge of the swamp instead of deeper in."

He shrugged. "Sure. It'll get us closer to Refuge City, if nothing else."

They climbed into the boat. She picked up the oars, then eyed the clear water jugs with longing. "I don't suppose we could spare some to wash our faces? And maybe our hair...?"

Her hair was plastered to her head with drying mud. Based on how his own hair felt, she probably not only found it depressing and disgusting, but also itchy as hell. He was deeply tempted, but said, "I wish, but we don't know when we'll get out of here."

She didn't take her gaze off the jugs. "Rule of thumb for water is a gallon per person per day. We've got five two-gallon jugs. So they can't be expecting this whole thing to take more than five days, maximum."

"Oh. Right." He was once again impressed with her unexpected practicality. He'd never joined the Boy Scouts, but if they were half as good as the Girl Scouts apparently had been, he should have. "But you never know what might happen. And we can't drink the swamp water."

"I know. We'll have to use that for bathing."

They both eyed the black swamp water. His inner monster who communicated in color flashed [cozy deep blue] followed by [relaxed pale blue] and [happy aqua]. Carter did not find that reassuring in the slightest.

"I guess it'd be better than being covered in mud," said Carter.

"I think it's only that color because of tannins. So it'd be like bathing in strong tea," Fenella said hopefully. Then she blew out a frustrated breath. "But I'm sure a one-day start isn't as good as it sounds when you're fleeing deranged kidnappers."

Or deranged wizard-scientists, he thought.

The all-shifter security agency, Protection, Inc: Defenders, which he sometimes freelanced for, had been stalked for a while by a mysterious and dangerous group of villains using both science and magic. Their plots tended toward the bizarre and baroque. Pretending to be a bunch of hunters enacting "The Most Dangerous Game" was exactly their style.

It felt deeply unfair that they'd gone after him too. He didn't even work there. He wasn't on the team. He just occasionally gave them a little technical help.

Of course, it was even more unfair to Fenella, who had literally nothing to do with any of this. Probably the sadistic bastards had grabbed her because they thought it would be hilarious to toss him in a swamp with his worst enemy.

She bit our enemies, growled a monster.

The enemy of our enemy is our friend, said another monster.

The monsters were being more coherent than usual. Normally they were a writhing, gibbering, screeching mob inside his head. Maybe the color-communication monster wasn't the only one who liked the swamp.

"Right?" Fenella asked.

It took him a moment to recall what they'd been talking about. "Yeah, we shouldn't waste any time bathing until we've already paddled all day. Once it's getting close to sunset, we can stop and bathe and forage some food—which I hope you can do, because I sure don't know what's edible in a swamp—and I'll build... something." As an afterthought, he said, "No, I do know one thing we can eat. Fish."

"We don't have a fishing pole or a net."

"I could make one. Though I'm not sure how tasty anything will be that we pull out of *that.*" He waved his hand at the black water.

"I learned about edible plants," she said. "I don't know how much I remember, though. I sure wouldn't try any mushrooms."

Glumly and muddily, they got in the boat.

"Ever paddled a boat?" Fenella asked.

"I rented a gondola in Venice once," Carter said. "What about you?"

"In Girl Scouts," she replied. Of course.

The little boat cut through the black water and the lily pads. They navigated around little islands and passed through canals lined with trees draped in gray, gauzy Spanish moss. It would have been beautiful and relaxing if he'd been with a friend or a date instead of Fenella Kim, and if he'd been in clean and swamp-appropriate clothes rather than a muddy suit, and if he'd had on sunscreen and cologne rather than mud and mud.

A bullfrog shrieked and dove off a lily pad, landing in the water with a loud plop. Swamp water splashed over his cufflinks. The bullfrog goggled at him from the black water.

On second thought, Carter thought, *I hate this place.*

"I think that's a Papa," Fenella said suddenly.

"What? Where?" He looked around, but didn't see any other human being, let alone a man who could conceivably be Fenella Kim's father.

"There. See? It's a Papa tree."

"What?"

"A Papa tree," Fenella repeated. "Papas grow on them."

Even given everything else going on, that was deeply surreal. "A… sorry, what?"

"P-A-W-P-A-W. They're fruit."

She must think I'm an idiot in addition to being a lunatic, he thought. *Great.*

"Oh. Right. I think I've vaguely heard of them." He was telling the truth, but he didn't think she believed him.

They paddled the boat toward the tree, which grew on yet another island. They got off the boat, testing the ground beneath their feet. To his relief, it didn't wobble.

The tree was laden with yellow-green fruit. Fenella looked up at it, then abruptly burst out laughing.

"What?" Carter demanded.

"I was just… picturing…" She was having trouble articulating between fits of giggles. "…a tree of dads… dangling from stems!"

A hot tide of embarrassment began to engulf him, then he too pictured it. The image was irresistibly funny. He also began to laugh. "With long… gray… beards! Like the Spanish moss."

She seemed to find this hilarious. "They could wear T-shirts with dad jokes!"

"You'd know they're ripe when the jokes are only funny if you're over forty."

She laughed so hard, she had to lean against the tree. He'd never seen her laugh like that. He'd never imagined that she was capable of laughing like that. And at *his* ridiculous joke, too.

It's a release of tension, that's all, he thought. *Because of the incredibly stressful situation we're in.*

She reached up, prodded a pawpaw, picked it, and tossed it to him. "Here. Have a dad."

He laughed as he caught it, and that didn't feel like a release of tension. The great and terrible Fenella Kim was unexpectedly funny.

He broke the fruit open. It came apart easily. Inside, it was yellow-white and smooth as an avocado, studded with shiny black seeds the size of almonds. It smelled tropical and intense, like a non-alcoholic daiquiri. He handed one half to Fenella. "Cheers."

The flesh was soft as custard and very sweet, with flavors that reminded him of banana, mango, and birthday cake. Without a spoon, he felt like he was eating a crème brulee by plunging his face into it. But he was hungry and tired and stressed out, and if he'd been served a crème brulee without a spoon, he'd have done exactly that.

He finished the pawpaw and looked up. She was polishing off her half in what he suspected was a slightly more dainty manner, but the bar was low. She looked up, wiped her mouth with the back of her hand, and said, "If they squish when you poke them, they're ripe. But they only keep a few days."

"Fenella Kim, you're a genius," said Carter. "I don't know what I'd have done in this swamp without you."

"You'd have been forced to hunt bullfrogs or starve."

"Then I do know what I'd have done. I'd have starved."

They shared another pawpaw, then took another few days' worth back to the boat. Now that he'd eaten something, he felt more clear-headed and less like he was running on adrenaline and fumes. *Get in boat and paddle, hopefully away from enemies rather than toward them,* was a perfectly reasonable strategy under the circumstances, but he could improve on it. As he paddled north, he pulled his thoughts together and considered what he knew about their enemies.

Several months ago, he'd helped his team—*the* team, he corrected himself—to rescue Ransom and his mate Natalie from a wizard-scientist named Elayne and her minions. And that hadn't been his first encounter with the wizard-scientists. By now he knew way more about them than he'd ever wanted to know.

Both the wizard-scientists and their minions were shifters who could transform into extinct or mythic beasts, the weirder the better. One of Elayne's crew turned into a giant armored prehistoric fish! And just to make it more fun, they all had special powers of some kind; the fish guy, for instance, could also induce vertigo.

Carter didn't have to worry that Elayne and her crew were after him; they'd been defeated and hauled off to shifter jail. But it gave him the general idea of what sort of enemies they'd be up against.

If they catch up with us, I'll have to defeat a wizard shifter leading a gang of assorted magical beasts and prehistoric animals, all of them with powers, he thought glumly. *The experiments that were done on me were supposed to give me powers, but they didn't. And I can't shift with Fenella around, so it'll just be one man armed with an oar.*

And Fenella, a monster growled.

She can fight, a monster hissed.

For once, his monsters had a point.

And one woman who can throw a mean can of soda, Carter agreed.

Fenella too seemed wrapped up in her own world. She paddled steadily, her dark eyes fixed on the horizon, her attention clearly turned inward. Even covered in mud, she was dignified and in control. She seemed like a very self-contained person.

If he'd imagined being lost and hunted in a swamp with Fenella Kim, he'd have pictured her refusing to go anywhere without her cell phone and makeup kit, while berating him about the time he'd tried to take over Little Bit and gloating over how she was going to take over Howe Enterprises. The last thing he'd have expected was a woman who fought like a snow leopard, remembered everything she'd learned when she'd been ten years old, had a whimsical sense of the absurd, and had never thought the worst of him, even back when they'd been enemies.

Back when we'd been enemies, he thought. *Does that mean we aren't anymore?*

Enemies don't feed each other, a monster put in.

Enemies don't make plans together, gibbered a monster.

Carter hated to admit that the monsters once again had a point, but he had to admit that being hunted in a swamp with Fenella Kim could have been a whole lot worse. Lots of people would have panicked or teased him for caring that his favorite coat was ruined or demanded that they do something stupid or refused to believe that the note meant what it said or screamed at him about the radio. She'd taken everything in stride, gotten over the radio incident, and even found them breakfast.

He vowed that once they stopped, he'd catch some fish and build something useful, since so far he'd done nothing but ruin their chance to call for help and freeze at the worst possible moment. If only Fenella hadn't charged out of the cargo bay, he could have shifted and then maybe they wouldn't be here now.

You could have shifted anyway, hissed a monster.

I wanted to shift, screeched a monster. *You didn't let me!*

Me too! Me too!

[reproachful dull orange]

Carter ignored them. His monsters didn't get why they needed to hide. They thought it would be totally fine for him to reveal himself as a grotesque monster to his teammates—the Defenders, he corrected himself—his family, Fenella Kim, and the whole wide world.

Never, he vowed. *I am going to get us out of this swamp and back to civilization, without the wizard-scientists ever catching up to us. Fenella Kim is never going to learn anything about me that's not already on the public record. She can go on believing we were kidnapped by movie-obsessed lunatics. Once she's safely home, we can go back to feuding or make up, but I will never let her find out what I really am.*

He had no idea how far they'd managed to travel when the sun lowered and the light turned golden, but whatever progress they'd made, they had to stop before it got dark. They couldn't build or fish or forage if they couldn't see, and he had absolutely no desire to paddle along bullfrog-infested waters at night.

They moored the boat on a non-floating island with plenty of trees and shrubs for Fenella to investigate for their culinary properties. They might also provide cover in case the wizard-scientists caught up with them, and Carter was forced to shift to fight them. It was possible. He'd managed to shift in the vicinity of his teammates—of the guys he freelanced with sometimes, he meant—without them ever seeing the monster that lurked beneath his skin.

"I'm taking a bath," Fenella announced the instant she set foot on land. "That way. Let's meet back at the boat when we're done."

"I'll go that way." Carter indicated the opposite direction. "If you see anything, yell. And watch out for alligators."

"Watch out for bullfrogs."

He hunted along the edge of the island for an area that wasn't too far to hear her if she shouted, wasn't too infested with goggle-eyed horrors, and had water that looked even vaguely clean. He had to settle for not too far away, scaring away the lurking batrachians, and water that, when he cupped it in his hands, did indeed look like strong tea rather than diluted mud.

Carter stripped naked, draped his clothes over a branch, and gingerly stepped into the water. It was tepid. Mud squished between his toes.

"Ugh."

[happy aqua]

[happy aqua]

"I'm glad *someone's* happy," he muttered sarcastically.

[very happy deep aqua]

Mud and brown water aside, it did feel good to wash up. He scrubbed himself from head to toe, crouching to duck his head and wash his hair. When he stood up, he felt much better. Like a snow leopard grooming itself, he'd always liked to keep himself meticulously clean. He was sure Fenella felt the same way—she never had a hair out of place in video or photos.

Fenella was, right now, bathing naked in the same water he was standing in. He wondered what she looked like beneath the tailored business suit. Her bone structure was delicate, but the cut of her modern suits didn't show off her figure. He couldn't tell whether her hips were wide or narrow, or whether her belly was flat or softly rounded. Nor did he have any idea of how big her breasts were, or the color of her nipples, or what they might look like bare, with water dripping down them…

A bullfrog gave a loud croak.

Carter hastily got out of the water, wondering where that fantasy about Fenella Kim had come from. He wasn't the kind of guy who automatically generated sexual fantasies about every woman he laid eyes on. She was attractive, sure. Beautiful, to be honest. And surprisingly sexy even when furious or covered in mud. But it wasn't as if anything would ever happen between them. There was still the matter of her hostile takeover. And that he could never tell her even the most basic facts about himself.

Not to mention that he was a monster. He could never inflict himself on any woman unless and until he managed to fix that.

He wiped as much water off as he could manage with his hands, put on his boxers (his only clean item of clothing) and surveyed the rest. Reluctantly, he decided that the water was cleaner than the mud, everything was ruined anyway, and he'd rather wear wet clothes than dirty ones. He scrubbed his clothing, then put it back on wrung-out and wet.

A flash of gold glinted in the corner of his eye. He lunged for the mini-welder he'd left on the bank, snatching it up and ducking behind a tree in a single smooth motion. It wasn't much of a weapon, but it was all he had.

There was no sound but an oddly familiar soft trill. Something small and gold flew down to him. Instinctively, he lowered the tool and raised his other arm.

A tiny golden dragonette landed on his forearm. She was a beautiful creature, lithe and gleaming, with a long tail she coiled around his arm like a rope of gold. Her wings were the translucent gold of a lazy summer afternoon.

Carter knew what she was because he'd seen a dragonette before. Some of the Defenders and all of the bodyguards in the west coast branch of Protection, Inc. had magical pets. Nick and his mate Raluca, and Lucas and his mate Journey both had dragonettes. But Doina was blue and Treasure was glittering diamond. Carter didn't recognize this little beauty.

She cocked an inquiring head and trilled again.

"Shhh!" Carter whispered. He had no idea what the dragonette was doing in the swamp, but if Fenella got a look at her, it would open up a bullfrog-sized can of worms.

Salutations, small fierce predator, growled a monster.

Little sister, hissed a monster.

[approving sky blue]

She would have pride of place on our shoulder, purred a monster.

Pretty little thing, pretty thing, gibbered a monster.

Keep her, keep her, screeched a monster.

"No!" said Carter. Then, remembering his inside voice, he thought to them, *No. She's not a pet. At least, she's not our pet.*

The dragonette gripped his forearm with her little claws and stretched out her neck. Carter put down the mini-welder and scratched her head, hoping to keep her quiet. The dragonette seemed to enjoy that, nuzzling his hand like a cat. Despite the metallic appearance of her hide, it felt more like suede than either metal or scales.

He noted with approval that unlike everything else in the swamp, the dragonette was impeccably clean. She probably groomed herself like a cat, unlike some magical pets he could name. He'd almost had a heart attack when Fenella had spotted the bright blue hairs that Merlin's pest of a bugbear had left on his coat. She'd instantly realized they came from a real animal, too, until he managed to convince her they were from a carpet.

Fenella was sharp as a tack. He couldn't let the dragonette get anywhere near her.

"Sorry, but you'd better take off," Carter whispered. "Go do… whatever you're doing."

When the dragonette showed no inclination to go anywhere, he stopped petting her and gave her a gentle shove. "Shoo!"

She jumped off his arm, flew to his shoulder, and nibbled gently on his ear. There was something oddly pleasant about her weight on his shoulder. He finally understood why Dali and Tirzah and Pete, who had flying kittens, liked to have them perch on their shoulders. But unlike Batcat and Cloud, this little beauty wouldn't shed all over his clothes.

The golden dragonette nuzzled him insistently until he petted her. Unlike Spike the cactus kitten, she wouldn't stab your hand if you accidentally rubbed her the wrong way. And she was so dainty and small, unlike Merlin's lumbering bugbear that knocked over furniture on a daily basis. She seemed to like the petting, making a soft crooning sound. Unlike Ransom and Natalie's teleporting puppies, the dragonette would never bark hysterically for no reason.

Really, this golden beauty was an ideal pet.

If you wanted a pet. Which Carter didn't. And even if he did want one, he certainly couldn't have one now, when he was running for his life and accompanied by a sharp-eyed, keen-eared, brilliant woman who absolutely could not learn that magic existed.

"You have to go," he whispered. "Seriously. Now."

The dragonette tried to crawl inside his shirt. It was wet and transparent, so it was in no way a hiding place, even if you ignored the lump she made.

The other magical pets could follow directions, sometimes. The people he knew who had magical pets said that instructions needed to be phrased simply, and the animals had to want to obey.

He lifted the dragonette off him, held her up so her summer sky-blue eyes met his, and said in a low but carefully articulated voice, "Go.

Away. Now. Don't. Come. Back."

No no no no no, howled an inner monster.

Keep her, keep her, screeched another.

You're making a terrible mistake, snarled a monster.

[angry reproach baked yam orange]

She belongs to us, hissed another monster.

"No, she does not," Carter said firmly. "She's lost. She needs to go home. Magical animals pick their own owners, and there is no way this little beauty has her heart set on belonging to a monster."

He opened his hands and tossed her into the air. "Go away!"

She opened her translucent wings, let out a tiny shriek, and flew away. In a moment, she was gone.

His monsters growled, roared, screamed, and color-flashed their disapproval. It made Carter's head ache.

[furious blood red]

[disappointed ash gray]

Gone, gone, gone, moaned a monster. *Gone forever!*

She loved us, and you sent her away, screeched a monster.

What have you done?! roared a monster.

"I've kept Fenella Kim from finding out what we are, that's what I've done," Carter whispered. "Now shut up!"

The monsters kept on wailing and screaming and snarling and flashing all the way back to the boat. He was surprised by how attached they'd gotten to the little dragonette in such a short time, and even more surprised by how attached he had. She had been an unexpected bit of color and joy in this dismal swamp, and now she was gone and he'd never see her again.

It was a choice he'd had to make.

He regretted it already.

CHAPTER 5

Fen pretended she was doing a tea bath treatment at a luxury spa. A fancy Korean spa where you could spend all day bathing in pools of assorted temperatures, then lie down in darkened rooms with floors of smooth heated stones or warm sand. Mud baths were a real thing. Why not tea-on-top, mud-on-bottom baths?

I am relaxing in an expensive luxury spa, she told herself. *The tannins in this exquisite imported tea are tightening my pores and AAAAAAHHH!*

She gulped back the shriek that tried to burst from her throat as a bullfrog's goggle eyes unexpectedly popped up from the dark water an inch from her body. Unlike Carter, she was not afraid of frogs. She liked frogs. Frogs were cute. Maybe her imaginary spa even featured frog baths.

All the same, she decided that she was done with her spa.

As she squeezed water out of her hair and wiped it off her skin, she wondered how Carter was getting on with his frog bath. As annoyed as she'd been over his incredible exploding radio, not to mention the condescending remarks with the subtext about her not being a genius inventor like him, she'd enjoyed his enthusiasm over the pawpaws. For a while there, she'd actually liked him.

She wondered how he'd clean up. She'd seen photos and video of him in his natural environment, the boardroom or the workshop, but he wasn't in a suit now. Right now, unless the frogs had scared him off, he was naked.

Carter naked...

Her imagination obligingly put together her personal observations, like his well-muscled thighs and long eyelashes and the injuries he'd collected along the way, into a complete package. (*His package is part of the package*, she thought with a giggle.) She could see him in her mind's eye, standing in the black water (but only up to his ankles), dripping wet and fully nude.

Droplets hung in his wet black hair and dotted his tanned skin like tiny diamonds. The muscles of his shoulders and forearms and chest and back gleamed as if they'd been oiled. His eyes were deep green with hints of brown, reflecting the lush foliage around him. The expression on his face was one she hadn't seen in a depressingly long time, that of naked lust for her, and only her. She could see *every* detail of his body in an imaginary surround-sound but for vision, his fine ass and his perfectly proportioned, fully erect, rock hard—

"Fenella?"

That was Real Carter, not Imaginary Carter. She knew because his voice wasn't rough and deep with uncontrollable passion, but sharp with annoyance... or was that worry?

"I'm fine!" Fen called. "I'll be there in a minute!"

"Take your time!" he called back. "Enjoy the bullfrogs."

She dressed in her soaking wet clothes—ugh, that was horrible—and put on her wet shoes, wondering all the while what had gotten into her. Not that she never had random sexual fantasies, she had random fantasies about pretty much everything, but Carter Howe was a new one. She'd never particularly had a thing about sleeping with the enemy, not even in her own imagination.

Fen picked her way across the island, half-expecting it to wobble beneath her feet even though they'd poked this one thoroughly to make sure it was solid. The air had cooled off and her wet clothes made her feel chilled.

And there was Actual Carter.

They stopped and stared at each other. Like her, he had washed his clothes and then put them back on wet. She'd assumed he would, but she hadn't accounted for what that would look like.

Forget Naked Wet Carter, it was Clothed Wet Carter that was really something. And forget wet T-shirt contests too, because he proved that wet button-down shirts were where it was at. The fine fabric was absolutely transparent and clung to him in a way that accentuated every sculptural bit of his body. His wet shirt made her notice parts of his body that she might not have paid proper attention to if he'd been shirtless, like his elegantly arched collarbones or the sexy little dips above and below them. She wanted to run her fingers along them.

And his hair, she *liked* his hair wet. He'd tried to smooth it back but it was already drying and coming loose, with locks hanging around his face, beaded with water exactly like she'd imagined. She thought of licking off that water and gave an involuntary shiver.

"You're cold." His voice was oddly husky and deep. He swallowed, cleared his throat, and said, "I'll make a fire."

She was relieved that he apparently hadn't noticed her staring at him. Maybe it had just been for a second, and had only felt like a long time.

Stop fantasizing about him, she ordered herself. That didn't feel very compelling, so she added, *At least don't think about licking him. That's swamp water, not shower water. It's gross.*

An image popped up of Carter inexplicably wearing that shirt in the shower, dripping with nice clean water. With an effort, she squelched it.

Focus, she told herself.

He was standing in an odd position, holding his heavy wet coat in front of him like a shield. He must be cold too.

"Yeah, we'd better warm up," she said. "Foraging in wet clothes seems like a great way to get pneumonia."

"Right. Right." He quickly turned his back on her and began collecting dry wood.

She found a space near a tree with low-hanging branches and ringed it with rocks. He put down the wood, she set it up to burn nicely, and he lit it with his mini welding torch. Orange flames blazed up, giving off a welcome warmth.

"I thought you could hang up your coat to dry," she said, pointing to a branch that extended over the fire.

"Oh, good idea." He carefully hung up his coat, using a branch stub to keep it in place.

"And your shirt, if you want." She spoke with some envy, because it wasn't like she could take off *her* shirt.

"Seems a bit unfair to you," he said. "You know, if you wanted to—"

"I'm not going to do a swamp strip-tease," Fen interrupted, but without anger. She appreciated that he'd noticed the double standard that allowed him to warm himself while she had to stand around in wet clothes.

"A swamp-tease?" Carter suggested with a grin. "Honestly, Fenella, it really isn't fair. And I don't love wearing wet pants. How about we both hang up our clothes, and keep our backs turned until we can get dressed again?"

It was a tempting idea. And really, what was the downside? That he might sneak a peek at her body? If he was the kind of guy who'd spy on a woman, he'd have done it when she was bathing.

"It's Fen," she said. "My friends—I mean, people who know me call me Fen."

"Seriously?" He sounded genuinely taken aback. "As in swamp?"

"A fen is a wetland with peat, sedges, and moss," she informed him, irritated. Her parents refused to call her by the name she preferred because they claimed it meant a swamp and had bad connotations. "Not a swamp. Or a bog. Or a marsh. Those are all completely different things. Fens are important ecosystems. And they're pretty."

Carter made a bullfrog-like gulping sound that was either suppressed laughter or a death rattle. Then he recovered himself. "Right. Fens *are* pretty. So how about turning our backs to change, Fen?" Her name rolled easily off his tongue, sounding so much more warm and friendly than the formal Fenella. Nobody but her parents called her that any-more. "I promise not to look."

"I believe you." She turned around. "You go first."

The fire was deliciously hot against her back as she sat on the ground and listened to the sounds of Carter getting undressed. They were distinctly squelchy, which shouldn't have been at all attractive, but because she knew exactly why they sounded like that, they were disconcertingly sexy.

Fwish-drip. That was Carter stripping off his clingy wet shirt, leaving his muscular chest bare.

Thud-squelch, thud-squelch. That would be Carter taking off his shoes and socks. She wondered what his feet looked like. She'd never seen them.

Fwish-squish. That was Carter taking off his pants. Now he was completely naked except for his—

Bwish. Oh God, that had to be Carter peeling off his boxers or briefs or whatever it was he wore to contain what had to be the world's most tempting cock. Now he was nude as she'd imagined him, only this time it was for real and he was right behind her.

This. *This* was the downside. She was sitting with her back to Naked Carter, and she wouldn't be able to think about anything else until their clothes dried off—*their* clothes, she was going to have to take off her clothes too, and then she'd be naked while Naked Carter was right behind her—

"Fen?" Once again, his voice had that husky roughness. "I'm done. Your turn."

"Okay. No looking." Her own voice also sounded different to her. She decided not to speak again.

Fen turned around, and immediately got an eyeful of Naked Carter sitting with his back to her. It was only a second or so before she spun around, remembering that she too had promised not to look, but that one second was burned into her eyes like she'd stared into the sun. Wet hair like black satin. The appealing vulnerability of the nape of his neck. Shoulder muscles to die for. Back muscles to die for. The groove of his spine that seemed made for her to trace with her finger. That amazing glimpse of his incredible ass…

She stared at the low branch his clothes were hanging from as if she was trying to set fire to them with her mind. Those were clothes that Carter wasn't in.

No. Don't look at them. Look at something else. Think of something else. Bullfrogs. The high note of the National Anthem. Cold oatmeal.

The swamp tease I'm supposed to be doing right now.

Fen gulped, and immediately hoped Carter hadn't heard. When he'd suggested the drying-off plan, she'd only thought of the social awkwardness. Now that they were actually doing it, she was excruciatingly conscious of the fact that she was going to be naked within touching distance of Carter who was already naked. The problem wasn't that it was awkward. The problem was that it was bizarrely, insanely, hair-tearingly hot.

Focus, she ordered.

Gritting her teeth, Fen took off her stiletto heels and placed them neatly by the fire. Grass and weeds gave under her bare feet. Everything was damp and squishy around here, which should have been the opposite of sexy, but right now it was making her think of the give of warm flesh under her hand, and the dampness that she could feel gathering between her thighs.

Stop it, she told her body.

Her body ignored her.

She had to reach beneath her skirt to peel off her nylons. They had been custom-made with a subtle geometric pattern, and were probably not worth keeping except as nets for very small fish. But the feeling of her own hands moving over her legs distracted her from annoyance at their tragic destruction, making her wish they were Carter's hands.

As she hung them up, she realized that she should have taken her panties off at the same time. Now she had to repeat the whole process of reaching up under her skirt while wishing it was Carter reaching there, pulling them down her legs while wishing it was Carter doing the pulling, hanging them up on a tree branch… at least that part was fine, as she didn't care who did the hanging.

And now she was standing there, fully dressed but with no panties. What a perfect scenario for someone, oh like say Carter for instance, to push her up against the convenient tree, with both of them so desperate that neither of them could even take the time to get her undressed.

Stop it, she told her mind. *He's your enemy—well, he's definitely your rival. He tried to take over your company. You are, right now, trying to take over his. He is the last person in the world you should even* think *about having sex with.*

Her mind ignored her. As she took off her blouse, she imagined Carter taking it off. When her fingers brushed against her nipples as she removed her bra, she imagined Carter teasing them with his clever inventor's fingers. When she removed her skirt and stood absolutely naked, touched by nothing but air, she imagined Carter standing up, striding toward her, and touching her everywhere, with his hands and his body and his mouth.

Fine, she thought. *I give up. I will sit here and silently stew by myself—well, unfortunately,* not *by myself—and plan on an epic session with my vibrator as soon as I get home.*

She had begun to imagine that session when her attention was caught by a flash of something metallic overhead. Her arousal vanished in a cold rush of fear.

Fen spun around. "Carter! Carter!"

"What, what is it?" As he leaped up, he snatched his pants and held them over his crotch like a wet, wadded up, extra-large fig leaf.

At that moment, modesty was the last thing on her mind. But Carter clearly cared a lot about it, so she put her forearm over her breasts and held her wet skirt over the rest of her relevant parts. "I think I saw a drone!"

"Where?"

“There.” She pointed. “It went that way. I didn’t get a good look at it, but it was metallic and moving fast. Those hunters are spying on us!”

He peered around, frowning. “Did you see what color it was?”

She had no idea why that would be relevant, but he *was* the tech guy. “Gold.”

“Oh.” Relief flickered across his face, then was replaced with alarm. “Hmm. Why don’t I go… look for it. Maybe I can, uh, disable it.”

“Disable it how? It was way too high to reach.”

“I better hurry.” He turned his back, yanked on his pants, grabbed his tools, jammed his feet into his shoes, and fled.

Fen was left naked and alone.

CHAPTER 6

I hate my life, Carter thought as he plunged through the swamp, wearing nothing but clammy wet linen pants and the trashed remains of his Ferragamo shoes.

He'd been within touching distance of the surprisingly sexy, remarkably beautiful, unexpectedly interesting, and completely naked Fen Kim, and not only could he do nothing but sit there listening to her undress and trying not to spontaneously combust, but he hadn't even gotten a good look at her when she'd shouted his name as he'd been too busy trying to cover up his hard-on. At least he'd been quick enough to hide it.

He *hoped* he'd been quick enough.

"Come on, you nuisancy thing you," he muttered. "Come out, come out, wherever you are."

The golden dragonette swooped into view, chirping happily. Carter could see how Fen had mistaken her for a drone, if she'd seen her high in the sky and moving fast. He waved his hands at her, trying to fend her off, but she dodged him, landed on his shoulder, and stuck her narrow head under his chin.

Inside his mind, his monsters set up a cacophony of rejoicing.

She's back, she's back!

Our little friend is back!

Hello, small beauty!

Welcome back!

Carter pried the dragonette off his shoulder, held her up, and looked sternly into her sapphire eyes. She squeaked in protest.

"You need to leave," he told her.

She squeaked louder and struggled. Her translucent wings looked so delicate, he was forced to let go of her in case he hurt her by accident. She promptly returned to his shoulder. Her little claws pricked his bare skin.

"I don't want a pet," he said.

We want a pet, growled a monster.

A sweet little sister, hissed another monster.

Not any *pet,* squawked another monster. *This pet.*

She wants us, put in a monster.

[happy aqua]

The little dragonette buried her head in his hair and wrapped her tail around his ear.

"Stop that," said Carter, but he could hear the futility in his own protest. This golden beauty had, inexplicably, chosen him. Like everything else in his life, there was nothing he could do about it.

But apart from the completely ridiculous figure he was making of himself, wet and half-naked with a tiny golden dragon winding itself around his head, and the fact that he had to keep her out of Fen's sight, he couldn't help wanting to keep her.

She was affectionate. She wouldn't shed. She was very clean—cleaner than him, right now. Her insistence on choosing him was touching. He knew from the other people with magical pets that you could teach them to be invisible in public, so it wasn't as if she'd always be this much of a bother. He still needed to get out of the swamp without Fen ever seeing her, but after that...

The dragonette poked her head out of his hair and chirruped.

Carter gave a sigh of resignation. "Okay, fine. I guess you've got me. Come here and let me take a look at you."

He held out his forearm. The dragonette jumped onto it, spread her wings, and preened. She really was a beautiful little creature, like a precious ornament come to astonishing life. The membrane of her wings was translucent amber, and the rest of her shone and glittered like purest gold. Carter gave a wry laugh as he recalled himself trying to shoo her away, when most people would never let her go.

Never, never, howled a monster.

In a distinctly Gollum-like voice, another monster gurgled, *She's ours!*

"'My precioussss,' huh?" Carter said aloud.

The dragonette gave a trill that sounded like approval.

"Okay. Precious it is." He raised his forearm, looking her in the eyes, and said, "Precious, you *cannot* let anyone but me see you. Don't come unless I'm alone. Understand?"

Precious gave an eager chip and booped his hand with her nose. Maybe she did understand. And that gave him an idea.

"Hang on, Precious. I have an errand for you."

Carter took out the writes-on-anything pen he'd invented and a piece of moldable plastic. He stroked Precious while considering what to write and who to send her to.

As far as he'd seen, the magical animals could go to people they'd met and places they'd been to, but their ability to find people they'd never met before was limited to the owners they wanted. He couldn't send her to the Defenders or anyone else he knew, because she wouldn't be able to find them. He couldn't send her to the nearest human, because that would be the people hunting them. He couldn't send her to just anybody, because they wouldn't know about magical animals and she might fall into bad hands.

He could try to get her to drop a message somewhere rather than tying it to her leg, but if he told anything even vaguely resembling the truth, it would sound like a bizarre prank and be ignored.

He absently chewed on the pen, thinking, then sighed and wrote.

IF YOU'RE READING THIS, YOU HAVE WON A NEW PHONE OF YOUR CHOICE, COURTESY OF HOWE ENTERPRISES

AND OUR LATEST VIRAL MARKETING CONTEST. CONTACT PROTECTION, INC: DEFENDERS IN REFUGE CITY AND TELL THEM YOU HAVE A MESSAGE FROM CARTER HOWE. GIVE THEM THIS. THE CODE WORDS ARE KIDNAP, SWAMP, PAWPAW, WIZARD.

Carter considered this message. If it reached the Defenders, they'd be as good as rescued. Ransom had the power to get information out of thin air, so he probably hadn't even needed to say that he was in a swamp with pawpaws. Just letting them know that he'd been kidnapped by the wizard-scientists was plenty.

Assuming it reached them, that was. It was a longshot, but it was all he had.

He signed the message, then nudged it at Precious. She gripped it in her talons and cocked her head inquiringly.

"Drop this near lots of humans," Carter said. "Outside of the swamp."

She chittered excitedly and launched herself into the air. He watched her spiral upward, a glint of gold, until she was lost from view.

"I'll be damned," he muttered. "I guess they really are that smart."

He returned to the fire, where he found Fen wrapped in his wet coat. The only bare skin showing was her face, but that only served to remind him of that dazzling glimpse of her nude. She'd covered herself with her hands and a wet skirt, but that had only accentuated her nakedness. He'd only seen her for a moment and he'd been distracted by surprise, trying to hide his hard-on and worried first about the supposed drone, and then worried about Fen seeing Precious.

And yet despite all that, the vision was burned into his mind with every detail sharp and clear as diamond. He'd never seen a more tempting sight. At that moment, he didn't care that she was trying to take over his company and had been annoying him for years. He'd wanted her more than he'd ever wanted anything in his entire life.

He tried to repress the thought that he still did.

"Well?" Fen demanded. "Was it a drone?"

"No." He fished frantically for a reasonable explanation—a

satellite?—and fell back on, "It was a gold helium balloon. God only knows how long it had been floating before it got blown here."

"Huh. It seemed like it was moving too fast for that."

"Well, you only caught a glimpse of it before it got hidden by the trees."

To his relief, she seemed to accept that. "Sorry I sent you off on a wild goose chase."

"Don't worry about it. You're alert, that's good." He hesitated, caught by a wild impulse to suggest that they hang up their clothes and not turn their backs, but that would only drive him insane with desire and make her deeply uncomfortable. Instead, he said, "Want to do the swamp-tease again?"

"I'm fine as I am," Fen replied. "The coat is wet, but the fire's warmed it. It can dry off on me as well as it can hanging up. But if you'd rather…"

"No, I'm fine. The pants can dry on me too."

Carter sat down as close to the fire as he could get himself, then reached for his bag of tools and parts. He spread them out on the dirt before the fire, hoping they'd give him an idea. His mind drifted as considered the objects and everything they could be used for. Images of turning gears and twisting wires floated across his mind's eye, then coalesced into an idea.

He set aside a battery, picked up his wire-stripper, and was soon lost in his work. Carter only looked up when he'd finished. The sun had set and the only light came from the fire. Fen was sitting beside him, silent and still and swallowed up in his black coat, watching intently. On the ground beside her were a set of huge leaves she'd repurposed as plates. One was piled with pawpaws and one with what looked like tiny corncobs skewered on twigs.

"You went foraging?" he asked.

She nodded. "Those little corncob things are cattail spikes. You can toast them like marshmallows."

"How long have you been sitting there? I must've been boring you to death."

"Not long, and not at all. I like watching you work. It's… peaceful. What did you make? It looks like a miniature hair-dryer."

Please please please please please don't explode, he thought, and turned it on. Just in case, he kept his body between it and Fen.

The device whirred to life.

Immensely relieved, he said, "Hold out your hands."

Fen looked nervous, but did so. She laughed with sheer delight as hot air warmed them. "It *is* a hair dryer!"

"A small one," he said modestly. "Battery operated. But now we don't need to wait so long for our clothes to dry. Do you want to toast the cattails or dry the clothes?"

"I love that both jobs involve getting warm. I'll take the clothes; I miss using things with batteries. Um. That's not what I meant!" She went bright red.

It took him a moment to think of what embarrassing thing used batteries. The image of Fen using a vibrator on herself momentarily deprived him of speech, so he was unable to protest that he knew what she meant.

"Anyway, it'll be great to not be wet," she said hastily. In the silence that followed, he was clearly not the only person who saw a double meaning in that. "Okay, you need to get toasting so I can have something to put in my mouth—I mean to stop myself from talking—oh God!"

Carter was torn between cracking up and rushing off to use the man's equivalent of a vibrator—his own right hand—on himself.

Fen with a vibrator. Fen getting wet. Fen opening her mouth to receive his…

He gave himself a little smack on the back of the hand: *Stop. Refocus.* All else aside, she was obviously deeply embarrassed.

"I'm glad you like the dryer," he said.

"I love the dryer." She'd been alternating blowing hot air over the hanging clothes and the wet coat she was enveloped in, but now she turned it on him. The heat went beyond pleasant and into luxurious. "Isn't that great? Thanks, Carter. Not just for making a dryer in the middle of a swamp, but for knowing that making a dryer was a fantastic use of your time and equipment. I know people call you a genius all the time so it doesn't mean anything to you… but you're a genius."

"*You* don't call me a genius all the time. So thanks. It means something, coming from you."

She gave him a startled look, and he realized that he'd spoken his feelings without thinking about what they'd sound like. Yesterday he wouldn't have cared what Fenella Kim thought of him. But now, after everything they'd been through together, he did. He cared a lot.

He wasn't sure how he felt about her knowing that, though. So to make it seem less… significant… he added, "I mean, you're not just anyone. You're a genius yourself."

She stiffened, all the warmth and playfulness vanishing. In words that seemed carved out of ice, she said, "I'll thank you not to condescend to me. I know perfectly well what I am."

Carter was genuinely bewildered. "What are you talking about? I wasn't condescending. I meant it."

She gave him a sharp look. "Oh? Exactly how do you think I'm a genius?"

"Who doesn't think you're one? I created Howe Enterprises, you created Little Bit, we both got on the cover of *Wired.* Anyone who thinks I'm a genius thinks you're one too. I guess unless they're a sexist, racist idiot who thinks only white men count. But if they're like that, then their opinions don't count." When she didn't reply, he added, "You don't think I'm like that, do you?"

"No." She shook her head for emphasis, sending locks of hair tumbling around her face. Her hair had dried into a sexy mess of tangled black. He'd always thought it was perfectly straight and sleek, but apparently it only was because she styled it that way. Left to its own devices, it was slightly wavy. "I've never thought that."

Carter was relieved. "Then…?"

She impatiently brushed a black strand out of her eyes. "You're an inventor. Howe Enterprises is a success because you invent new things and build prototypes of them yourself. I'm a businesswoman. Little Bit is a success because I think of little improvements on existing products and I tell the tech people on my staff what they are, and they build them for me."

Carter was starting to get frustrated. "I *know.* That's its whole thing." Imitating the crisp tones of the actor who said her slogan in commercials, he recited, "'Little Bit is just a little bit better.'"

"So, you're the genius. I only think of little fixes and market them."

What she was saying was so foreign to his understanding that it took him a moment to realize that she wasn't putting him on. At last, he said, "Are you seriously saying you think doing what I do takes more intelligence than doing what you do?"

"*I* don't, but everyone else does."

"I don't."

Her dark eyes widened as she took in his sincerity. "You don't?"

"I don't."

Suspicion flickered across her face. "That's not what you told *Wired.*"

"Our companies were—are—rivals," he pointed out. "I could hardly tell *Wired* I thought yours was exactly as good as mine. Our stock would drop and yours would rise."

"But if it wasn't for the stock...?"

"Fen," Carter said. "Would you like to know a secret?"

"Sure."

"Have you ever noticed that I'm never photographed in my kitchen?"

She nodded, which pleased him. She'd been paying close attention to him, apparently. "I figured you had something embarrassing in there, like hundreds of bottles of Soylent and no actual food."

"I do, but it's not that disgusting stuff. My microwave is a Little Bit Hotter 500. My smart coffeemaker is a Little Bit Smoother 300."

"Just wait till you try the Little Bit Smoother 300 Deluxe," Fen began, then stopped short, staring at him. "Really? You use my kitchen equipment?"

"Well, Howe Enterprises doesn't have a kitchen division—" Carter barely cut himself off before he said *yet*. He'd gotten to like Fen, but he still had a business to run, and she was still his rival. "And I'd hardly use TicTech crap."

"Oh hell no," she said. "I call the Eldon McManus espresso machine the Little Bit Burnt."

Laughing, Carter agreed, "I call it the TicTerrible. But the Little Bit Smoother 300 makes absolutely stellar coffee, it never spills water or coffee grounds, and it's easy to use even before you've had coffee."

Visibly pleased, she said, "I tested it on sleep-deprived college students. If it took them more than six seconds to program what they wanted, it went back to the drawing board."

"And I love the self-cleaning function on the Little Bit Hotter 500. Even my teammates—uh, even some of the worst slobs at my company have failed to trash it, and believe me, they've tried."

"That's why we use college students as testers. If they can't wreck it, no one can." Her gaze drifted upward, as if she was considering something, then returned to him. She seemed to struggle inwardly, then spoke as if she was confessing to some truly shameful crime. "I like your phones."

Carter had heard that before. He'd heard it from friends and family, from product testers, from journalists, from random strangers, and, most gratifyingly, from other inventors. But it had never filled his heart with such pride and delight as when he'd heard it from Fen. Inside his head, his monsters purred and rumbled and preened. "You do?"

"If it wouldn't make Little Bit look bad, I'd buy one." Quickly, she added, "As a second phone. Just for games and stuff like that. I still think my Little Bit Faster is better for actually communicating with people, which is still the primary purpose of a phone."

"The Little Bit Faster does have a good texting system," Carter admitted.

"And calling."

"And calling. But nowadays phones are primarily miniature computers. Communication isn't their main purpose. Using the internet and gaming and taking photos and videos is."

"Which would you rather be able to do right now, video some bullfrogs or call for help?"

He spread his hands wide. "Okay. You got me."

Her triumphant grin made his defeat worthwhile. She practically glowed. Her hair, now dry, was a glory of rippling waves that a hairdresser would spend hours to achieve and still never get right. It framed her face like a black velvet setting for a perfect pearl. He wanted to touch it so much that his hands clenched involuntarily, nearly sending the cattails into the fire.

"Careful!" Fen exclaimed.

"I think they're done. Here, try one." He offered her a twig.

"Making me your product tester, huh?"

"Not at all. One person's opinion says nothing. They could be an outlier." He picked up another twig. "Three, two, one, test!"

They bit into the cattails and chewed thoughtfully. The spikes were chewy and stringy, like old asparagus, and the flavor reminded him of cabbage. Fen made a face, but swallowed valiantly.

"On a scale of zero to ten, with zero being 'I spit it out' and ten being 'the best thing I've ever eaten,' how would you rate this?" he asked.

"I give it a four for flavor and a two for texture," she replied. "You?"

"Four, that's generous. I give it a three for flavor and a two for texture."

Speaking in the precise tones of a market researcher, Fen inquired, "What would make you more likely to buy this product?"

"Being lost in a swamp with nothing else to eat."

"Excellent, we'll market it to survivalists. 'When you're lost in a swamp, cattail hits the spot!'"

"Sold," said Carter. "I'm glad we have some pawpaws left for breakfast, though."

"We've got enough to have some for dessert tonight."

They finished choking down the toasted cattails, then broke open a pair of pawpaws. Fen ate daintily, holding her hair back from her face with one hand. Carter also ate with one hand, using his other to aim the hair dryer on his clothes, but he too tried not to get the custard-like pawpaw all over his face. He might be lost in the swamp, but he didn't want her to think he was some kind of barbarian.

"Turn around?" she suggested when they finished. "My clothes are dry."

"So are mine."

The back-turned reverse strip-tease was only marginally less sexy than the one where they'd both gotten naked. They scrambled into their clothes, but he still had plenty of time to listen to Fen pulling on her skirt and blouse, and to imagine what she looked like doing it. Spontaneous combustion was a definite risk.

"Done?" he asked.

"Done."

They turned and faced each other. Her rumpled business suit looked like it had been plastered with mud, then rinsed off in swamp water, then blasted with a jerry-rigged hair dryer. Carter didn't even want to think about what his suit looked like.

But she was looking at him with a desire that matched his own. He could see it sparking in her dark eyes, feel it rising off her skin like smoke. It was unmistakable. And he knew that she felt his desire for her, the same way he had felt hers for him. Maybe you could only feel it this clearly when it was mutual.

"This is such a bad idea," Fen murmured in a husky tone that drove him wild.

"Terrible," he said.

She took a step forward. He could feel the warmth of her breath when she said, "It's sleeping with the enemy."

"Never a good move," he agreed.

"We absolutely shouldn't do this," she purred.

"Definitely not."

He bent down. She put her hands on his shoulders. Time seemed to stop with them caught in that moment, touching but apart. And then they were clutching at each other, bodies pressed together and lips locked.

For a moment, he forgot where he was. He practically forgot *who* he was. There was nothing in the world but her pliant body melting into his, her tongue caressing his, her sharp little teeth nibbling on his lip, the taste of pawpaws, the scent of her, and the force and flame of their mutual lust.

"Let's do the strip-tease again," whispered Fen. "And this time, let's watch."

Her eyes looked huge, the irises swallowed up by the pupils. A light danced in that utter darkness as she reached behind her back to undo the fastenings on her blouse.

Carter felt dizzy with the intensity of his desire. He knew what the strip-tease would lead to, and he wanted it so much that not having it would cause him physical pain. All he had to do was say yes, and he could make love to Fen. He could run his fingers through her tousled black hair, he could reach between her thighs and feel exactly how wet she was, he could see what she looked like when she came under his touch. He could breathe in the scent of her arousal, and it drove him wild.

But she wanted Carter Howe, genius inventor and businessman. She had no idea of the monster that lurked beneath his skin. If she did, she wouldn't invite him to strip with her, she'd run screaming. He couldn't have sex with her—he'd be doing it under false pretenses.

He wished he hadn't remembered that, and then hated himself for having that thought.

It was as hard to do as if he was in some dream where the air had solidified like gelatin, but he forced himself to take a step back. "Wait. We—We can't—"

"It's all right." Fen touched his cheek, smiling wickedly. "We'll only use our hands. And I know you're good with yours."

The thought of her curling her fingers around him sent a wave of lust crashing over him. He wanted so much to say yes. He *was* good with his hands. And he bet she was too.

I hate my life, Carter thought.

Feeling like he was throwing himself head-first into a pit of bullfrogs, he said, "No. Wait. I—"

As she dropped her hand, looking at him quizzically, he ground to a halt. A wave of cold horror hit him as he realized that he was either going to have to tell her there was something she needed to know first and then tell her what it was, or else turn her down flat. He couldn't say "Not yet," and then string her along waiting for a revelation that would never come.

Tell her, growled a monster.

No, show her, shrieked another monster.

The monsters all seemed to like that idea. They began chanting, screaming, hissing, bellowing, and snarling, *Show her! Show her! Show her!*

[eager electric blue]

Carter's head felt like it was about to explode. He clutched at it involuntarily, then saw Fen staring and dropped his hands.

"Uh…" He fished for something, anything to say. Nothing presented itself.

Trapped in a swamp and hunted like an animal with a gorgeous, brilliant, funny woman who wants to have sex with me, and I can't either say yes or tell her why not, he thought. *A gorgeous, brilliant, funny woman who will never want to have sex with me again, because I responded to her incredibly hot invitation by backing off and grabbing my hair like a lunatic.*

"I have a headache," he said at last. It was true, but it made him feel like a liar. "I know that sounds like a bored housewife in a movie from the fifties, but…"

"No, no. You have a head injury. Why don't you lie down?"

Before he could protest, she'd pulled him down to the slightly squishy ground. Her sympathy and belief made him hate himself. "I'm fine. I was making a fuss over nothing,"

"Don't be ridiculous," she said crisply. "You got knocked unconscious twice in a single day. Now put your head in my lap. I promise not to hit on you."

Seeing no alternative, he lay down with his head in her lap. She began to stroke his hair, her slim fingers combing through every tangle. He relaxed as she gently rubbed his forehead and temples, avoiding the injured area. It felt incredibly good, tender and sensual without any performance pressure.

A deep sigh escaped him as he melted into her caress. He'd been too distracted by things like being kidnapped and trying to shoo away a dragonette to pay attention to it before, but his head did ache, and not only because of the monsters. His whole body felt, unsurprisingly, like he'd been punched repeatedly and thrown around an airplane.

"Thanks, Fen. You ever thought you'd stroke the forehead of your chief business rival?"

"Only if I was trying to plant a surveillance chip in his hair."

He laughed. "Well, now's the time. I'd probably assume it was a leaf."

"I didn't bring one. What a missed opportunity."

He gazed up at her as she rubbed his neck, taking out the stiffness. A truly incredible number of dangling swords of impending doom hung over him, but whenever he started to worry, her fingers would move and he'd be drawn back into a warm bubble of contentment.

"I'm sorry I tried to take over your company," he said. "I used to be a real jerk."

"Used to be?" She tapped his nose, taking any sting out of her words.

"I've gotten much better," he protested.

"Well, I'm not sorry I tried to take over yours. You deserved it. But I'll drop it as soon as we get out of here."

"Thanks. You weren't going to get it anyway, but it'll save us both a lot of money in lawyers' fees."

"Was too," she said.

"Were not."

"Was too."

"Were not." He rolled over and pulled her down so she lay beside him. She laid her head on his shoulder, and he tugged on his coat to cover them both. "Comfy?"

"Mm-hmm."

She snuggled in closer. He held her tight, marveling at the chance that had brought them together. It would never go any further than this. Eventually he'd have to end it before it got serious enough to hurt her, and break his own heart. But for now, for this one precious moment, he'd enjoy what he had and not think about the future.

"The stars are so bright," she said.

With no artificial light and their fire dying down to coals, the stars shone brilliant against the absolute blackness of the night sky. He could even see the glitter-dust sweep of the Milky Way.

"When I was a kid, I had glow-in-the-dark sticky stars on my bedroom ceiling," he said.

"Lucky. I wanted those. My parents wouldn't let me."

"Neat freaks?" Carter asked sympathetically.

"Perfectionists. My father was a Korean diplomat who met my mother when he was posted to England. She was English aristocracy, the sort with a huge ancestral manor they can't afford to maintain. He got a job in DC and they settled down in the US. I grew up in a big posh house where nothing could be messy or tacky or ugly. No pets, no ripped jeans, no glow-in-the-dark stars."

"No Babysitters Club." He was beginning to get an inkling of why Fen, or at least the public persona of Fenella Kim, was the way she was.

"Classics, literary fiction, and highbrow nonfiction only."

"What did they expect you to read when you were a little girl, *Moby Dick*?"

"Oh, no, I got all the best, most award-winning, and age-appropriate children's books." Fen huffed a soft, warm chuckle against his throat. "Guess what those were like."

"Stultifyingly boring and full of improving moral lessons?"

"Sometimes. But mostly they were depressing. I got books about grandmas dying of cancer, grandpas dying of heart attacks, sisters dying of leukemia, best friends dying of freak accidents, and dogs dying of rabies, grief, getting hit by a car, and getting shot by racists. In retrospect, I'm lucky it didn't turn me off reading."

"It should've turned you off your parents," said Carter.

She shrugged. "They were brilliant and did everything perfectly. I was this gawky, absent-minded girl who lost her homework and flunked classes and generally didn't measure up. They had sophisticated conversations about politics and current events at the dinner table, and God help you if you got bored and spaced out. They used to ask me to repeat what they'd just said when they thought I was daydreaming, and I don't think I ever managed it. Most of the time I didn't even remember the general topic."

Carter was indignant on young Fen's behalf. "It's not fair to expect a kid to keep up with an adult diplomat's conversation about politics."

He felt rather than saw her turn to look away from him, up into the night sky. "Yeah, I get that now. But enough about me and my parents. What was your family like?"

"Warm," he said, after a moment of thought. Normally he could easily describe his family without having to consciously edit out any reference to shifting. But lying there on the slightly damp grass with Fen in his arms, he felt like he was doing everything for the first time. "Relaxed. A bit chaotic. There were always a bunch of uncles and aunts and cousins and foster kids and so forth around. We had a big house, but people were still always unexpectedly showing up and sleeping on the sofa. I took over the attic so I didn't have to share a room. I always had bits and pieces of things I was building lying around, and I was sick of them getting stepped on and moved around."

"Did they appreciate what you could do?" She sounded so concerned for the young Carter that he rushed to reassure her.

"Oh, sure. It wasn't like there was so much going on that I got ignored. I like things more organized and less noisy, that's all. If I can't keep everything exactly in its place, I can never find it again." A yawn stretched his jaw so wide that it gave an audible pop. "We should get some rest. I already set my watch alarm for dawn."

"How do you know when dawn is? We don't know the time zones here."

He smiled. "It's light-sensitive; it's set to the sun."

"You're so smart," she said, and snuggled in close. Before he could tell her she was too, her breathing evened out into sleep.

He lay awake a while longer, knowing he needed to get as much rest as possible in case he had to fight tomorrow but unwilling to miss a minute of having Fen in his arms. It wasn't only the pleasure that went bone-deep, but an unexpected tenderness. She felt so *right* there; he felt so right holding her. And he might never get this chance again.

As he drifted off to sleep despite himself, he wondered if Precious had delivered his note.

CHAPTER 7

Fen awoke hot and sweaty yet strangely content. A song was playing and warm arms held her tight. She stretched luxuriously, thinking vaguely that she should probably get up and turn on the air conditioning, but it felt so good to lie at ease, draped all over the body of…

…Carter Howe!

She sat upright with a gasp as she remembered where she was. Carter lay on the grass in the pale dawn light. His watch was playing Green Day. He blinked, glanced down at it and turned it off, then saw her. His hazel eyes widened as she watched him replay the day before in about two seconds. She expected him to jump to his feet as he regretted everything and rushed to distance himself, physically and emotionally.

Instead, he reached up and ruffled her hair. She instantly understood why cats purred when people did that as she leaned into his touch.

"You're beautiful in the morning," he said. "Definitely the highlight of the swamp."

So he didn't regret their kissing and cuddling, nor was he going to pretend it hadn't happened. Well, well, well. If he had no regrets, she certainly wasn't going to pretend she did.

Fen leaned down and kissed him. Neither of them had brushed their teeth, but just this once, she didn't care. And once they got going, she forgot all about that.

But she didn't forget that they were being hunted by mad movie fanatics. Neither, evidently, did he. They broke off simultaneously, then packed their stuff into the boat. After a check of the leaf compass, they set off north, or at least approximately north.

The swamp was especially noisy in the early morning. For a while the frogs were so loud they couldn't even talk, and once the frogs shut up, the birds began. But she didn't mind. She was inexplicably, absurdly, ridiculously happy. Who would have ever thought she'd feel so good being chased through a swamp by armed lunatics, in ruined clothes and swamp water-washed hair, with none other than her hated rival Carter Howe?

She mentally crossed off the 'hated.' Fen had a lot of feelings about him, but hatred was no longer one of them.

"How's your head?" she asked.

"Much better." There was an odd note in Carter's voice, and she twisted around to get a better look at him. He looked as deeply conflicted as he'd sounded.

"Are you sure? You're not just saying that to preserve your Manly Man credentials?"

He shook his head and gave her a smile that looked sincere. "I'm sure. See, I shook my head and it didn't make me feel like it might fall off."

"Always a good thing." Fen offered him a pawpaw. "Can you manage a dad while you're paddling?"

He grinned. "No, thanks. I'd either get it all over my face or drop it overboard and feed the batrachian horrors. You?"

"Same," Fen admitted. "Let's keep on now and take a lunch break later."

"Sounds good."

They paddled on together, talking easily about many things: movies that were overrated and movies that were rated exactly as highly as they deserved, how they first got interested in science and technology, and which set of Star Wars movies was the best. They played Twenty Questions, debated over which of TicTech's products were the most poorly designed and which of Eldon McManus's ideas were the most harebrained, and fantasized over meals they'd eat once they escaped the swamp and its limited menu of cattail spikes and pawpaws.

They did not discuss the kiss or what was happening between them, for which Fen was guiltily grateful. She had no idea what their relationship was becoming, whether it would last, or even whether they'd kiss again, but she had a strong feeling that nothing would ruin it faster than an in-depth feelings discussion before an audience of bullfrogs.

During their quick lunch stop, Carter constructed a fishing line to trail behind the boat. When the sun touched the horizon and the light turned to deep gold, they found a non-floating island with plenty of shrubbery to hide both the boat and their fire, docked the boat, and pulled up the line.

"A fish!" Fen exclaimed.

He held it up as if he was posing for a photo, then took out his multitool and began to clean and filet it. Fen watched, impressed. She'd have expected him to be squeamish about it, but he'd obviously done it before.

"Did you ever work as a chef?"

He glanced from his careful work deboning the fish. "My family was into hunting and fishing. It was..." He came to one of those abrupt halts that tended to happen, she'd noticed, when he talked about his own life. He never did that stop-and-backtrack when he was discussing, say, movies. "Well, I learned some things."

What are you leaving out, Carter? Fen wondered. *How could you go hunting and fishing with your family, enough to clean a fish like an expert, and still be less comfortable in nature than a former Girl Scout?*

But she didn't press him. She was still overflowing with goodwill and sexual chemistry, not to mention the promise of a fish dinner and the hope of making out afterward. No need to spoil a good thing with unwanted prying into his personal life.

She went foraging while he figured out how to cook the fish, and returned with watercress and a handful of elderberries.

"I saw some mushrooms too, but I was only ninety-eight percent sure they weren't poisonous," she explained, showing him her bounty. "So I left them."

"Good call," he said, turning the fish over on a handmade rock oven. "Though I guess we could've tested them on the bullfrogs."

The fish came out hot and flaky. Even without salt or seasonings, it was one of the most delicious meals she'd ever had. There was enough for both of them, especially when supplemented with the watercress as a side salad. They ate the tart elderberries for dessert.

"If I had been a chef, I'd have charged a lot for that meal," said Carter contentedly.

"And I'd have paid it." Fen warmed her hands over the crackling fire. The sexual chemistry between them was crackling as well. Now that he'd clearly recovered from his headache and they were both well-fed, it was time for some wild and passionate swamp sex. "Now that we've had such an expensive dinner, I don't see the point in paying the restaurant for after-dinner drinks. I've got a nice bottle of whiskey at home. Want to come over and have a drink at my place?"

For an instant, he looked like there was nothing he wanted more. He started to lean in, then jerked back with an expression that told her there would not be any swamp sex that night. "Um... Look, Fen..."

She was hurt. Wasn't she good enough for him? Did he suddenly notice that she smelled like swamp water? Then she told herself that there were plenty of reasons he could have for wanting to take it slow. She was an adult, not a teenager, and she was going to act like one. "Or we could hold off until we're out of the swamp. I get it if you'd rather take a rain check until we're not being chased by lunatics through schools of bullfrogs."

She'd hoped he'd smile and agree. Instead, he edged away from her. Judging by the look on his face, she might have been a bullfrog herself.

"I don't think that's a good—" He broke off and clutched at his head.

"Are you all right?" Fen asked, worried.

Then the penny dropped. He'd made that exact same gesture the last time they'd come close to making out. She'd taken it at face value, given that he'd been repeatedly hit over the head. But it was deeply suspicious that these headaches came on only when she tried to get close to him.

Had she been right about him all along? Was he the sort of immature playboy who'd fake a headache rather than be straightforward with a woman?

Stiffly, she said, "If you're not interested, just say so. Don't pretend you have a migraine."

"Stop it!" Carter yelled.

She stared at him. "*Excuse me?*"

He let out a groan, his hands dropping from his head. "I wasn't talking to you. I mean—"

Before he could finish his sentence, a strange sound pierced the air, halfway between a birdcall and a windchime. Something golden darted down from the dark sky.

Fen had seen it before; she recognized both the color and the movement. She'd thought it had been a drone, and Carter had said it was a helium balloon.

It was neither. The golden thing was alive. As she stared, incredulous, taking in the gleaming golden hide, the slim body, the four clawed legs, and the translucent bat-like wings, she couldn't deny that she knew exactly what it was. The impossible little creature was a dragon the size of a cat.

"That's a..." Fen began, but her voice trailed off. Even though it was right in front of her, she couldn't bring herself to actually say the word *"dragon."*

The tiny golden dragon held something shiny in its two front... paws? Hands? Feet? With a squeak Fen couldn't help but hear as triumphant, it released what it was holding. Carter automatically opened his hands, and the thing smacked into them. It popped open when it hit, revealing that it was a beautiful brass compass. A piece of plastic followed the compass and bounced off it, landing somewhere in the weeds.

"What the actual fuck," said Fen, finding her voice at last.

Carter found his voice as well. "She's not mine!"

Fen stared at him. She'd thought that he, like herself, had been struck dumb with the sheer *what the actual fuck* of it all. But his words, not to mention his expression like he'd been caught with both hands in the cookie jar and chocolate chips falling out of his mouth, gave her an unpleasant sinking feeling, as if the island was floating after all and had just sprung a leak.

"Why would you say that?" she inquired.

He recovered quickly, but she knew what she'd heard. Brandishing the compass, he said, "It did give me a present." Meeting her icy stare, he hastily said, "Kidding! It dropped the compass and I caught it automatically."

The dragon was flying in circles above them, squeaking. The firelight gleamed off its golden flanks and shone through the translucent membranes of its wings.

"It's a dragon," said Fen, distracted from Carter's perfidy by sheer wonder. "A tiny baby dragon. They're real."

"No no no," he babbled. "There's no such thing as dragons. It's a… flying swamp lizard. I think I read about them in *Ranger Rick* when I was a little—"

She only realized that he had been subtly edging away from the tiny dragon when the little creature gave a frustrated squeak and darted at him. He tried to duck away. Fen, thinking he was being attacked, lunged to try to grab it. The tiny dragon dodged her and landed on his shoulder. But rather than attacking him, it nuzzled his neck, making happy chirruping sounds.

"Shoo!" Carter commanded.

The little dragon responded by nuzzling him harder. Also by licking his neck, wriggling around on his shoulder, and generally behaving like the world's smallest golden retriever. With wings.

"It knows you," said Fen.

"No. No, absolutely not. Of course it doesn't. How could it?"

He pocketed the compass and gave the golden dragon a desperate push. The little creature clearly thought this was a game. It leaped onto his other shoulder and playfully booped his cheek with its nose.

"Umm," he said. "It's friendly, isn't it? I think I remember that those flying swamp lizards—"

His words lit a fire within Fen. More precisely, they lit the fuse of a stick of inner dynamite. She had no idea what was going on and she hated not knowing what was going on. Carter was lying to her, and she hated being lied to. And to think that she'd kissed that dragon-owning liar! In her mind's eye, she saw the dynamite exploding in slow motion, blasting him into the middle of next week.

"You liar!" Fen prided herself on never yelling—it gave men an easy excuse to call her hysterical—but if ever there was a situation that justified screaming, it was this one. "You absolute, barefaced, shameless LIAR! You said it was a helium balloon when you KNEW it was a dragon! You never read about any flying swamp lizards because THERE'S NO SUCH THING!"

"Shhhh!" Carter hissed. "There's people hunting us. We don't know how far away they are."

Her voice had risen without her intending it to do so, but at that, she inflated her chest and deliberately screamed at top of her lungs. "THERE ARE NO KIDNAPPERS! THERE'S JUST YOU AND YOUR MINIONS AND YOUR BABY DRAGON! YOU STAGED YOUR OWN KIDNAPPING AND NOW YOU STAGED MINE! I BET YOU SPENT HALF YOUR FORTUNE TO HAVE THIS DRAGON GENETICALLY ENGINEERED SO YOU COULD PLAY SOME FUCKED-UP GAME WITH ME IN THE SWAAAAAAMP!!!!"

Carter stepped forward, trying to clap a hand over her mouth. The golden dragon darted at his hands, delighted by this new game.

Fen dodged him and took a few steps back. Her foot landed on something hard, and she remembered the bit of plastic the dragon had dropped. She bent to pick it up, then ducked again, avoiding Carter's grab for it. Fen read it aloud, her eyes flickering back and forth so she could glare at him at the same time.

"'If you're reading this, you have won a new phone of your choice, courtesy of Howe Enterprises and our latest viral marketing context! Contact Protection, Inc: Defenders in Refuge City and tell them you have a message from Carter Howe. Give them this. The code words are kidnap, swamp, pawpaw, wizard.'" She shook the bit of plastic at him. "And there's your extremely famous signature at the bottom!"

Shaking it wasn't good enough. She hurled the plastic at him. It bounced off his forehead.

"Hey!" Carter yelped.

The little dragon flapped its wings and hissed.

Fen took another deep breath. Yelling was surprisingly satisfying. "VIRAL MARKETING? IS THAT WHAT THIS IS?!"

"No! No, of course not!" He sounded sincere, but then he always sounded sincere. He probably sounded most honest when he was lying the hardest. "I was trying to get help, and I thought 'Help, I've been kidnapped' would sound like a prank."

"TRYING TO GET HELP BY SENDING YOUR PET DRAGON?!"

"Will you please lower your voice?!" Carter hissed.

She was in no mood to do so. And besides, she had one more thing she wanted to shout. Inflating her lungs and raising her voice to the absolute maximum, she shouted, "AND YOU HAD THE NERVE TO KISS ME WHEN YOU WERE LYING TO ME ALL ALONG!!!!"

He made another try at putting his hand over her mouth, but was again hampered by the dragon.

Fen bared her teeth. "Do that and I'll bite you!"

He lowered his hand, but kept it ready. "And we both know you could probably take off a finger. Look, Fen, I'll explain every—I'll explain. But there really are people after us—well, after me—so please don't shout."

The fire of righteous anger filled her, but she also felt oddly relaxed.

It was as if she'd opened a gate that had long been under pressure, releasing a pent-up flood. "Fine. Explain. Start with the baby dragon."

CHAPTER 8

Carter had always prided himself on honesty. If he couldn't tell the truth, he at least tried to omit information rather than outright lie. He'd had to keep shifters a secret from non-shifters, of course, but it wasn't as if non-shifters commonly asked questions like "Can you turn into a snow leopard?" He simply didn't mention that he could, and that was that.

After he'd been kidnapped (the first time) and turned into a monster, he was confronted with keeping a different secret. He had to give the public some explanation, but he was so unused to making things up that he resorted to a story which, in retrospect, could have been more plausible.

And then there was the matter of what exactly had happened to him when he'd been kidnapped. His family and teammates—the guys he contracted for sometimes—already knew he was a shifter. The Defenders additionally already knew, more or less, what had happened to him, because, more or less, it had happened to them too. And he could hardly lie to his family. So he'd simply refused to give any details other than that his captors had experimented on him and killed his snow leopard. His family, naturally, had been so horrified and sorry for him that they hadn't tried to make him say more.

You should've told them about us, growled a monster.

Yes, yes, hissed another monster.

You should've shown *them us,* screeched a third.

Even the thought of revealing his monster self made Carter feel like he'd been punched in the gut. His snow leopard had been beautiful and sleek and dangerous, agile and lithe and quick. His leopard had been *him*—the truest, deepest, most primal part of him.

And now that truest, deepest part of him was a hideous, disgusting, destructive, unwanted, out of control, repulsive—

Hey! The monsters snarled and shrieked and hissed a chorus of disapproval.

Carter gritted his teeth so hard they felt like they might shatter. He'd lied to Fen that Precious was a helium balloon and a flying swamp lizard, but he wouldn't lie any more than he had to. As far as he could manage, omission was the name of the game.

The monsters in his head broke into an uproar that threatened to split his head open.

STOP LYING!

TELL THE TRUTH!

YOU CAN TRUST HER!

SHE ALREADY KNOWS ABOUT PRECIOUS!

SHE'S READ YOUR NOTE!

[insistent orange]

And then all the monsters began to chant and hiss and growl and screech and snarl and scream and color-flash the same thing.

TELL HER!

TELL HER!

TELL HER!

TELL HER!

TELL HER!

"All right!" Carter said aloud. He dropped his hands down from where he'd been clutching his head. He had a splitting headache, and he knew the monsters wouldn't give up until they got what they wanted. "I'll tell you everything."

And he would. It wasn't as if he had any choice. But in the deepest, quietest, most private recesses of his mind, the one place he had left where the monsters couldn't reach, he thought, *I'll tell her everything... except that I'm a monster.*

Precious rubbed her head under his chin, and he couldn't help feeling cheered. She'd given away the game, but he couldn't blame her. She couldn't stand to stay away from him, and as baffling as that was, it moved him too.

"She's a dragonette," said Carter. "Not a baby dragon. She won't ever get much bigger than this." She banged her head into his throat, making him cough and then chuckle. "Her name is Precious."

Fen looked as though she wanted to object, but couldn't find anything specific to pick on. She settled on, "Does that make you Gollum?"

"Do I look like Gollum?" Seeing the gleam in her eyes, he said, "Don't answer that."

The faintest snicker escaped her lips. "I know not to call anyone anything that can turn into 'no you.'"

"I would never," he said with perfect sincerity. "Even when you were covered in mud, you looked like..." He fished for another *Lord of the Rings* comparison. Both movies and books were sadly short on female characters, and none of them looked like Fen. He settled on one who was at least dark-haired. "...like Arwen covered in mud."

"I'll take that," she said grudgingly. "Where'd your precioussss come from?"

"I don't know—" Seeing her draw in a deep breath, no doubt to scream at him, he hastily added, "I mean, I don't know where she *originally* came from. The first time I ever saw her was yesterday—when I went off by myself, she flew down and sort of glommed on to me."

"But you already knew what she was. You claimed she was a drone and ran off to meet her."

"I guessed what she was," he corrected her. "I'm pretty sure she was one of a bunch of magical animals—"

"*Magical animals*?!" She sounded equal parts outraged and

disbelieving.

"You're the one who knew she wasn't some kind of rare lizard. Look for yourself." He pried Precious off his shoulder. "Fen, hold out your arm. Precious, go visit Fen."

Fen scowled, but offered her forearm. Precious lifted off and landed on it. She cocked her head, looked inquiringly at Fen with a sapphire eye, and trilled. Cautiously, Fen petted her. Precious stretched her wings and wriggled with pleasure.

Carter made sure to keep a straight face. If he smiled, Fen would probably drown him in the swamp. But as he'd guessed, Precious could melt even the prickliest, chilliest, angriest heart. Fen looked positively happy as she stroked the golden dragonette, marveling, "Her skin's so soft and warm. I thought she'd feel like a snake, but it's more like suede."

"Technically it's hide, not skin," Carter said absently.

He shouldn't have said anything. Fen's head whipped up and she fixed him with a glare again. "Don't think you can get out of explaining this by distracting me with your little pet."

"I was trying to explain," he protested. "You keep interrupting me."

She glared some more, then boosted Precious on to her shoulder and folded her arms. "Fine. No more interruptions. Tell me the entire story, from the beginning. I want to know every detail about every bizarre thing going on right now. And include your desert island lie, because I have a feeling that's part of it."

Precious flew back to his shoulder, where she flapped her wings and hissed at Fen.

"Is she defending you?" Fen asked incredulously. "Just how smart is she?"

"I don't know if she understood that you were calling me a liar, but she could tell you were mad at me. She obviously didn't get what I was trying to do with the note, but she does seem to understand feelings."

"Figures." Fen sat down on the grass and fed more sticks into the fire. "I get dumped in a swamp, and you get a beautiful little empathic dragon."

"I got dumped in the swamp too," Carter protested.

He sat down on grass that squished unpleasantly. She pointedly scooted away from him. The moment when they'd kissed kept replaying in his mind. It had been one of the very best moments of his entire life, and now she was furious with him again and he had to lie to her again. And not only did he have to lie to her, but she probably wouldn't even believe the true parts. And they were still lost and hunted in a swamp.

And she'd never let him kiss her again.

That's your *fault,* hissed a monster.

We told you to be honest, screeched a monster.

[guilt-trip purple]

"Okay. I'll start at the beginning. This is going to be hard to believe, but keep in mind..." He indicated Precious. "Dragonette."

Fen impatiently gestured to him to get on with it.

"Magical animals exist. Dragonettes. Bugbears. Kittens with wings. All sorts of strange little creatures... and sometimes not so little. They're very rare and hidden, and the people who know about them keep them secret for their own protection. They don't want them to get locked up in secret labs and experimented on. With me so far?"

"Sure," said Fen, a little grudgingly. Then, softening a bit, "Kittens with wings sound adorable. I'd love to pet one."

"They're unbelievable nuisances," said Carter. "Like toddlers that will never grow up, and can fly. Nothing's safe from them. And bugbears are even worse. Remember in the plane, when you saw blue hairs on my coat and asked if I had a blue cat, and I said they were from a carpet? You were right, they were animal hairs. Only they were actually from a bugbear."

"And a bugbear is...?"

"A hairy thing the size of a Saint Bernard, but blue. It steals chocolate, breaks things, and sheds. A guy I know has one." He paused, watching her for a reaction. "Do you believe me?"

In a perfect mimicry of his gesture and inflection, she indicated

Precious and said, "Dragonette." Returning to her own voice, she said, "How did you get involved with the magical animals, though?"

He took a deep breath. This was the part he wished he could avoid. Choosing his words carefully, he said, "Because cute little animals like Precious aren't the only magic in the world. There's also shifters—people who can shapeshift into animals. It runs in families, usually. Shifters live alongside regular humans, but they keep their abilities absolutely secret from non-shifters. It's for the same reason magical animals are secret—no one wants to get locked up and treated like a lab animal."

Fen looked deeply suspicious. "Uh-huh. And this relates to you how?"

Here goes. His stomach was tied up in knots. He struggled to keep his breathing under control. "I was born a shifter. My whole family can turn into snow leopards. When I disappeared for a year, it was because I'd been kidnapped and experimented on by a black ops agency. When you're a shifter, it doesn't just mean you can become an animal. There's a part of you that *is* that animal. It's a voice in your mind, a place in your heart. It's the deepest, most primal, most *you* part of you. That was my snow leopard. And they killed him. I'll never become a snow leopard again. I can't prove any of this to you."

He waited for her to say "How convenient" or something along those lines. But she didn't. She kept still, looking at him with those dark eyes of hers. They were wells of emotions he couldn't understand.

Unable to bear the suspense, he said, "Go on, get it over with. Call me a liar. Just don't scream it."

He was bracing himself so hard for it that when she leaned over and put her hand over his, he almost jumped out of his skin. "What's that for?"

"It's a thing humans do to express sympathy, you weirdo." She squeezed his hand. "I'm not going to call you a liar. I believe you."

"Why?" he blurted out.

"Because when you said they killed your snow leopard, you didn't sound like you were lying or fucking with me. You sounded like it broke your heart."

Carter felt like he'd been punched him in the gut. He'd tried so hard to keep his emotion under control, but either he'd done a terrible job or sharp-as-a-tack Fen Kim had seen right through him. "Yeah. It did. Let's talk about something else. I mean, I'll explain the rest of it, but let's table the exact details about what they did to me."

He felt equal parts guilty and relieved when she nodded. "No problem. Believe me, I have lots of questions that have nothing to do with that."

"I bet you do. Okay, you asked how I knew about the magical animals. A while back I helped some other shifters break into another secret lab that was experimenting on people. It also had a bunch of magical animals in cages. Some of them got adopted by the team I was with, and some of them escaped. I'm pretty sure Precious is one of the ones that escaped. I really did meet her today. They have a way of finding people they want to attach themselves to."

Precious squeaked and nibbled on his ear.

"Lucky," Fen said wistfully. "I'd love to have a tiny dragon. She even brought you a present."

"A useful one, too. Though I wish she'd brought me a cell phone."

"Could she?" A wild hope gleamed in Fen's dark eyes. "How smart is she? She knew to bring you a compass when you were lost..."

He had to shake his head. "I think that's a coincidence. It's pretty and shiny. I tried to get her to drop off a message, and you saw how well that went."

She picked up the message from where it had fallen after she'd bounced it off his head. "What's Protection, Inc: Defenders?"

"A bodyguard agency. They're the guys I helped rescue from the lab that had the magical animals. I help them with technical stuff sometimes. One of them has that infernal nuisance of a bugbear."

"Are they shifters?"

He nodded. "But they weren't born shifters like me. The lab experimented on them and made them into shifters. It really messed them up, too. The scientists were trying to give them powers apart being able to turn into animals, and they had some nasty side effects. But one of the bodyguards has the power of finding things. Information. People. I figured if the message got to him, he could probably find us."

She looked at the plastic strip with new interest. "I get kidnap, swamp, and pawpaw. But what's wizard?"

Carter had been dreading this part. He hesitated, and she pounced. "You don't want to tell me. What is it, a code word for your viral marketing scheme?"

"There is no viral marketing scheme."

"What then? A code word for 'a civilian learned about shifters, be ready to wipe her memory?'"

"No! What sort of monst—horrible person do you think I am?" As an afterthought, he added, "Anyway, no one can wipe anyone's memory. That's not a thing."

"Then—"

He held up his hand, stopping the apparently limitless flow of her ideas about terrible things he might do under the code name of "wizard."

"I didn't want to tell you because out of all the things you're not going to believe, it's the hardest to believe. But since you're obviously going to keep on guessing that it means something awful about me, I'll tell you what it does mean. It's not a code word. It actually does mean wizard. That's who's really after us—well, after me. The note about hunters and the most dangerous game is just some weird mind-game they're playing with me."

He braced himself for her to scream "LIAAAAR!!!"

An incredulous grin cracked her face. "Wizards? Like Harry Potter?"

"More like Voldemort."

She leaned forward, resting her chin on her fists, for all the world like she was watching the opening credits in a long-awaited movie. "Go on."

Carter searched her expression for disbelief or mockery or anger, but found none. "You believe in wizards?"

She made a face. "Not until now. Don't you go telling the magazines Fenella Kim sleeps with a window open because she expects a letter from an owl!"

"I would never," he assured her. "I knew that wasn't what you meant."

"Well, I did when I was eight," she admitted. "But what I meant is that I believe *you,* Carter. I don't know why I do, given how much you've lied to me, but everything that's happened is so weird that wizards make as much sense as anything. Also, I've noticed an interesting pattern with your lies."

Alarmed, he asked, "What's that?"

"I probably shouldn't tell you," she muttered. "It'll be teaching you to lie better."

"I swear..." he began.

"Don't bother. If you're telling your secrets, I may as well tell you something I've been keeping from you." Her grin was surprisingly warm. "Your lies try to make things sound more plausible than they are. 'Crashed on a desert island' isn't *likely*, but it's a lot more believable than 'kidnapped and experimented on.' Helium balloons and rare lizards are more plausible than dragonettes. 'Wizards' are even less likely than 'man-hunting lunatics.' Given that, I think your wizards are the unlikely, implausible, unbelievable truth."

It was unlikely, implausible, and unbelievable, but Fen believed him. In the flickering light of their swamp cookfire, her openness to whatever weird story he was about to tell was written all over her face.

"It's hard for *me* to believe," he admitted. "You have to understand, shifters are normal to me. But up until I got kidnapped, all the shifters I'd ever known turned into ordinary animals. I'd never heard of magical animals outside of fantasy books, or of shifters who turned into anything that didn't exist. I knew we had to keep shifting a secret, but I'd never met anyone who'd actually gotten captured by a lab. I didn't even think of shifting as magic. I thought of it as a bit like having an unusual genetic trait like six fingers, and a bit like belonging to the world's coolest secret society."

"When did you find out about Voldemort?"

"After I got kidnapped. The black ops group that took me was experimenting on shifters, and on turning ordinary people into shifters. I got broken loose by two other people they'd captured." He kept his voice as even as he could, but it wasn't easy to talk about.

"I don't need the details about that," Fen said. She was obviously picking up on how stressed he was getting. "Just jump ahead to Saruman."

He forced a smile. Her fantasy references did amuse him, but there was more going on than not wanting to talk about a traumatic experience. Once again, he was leaving out crucial information, and it wasn't the sort that she was assuming.

If she ever found out what sort of person I really am...

He plunged ahead, speaking quickly to drown out his guilt and his secrets and the shrieks of his monsters. "Thanks. Well, the people who broke me loose were with an all-shifter private security agency on the west coast called Protection, Inc. I owed them a favor, so I offered to fly them or their whole team anywhere, anytime, with no questions asked. They called in the favor a while later to ask me to fly them to the lab I mentioned before, the one with the magical animals."

Precious, who had been napping in his lap, stirred in her sleep. He stroked her until she settled down.

"That lab was also experimenting on shifters and turning ordinary people into them, but it was under different management from mine. They called themselves wizard-scientists, and they really could do magic, not to mention weird science. We blew up the lab, but some of the wizard-scientists escaped. That place I do tech support for, Protection, Inc: Defenders, is the guys who got turned into shifters there. The wizard-scientists have been stalking them ever since, one by one. I figured I was exempt since I'm not actually part of their team, but obviously not." He waved his hand, indicating the swamp.

"Wait." Fen's eyes narrowed. "You think the guys who dumped us here are wizard-scientists? Those guys in the plane were them?"

"Not exactly. I think they're employed by wizard-scientists. This is exactly the sort of trick they'd pull."

"Did you know this all along?" Fen asked indignantly.

"Yeah, but it wasn't like I could tell you. What would you have said if I'd told you in the plane that we'd been kidnapped by wizard-scientists?"

"Bitten you, probably," she admitted. "If I could reach."

Carter spread his hands. "See? I was hoping to get us both out and send you on your way without you ever finding out. And if it wasn't for Precious, I might've been able to."

She frowned. "So are we being hunted or aren't we?"

"Oh, we're definitely being hunted. Just not in the way you've been thinking. I'm still hoping we can get out of the swamp before they catch up to us. But if not, based on what happened to the other guys, we'll get chased around and menaced by the most bizarre shifters you can imagine—those will be the wizard-scientists' minions—and when they think we've been beaten into submission, they'll tell me to join them or else."

She blinked a few times, taking this in. He didn't blame her. It was a lot, even for him. "What sort of bizarre shifters? Dragonettes? Big dragons?"

"If only. The last time one of the Defenders got attacked by them, the wizard-scientist was this awful woman named Elayne who could turn into a harpy. She also had the power to manipulate shadows and make them solid, so literally every shadow you walked by could grab you."

"Ugh!" Fen shuddered. "Something so creepy about that."

"This all went down in an amusement park after dark, so it was even creepier. And she had henchmen who were shifters she'd created in a lab, so they had weird shift forms *and* special powers. One of them could give you vertigo, one could tell if you were lying, and so forth."

"And their shift forms were…?"

"One could turn into a chupacabra."

Her eyebrows rose. "A goat-sucker? Those are real?"

"You mean, other than her? Got me. And there were two dinosaur shifters. One was a giant lizard-bird, and one was this enormous armored fish." Carter laughed. "The fish couldn't breathe on land, of course. You'd think the guy who could turn into it would have stayed human and used his power to give us vertigo. But no. He kept turning into a fish and trying to flop after us or whack us with a fin for as long as he could hold his breath. At one point he got into a swimming pool he could barely fit into and stayed there for ages. Elayne had to order him out."

"What was up with him? Did he just really like being a fish?"

"I guess so." He'd been amused at the memory, but her question made a pain go through his chest. Probably the fish guy... what had his name been? Boris? Morris? ...*had* loved his shift form. It wasn't one Carter would have wanted, but he understood the feeling. He'd loved being a snow leopard.

"We should get some sleep," he said.

"What if we get attacked by a chupacabra?"

"We won't. Elayne and her gang got arrested and tossed in a special shifter jail. And the wizard-scientists love mind games. Whoever's after us probably did give us a head start, to wear me down before they make their big move. Anyway, if we stay up all night, we'll be exhausted tomorrow, and then it'll be harder to fight if they do catch up."

"All right." Fen poked at the grass, searching for a comfortable spot, then looked back up at him. "One more thing..."

When she didn't finish, he said, "Go on."

She shook her head in frustration. "I forgot it. I'm so stupid!"

"I laid a lot on you. It's easy to lose track of it all."

She seemed unsatisfied, but returned to prodding the earth. Finally, she lay down on it. He lay down beside her. Precious immediately curled up in his arms, a velvety-warm, comforting weight.

He closed his eyes, but he couldn't sleep. It should have been a huge weight off his mind that Fen knew about shifters and him and what was really going on, but it wasn't. That things he hadn't told her loomed larger than everything he'd revealed. And he still couldn't kiss her, and he still couldn't tell her why.

"Carter?"

He jumped, knocking Precious off his chest. She gave a squeak and flew upward to perch on a tree branch. "What?"

Fen lay beside him, wide awake, staring directly into his eyes from about six inches away. Her gaze felt like a laser beam burning right into his soul. "I know you want to sleep, but I have one more question. Answer it honestly, and then I promise to leave you alone."

"Okay," he said warily.

"If I kissed you right now, would you you grab your head and pretend you have a migraine? Or would you kiss me back?"

CHAPTER 9

Carter looked pole-axed. Fen regarded his expression with some satisfaction. She didn't *really* want revenge on him anymore, but she was due some payback after how hot-and-cold he'd been with her.

He spluttered like she'd tossed a cup of swamp water in his face, tried to pull himself into a dignified posture (impossible, given that he was lying down), and finally said, "Okay, first of all, I didn't ever pretend to have a migraine."

"Oh? You just coincidentally get one whenever it looks like we might kiss?"

He ran his hand through his hair. It was very unfair that his hair fell into sexy rumpled waves when he did that, instead getting messy like when she did. "It's not coincidental, no. It's because I feel conflicted."

"Being conflicted gives you a headache?"

"In this case, yes." He rolled over, propped himself on his elbows, and looked into her eyes. Reflected flames shone in his hazel eyes. "It has to do with they did to me when I was kidnapped. When they killed my snow leopard."

"Oh!" It hadn't occurred to her that he'd been having flashbacks or some other trauma-based reaction. She immediately felt guilty for giving him a hard time about it. "I'm so sorry. Forget I asked. Just know that the door is open if you ever want to, uh…"

"Step into your bedroom?" He gave her a wry smile. "Look, Fen, I didn't mean to lead you on and then push you away. For what it's worth, you're the sexiest, most beautiful, funniest, most resourceful, bravest, smartest—"

"Oh, stop," she said uncomfortably. "You don't have to lay it on with a trowel. You think I'm sexy, I believe that."

Carter seemed puzzled and even a bit hurt. "What are you talking about? I meant every word I said. I'm too much of a hot mess to have a relationship right now, but you're fantastic. Of course I think you're sexy, but you're more than that. You're kind. You're fun. You're brilliant—"

"I said stop!" Her words rang out, loud in the still and humid night. For no reason at all, her eyes stung.

"Fen..." His voice was very gentle, which inexplicably only made it harder to keep back her tears. "Who told you that you weren't smart?"

She scrubbed angrily at her eyes. It was ridiculous for an adult woman to cry when she thought about true things people had told her when she was a little kid. "My parents, who else? And my teachers. Sort of. And they didn't say I was stupid. They said I was careless and lazy."

"You are the least careless and lazy person I've ever met." Carter actually sounded like he believed it.

She took a deep breath, trying to steady her voice. "Yeah, I don't seem like that *now.* That's because I've spent years and years trying to make up for it. I have reminders to myself. I have phone alarms—yours are good, I have to say. I have calendars. The most important part is that I have a fantastic assistant who remembers and keeps track of things for me. But I'm still lazy, to tell the truth. I work hard at things when I'm interested in them, but I'm not a hard worker in general."

"That doesn't make sense," Carter said. "If you work hard, you're a hard worker."

He didn't understand. She tried another angle. "When I was a kid, my grades were all over the place. I was outstanding at the things I was interested in, but I was barely scraping by in classes I easily could have gotten As in if I'd cared enough to try harder. My parents were always telling me I couldn't skate by forever by doing great in one area to make up by being terrible in another, because it averages out to being just a little bit better than average. And I thought, 'Maybe I can. Maybe just a little bit better is actually a big deal.' And so… Little Bit."

"Of course it's a big deal! Little Bit is a brilliant concept. And you are a brilliant woman."

He sounded so sincere. She wanted to believe him, but he clearly wasn't understanding the basic issue. "Okay, yeah, I'm very smart in some very specific ways. But it doesn't come easily to me. Things that actually brilliant people just… do… I struggle with. If I'm not interested in something, it's basically impossible to just do it anyway. I forget things all the time, even really important things. I lose things, even valuable things. I'm incredibly careless. And absent-minded. I can go to my bedroom to get my shoes and then leave my bedroom with a book and then go back to get my shoes and put the book back on the shelf and go out and then go back to put on my shoes and come out with a tube of lipstick and, well, you get the picture."

Carter was frowning at her, but not as if he was annoyed. He seemed very intent. "Fen, were you like that when you were a kid?"

"Yeah, I've always been like that. I lost my homework, I forgot to do all the projects that weren't about things I was interested in, I lost my report cards." She shrugged. "My parents were incredibly organized, intelligent, focused people. I was such a frustration to them."

"Did they ever have you tested for ADHD?"

She shook her head, frustrated that he *still* didn't get it. "No, I don't have that. I've never had any trouble sitting down in one place. And if it's something I actually care about, I have no trouble focusing on it. In fact if it interests me, I get so focused on it that I forget about everything else."

Carter's eyes gleamed with excitement. "Fen, that is the definition of an attention deficit! I have it, and you've exactly described what I was like before I started taking medication for it."

Fen already knew that about him. He mentioned it sometimes in interviews. But it didn't seem relevant to her. "Yeah, you may have ADHD, but you're still naturally brilliant. I'm the one who has to work at everything."

"Fen. I still have to work at everything. But I had to work a whole hell of a lot harder, and I still wasn't very successful, until I got diagnosed and put on meds. Look." He sat up, picked up his bag, and pulled out a little orange bottle of pills. "See?"

"Oh, is that what those are for?"

He nodded. "Weren't you curious?"

With dignity, she replied, "I don't snoop around people's personal medical stuff."

Carter grinned, unabashed. "But you *were* curious, weren't you?"

She snorted. "I figured they were for something boring and gross, like toenail fungus."

"I don't have toenail fungus!"

She couldn't resist saying, "Maybe you didn't when you arrived, but after bathing in swamp water…" He looked so horrified at the idea that she relented, saying, "It probably takes a while to set in. I'm sure if you get checked up once we get out, you can get some kind of disinfectant to prevent it."

"I'll *bathe* in disinfectant the instant I get away from this swamp," he vowed. Then he rattled the pill container at her. "But back to my meds. And ADHD—emphasis on the attention deficit. I don't think either of us has the hyperactive part. I'm positive one of my teamma—one of the guys in Defenders does, but it doesn't seem to bother him any. He's the one with the bugbear."

"Of course he is." Fen still hadn't completely processed all the mind-blowing stuff about bugbears and shifters and wizard-scientists. She glanced upward. Precious the dragonette was still perched on the tree branch, watching them with her gleaming sapphire eyes. Fen had touched her. She was definitely for real.

It was so typical of her life. Carter got the beautiful golden dragonette,

Carter got the diagnosis that made his mind make sense, and she got…

Carter snapped his fingers, jolting her back to the conversation. "Where'd you go just now, Fen? Quick, tell me what you were thinking."

"You don't want to know."

"Yes, I do. Go!"

"You asked for it," she warned him. "I wish I had a dragonette. I wish I had a diagnosis. It'd be nice to think I wasn't just careless and lazy."

Fire blazed up in his eyes, and it wasn't only reflected from their campfire. He grabbed her by the shoulders, making her jump. "Listen to me, Fen. You are NOT careless. You are NOT lazy. You ARE brilliant."

The force in his words and the intent behind them seemed to crack something open in her. She didn't immediately believe that he was right. But she did believe that he believed it, and that stunned her into silence.

"I can't give you a dragonette," he went on. "I can't give you a diagnosis, because I'm not a doctor. I can't even give you my pills to try out, because it's not a good idea to take someone else's meds with no medical supervision even if we weren't being chased through a swamp by wizard-scientists. But I'll give you what I can, which is the name of my doctor so you can get yourself tested as soon as we get out of this place. I think you'll be very pleasantly surprised with the results."

Fen swallowed. For the second time that night, her eyes stung with unshed tears. She couldn't do more than whisper, "Okay. I'll do it."

"Good." He dropped his hands from her shoulders. But neither of them lay down again. They sat facing each other in the dark night, lit by flames and moonlight.

For what seemed like a long time, they sat in silence. Her thoughts bounced and zig-zagged around in a way that she suspected would have been the case whether she had ADHD or not, all things considered, moving from Carter to shifters to attention deficits to her parents to wizard-scientists to dragonettes to toenail fungus to diagnostic tests and back to Carter again.

"You're right," she said.

He gave her a catlike, satisfied, Carter Howe smile. "Yes, I am."

"You're a hot mess."

The smile instantly switched to indignation. "What?"

"You said it yourself," she pointed out. Now it was her turn to smile. "But guess what? I don't care. I'm not going to push you, but my bedroom door is open and it's going to stay open. You can walk in right here, right now. Or you can wait till we get home and bathe in disinfectant and then moisturize and apply your expensive cologne and manicure your eyebrows—"

"I do not manicure my eyebrows!"

"Liar. Anyway, either way, my door is open and it stays open. But I'm not going to push you and give you a headache. You sort your own stuff out, or let me help you with it if you want." She paused, hoping he'd agree to let her help, but he didn't speak. "Whatever you want. But the ball's in *your* court, Carter Howe."

He didn't speak for a long moment. Finally, he said, "Would you still want me to walk in if there were things you didn't know about me?"

"I *know* there's things I don't know about you."

He blew out an exasperated breath. "Not like that. I mean... Bad things. Upsetting things. Gross things."

"Carter, there are bad, upsetting, gross things you don't know about me. Every person alive has bad, upsetting, gross things they'd rather not have anyone know about."

"Not like mine." He eyed her, frowning. "I assume."

Fen shrugged. "Since you're not going to tell me what they are and I don't want to tell you gross stuff about me, I guess we're at a deadlock. So I'm going to lay out *my* dealbreakers. Are you a serial killer?"

Carter rolled his eyes. "No."

"Are you a cheater?"

"No!"

"Do you have toenail fungus?"

He laughed, then glumly looked down at his muddy feet. "I mean, probably."

"Then as far as I'm concerned, we're good."

He took a deep breath, then another. "Okay."

"Okay, what?"

"Okay." Once again, there was fire in his eyes. "I'm coming in."

He leaned forward and kissed her. She might have expected him to be hesitant or shy, given how conflicted he'd said he was, but he wasn't. Carter kissed with confidence and passion and wholeheartedness, and she responded in the same manner.

The sexual chemistry she'd felt before was palpable, crackling around them like static electricity and sending delicious little shocks down her nerves. She felt like a match that had been unexpectedly struck, flaring into hot and brilliant life. It was instantly unbearable that every part of her wasn't touching every part of him, that there were clothes in the way, that she could only touch and be touched lips to lips and hands to hands.

Fen slipped her hands up his shirt, caressing his chest, teasing his nipples. He did the same to her. And all the while they kissed, hungrily, unable to get enough of each other. She was on fire, every inch of her skin impossibly sensitive to his touch.

Without remembering when it had happened, she found that she was sitting in his lap, rubbing herself against his steel-hard erection, making little moans and gasps of desire. He was panting too, clutching her tight, their faces pressed together.

"I can't—" he gasped, as she muttered, "Wait, wait, we shouldn't—"

For the first time since they'd begun they pulled slightly apart. She had no idea how much time had passed. A few minutes? An hour? It felt at once like an eternity in Heaven and only a few perfect seconds. The pale moonlight and flickering firelight made transformed Carter into some magical being of silver and flame. His eyes glimmered in colors she couldn't name, and his tousled black hair had glints of ruby and ivory. Reflected flames danced in the depths of his eyes.

"We should use our hands," she said.

He stroked her face, a touch so sensual and so tender that she shivered.

"I'm good with my hands."

"Famously," she said. "Show me."

He took her in his arms and lowered her down to the ground so they lay side by side, with one of his arms cradling her and one between her thighs. She did the same, gripping him in her hand. He gasped.

"Maybe I'm good with my hands too," she said.

He swallowed, his voice coming out thick and husky. "Oh, you are. You already are."

As she slid her hand up and down, feeling the soft skin roll over the hardness underneath, he touched her with clever fingers. Her slick folds parted for him and she moved to give him better access, tilting her hips as she felt her heart pound. He rubbed her swollen, throbbing clitoris, making her gasp, finding a rhythm that suited her even as she found one that suited him.

"Slow down," she gasped, just as he said, "Wait, wait!"

They laughed, slowing, as she said, "I don't want to go off like a rocket."

"You can," he said. "You've got multiple chances, right? Unlike me."

"Not now. I'm too tired. I'll fall asleep. And I want this to last a bit longer."

"Me too. Let's go a bit slower."

They tried, but soon they were both caught up in an urgent rhythm, unable to recall why they'd wanted to slow down.

"Come on," she heard herself muttering. "Harder, harder, yes, like that, like that!"

Her climax hit her like a freight train. For a moment she forgot where she was, almost forgot who she was, lost in a tide of ecstasy. When she remembered what she was doing, she found that he was also gasping, on the edge. His hazel eyes were open wide, and he was looking straight at her. There was passion in his gaze, and desire, and excitement, and tenderness, and…

Love? Could it be?

His body tensed and his eyes closed as he came, crying out her name.

They kissed again and cleaned up as best they could with leaves, then rolled over and lay down again on a slightly less damp patch of grass. She snuggled in closer to him, trying to fit every part of her body into every part of his. After that fantastic sex, she was utterly relaxed, ready to fall into what she suspected would be the best swamp sleep ever. But she wanted to enjoy every moment of cuddling with Carter, who was as good at that as he was with his hands.

Dreamily, she said, "That was better than the best vibrator I've ever had."

"I should hope so," he said, sounding indignant. Then he added, "I could make you a vibrator that's better than your best. For when either of us is gone on a business trip, you know."

"Gonna base it on your dick?" she teased.

"Maybe," he shot back. "I'll wait to see if you actually like mine, though."

"You want me to do some product testing before you design the prototype, huh?"

"Exactly."

She dropped her hand lower. "I feel very confident about the original model."

CHAPTER 10

Carter awoke with a sense of happiness, peace, and well-being that he hadn't had in years. Fen was nestled in his arms, fast asleep. He didn't dare move for fear of waking her, so he stayed completely still.

She was warm and breathing gently, her eyes closed. The pearly dawn light touched her skin with a lovely luminescence. The fringed half-moons of her eyelashes were echoed in the fine arches of her eyebrows. Her mouth was slightly open, making him remember what it had felt like to touch those sweet lips with his own. One of her hands was curled around his forearm, with those fingers that had driven him wild the night before now relaxed in sleep.

I'm crazy about her, he thought. *If we weren't being chased, I could lie here and hold her all day. Everything about her is a marvel.*

He couldn't believe he'd spent years disliking and periodically sending hostile emails to her without ever actually meeting and realizing how wonderful she actually was. And all that time, the people who deserved the emails were her awful parents. How dare they convince her she was lazy and careless! How dare they assume her struggles with attention were some character flaw and blame her for it!

He must have made some indignant noise, because her eyes opened. She blinked up at him and smiled. "Morning. How's your head?"

"It's absolutely fine."

And it was. There wasn't a peep from his monsters, other than a faint background rumble that might have been purring.

Carter did feel guilty for letting her assume his headaches were due to sadistic experimentation rather than a horde of inner monsters screaming at him. But then again, the monsters were the result of sadistic experimentation, so it wasn't really a lie.

"I supposed we should get up and start paddling." She sighed. "I want to lie here with you all day, though."

"Me too, Fen. Me too." He leaned down to kiss her.

Just before their lips could meet, something hard bounced off his head.

Carter lunged to cover her with his own body. Unfortunately, since she was mostly lying on top of him, that involved dumping her onto the ground.

She let out a startled, indignant yell. "Hey!"

"There's something—" He broke off as he saw the object that had hit him, which was still rolling across the grass. It was a polished steel tube that had come open when it had hit either his head or the ground, spilling out a small flask and... was that a pair of steel shot glasses?

Precious landed with a triumphant trill. She picked up a shot glass in her delicate claws and dropped it beside his face, for all the world like a cat presenting her owner with a freshly killed mouse.

"Never mind." Carter sat up and helped Fen up as well. "Sorry I dumped you. Precious dropped another present on my head."

Fen peered at it. "Is that a shot glass?"

"Looks like it. The real question is, what's in the flask?"

Fen pounced, unscrewing and sniffing at it. "Smells like very nice whiskey to me."

Carter took and sniffed it. "I'd say the same. Let's save it for tonight, if we're not out of the swamp by then."

She didn't reply. He glanced at her and caught her with a surprisingly pensive expression. Slowly, she said, "Yesterday morning, I'd have said I couldn't wait to get out. But now... Oh, I know we're still in danger, but we haven't even seen the people who are after us. I think we've lost them. And after last night, I kind of don't want to leave. I know we can keep seeing each other—and I want to—but I can't help wondering if things will change once we're out of this weird situation."

"And that makes you want to stay?"

She nodded. Her deep brown eyes were wells of sincerity.

You'd rather stay in a swamp than risk damaging your relationship with the man you don't know is a monster. He gritted his teeth against a surge of guilt.

"Nothing will change," Carter said, shying away from diving deeper into what she was trying to say. "I promise. We'll eat lobster and steak instead of cattails and pawpaws, that's all. And we can have sex when we're actually clean. Won't that be nice?"

"I could definitely do with a shower," she admitted. "But if we're not out by tonight, I'll settle for another swamp water bath. And after that, my door's still open."

"Your 'door,'" he said, holding up his fingers in a quote gesture.

Fen gave him a smile that made all the blood rush to one particular part, leaving him literally weak at the knees. "My 'door' is always open for you, Carter."

He glanced at the sky, wondering if they had enough time to risk a quickie before they started paddling again. Maybe they did. The sun hadn't even risen yet. And she was right, they probably had lost their pursuit. From what he'd seen of the wizard-scientists, they wouldn't have been able to resist fucking with them since long before now.

"How about right—"

There was a tremendous splash, and a wave of swamp water crashed over them both. He grabbed Fen and hauled her away from the shore. She was gasping and spluttering, as was he. A piercing shriek from above and water dripping down on his head told him that Precious had also been drenched.

Carter dashed muddy water out of his eyes and stared out at the swamp. His heart sank right down into his shoes even as his adrenaline spiked.

An armored prehistoric fish loomed up out of the black water. It was so big and the water was so shallow that most of it protruded from above the surface. Its immense toothy jaws gaped wide, then snapped shut.

"What the actual fuck?!" Fen screamed.

The great fish lurched forward, but it was mired in mud and shallow water. It flapped its fins in apparent frustration, once again splattering them with muddy water.

"It can't get to us," Carter said, vainly wiping at the mud on his face. "See? It's too big."

"But what *is* it?"

Carter was so furious that he had to unclench his jaw to speak again. "Remember the wizard-scientists who chased the Defenders around an amusement park? That's Boris the Dunkleosteus."

The armored fish vanished. A man rose from the water, dripping and muddy. Carter had remembered that he was a big guy, but not exactly how big. He was tall and broad as a pro wrestler, though not particularly muscular.

The Dunkleosteus shifter wiped the mud out of his eyes and said, "It's Norris, actually."

Carter's mind was racing. In his human form, Norris had the power to give people vertigo. But Carter, who had always been extremely resistant to motion sickness, wasn't too affected by it; it put him off-balance, but he could still fight. And though Norris was a big guy, he hadn't seemed like much of a fighter before. Carter wouldn't need to shift. He could rush him and punch him out, which was what he'd done the last time. He just needed to bide his time and take him by surprise, so he didn't rush straight into the jaws of a fish that could swallow him in a single gulp.

Carter spoke calmly. "Fen, this is the guy who can give you vertigo. If you start to feel sick, that's why. But it won't actually hurt you."

"Whoa, whoa," Norris broke in. "I'm not here to attack you."

"Yeah, right," snapped Fen. She was gripping a branch in one hand and the steel canister in the other. "You came to wish us a happy swamp day!"

Norris took a step forward. She hurled the canister at him. He ducked, and it bounced off his shoulder instead of his head.

"Ow!" Norris yelped.

"Good aim, Fen," remarked Carter. "I know a circus that would want to recruit you as a knife-thrower."

"I wish I had a knife to throw," she snarled. Not taking her gaze off Norris, she crouched, felt along the ground, and straightened up with a rock in her hand. "Get lost. Go tell your wizard-scientist boss I have a big rock waiting for her."

"Hey, hey!" Norris gave her an imploring look. "I'm not with the wizard-scientists anymore. Elayne—that was my former boss—is still in shifter jail."

"*You're* supposed to still be in shifter jail," Carter pointed out.

"I know," said Norris. "But I had to come warn you—"

In a flash of gold, Precious dropped out of the sky like a hawk and dive-bombed him, screeching. Norris flung up his arms, covering his face and head.

"Precious!" Carter shouted, alarmed. "Get away from him!"

The little dragonette ignored him, clawing at Norris's shirt-sleeves and shrieking.

"Call it off!" Norris's voice was muffled. "I don't want to hurt it! I don't want to hurt any of you! I'm your biggest—ow, stop!"

A tiny gray creature leaped out of a tree. It glided smoothly through the air with wing-flaps outstretched, landed on Norris's shoulder, and vanished down the front of his shirt.

"What the hell was that?" Carter said, though he didn't expect anyone to answer.

"A sugar glider," said Fen. "They're kind of like flying squirrels. I love them."

"Augh! Get it off me!" Norris was trying to gently bat away the creatures attacking him, but was hampered by his obvious unwillingness to do anything that would hurt them. Not to mention by the fact that he had one flapping around his head and one inside his shirt, and he didn't seem to have the best hand-eye coordination. "Stop! It tickles! Help!"

Fen and Carter looked at each other.

"I know he's a bad guy, but…" Fen began.

Carter was thinking along similar lines. "His fish form is basically helpless on land, so long as you don't get too close. And if he tries anything as a human, we can take him."

"Precious and a sugar glider are taking him right now," Fen said drily.

"Norris!" Carter yelled. "Promise you won't attack us, get on the island, and I'll call them off!"

"I don't *want* to—hee hee!—attack you!" Norris shouted back, flailing his long arms. "I already—ugh, stop!—told you that! I'm here to help you!"

Once again, Carter and Fen exchanged glances.

"I'm honestly curious to hear what he has to say," she said.

"Fine," said Carter. "Norris, get over here."

Norris waded on to the island. Fen and Carter kept a wary distance from him so if he suddenly became a Dunkleosteus, he wouldn't be able to bite them. Carter whistled to Precious, who reluctantly left off clawing Norris and flew to Carter's shoulder. She clung to his wet shirt and preened in a self-satisfied manner.

"Good girl," he said, scratching her head.

"Can you please call off the flying squirrel?" Norris pleaded, vainly trying to grab the small moving lump under his shirt. "It's tickling the hell out of me."

Carter shook his head. "That's not ours."

Fen started to step forward. Carter grabbed her arm. "Don't get close to him."

"I swear," Norris began, sounded both exasperated and on the verge of uncontrollable tickle laughter.

"Here, sugar glider," Fen called. "Get out of that weird man's shirt. It's all wet and muddy and gross."

The lump crawled upward, emerged from Norris's collar, and leaped. The sugar glider's furry gray gliding flaps spread out, and it sailed straight for Fen. She caught and held it, petting its black-striped head. It gazed at her with adoring eyes as black as engine oil and chittered softly at her.

"Hello, darling," Fen crooned, stroking it. "What a sweetie. And so tame! He must be someone's pet."

Norris gave her a startled glance. "It's not your pet?"

She shook her head. "Never seen him before in my life. In fact, I've never seen a sugar glider in real life before. I've only ever seen photos and videos."

Tiny friend, crooned a monster.

Pretty pretty furry friend, pretty furry friend, gibbered a monster.

[approving blue]

Carter was getting a suspicion about what might be going on. "They are real animals, right?"

Fen stared at him as if he was a complete lunatic. "As opposed to what?"

He pointed to Precious.

"Oh. Yes, they're normal animals." The sugar glider squeaked. She added, as much to the little creature as to Carter, "Normal but incredibly adorable animals."

To his horror, he caught himself exchanging glances with Norris over her head. The horror instantly switched to annoyance when Norris, who clearly had never been acquainted with discretion, blurted out, "That one's probably magical though."

Her eyebrows rose. "Really? What makes you say that?"

Norris waved a big, muddy hand at Precious. "He's got a magical pet, you've suddenly gotten an animal attaching itself to you, and your sugar glider joined his dragonette in attacking me because both of you thought I was a danger to you. It's obvious."

From the look in her eyes, it was clearly less obvious to her. "So, this is a known thing that happens?"

"Yeah, his whole team—well, most of his team—has them."

"They're not my team," Carter snapped. "I just work with them sometimes. Anyway, we can check the sugar glider for magical powers later. Right now I want to know exactly what you're doing here, Norris. And make it fast; we're being hunted."

"Yeah, I know," Norris said. "That's why I came."

"To help hunt us?" Fen demanded, clutching her sugar glider protectively.

"To warn you!" The Dunkleosteus shifter scratched his head. "I guess I'm too late for that, though, if you're being hunted already. But don't worry. I'll protect you."

"*You'll* protect *us,*" Carter said, his voice heavy with sarcasm. "I seem to recall that the last time I saw you, you were doing your best to murder me and my—the team."

"Hey, no," Norris protested. "I did help Elayne lock your friends in a cellar full of animatronics, and I did turn into a Dunkleosteus and jump into a swimming pool they were in, and yeah, I gave them vertigo and blocked their way when they tried to leave—I admit all that—but I never tried to kill anyone. And I feel bad about the things I did do. Especially when I realized who you were!"

The look that came into his eyes was one that Carter was all too familiar with. It was starry-eyed, awestruck, and slightly nervous. He'd seen it often, but never before in a swamp.

"I didn't realize it was you in Tomato Land," Norris went on.

"Tomato Land?" Fen echoed.

"That was the theme park he attacked us in," Carter said absently. He was busy trying to remember exactly where Norris had been during all that confused fighting in a poorly lit area. Had he seen Carter shift?

"I mean, I did hear your name, but I didn't realize you were Carter *Howe,*" Norris went on. "And I didn't recognize you because it was dark and people were fighting and it was pretty confusing, and the closest I ever got to you was when you punched me out."

"You punched him out?" Fen said, looking from Norris to Carter.

Norris rubbed his jaw in painful memory. "Yeah. He's got one hell of a right hook. Anyway, Carter, I never would have taken the job if I'd known Elayne intended to do anything to *you*."

"He's a fan," said Fen to Carter. She seemed to be trying not to laugh. "I bet he loves your phones."

"I do," said Norris earnestly, then turned his star-struck gaze on her. "I love your products too! I have a Howe phone, of course, but I have a Little Bit Sharper TV. I was so thrilled to see that not only was Carter Howe here, but so were you! I mean, not thrilled you're in danger, that's terrible, but thrilled to meet you. I have the edition of *Wired* magazine that has both of you on the cover! Once we're out of here, would you both autograph it for me?"

There was a long silence. Uncharacteristically, Carter was absolutely at a loss for words. So, apparently, was Fen.

"Hey!" she said suddenly. "You came here, so you must've come from somewhere. Where are we? And which way is out?"

Norris looked apologetic. "We're somewhere in Georgia. I mean, I think it's probably still Georgia. And I'm not sure which way is out. I didn't follow a map to get here. I followed you."

"How?" Carter asked blankly. "We came on a plane."

"It's my other power." To Fen, he said, "We all have two. Not counting shifting."

Except for me, Carter thought glumly. *I got a curse instead. Lucky, lucky me.*

"One of my powers is inflicting vertigo," Norris went on. "The other is finding people. But I don't actually know where they are. It's more of a directional pull. I think about someone, and I can feel that they're..." He pointed. "*That way.*"

Carter was getting a directional feeling himself. It was the sensation of slowly sinking into the ground. "So you walk in the right direction until you get there?"

Norris beamed at him. "You got it! A car works too. Though I prefer to swim. Once I found out you were in danger, I thought to myself, "Where's Carter Howe?" And I got that pull. So I started driving. I was so thrilled when I hit a lake, because then I could become a Dunkleosteus and swim to you."

Under her breath, Fen echoed, "Become a Dunkleosteus."

"My finding power only works in human form, unfortunately, so I'd turn back into a man periodically and recalibrate," Norris explained earnestly. "Anyway, after the lake I got to the swamp, but I didn't travel exactly in a straight line because I was keeping to water deep enough for a Dunkleosteus as much as I could. And it wasn't like I could mark my path anyway. But I could lead you out. It just wouldn't necessarily be the same way I came in. I'd have to focus on finding someone who definitely isn't in the swamp."

Even more under her breath, Fen murmured, "Someone who definitely isn't in the swamp."

Carter shot her a furtive glance. Her eyes glittered with unshed tears—tears of laughter, he realized after an instant of concern. She was *this close* to dropping to the grass and rolling around on it, laughing so hard that she cried.

He seized the moment. "Fen, can you excuse me and Norris for a moment? I have to talk to him about something that involves some third parties."

It's true, he told himself defensively. His monsters were third parties.

Fen was too busy trying not to throw herself to the ground and howl that she did nothing but wipe her eyes and nod.

He marched up to Norris, grabbed his arm, and yanked the startled Dunkleosteus shifter out of earshot. Once he was sure Fen couldn't overhear, he realized that he wasn't sure what to say himself. He could hardly ask Norris if he'd seen his shift form when he wasn't even sure if Norris knew he *had* a shift form.

Carter settled on saying quietly, "What do you know about me?"

The starstruck gleam in the other man's eyes tipped Carter off that he'd asked the most useless possible question, even before Norris began, "You're a genius inventor, you founded Howe Enterprises, you make the best phones—"

Carter cut him off. "Not that stuff. I mean, what did Elayne tell you about me?"

"Nothing. I told you, I had no idea you'd be there."

Carter repressed the urge to clutch his hair and scream. "What do you know about me now? In terms of magic shifter stuff."

"Oh, got it." Norris gave an earnest nod. "I know you were born a snow leopard shifter, but you got captured and experimented on, and something went wrong. I don't know exactly what."

Carter waited for more, but Norris only stood there gazing at him worshipfully, no doubt thinking about phones. With immense relief, he realized that Norris hadn't seen him shift at Tomato Land and hadn't talked to those of Elayne's group who had. There was nothing he could give away to Fen.

Except for this conversation, which had nothing to do with third parties. Dammit.

"And my boss?" Carter asked, somewhat at random. "What do you know about him?"

"I thought you were the CEO." Norris looked puzzled.

"I am, of my own company. I meant Roland Walker. The boss of Protection, Inc: Defenders. He's a big black guy with a short gray beard. What do you know about him?"

"Oh, him. I saw him at Tomato Land. He turned into a phoenix. Pretty cool. Though not as cool as a Dunkleosteus."

"Right," Carter sighed. "A gigantic fish that can't breathe or move on land is *much* cooler than a bird of fire. Okay, let's get back to Fen before the wizard-scientists show up."

They returned to find her crooning over the sugar glider. She had him cupped in her hands, their noses almost touching. Fen glanced up at them. "I've named him Sugar."

"Good name," said Carter.

Norris tentatively reached out to pet Sugar's head. "Cute little thing."

Carter glanced upward. Dawn was breaking, changing the gray-white sky to blue and decorating it with streaks of gold and pink. "We should get moving. Fen, if it's okay with you, Norris could come along with us and tell us what's going on while we paddle."

Her eyes glinted with suppressed laughter. "Oh, sure, it's fine with me. Hey! Norris, can you tell us which way the Most Dangerous Game guys are, so we can make sure we're going away from them?"

"The who?" Norris asked.

"Our kidnappers, we'll explain later," Carter said impatiently.

"No, sorry. I can only do people I've met. But I could find the wizard-scientist who contacted me!" He frowned, concentrating, then pointed. "He's that way."

Fen and Carter instinctively stared in that direction. Fen asked, "Can you tell how far away that way?"

Norris shook his head. "He could be behind that tree, or he could be in Australia. No idea."

"That is the most useless power," Carter burst out, aggravated.

Norris looked wounded. "Hey! I found you guys, didn't I?"

Peaceably, Fen suggested, "Let's keep heading north."

The three of them piled into the boat, which sank noticeably under Norris's weight. He offered, "I could turn into a Dunkleosteus and swim beside you."

"Maybe later," said Carter, and handed him an oar.

Fen sat in the middle of the boat as Norris and Carter began paddling north. Sugar scampered up her arm and perched on her shoulder. Carter eyed the little creature, wondering if Norris was right that it was magical. It *did* seem odd for a random animal to adopt Fen in the middle of a swamp, let alone tickle Norris on her behalf, but otherwise it showed no sign of being anything but cute.

Cute is enough, purred a monster.

"Okay, Norris," said Fen. "Begin at the beginning. What are you doing here?"

Norris seemed to ponder that. "You mean when I found out you were being targeted? Or earlier than that, when I became a Dunkleosteus? Or do you want the very beginning, when my grandmother gave me a book on marine biology when I was nine, and I was so inspired that—"

Carter repressed the urge to clutch at his head. He saw Fen's fingers twitch, and guessed that she was thinking of hurling something at Norris's head. Since the closest thing to her hand, which she was trailing in the water, was a large floating bullfrog, Carter hurriedly said, "Let's go with how you became a Dunkleosteus."

Norris looked mildly disappointed, having evidently geared up to tell them his life story, but said, "I'm a marine paleontologist, and I was trying to get a grant for a research project on reconstructing DNA from a Dunkleosteus tooth. It was very difficult, expensive, experimental work, and I'd been at it for years with no success. Then I got approached by this woman named Elayne. *She* was supportive."

"I bet," muttered Carter.

"She took me on a tour of her lab," Norris went on. "It was amazing. So advanced! I couldn't believe I'd never heard of her or her research group. And then she told me her secret: she was using magic."

Fen glanced up, fascinated. "How'd she convince you it was real?"

"She turned into a harpy," said Norris. "That was very convincing. Then she offered me a deal: if I worked for her in her lab, and also did some, um, other types of work for her, she'd give me the power to turn into the dinosaur of my choice. That is, of my choice from the ones she had available. She needed DNA to make it work."

"You *chose* to be a Dunkleosteus?" Fen asked.

Simultaneously, Carter said, "So you could've been a T-rex or a pteranodon or anything, and you picked a *fish?*"

Loftily, Norris replied, "She didn't have a Dunkleosteus available as an option at that time. I had to work for her for years before we got a good enough sample to use on me. And even then, she made a big fuss about it not being practical. But I pointed out that she didn't have any marine shifters and you never knew when you might be able to use one, and she finally gave in. So yeah, my finding power isn't the most practical and I don't like using my vertigo power—it's kind of mean—but who cares? I wasn't in it for the powers. I just wanted to be a Dunkleosteus!"

"You just wanted to be a Dunkleosteus," Fen murmured. She was clearly about to get the giggles again.

"They're my favorite dinosaur," said Norris. "It's so amazing to be able to turn into one!"

As Norris rhapsodized about the coolness of the Dunkleosteus, Carter couldn't help being jealous. Norris loved his shift form as much as Carter had once loved being able to turn into a snow leopard.

"Anyway, I got what I wanted, but I didn't realize exactly what sort of other work she meant for me to do," Norris went on. "I'd assumed it was stuff like locating underwater fossils—things that would make sense for a Dunkleosteus to do. But no. Out of all the marine paleontologists she could have approached, she picked me because I'm a big guy and she assumed I'd be good at pushing people around. Just because I'm big doesn't mean I'm a bully!"

"I get it, Norris," Fen said unexpectedly. "From the opposite direction. People look at me and think, 'Skinny Asian woman, she must be a pushover.'"

"I would never think that," Norris assured her.

She gave him a remarkably sweet smile. "I believe you."

"The very first mission she sent me on, I got punched out and arrested," Norris went on glumly. "Honestly, I deserved it. I should have walked out once I realized what Elayne wanted me to do. But she'd threatened us all that she could take away our shift form, and I—" he shot a guilty glance at Carter. "I love mine so much."

He kept a tight grip on his feelings, hiding them behind an expressionless mask and an impatient gesture at Norris to get on with his story. He didn't look at Fen; he didn't think he could bear to see her sympathy.

"So there I was, in shifter jail," Norris continued. "They separated

Elayne's group so we couldn't plot together. I was relieved. I didn't much like any of them, and I especially didn't want to hang out with Elayne. One day, this weird-looking guy showed up. He was dressed like a guard, and he had a long, scraggly gray beard and long, scraggly gray hair. He said his name was Balin and he was a wizard-scientist and a colleague of Elayne's, and he'd break me out if I'd work with him on just one job. I asked him what it was, and he said it was sort of a continuation of my last one. I told him there was no way I was going up against that hellhound again, and he said he wasn't interested in the hellhound. He asked me if I knew the name of the man who'd defeated me. I said yes, of course!"

Turning to Carter, Norris said, "The guards had already told me who you were. I mean the real guards. I felt *terrible.* So I thought, I could tell the guards—I mean the real guards—about this guy, so they could warn you. But then I thought, what if this guy Balin *is* one of the real guards? What if there's a vast wizard-scientist conspiracy to infiltrate shifter jails? What if any warning I try to send from within the jail gets lost? So I said sure, I'd do anything for him as long as he broke me out."

"Great," Carter muttered. "Let me add this to my list of things to do as soon as I get out of this swamp: warn the Defenders that Elayne's whole gang is out."

"I don't think they are," Norris assured him. "Balin said I was in the lowest-security wing, so he was starting with me. He magicked my cell open, and all these alarms started going off, and there was this bright flash, and I was outside. I asked myself, 'Where is Carter?' And I ran straight to you! Apart from the parts where I drove and swam."

"Huh," said Carter. "And that was the last you saw of Balin?"

Norris nodded. "I assume he expected me to wait for him."

Fen gave an inelegant snort of poorly suppressed laughter.

"I bet he did," Carter muttered.

As they rowed on, Norris made light conversation mostly consisting of praising their products (Carter did enjoy that) and telling them marine dinosaur facts, and Fen alternated between stifling laughter, petting Sugar, and egging on Norris.

Carter had time to think. Much too much time to think. His main thought was, *There goes any chance of Fen and me having sex again.*

CHAPTER 11

By the time the three of them (five if you counted Precious and Sugar) stopped at an island with a pawpaw tree for a lunch of pawpaws, Fen felt distinctly punchy. In the last twenty-four hours, she'd had the greatest sex of her entire life, thrown a flask holder at a giant prehistoric fish, acquired the greatest pet of her entire life (also the first, but she couldn't imagine anything topping her darling Sugar), and involuntarily attended a college seminar on marine paleontology.

She'd spent the first half of the boat ride trying not to burst out laughing every time Norris opened his mouth, and the second half being painfully conscious that Carter was *right there* and there was absolutely no way they could have sex now that they had a third wheel present.

That is, she thought, *a third fin.* She barely managed to gulp down a howl of laughter.

Carter picked up a pawpaw with an air of grim resignation. "Norris, didn't it occur to you to bring any food into the swamp?"

"I figured I could eat fish," Norris replied. Unnecessarily, he added, "As a Dunkleosteus."

"We know," muttered Carter. "Everything is a Dunkleosteus as far as you're concerned."

Fen forced herself to take a bite of pawpaw, then offered the rest to

Sugar. The sugar glider seized the pawpaw, which was almost as big as he was, and daintily began to eat. Fen smiled ruefully. "Just wait, little guy. You won't enjoy them one-tenth as much when they've been 90% of your diet for a week."

Carter stared at his pawpaw, then put it down without even breaking it open. "He can have mine."

"You need to eat," Norris said, dividing a concerned look between them both. "You have to keep up your strength. Or—wait! I know! I'll catch some fish for you!"

Without waiting for a reply, he jumped to his feet and leaped off the island, transforming into a Dunkleosteus in mid-air. Fen caught a surreal glimpse of an immense armored fish sailing through the air before he landed in the water with a tremendous splash. She and Carter were drenched in a wave of black swamp water.

"Goddammit," Carter swore, dashing water out of his eyes. "I can't believe that idiot!"

"Bullfrog," warned Fen, pointing to his lap.

He jumped to his feet, sending the surprised bullfrog tumbling down. It let out a shriek, then dove into the water.

"Ugh. Ugh. UGH," moaned Carter. "What did I do to deserve Norris?"

"I didn't do anything, and I got him too," she pointed out, plucking a slimy water weed off her shoulder.

Lowering her voice, though she couldn't see either the fish or the man, she added, "It'd be mean to ditch him and take the boat, right?"

"Probably, but I'd vote for it if he wouldn't just use his power find us immediately." Carter glanced around. "Hey, where did Precious and Sugar go?"

"I guess they flew off." She didn't see them anywhere. "I bet they left the instant they saw Norris run for the water. I would've, if I'd had wings or patagium."

"What's patagium?"

"The skin flap that flying squirrels and sugar gliders use to—"

Fen was interrupted by a man's yell. "We win!"

She whipped around, then froze in shock and horror. A boat had emerged from the swamp behind them. The five men in it were the same men who had kidnapped them. They wore camouflage and carried rifles.

Fen had only an instant to take this in. The next moment, the nearest man (Bill, the one she had kicked in the nuts and bitten) raised his rifle, aiming it at her.

Carter moved quick as thought, lunging at her and shielding her with his own body. The rifle cracked as they fell together.

His body covered her, pressing her into the soft earth. She could feel the impacts as more bullets struck his body. Not a single one touched her.

"No!" Fen screamed.

How many times had he been shot in his effort to save her life? Four times? Five? Could a man survive that?

Filled with grief and rage, Fen struggled to get out from under him. She heard herself screaming, "Let me at them! I'll rip their balls off with my TEETH!!!"

"No!" Carter snapped. "They have guns! I'm covering you. Just hold still."

For a man who'd just been shot multiple times, his voice was surprisingly strong. He sounded angry and worried, but he didn't sound like he was dying.

"Are you hit?" Fen asked. "I felt you get hit… I think."

"So did I," he said. "I think."

He moved slightly, giving her enough room to move her head. Previously her face had been crushed into his shoulder. She smelled swamp mud and swamp water and the tiniest bit of Carter's own distinctively Carter scent, and also a strong chemical odor like wet paint. What she didn't smell was blood.

"Move up a bit," said Fen. "I can't see."

He lifted himself up a bit more. Now she could see his chest, his face, and some of his side. Bright orange liquid, the color of a traffic cone, dripped from his head and down his cheek. His side was smeared with a mixture of mud, sky blue liquid, sunflower yellow liquid, and lavender liquid. But no blood. Unless he was an alien. But she'd seen his blood before, and it was a normal color. For a human.

Carter was also staring down at himself. In a tone that combined sudden understanding and absolute fury, he said, "Oh."

He sat up. So did she. Now she could see that he was splattered with paint in five different colors. One of the men had scored a hit to his heart with pink paint the color of a Barbie Dream House.

"Those were paint guns," said Fen, unnecessarily.

She glared at the laughing, cheering, whooping men in the boat. They'd put down their guns and were giving each other high-fives.

"YOU MISERABLE FUCKERS!" she yelled. That didn't even come close to expressing her feelings, so she tried again. "YOU ABSOLUTE BLOODY WALNUTS!"

The men laughed harder.

Fen leaped up and rushed into the water, planning to tear them limb from limb with her bare hands. Carter was right there beside her.

One of the men hurriedly turned on the outboard motor. The boat began to zoom away in a wake of black water and mocking laughter.

It crashed into a Dunkleosteus.

The great prehistoric fish had reared up out of the water right in front of them. It was a game of small boat vs enormous armored dinosaur, and the boat lost decisively. There was a spectacular rending crash and a whole lot of unmanly screams. The next instant, dented boat pieces were sinking and five kidnappers were flailing in black water, looking terrified. Norris loomed over them, periodically snapping his immense toothy jaws. Every time he did, the mighty hunters screamed and thrashed, trying desperately to get away from him.

It was too much. Fen staggered out of the water and onto the island, and did what she'd been wanting to do all day. With no regard for her dignity, not caring in the slightest who was watching, she flung herself down on the ground and rolled around, howling with laughter. Every now and then she wiped the tears from her eyes to get a better view at Norris ponderously swimming in a circle around the shrieking, flailing manhunters. He was clearly enjoying himself immensely. But probably not as much as she was.

Carter did not throw himself to the ground and roll around. But he did sit down beside her and laugh until tears came to his eyes.

After a while, she subsided into the occasional fit of giggles. She sat up and wiped her eyes. "My sides literally ache."

"Mine too." Carter gazed at the frantically swimming men. They were clearly getting tired. Norris flapped his fins at them, sending them into a spasm of redoubled efforts. "I don't think I've laughed like that since I was a little kid."

"I don't think I've *ever* laughed like that."

Fen eyed Bill, remembered how she'd thought Carter was dying beside her, picked up a pawpaw, and hurled it at him. It hit him on the head and splattered. All the men screamed before they realized that his head hadn't exploded, then spluttered angrily when they figured it out.

"That was very satisfying," said Fen with a contented sigh.

"You have great aim." Carter lay back, folding his arms behind his head as if he was on a beach holiday. She imitated him, and they lay and watched Norris menace the mighty paintballers.

Sugar launched himself from the pawpaw tree, landed beside Fen with a tiny thump, and dove into her blouse. He wriggled around, got himself settled into her cleavage, then peered out to watch the show with her.

Fen tickled him behind the ears. "So that's where you went. I wonder… Hmm."

She and Carter looked at the pawpaw tree. There was no sign of Precious. Fen whispered, "Think she's smart enough to know no one but us should see her? No, wait. The wizard-scientists already know about her, right? Or at least, about magical animals in general."

"I'm not so sure now that these guys are from the wizard-scientists,"

Carter whispered back. "I know what Norris said, but I've only ever seen the wizard-scientists use shifter minions. And real weapons. I can't see them messing around with paint guns."

"Who else could they be?" Fen whispered. "You don't think they really could be… exactly what they said they were?"

Carter pointedly looked at the thrashing men. One accidentally swam into Norris's fin and got contemptuously flipped over. He let out a high-pitched shriek. "Don't they seem more like Most Dangerous Gamers than super-powered henchmen?"

"They do," she admitted. "Think they'd confess by now?"

"Probably. But let's give it a little more time. I want to make sure they're so worn out that if they try to attack us they'll fall over."

"Good idea." She nudged him. "And also, you don't want to miss a minute of them getting chased in circles by a Dunkleosteus."

With dignity, Carter said, "Norris was kind enough to warn us, even if he might've been wrong about what was going on. I don't want to deprive him of his fun."

"Hey!" Fen exclaimed. "Remember we said we were saving the whiskey for a special occasion? What could be more special than toasting the downfall of our enemies while we watch them getting chased around a swamp by a prehistoric fish?"

"Nothing. Nothing could possibly be more special than that."

They found the flask and cups, poured out a shot each, and lifted their glasses.

"HEY!" Fen yelled, loud enough that even the frantically swimming kidnappers looked up. "WE'RE TOASTING YOUR DOWNFALL!"

One of the kidnappers gave an angry yelp. "That's my flask! How'd you get my flask? I thought it fell off the boa—" His sentence was lost in a splutter as Norris flapped a fin, sending a wave of swamp water into his mouth.

Carter and Fen looked at each other. A spark of glee danced in his hazel eyes. He took out the compass Precious had brought him and held it up. "Anyone recognize this?"

"That's my compass," yelled a floundering kidnapper. "I thought I lost it in the swamp! How'd you—" Norris snapped at him, making him break off and swim away frantically.

In a lower voice, Carter said, "To Precious, the prettiest little thief."

"To Precious." They clinked their glasses and sipped.

Fen had known the whiskey would be good, but it was even better than she'd expected. "This is Jack Daniels Blue Label single malt. Good stuff. And worthy of my toast. To Sugar, the cutest thing to ever come out of a swamp."

They clinked and drank again.

"To you," said Carter softly. "The smartest, sexiest, bravest, funniest, all-around best person to be trapped in a swamp with. I'm so glad I got to know you."

"To you," said Fen. "The guy who's terrified of bullfrogs but not bullets. The guy who's too sexy for the swamp. The guy who makes me not care that I'm in a swamp. Here's to you."

"Here's to us," said Carter.

They clinked and drank. The warmth of the fine whiskey filled her belly, and the warmth of being with Carter and knowing they cared for each other filled her heart.

Was this love? If she counted days, it was far too soon. But it felt neither sudden nor shallow, but like something she was consciously realizing long after it had already begun. How could she not love a man who'd throw his body between her and danger, then join her in a toast to the downfall of their enemies?

She wondered if he felt the same way as her. Her heart said he did. Her heart said this kind of feeling had to be mutual. Her heart said she should tell him, and hear him say it back to her.

But another part of her was afraid. It was the part that whispered, *Careless, lazy Fen Kim. Daydreamer Fen Kim with her head in the clouds.*

What if she was imagining the whole thing? What if this was just a swamp interlude that would fall apart once they were out of the swamp?

If Carter loved her, wouldn't he have said so already? He was so confident, he wouldn't be held back by the kind of doubts she had.

"We should probably let them get out of the water," said Carter, indicating the kidnappers. They were so exhausted that their heads were repeatedly slipping below the water.

Fen would have enjoyed that sight more if she hadn't been hoping Carter was contemplating telling her he loved her rather than watching the kidnappers. Hurriedly, she said, "Yes. You do it."

He got up, stretched in a leisurely fashion, and shouted, "Will you all give me your word you won't attack us if we let you get on the island?"

The kidnappers all shouted their agreement, some of them swallowing water as they did so.

"And will you tell us everything you know about what this was about?" Fen added.

They agreed to that too, spluttering and choking.

Carter whispered, "Want to do the honors? Just don't give away that he's a shifter."

Fen nodded. She strolled to the edge of the bank, pointed at Norris, and shouted, "Shoo!"

Immediately, he plunged back down into the water's depths. The exhausted kidnappers thrashed their way to shore, where they all collapsed, panting and gasping and spitting out swamp water. An array of goggle-eyed bullfrogs that had been scared away by Norris popped up and watched the kidnappers in a mocking manner.

Fen and Carter stood over the miserable, gasping kidnappers.

"What's all this about?" she demanded. "One lie, and I'll call back the—er—"

"The Great Swamp Shark," Carter put in smoothly. "And just so you know, it's getting near his dinner time."

Several of the kidnappers made gulping noises, like bullfrogs. One of them, staring bullfrog-eyed at Fen, said, "You have a rat in your shirt."

"He's a sugar glider," she said, petting him. "I have a way with animals."

"As you saw," put in Carter. "Now tell us everything. Out with it, or you go back in the water!"

Four of the kidnappers looked at the fifth. It was Bill. Fen supposed he was their leader. She was pleased to note that he had a sodden bandage on his hand where she'd bitten him.

He puffed out his chest, as much as he could while flopped on the ground, and said, "I run a secret society for men who want to go back to their roots as real men. Modern men have lost their way. They take orders from women. They depend on technology like cell phones, instead of spears and stones and their own strength, like the cavemen of yore."

"Did the cavemen of yore play paintball?" Carter inquired.

"Or use outboard motors?" asked Fen. "Or airplanes?"

Defensively, Bill said, "They would have if they'd had them. Anyway, my society puts us back in touch with our true selves: Man the Hunter!"

The kidnappers loudly chorused, "Man the Hunter!"

Carter and Fen jumped. Several of the kidnappers looked embarrassed.

"Er, anyway," Bill went on. "I lead them on hunting trips and so forth. Also, I'm a nutritional consultant for men going on the caveman diet, which is very popular nowadays with high-powered alpha men like CEOs."

Carter made a choking noise. He sounded in danger of doing a Fen-style roll on the ground laughing fit.

Fen asked, "Is that what alpha CEOs call the paleo diet?"

"Pah!" Bill exclaimed. "Paleo is for wusses. REAL men do it caveman style. First thing in the morning, you make a smoothie with raw beef liver—"

Carter made another choking noise, this one sounding like Fen felt at the idea of that. To distract herself from imagining how that tasted, she said, "First time I've heard of cavemen using blenders."

Icily, Bill said, "They would have if they'd had them. Anyway, I was in very, very high demand. One of my clients is Eldon McManus, the CEO of America's greatest tech company, TicTech."

"Eldon McManus?" Fen exclaimed. Suddenly everything fell into place. "*He's* behind this?"

"No wonder their products are so awful, if Eldon drinks liquefied raw liver for breakfast!" Carter exclaimed.

Scowling, Bill said, "I'll have you know, Eldon a true alpha male. I told him about Man the Hunter, and he was very interested. He proposed that I pit my alpha hunters against the epitome of tech-happy modern man and modern woman—you two—in a battle supreme from which only one could emerge victorious!"

Fen waited for the rest of it. There was an awkward pause, and Bill said defensively, "And we did! We won. Your little tech toys were no match for our—"

"Paintball rifles?" Carter put in.

"Hunting skills," sneered Bill.

Fen and Carter looked at each other. Carter spoke first. "How much did he pay you?"

"What?" Bill asked blankly.

"Eldon," said Fen. "How much did he pay you to kidnap us?"

This seemed to offend Bill. "Nothing! It was purely a skills test. We can all afford to take some time off work, and Al here owns a plane."

Al nodded vigorously. "I flew everyone here."

"What the hell kind of work do manly cavemen do?" asked Fen incredulously.

"I'm a private nutritional consultant, like I said," said Bill. "Al's a private trainer, Jim's a life coach, Horace is the activity coordinator for an exclusive country club, and Bob's a podiatrist."

"How convenient," she remarked. "Bob can treat your toenail fungus in prison."

Bob's voice rose in a squeak. "Prison?!"

"Yes, prison," snapped Carter. "For kidnapping, assault, industrial espionage, and conspiracy to manipulate the stock market."

"Industrial espionage?" Jim repeated, bewildered. He was the one Fen had nailed with a can of Sprite, and he had a soggy bandage on his head.

"What conspiracy?" Al demanded, sounding worried.

"Eldon scammed you," said Fen. "Remember when Carter disappeared for a year, and then he reappeared with a story that most people didn't believe, and Howe Enterprises' stock crashed and the company nearly went under? Your Most Ridiculous Game thing was an excuse to get you all to commit the crime and leave his hands clean. Eldon wanted us both to disappear for a while and then reappear with a story that absolutely no one would believe. We'd look like lunatics, and Little Bit's and Howe Enterprise's stock would crash. Then TicTech would reign supreme, as the cavemen say."

A dead silence fell. The kidnappers squirmed and shot nervous glances at each other.

"I don't know anything about any of that," said Al.

"Me neither," said Jim.

"It wasn't kidnapping and assault," said Horace. "It was a prank. A boys will be boys kind of practical joke."

Fen fixed them with a glare that made all five of them shrink back into the mud. "It was kidnapping. And assault. And battery. And if I hadn't happened to have spent some time in this very swamp—er, swimming with Great Swamp Sharks, it's the extreme version of swimming with dolphins—and if I hadn't gotten close to one particular Great Swamp Shark, you'd have gotten away with it."

Carter added his glare to hers. "If you don't want to be on the hook for the conspiracy part, you can testify about who hired you."

The kidnappers all shot each other nervous glances. Belligerently, Horace said, "It's our word against yours!"

A wave of muddy swamp water crashed over them as the Dunkleosteus heaved itself out of the water. The kidnappers shrieked and tried to scramble away as Norris lunged for them, his great jaws snapping.

"Horace, you moron!" Bill yelled, and smacked him hard across the back of the head. "Take the deal before she feeds us to that thing!"

"All right, all right!" Horace gasped. "Call it off! I'll testify!"

Fen snapped her fingers at Norris, who dragged his great bulk back into the water. Like the Cheshire Cat, his toothy jaws were the last thing to disappear.

Carter beckoned to her to step away from the kidnappers. They went far enough away that they could watch them while being able to speak privately.

"We have to figure out what to do with them," he whispered. "Their boat is destroyed, and we can't tie them up."

"We could ditch them on the island," she whispered back. "They might swim for it, though."

His grin lit up his entire face. "Not if they think Norris is guarding them."

They returned to the kidnappers.

"Listen up," said Carter. "We're leaving you on this island with the Great Swamp Shark guarding it. You'll be safe as long as you don't go in the water."

"Or too near the shore," Fen added. "As you just saw."

"The sooner we get out of the swamp, the sooner you'll be rescued," he said.

"And by 'rescued,' he means arrested," she put in. "Still, better than getting eaten. Right?"

The kidnappers unenthusiastically nodded.

"So where are we, and which way is out?" Carter asked.

"Georgia," said Al. "Or maybe Florida. The swamp's right on the border. Keep heading north, and you'll be out in a day or so. It'd be faster if you had a motorboat, but…"

"You can't leave us here for two days," said Horace. "There's no food! It'd be murder!"

"A two-day fast won't kill you," muttered Carter.

Fen, concerned that Horace specifically might resort to cannibalism without an afternoon snack, pointed to a gnarled tree. "See those fruits? They're called pawpaws. And see those reeds? Those are cattails. Every part is edible. What kind of survivalists are you, anyway?"

"We're hunters," said Bill. "Foraging is women's work."

Fen gave up. Maybe they deserved to be cannibalized. "There might be some swamp roaches you can hunt. Leave the bullfrogs alone, though. Remember, the Great Swamp Shark is patrolling the beaches."

She knew a good parting line when she said it herself. Beckoning to Carter, she strolled away. They got into the boat and paddled north, leaving the kidnappers to their small island.

When they were absolutely, definitely out of sight and earshot of the kidnappers, Fen once again began to giggle. Carter laughed too. They were both covered in mud and paint, they smelled like a chemical spill in a swamp, neither of them had eaten lunch, and pawpaws were probably still on the menu. But her heart was light and she could tell that his was too. Despite the coating of grime and paintball paint, he seemed to shine like a beacon. If she hadn't known that Norris would appear at any moment, she'd have been tempted to ask if he'd like to jump overboard, wash off, and find an island for a quickie.

"Great Swamp Shark!" Carter said, laughing.

"Man the Hunter!" gasped Fen.

And then, both at once, they said, "TicTech!"

Carter wiped at his eyes, smearing more paint across his face. "All's well that ends well, I guess. Tell you what. Once we get out of this godforsaken swamp, let's book a suite at the fanciest hotel in the city, have a very long bath, and spend at least one day doing nothing but having sex and eating food that doesn't come from a swamp."

She stuck out her filthy hand. "It's a deal."

They shook hands, then had some difficulty letting go. The paint got sticky as it began to dry.

"Let's take a swim," she suggested. "It's not like there's any rush now."

Before he could reply, there was a musical trill and a flash of gold. Precious flew through the swamp, gleaming in the afternoon sun. She dove toward him, but let out a squeak and veered off at the last minute, landing on the edge of the boat instead. The dragonette eyed him disapprovingly, then raised her muzzle to the sky and let out a very loud, long trill.

"What's with you?" Carter asked, reaching out to pet her. Precious hopped away from his hand.

"I think she doesn't want you to get her dirty," said Fen, grinning. "Like master, like dragonette."

"I'm surprised Sugar doesn't mind, then."

"Carter, my cleavage is the only part of me that's not covered in paint or mud." She grabbed his hand. "Come on. Swim time!"

He froze. "Wait. I hear something."

Precious trilled again, but Fen could hear something over her clear call. It was the distinctive putt-putt-putt of an outboard engine.

"Civilization!" Fen exclaimed in delight. "Hey! Here! Over here!" Then, remembering, she whispered, "Carter, tell Precious to get out of sight!"

"Precious, take off!" Carter ordered.

The golden dragonette launched into the air, but she didn't hide. Instead, she looped and dove and glided, soaring and tumbling and trilling at the top of her little lungs. It would have been a wonderful sight to see if Fen couldn't hear for herself that the boat was getting closer and closer.

"Precious!" Carter hissed. "Get out of here! Hide!"

But it was too late. Fen could see the approaching boat now, and Precious was still flittering and trilling, having the time of her life.

A man at the prow of the boat pointed straight at the dragonette, exclaiming, "Look!"

CHAPTER 12

Fen shot a glance at Carter, hoping he'd have a better idea to explain Precious than the absurd "flying swamp lizard" excuse he'd attempt to fob her off with. But he was staring at the approaching boat, looking utterly pole-axed. There would clearly be no help coming from that direction.

Maybe it wasn't too late. Maybe if the dragonette flew away now, she could be passed off as an optical illusion—a swamp mirage.

Precious swooped down, landed beside Carter, and gave a crystal-clear trill.

Fen waved to the people in the boat. "Hey, can you help us? We're lost. Our cool new dragon-shaped drone there doesn't have GPS."

The man who had pointed at Precious beamed at her. With apparently sincere approval, he said, "Dragon-shaped drone is a *great* idea. Why didn't I ever think of that?"

His comment was so baffling that Fen could only stare at him. He had rumpled blond hair, bright blue eyes, an even brighter smile, and a lithe gymnast's build. He wore blue jeans and a T-shirt with a picture of a T-rex wearing a T-shirt, captioned T-REX. As the boat came closer, Fen could see that the T-shirt the T-rex was wearing also had a picture of a T-rex wearing a T-shirt, captioned T-REX. When she squinted, she could almost see that the T-shirt within the T-shirt also had a T-shirt, and so on to infinity. The effect was hypnotic.

"Merlin…" another man sighed. He was a burly, handsome black man with silvering hair and beard. His demeanor of effortless command made it obvious that he was the boss, and his tone made it obvious that Merlin was a complete loose cannon of whom he was nonetheless very fond. Fen had several employees to whom she was always sighing "Juan…" or "Lydia…" in identical tones. She warmed to the boss immediately.

A muscular Latino man with a military haircut and bearing elbowed the T-rex guy aside. Eyeing Carter, he said, "You're a mess. What did you do, dive into the swamp head-first and then go finger-painting?"

"Pete…" began the boss. This tone was more warning than indulgent.

"Hey!" Fen exclaimed, her temper flaring. "We're the victims of a crime—we were kidnapped and dumped here—and you're going to insult us for being *dirty?* In a *swamp?!*"

A slim white woman with rainbow-dyed hair stepped forward. Even that simple movement had an astonishing grace. If she wasn't a dancer or an acrobat, Fen would eat… well, not a bullfrog… another pawpaw, maybe. With a teasing grin, the rainbow-haired woman said, "Say something, Carter."

Fen twisted around. "Carter? You know these people?"

Carter had the oddest expression, as if he was torn between being astonished, pleased, and disbelieving. Clearing his throat, he said, "They're my tea—uh, they're people I work with. Sometimes. They're the ones I told you about. The Defenders."

A tall man with auburn hair and a professorial air said dryly, "And are you going to introduce your companion, Carter?"

"Like you don't already know, Ransom," Carter snapped.

Ransom replied, "As a matter of fact, I don't. We were only looking for you."

Merlin straightened his T-rex T-shirt and offered Fen his hand. "Please to meet you! I'm Merlin Merrick."

She shook it automatically, covering his palm with mud and blue paint. "Fenella Kim."

It wasn't as if Fen wasn't used to her name causing a stir. She was famous, after all. But she wasn't used to it getting the reaction it provoked from the Defenders.

Merlin, Pete, and the rainbow-haired woman burst out laughing.

Ransom remarked, "As a high school student once wrote in an English paper, 'And then the hand of fate stepped in.'"

Only the boss managed to react like a normal person, though even he had an amused twinkle in his eyes. He said, "Pleased to meet you, Fenella. I'm Roland Walker, and I'm the boss of this odd crew. Take no notice of them. They're laughing at Carter, not you."

"I know they're laughing at Carter," Fen snapped. Far from being quenched by his words, her anger burned hotter. Turning to the rest of them, she said, "Odd is a nice way to put it! Let me tell you, Carter put his own body between me and men with guns! Sure, they weren't real guns, but he didn't know that. They were kidnappers and assaulters—that blood on his head is plenty real—and he defended me from them, even though for all he knew, it would cost him his life. That's where the mud and paint came from. Oh yes, so hilarious. Ha ha."

"Fen..." Carter began.

But she wasn't finished. Glaring at the Defenders, she added, "HA!"

They were all silent, looking properly abashed.

Carter caught her by the wrist and turned her around. To her surprise, he was smiling. "Fen, it's okay. They're weird and annoying and tactless, but they don't mean any harm. And they did come to rescue me." Turning to the Defenders, he said, "Right?"

They nodded.

"We're not laughing at Carter as a person," Merlin assured her. His smile practically lit the swamp. "We're laughing because he was so mad at you over you trying to do a hostile takeover of his company, and then he somehow got trapped in the swamp with you, and now you don't seem hostile anymore. You're not, are you?"

"No," she admitted. "And the hostile takeover is off."

"See?" Merlin spread his hands wide. "That's all."

"It is pretty funny to see him covered in mud and paint, considering how fussy he is about his clothes," put in Pete. "I have a thirteen-year-old daughter who thinks less about how she looks."

Fen gave him a freezing glare. "I'm fairly certain your thirteen-year-old daughter isn't the CEO of a Fortune 500 company whose stocks rise and fall depending on people's trust in her. I expect she's never had to consider that if her image isn't exactly right, her many employees might find their livelihoods in danger."

"Fen..." Carter's smile had widened into a grin. Despite his team's sarcastic remarks, he seemed quite pleased. "Much as I love your defense of me and my wardrobe, they really do mean well. Even Pete. Probably." Turning to the team, he said, "Can we stop bickering and get out of this swamp?"

Roland beckoned to him and Fen. "Pile in."

They clambered into the boat. Ransom, who was steering, turned it around and started it up. As the boat motored along the swamp, Fen sank down, relieved to no longer have to paddle.

"So you got a magical pet," said Merlin, trying to coax Precious on to his hand. "Now you'll be much more understanding when Blue eats your chocolate, or steps on your shoes, or shreds your reports, or sits on your laptop, or—"

"I will not," Carter interrupted. "Precious is very well-behaved. And she doesn't shed."

"Hi," said the rainbow-haired woman, offering Fen a slim hand. "I'm Natalie Nash, the team's newest bodyguard. I used to be a target girl and acrobat at a circus, and..." She glanced at Precious. "I assume Carter told you about magical animals."

"I did." He gave Natalie a strangely intense stare. "I also told her about the existence of shifters, and that I used to be a snow leopard, and that you're all shifters. But that's it. I didn't tell her what animals you shift into. For instance."

"Ah. Gotcha." Turning back to Fen, Natalie said in tones of pride and brimming happiness, "I turn into a Gabriel Hound."

If that was supposed to be meaningful to Fen, it missed the mark. "A what?"

"A Gabriel Hound. It's a big white dog with wings. Ransom's my..." She glanced at Carter, who was giving her a ferocious glare. "My boyfriend." Natalie turned her thousand-watt smile first on Carter, then on Fen. Carter's glare subsided.

Fen, baffled, decided that this team certainly had some *interesting* workplace dynamics. She made a mental note to ask Carter about that little exchange later, then instantly forgot it when Natalie added, "He turns into a hellhound."

"A... Sorry, he turns into a *what?*"

"A big black dog," said Ransom. After a moment, he added, "Without wings."

Under normal circumstances, Fen would have thought she was being made the target of an elaborate practical joke. Carter had said the team were all shifters, but she couldn't help glancing at him for confirmation.

"It's true," he said. "They're all unusual types of shifters. It's because they were created in a lab. Pete's a cave bear."

Fen glanced at Pete, impressed. "I saw a reproduction of a cave bear in a museum once. It was enormous. Bigger than a grizzly!"

Pete only nodded, but she imagined that she could see a hint of the bear in his broad shoulders, brown hair, and air of steady strength.

"And I'm a raptor," put in Merlin.

"What kind of raptor?" Fen couldn't remember if all birds of prey were considered raptors, or just some of them.

"Well, that depends," said Merlin. "I could show—"

Carter glared at him. "DON'T."

Sugar poked his head out of Fen's cleavage and peered at the new people with wide black eyes. Merlin was immediately distracted.

"Hiya, cutie," he said, offering his hand. "What's your name?"

"Sugar," said Fen. "He's a sugar glider."

Merlin nodded, clearly already having identified him. "And what's his power?"

"Power?" Fen echoed, puzzled. "He can glide."

"I don't think he's a magical animal like Precious here," Carter put in. Hearing her name, Precious stretched her wings and chirruped. "He seems to be an ordinary sugar glider who took a fancy to Fen."

Ransom glanced over his shoulder and briefly said, "No."

Fen waited for him to elaborate. When he returned to steering, she said, "No, what?"

The tall man's cool grey eyes moved from Sugar to Fen as if he could see right through them both. "No, he's not an ordinary sugar glider."

Once again, Fen waited. Once again, Ransom said nothing more and returned to steering.

Irritated, Fen said, "And I suppose your power is making enigmatic pronouncements without elaboration?"

Merlin laughed. Pete grinned. Roland smiled.

"You got it," said Carter.

"His power is knowing things." Natalie's voice had a distinct edge to it, and she bristled protectively. "If he says something, it's so. And if he doesn't say something, it's because he doesn't know."

Ransom laid a hand on Natalie's shoulder. The harsh angles of his face softened as he touched a bright blue lock of her rainbow hair. To Fen, he said, "I know Sugar's a magical animal of some kind. But I don't know what he can do. You'll find out. I didn't know what mine could do right away, either."

"You have a magical sugar glider too?" Fen asked.

He shook his head. "Natalie and I have a pair of teleporting huskies."

"I have a cactus cat," Pete volunteered. His voice softened with fondness. "He's a flying green cat who can shoot cactus spines at people."

"I have a bugbear!" Merlin said with pride.

"And we're all thankful you left him at home," said Carter. With mild alarm, he glanced around. "He is at home, right? He's not waiting for you on shore like a sailor's wife in a ballad, only blue and hairy instead of fair and comely?"

"No," Merlin said. "He's home. Roland thought he wouldn't fit on the boat."

That reminded Fen that Roland was the only person who hadn't mentioned his shift form, so she asked, "What do you turn into, Roland?"

Before he could reply, Precious let out a shriek and Sugar gave a frantic chitter. His little claws dug into her chest as he scrambled out of her blouse and launched himself into the air. Precious was already aloft.

"Wise creatures," said a strange man's voice.

Carter flung himself on top of Fen, squashing her to the rather wet bottom of the boat. For the second time in about an hour, she could see nothing because he'd used his own body as a shield to protect her from danger.

I love him, she thought. *Even if it's too soon. Even if he doesn't love me back. I love him.*

She had no time to think over or second-guess her realization, because the man spoke again. His voice was loud and somewhat pompous. "Stop that. Both of you, sit up at once."

"Why, so you can shoot us?" Carter demanded. His voice was muffled, and she could feel his chest moving against her back as he spoke.

"I have no intention of doing anything so wasteful," replied the strange man. "And in case it's escaped your notice, your associates are unable to assist you. They will be witnesses, nothing more."

In fact, she had heard nothing from anyone but Carter and the unknown man, and had felt nothing but Carter's body atop hers since the first moment the man had spoken. What was everyone else doing?

"Merlin?" Fen whispered. "Roland?"

There was no reply.

Carter gave a muttered exclamation of annoyance and disgust.

"What?" Fen whispered.

In an ordinary speaking tone, he said, "I was trying to get Merlin's gun—he's the closest—but it's turned to stone."

Fen, uncertain that she'd heard him correctly, said, "It's what?"

Carter moved off her and sat up. She rolled over and blinked up at him. He held up a gun made of shiny black rock. Everyone else on the boat was absolutely still in the positions she'd last seen them in, as if they were playing freeze tag.

For a moment she was utterly baffled, and then it came to her. "Is this the wizard-scientists?"

"Correct," said the male voice. "Sit up and witness."

She looked at Carter. "Should I?"

Glumly, he said, "You may as well. The bottom of the boat won't be much protection if—"

The boat bumped gently into something and stopped moving, though the engine continued to run. Carter reached out and turned it off.

Fen sat up. The boat had run aground on an island. A man and a woman stood on the island, smirking at them. The woman was Asian and in her twenties, with black hair in a bob. She wore leather armor straight out of a Renaissance Fair. The man was white and older, with long straggly gray hair and a long straggly gray beard. He wore a long white garment something like a doctor's coat and something like a wizard's robe, embroidered all over with strange black symbols.

The pair had nothing in common, and yet they struck Fen as being two of a kind. After a moment, she placed it. They both looked incredibly smug.

"My name is Balin," announced the man. "I am one of the ancient order of wizard-scientists, and I am here to claim my Dark Knight."

CHAPTER 13

The worst thing about the wizard-scientists, Carter thought, was being forced to take them seriously. They were pompous. Their collective name was ridiculous, and so were the individual names they took on. They wore absurd costumes. They ought to be a joke.

He'd also seen them nearly kill several of the Defenders, and drive others near to madness. Worst of all, they had no regard for innocent bystanders, but would ruthlessly cut down anyone who stood in their way. When they'd kidnapped Roland, a woman had tried to defend him. They'd taken her along with him, and their experiments had killed her. As far as Carter could tell, it had broken Roland's heart as surely as if he'd been a shifter who had recognized his mate at first sight, and then discovered that she'd died alone at the hands of his enemies, before he could even learn her name.

Fen was an innocent bystander. She had nothing to do with the wizard-scientists, but if they decided she was a problem, they'd murder her as casually as if they were swatting a fly. They could do it, too. Just one of them had taken out the entire team of Defenders, apparently without even breaking a sweat.

"So it *was* you guys all along?" Fen asked. "Did you put Eldon McManus up to hiring the hunters, or was that whole thing a lie and Eldon had nothing to do with it?"

Balin's lip curled in scorn. "I would never dirty my hands with such fools. No, I merely utilized an existing situation. When I learned of your rival's scheme, I decided to allow his chosen hunters to exhaust and harry you before I stepped in myself."

Fen glanced around nervously. "Where'd Sugar and Precious go?"

"Your little pets have fled," said Balin. "Like your so-called friends, they have no true loyalty."

"Bullshit!" Fen snapped.

"Don't say another word," Carter hissed at her. "And don't do anything. They'll kill you."

Her elegant eyebrows arched in disbelief as she stared at the pair in their idiotic costumes, but he jerked his head at the frozen Defenders. She gave a reluctant nod. Carter was immensely relieved that she wasn't going to try to do anything heroic. He had a horrible vision of her hurling a pawpaw at Balin and getting vaporized on the spot.

His monsters broke into an angry inner chorus.

Shift, hissed one. *Shift and protect her!*

Yes, shift, growled another. *Slay the wizard!*

The monsters began to chant in unison. *Slay! Slay! Slay!*

[murderous crimson]

[urgent dandelion yellow]

Carter resisted the urge to clutch his head. He didn't have any better ideas—yet—but shifting was a bad one. Balin would freeze him, and then he'd be a frozen monster. In front of Fen. And the Defenders.

Shift and attack before he can do that!

Bite his head off!

Rip his throat out!

Crush him!

Choke him!

Tear him limb from limb!

[murderous crimson]

[murderous crimson]

The other thing Carter knew about the wizard-scientists was that they liked to speechify. If he could get them talking, maybe he come up with an idea for defeating him that didn't involve turning into a monster in front of everyone.

"*Who* are you, again?" Carter asked.

"Balin," the wizard-scientist repeated irritably. "Of the wizard-scientists."

The woman beside him cleared her throat meaningfully.

"And this is my minion—"

"What did we talk about?" she demanded, glaring at him.

"My associate," he said grudgingly. "Eunice. She's a gargoyle. Don't even think of using one of your pitiful gunpowder weapons against us. She's already turned them all to stone."

Eunice smirked. "Your cell phones too."

Carter wasn't surprised. The wizard-scientists often allied with gargoyles, who made it impossible to either use guns or call for help.

"We wizard-scientists are an ancient order," said Balin, making a grandiose gesture. "We trace our lineage back to the days of our greatest enemy, King Arthur."

"King Arthur?" Fen exclaimed, then shot a guilty glance at Carter. "Sorry. I'll keep quiet."

"No, no," said Balin. To Carter's intense relief, the look he was giving Fen was weirdly approving. "You may ask questions, fair maiden."

Her eyebrows rose at that, but she didn't comment. Instead, she said, "King Arthur was real?"

"He was. And so was Merlin—not that yellow-haired fool in the boat, the one he named himself after. The original Merlin was the first shifter. He and King Arthur allied. They fought the original order of wizard-scientists—we were wizard-alchemists back then—and defeated us. We were scattered to the winds, our power broken, and Arthur's ideas triumphed. It is only recently that we regained our strength, regrouped, and began work on our master plan."

The surest sign of a wizard-scientist is the unironic use of the phrase 'master plan,' thought Carter.

Balin gave Fen an expectant look. She played along. "What's your master plan?"

"To rule the world, of course," said the wizard-scientist.

Of course, Carter thought.

"We shall create a Golden Age in which wizardry and science rule! But to do that, we must have knights, like the knights of Arthur of old. Our own knights—*Dark* Knights." Balin cast a scornful glance over the people frozen on the boat. "There you have a pathetic selection of failed Dark Knights, poorly chosen by wizard-scientists who were brilliant and powerful, but lacked wisdom."

He pointed scornfully at Pete, who was frozen in the act of checking his now-stone gun. "Peter Valdez, who chose the love of a cripple bound to a rolling chair over the glory of being the Dark Knight Rage."

Pete didn't move—he couldn't—but Carter saw fury burn in his brown eyes. Carter was pissed off too. Pete's mate Tirzah wasn't bound to her wheelchair. It was an assistive device that freed her to get around, not some kind of mobile prison.

The wizard-scientist's skinny finger moved to Merlin, who was poised on his tip-toes with his hand upraised; he'd been caught in the act of reaching up toward the flying Precious. "Merlin Merrick, who chose the love of a ruined warrior over the glory of being the Dark Knight Deceit."

Merlin's bright blue eyes sparked with anger. Carter could see that he wanted to shift and go for Balin's throat, and Carter would have gladly joined him. Merlin's mate Dali, wasn't ruined—what an awful thing to say. She was a highly skilled veteran with a prosthetic hand, and if she'd been there, she'd probably have pitched Balin into the swamp. Head-first.

"And Ransom Pierce." Balin practically spat out the name as he stabbed his finger at Ransom, who was gazing down at Natalie with the beginning of a smile. "He's the worst of all! He could have been the Dark Knight Despair, and he threw it away for the love of that garish little guttersnipe!"

Balin jabbed his finger at Natalie, whose rainbow hair shone bright as she crouched in one of the acrobatic poses she often absent-mindedly adopted, balanced on the ball of one foot with her other leg stretched out like a kung fu master. Ransom's eyes smoldered like the fiery gaze of his hellhound, but Natalie's glittered with amusement.

Carter wished he could find the humor in the situation. He was torn between terror for the others and especially for Fen, the only person present with no shift form and no special powers, and a frantic mental search for a plan to get out of this disaster. So far, he hadn't come up with anything other than to play along and keep Balin talking until he thought of something. So far, nothing had come to mind.

You can shift, shrieked a monster.

You're not frozen, another monster gibbered.

You don't need guns when you have talons, screeched a third.

[urgent dandelion yellow]

Maybe he hasn't frozen you because he can't, hissed a monster. *You have some resistance to their powers, remember?*

It was true. Once before, Carter had been able to move when a wizard-scientist had frozen everyone else in place. It probably had something to do with having so many creatures crammed into him, when the others had only one. But it wasn't as if he was completely immune to wizard-scientist powers. It had only been that one time, and that one power.

COWARD!

The monster's voice was so loud that he jumped.

"Are you even listening?" Balin demanded. "What did I just say?"

"You called Natalie a guttersnipe," Carter said.

"No!" Balin glared at him. "You missed the last five minutes, you careless fool. You, maiden, tell him what I was saying."

"He was telling us about the glorious future we'd have when the wizard-scientists ruled." Fen's lips twitched slightly; like Natalie, she clearly found the situation a bit funny as well as frightening. "It was… er… glorious!"

That seemed to satisfy Balin. He nodded, his beard bobbing. "Join me, Carter Howe, and that glory will be yours. I know what happened to you in the laboratory. That was most ill-advised, but not irrevocable. I can fix it."

The monsters began to scream and jabber and growl inside his head. Carter couldn't understand a word they were saying. They were an incoherent, raging mob, screeching so loudly that he felt like his head would explode.

And then, in an instant, they fell silent. Carter opened his eyes, which he realized had been squeezed shut. He was on his knees, clutching at his head. Fen was kneeling beside him, urgently calling his name.

"I'm all right," he said, letting his hands drop.

She took a long look at him, then fixed a truly murderous glare on Balin. "Do that again, and I'll wring your beardy little neck."

"Fen! Don't provoke him." But Carter was touched by her protectiveness. She'd believed that Balin had done something to hurt him, and she'd threatened Balin in return.

"I didn't do that," Balin said. "Eunice did."

"Then I'll wring her neck," snarled Fen. Her hands clenched on air.

Eunice smirked at them both. Carter waited, his pulse thundering in his ears, for her to reveal that she hadn't inflicted pain on him, but had removed it by silencing his inner monsters. How in world would he explain that to Fen and the Defenders? Maybe he could claim he had no idea what they were talking about…?

"I can silence, and I can kill," said Eunice. "I could do it right now. But I won't. I'm going to do something else instead."

Balin explained, "Eunice went through a similar process to that of your sad, damaged associates, but hers was much more successful. She retained her natural gargoyle powers over stone, but also gained others. One was control over others' inner animals."

Carter eyed the woman. She looked so… ordinary. Other than her costume, he wouldn't have given her a second glance. At a Renaissance Fair or a fantasy convention, she'd have blended into the crowd. But if

Balin was telling the truth, she had the most terrifying power he'd ever heard of. Just the thought of someone else controlling his inner animal made his skin crawl. It was as if she could reach into his very soul and force it to do her bidding.

But if she could really kill his monsters…

Carter hated himself for being tempted. The wizard-scientists were evil. They were murderers. They ruined people's lives. And they had an absolutely dreadful fashion sense.

But he *was* tempted.

Balin interrupted his thoughts. "I shall not make the mistakes of my colleagues. I will not push you to choose immediately, and force you into a foolish, impulsive decision. Instead, I will give you some time to decide. When we meet again, you will make your final and irrevocable decision."

"I've taken control of your inner animals already." Eunice gave him a hard, fierce smile, showing a lot of very white teeth. "Until you make up your mind, you'll slowly transform into a monster."

"What?" Carter blurted out.

That's impossible, he told himself. *It's a mind game. Don't fall for it.*

Eunice's toothy grin widened. "It's reversible. But only by me. Don't wait too long!"

"I won't wait at all," he said promptly. "My answer is no."

Balin gave an airy wave of his hand. "I told you, I don't want a foolish, impulsive decision. I want you to take your time and think it over. Only then will you be able to take in the offer I make and the price of refusing. And now I will return your associates to their senses so they can see and recoil from the monster that you are. I alone will treasure you and lift you to glory. When you're truly ready, you shall make your choice. And then you will take up your true place among us, as the Dark Knight Pride."

Balin made a grand gesture, unfreezing everyone on the boat.

Merlin almost fell over, but recovered into a graceful flip that propelled him off the boat and onto the island. He immediately shifted, becoming a sleek black velociraptor.

Natalie, who like Merlin had once been a professional acrobat, leaped off the boat in an astonishingly high jump. She shifted in mid-air, becoming a huge white hound with feathered wings and eyes like pieces of a summer sky.

Pete vaulted off the boat. He too shifted as he moved. His massive cave bear hit the island with an enormous thud.

Ransom stepped off the boat and on to the island. A cloud of smoke rose up and a black hound the size of a pony stepped out. The hound was wreathed in smoke, and it glared at Balin with eyes made of pure fire, like windows into Hell itself.

Roland spread his arms wide, as if in a gesture of invocation. Flame blossomed in his palms and raced up his arms. For the blink of an eye, he was a man with wings of fire. Then he was gone, and a fiery phoenix blazed across the sky.

It all happened so fast that Carter had no chance to warn them. All five of the Defenders went straight for Balin and Eunice. Despite Carter's sinking feeling that it was a useless attack, he couldn't help feeling warmed by how instantly they'd all jumped to his defense.

Fen, who had unfrozen in a kneeling position, scrambled to her feet, staring. "What the actual fuck."

When the Defenders were about to reach the wizard-scientist and the gargoyle, Eunice gave a fierce, toothy grin, and everything fell apart.

Roland, who had been diving down as a phoenix, shifted to human form in mid-air. He hit the ground hard.

Natalie, who had also been diving in her Gabriel Hound form, veered off and plunged into the swamp. She vanished into the black water with a tremendous splash.

Merlin shrank to the size of a gecko. Since his power was to change his size, this didn't seem to throw him much. He kept on running, darting to veer around a bush that was suddenly an obstacle. Then he became the size of a T-rex and crashed into the trees he'd been about to run between. He fell to the sand and struggled to get up, clearly dazed.

Ransom became a man again, his face taut with pain and fear. He managed a single step forward before falling to his knees, pale and shaking.

Pete swerved off course, charged in a wide circle around Balin and Eunice, and ended up facing the boat again. He let out a tremendous roar and charged straight at the boat. The cave bear's eyes were mad with rage and fixed on Fen.

None of the other Defenders could fight at all now, let alone take on a mind-whammied cave bear. If someone was going to put their body between Fen and the maddened prehistoric beast, it would be Carter or no one.

He had only a split second to think, but the adrenaline surging through his body made time seem to slow. He had just enough time to think, *Fen will see me. Everyone will see me. This is the end of everything.*

He pushed her toward the back of the boat, shouting, "Get down!"

Then he jumped from the boat on to the island, putting himself directly in the path of the charging cave bear.

Carter shifted.

CHAPTER 14

Carter pushed Fen harder than she thought he'd intended to. She stumbled backward, tripped, and sat down hard in the back of the now-empty boat.

After the many, many things she'd just seen that she could barely believe were real, the most horrifying was Carter jumping to put his body between her and the gigantic charging bear. But it was very easy to believe that he'd give his life for her. It was the third time she'd see him throw himself between her and danger, without regret or hesitation.

Fen leaped to her feet, screaming, "Carter, no! Get in the water!"

She didn't think he even heard her. She could barely hear herself over the cave bear's roar. And the expression on his face when he'd pushed her made her think he was beyond listening. He'd had the spookily calm, set expression of a man about to throw himself on a grenade.

Well, she wasn't about to let him die for her. She lunged for him. There wasn't enough time to turn the boat around, but if she dragged him into the swamp, they could swim away and hope the cave bear wouldn't swim after them.

She caught him by the arm. He screamed. Instinctively, Fen yanked her hand away. How could she have hurt him that badly? He sounded like he was in agony.

Carter fell to his knees as his scream turned into a spine-chilling howl. He writhed in pain, then seemed to expand. His clothes exploded off his body.

He was shifting, like the Defenders had. Like he'd told her he could no longer do.

She backed away, worried and baffled. The others had become animals in the blink of an eye and it hadn't seemed to hurt them, but Carter was still changing. His eerie howl modulated into a shriek so loud that it hurt her ears. Something had to be wrong.

And what *was* he, anyway? She couldn't tell. There was a batlike wing, but only one. There were legs like a great cat or maybe a wolf—far too many legs, and not in the right places. As she watched, a leg vanished and was replaced by a great feathered wing that beat at the ground. A tentacle lashed out, hitting the ground and sending up a spray of mud.

Fen jumped back, confused and scared, desperate for help for Carter and longing for someone to tell her what the hell was going on. And the cave bear! They were still getting charged by a giant bear… or were they? When she looked around, she saw that the bear was gone. Where she'd last seen him, only Pete stood on the beach, staring at the writhing mass of ever-changing body parts that Carter had become.

Natalie, now human again, climbed onto the beach, dripping wet and with her previously rainbow hair plastered with mud. Ransom was getting up, still pale but now calm and collected. Merlin had also returned to his human form and had gone to help Roland to his feet. Unlike Carter, none of them had destroyed their clothes when they'd shifted, but were all back to wearing whatever they'd had on before.

Balin and Eunice were still standing where they'd been when it all started, smug and untouched after kicking the asses of a velociraptor, a cave bear, a phoenix, a Gabriel Hound, and a hellhound. Fen wanted to murder them, but she clearly wouldn't stand a chance. Gritting her teeth, she ignored them and turned to Pete, who was closest.

"What's wrong with Carter?" she asked. "Did those assholes do this to him?"

Pete, still staring down at Carter, said, "I have no idea."

"I think this is his shift form," said Merlin. "He definitely has one, but he wouldn't say what it was or let us see it."

"He told me he didn't have one," Fen said.

"Oops," said Merlin, then bent down and said, "Sorry, Carter!"

"I did nothing," Balin called. "The Dark Knight has been a monster for years."

The mass of parts that was Carter's supposedly nonexistent shift form finally stabilized. Even then, Fen had trouble taking it in. It was bigger than the giant bear and had six legs, a snapping beak on one end and a fanged jaw on the other, a single feathered wing, way too many eyes, and a mass of writhing, thrashing tentacles. It looked deeply *wrong*--and painful, too. It was still letting out a high keen of pain and misery as it staggered to its feet, then charged Balin and Eunice.

Balin made a gesture. Nothing happened. Fen was delighted to see him look slightly panicked. "Eunice!"

In the blink of an eye, Eunice changed from a woman to a weird batlike creature, humanlike but with wings and talons and a tail, black as obsidian. She spread her wings, leaped into the air, and reached down with unnervingly elongated arms to grab Balin and lift him out of the way.

The swamp erupted. A wave crashed over Balin, sending him sprawling. It was followed by the enormous form of a Dunkleosteus as it heaved itself onto the island.

"Norris!" Fen exclaimed in delight.

Norris opened his huge jaws and snapped at Eunice. She flew upward just in time. Ponderously, Norris dragged himself toward Balin. The strange beast that Carter had become was also going for the hapless wizard-scientist.

"Eunice!" Balin shrieked.

The gargoyle swooped down, grabbed Balin, and flew upward with him. She was just in time. Several of Carter's tentacles slammed into the ground where he had been.

Norris opened and closed his mouth. His gills pulsed open and shut as he dragged himself back into the water, unable to breathe on land. Once he was back in the swamp, he lifted his head above the water and flapped a contemptuous fin.

"Get the traitor, Eunice," hissed Balin. "Lock him in fish form."

"Already done." Eunice grinned toothily. "The monster's locked in, too. And everyone else is stuck in their human forms. I've trapped them all."

"Good." The wizard-scientist glared down at them all as he dripped from above. "Let our Dark Knight's supposed friends get a good taste of what he really is. Dark Knight Pride, soon you must decide which you prefer: being a monster from whom everyone flees screaming, or being a whole man and an honored knight."

Balin stabbed a skinny finger at Norris. "And you, piscine traitor, will stay as you are until and unless you show up with the Dark Knight when he's ready to choose, at the place I will arrange with him. And by 'show up,' I mean in person. Or should I say, 'in fish.'"

Balin laughed at his own joke. So did Eunice.

"The rest of you will regain your ability to control your shift forms when we leave," Eunice added. "We don't care about you. Our only interest is in the monster knight."

"When you wish to make your decision, all you need to do is say 'I, Carter Howe, summon you, Balin!' I will send you a message telling you where we shall meet."

"Not doing it," said Carter.

Balin pretended not to hear him, declaiming, "Soon, Dark Knight!"

Eunice flapped off with him. Within moments, both were out of sight.

There was a long silence. Fen wasn't sure what everyone else was doing, but personally, she had a lot to take in. And while she filed away most of it to think about later, when she wasn't in a swamp, one thing stood out to her.

She marched up to the weird beast he had become and said, "Carter Howe, you lied to me. AGAIN! Turn back into a man this instant. I want to give you a piece of my mind, and I'm not even sure which end I'm talking to."

She thought she heard a snicker from someone, possibly Merlin. She ignored it. Carter's lies weren't funny to *her.*

"Carter!" Fen snapped.

The beast gave a faint moan. It struggled, legs and wings and tentacles thrashing. The moan became a cry of pain, which cut off sharply when the beast vanished. In its place, Carter sprawled naked on the sand, face-down with his head buried in his arms.

Her anger changed to concern. She put her hand on his shoulder. "Carter! Carter, are you all right?"

He twitched slightly but didn't lift his head. His words were muffled as he spoke into the crook of his elbow. "You're still here?"

Stung, she snapped, "What did you think, I'd run off with Norris and jumped in the swamp?"

"No—I just meant..."

Oh. He thought she was rude to sit there staring at him while he was completely nude. "I've already seen you naked, remember?"

She glanced around. His own clothes were scattered, muddy shreds. The Defenders were all standing around uselessly gaping at him instead of helping out.

"Hey! Don't just stand there!" She mentally measured them. "You, Pete. Give him your shirt. It's big enough that it should cover his, er, well, you're the biggest."

"*Pete's* still here?" Carter asked.

"Yes, of course, where did you think—" Fen broke off, realizing what was going on. Either he'd hit his head at some point in all the commotion, or that awful, painful shifting had left him dazed. Gently, she said, "We're all here. Just lie still."

"You're *all* here?" He sounded incredulous.

Roland came limping up, supported by Merlin. Roland was so big and dark, while Merlin was comparatively short and extremely blond, that they looked a remarkably odd couple. But Merlin supported his boss's weight with ease.

"Carter," said Roland. "Open your eyes and look at us."

His deep voice had a note of command that made it impossible to disobey. Carter sat up, dropping his arms from his face.

CHAPTER 15

When Carter had thrown himself between Fen and the hunters' guns, he'd known he might be sacrificing his life to save her. He'd been fine with that. Everyone had to die some time, and Fen was more than worth dying for. He'd felt no regret or fear, only calm determination.

When he'd shifted in front of everyone, he'd known that he was embracing a fate worse than death. With his luck, he'd live on, alone, knowing that people he cared about had seen the monster that he was. Even the bone-snapping, muscle-ripping agony of the transformation itself paled in comparison to his shame and misery at the knowledge that he'd been seen.

He'd been seen, but he refused to see in return. It was bad enough knowing what everyone thought about him. He didn't have to actually watch them recoil in horror and revulsion.

But then he'd heard Fen's voice, and it wasn't a scream of horror or an exclamation of disgust. First she'd sounded worried, and then she'd sounded pissed off, and then she'd returned to worried. Who would worry about a monster? Who'd be angry at a monster?

He'd been unable to process it, just as he was unable to believe that any of the Defenders had stayed with him until Roland spoke. But when Roland gave you an order, it was hard to disobey. Bracing himself for what he'd see, Carter opened his eyes.

Fen knelt beside him. Her beautiful face was tense, and she had a hand outstretched as if she wanted to touch him but something held her back. The fear that a tentacle would grab her, probably. It was incredibly brave of her to not have run away already, and that touched him deeply.

Roland was standing over him, leaning most of his weight on Merlin's shoulder. It was so rare to see the Defenders boss need help that it drove all else from Carter's mind.

"What's the matter, Roland?" Carter asked. He was already calculating the time it would take to get to a hospital in a motor boat in case Roland had internal injuries or—

"I twisted my knee when I hit the ground," Roland replied. "It's nothing serious."

Only then did Carter register his expression. He looked deeply exasperated, but not horrified or repulsed. It was a very similar expression to the one he'd worn when he'd discovered that Merlin had procrastinated on filing his reports until he had a stack of half-done ones in his office, and then his bugbear Blue had eaten them.

But Roland was a twenty-year Army veteran. He was a mature, experienced man with a wealth of life experience, including a tragic loss. It would take more than a hideous monster to faze him.

But Merlin was different. He was young, even younger than Carter. His bright eyes and hair matched his sunny nature. Surely he would recoil from...

...but he wasn't recoiling. He was examining Carter with cheerful curiosity and interest, as if he'd discovered some fascinating and distracting object.

On second thought, that made sense. Merlin was interested in *everything*, from sea slugs to obscure Japanese soft drinks to the world's most horrifying sports mascots. It obviously took more than a grotesque monster to scare him off.

The other Defenders had gathered round as well. Carter made himself look up at them. Ransom had once been repulsed and horrified by his own inner beast, so he'd surely be repulsed and horrified by a creature far worse than a hellhound. Natalie's rainbow hair and beautiful Gabriel Hound matched her joyous nature; she'd be naturally repelled by something as disgusting and monstrous as Carter's true form. As for Pete, he had a teenage daughter he protected from all dangers, so he wouldn't want anything to do with a rampaging horror…

…but even as Carter thought all that, he was looking at their expressions. To his bewilderment, not one of them looked horrified or disgusted or afraid. They looked concerned. Worried. Annoyed. Frustrated. Curious.

If he had to sum up the emotional atmosphere of the entire group, Fen included, he'd have thought it like people watching their daredevil friend wipe out on a dangerous stunt they'd warned him against.

He didn't believe it. He *couldn't* believe it.

"Hey!" Fen said sharply. "What about that shirt? He needs to get some clothes on. He's hurt. He's dazed—see, he can't track a conversation. He needs to stay warm."

The swamp was as hot as ever, but Carter appreciated the thought. He was about to point out that he was neither hurt nor dazed and he was tracking the conversation perfectly well, but Merlin spoke before he could get a word out.

"We brought a whole set of spare clothes," Merlin said. "Just in case."

"I'll get them," said Natalie. She ran lightly to the boat, took out a backpack, and brought it to Carter. "Here you go."

"Give me that." Fen seized the backpack before Carter could even reach for it. "And turn your backs. Can't you see you're embarrassing him?"

The Defenders politely turned their backs, though Carter caught half of them grinning as they did so. Fen removed the clothes and placed them on the backpack so they wouldn't get muddy. She lifted the black shirt and was starting to put it on him when his mind finally caught up to what was going on.

"Why are you still here?" he asked.

She gave him a look like he was an idiot, then seemed to remember something and replaced it with a kinder one. "We're on an island. But we're going to leave soon. Once you get dressed."

"Fen. I don't have a concussion. You can talk to me like a normal person."

She shot him a dubious glance as she buttoned up the shirt. "I will if you want, but you're sure not acting like it."

"What I mean was, why are you *right here?* Sitting down here, next to me?" He took the boxers from her hand, got up, and pulled them on himself.

She stood up with him. "Because you were hurt. It wasn't like I could run and get a doctor."

"A doctor?" Carter echoed, baffled.

"It was obviously painful for you to turn into whatever that was that you turned into. I thought you might be stiff." She paused, her eyes flickering as she replayed what she'd just said, and hissed, "As in 'stiff and sore.' Not… you know. Are all men twelve at heart, or what?"

He couldn't help smiling. "Yes. We are. But I wasn't even thinking of that. You're the one with the dirty mind."

"Dirty mind, I like that coming from a man who—" She dropped her voice to a whisper. "A man who promised to make me the world's greatest vibrator."

"You're the one who'd be using it," he retorted.

"Right, put it on me. NOT LIKE THAT. Anyway, don't distract me. I'm trying to be mad at you."

He felt his eyebrows rise. "You're *trying* to be *mad* at me?"

"Yes," Fen snapped. "You told me you weren't a shifter anymore, you liar."

He bent and put a pair of black pants on. Then socks. Then shoes. He had the irrational feeling that if he avoided her gaze for long enough, she'd forget the question or disappear or something. When he finally straightened up, she was still there, her dark eyes fixed on him like lasers, her arms folded across her chest.

"Well?" she demanded, then inflated her lungs. Her voice rang out like a cross between a foghorn and a bugle. "LIIIIIIAAAARRRR!"

Stung, he snapped back. "Of course I lied! I couldn't say I was a shifter because you'd ask me to prove it, and it wasn't like I could shift to show you... *that*."

"You could have told me you were a shifter, but you couldn't demonstrate it!"

"Would you have believed—" he began.

"YES!" Fen shouted. "That's no harder to believe than that you used to be a shifter and weren't anymore! YOU LIAR!"

"I didn't lie to you! I said my snow leopard was dead, and was true, so—"

"YOU'RE A GIANT LIAR AND THAT'S A GIANT EXCUSE!" She yelled that so loudly that Carter felt like his hair was blowing back.

Stop lying, hissed a monster.

Stop lying, growled a monster.

Stop lying, screeched a monster.

[stoplight red]

His ears were ringing. He wanted to put his hands over them, but he felt certain that if he did, Fen would break the sound barrier.

"Just... give me a second, all right?" Carter tried to pull his thoughts together. Everything felt like too much to take in. The only conclusion he could come to was that he *had* lied to her, however valid his reasons had been, and she did deserve an apology.

He straightened up, took a deep breath, and looked her in the eyes. "You're right. I did lie to you, and I shouldn't have. You were always honest with me, and I wasn't honest with you. You're right to be angry. I deserve it. I was wrong and I apologize."

She gave him a very close look, as if she was examining a new product for flaws, then gave a satisfied nod. "Apology accepted. But why on earth didn't you just tell me that you were a shifter, but you couldn't demonstrate because it was excruciatingly painful?"

Confused, he said, "Because that would have just been a different lie?"

It was then her turn to seem confused. "Wait, that wasn't why you didn't want to do it? It looked absolutely agonizing. You were screaming!"

"Yeah, it hurts. But I do shift when I have to. It wouldn't have stopped me from proving it to you if I'd had to." He paused, then heaved a sigh when he realized that for whatever reason, she wanted him to say it himself. "I really could become a snow leopard once. My leopard was beautiful and agile and strong. And he was me: the most primal, most... *me*... part of me. I loved him."

He had to stop there for a moment, unable to look in her eyes. With his gaze fixed on the mud and weeds at his feet, he went on, "When I was kidnapped, they didn't just kill my snow leopard. They put other animals in me. I don't even know what they all were. But I was supposed to be able to shift into any of them. It didn't work out that way. They all got mixed up together inside me. They're horrible, grotesque, disgusting monsters, and they're *in* me. They *are* me. I'm a monster."

He waited for the sound of her footsteps walking away. Instead, a pair of very familiar hands cupped his cheeks, then slid around to the back of his head and pulled him down. Their faces were so close together that he could feel her warm breath on his face as she said, "Carter, you are not a monster. You're a man who had a horrible, traumatizing experience that changed you. Something bad was done to you. That doesn't make *you* bad."

It was impossible to deny the sincerity in her face or her voice, in her body language or in her nearness. But her words felt impossible. He pulled out of her grip. "But you saw me. You saw the monster."

"I saw a man choose to do something physically and emotionally painful to save my life. And I saw a weird creature, sure. But it was just one of a whole bunch of weird creatures!" Fen waved her hand at the Defenders who, Carter noticed for the first time, were all watching and listening. "I saw a dog with wings! I saw a size-changing velociraptor! I saw a ginormous bear and a fire bird and a giant smoke dog! And a prehistoric fish with armor plates and way too many teeth! Oh, and let's not forget Eunice. Do all gargoyles look that weird? Because she was super weird."

"But..." Carter began, then fell silent. It had never even occurred to him that anyone could perceive a gargoyle or a phoenix to be as monstrous and strange as the monster that he was. But Fen clearly did.

Merlin piped up from where he was sitting beside Roland, who had his injured leg propped up on a gnarled tree root. "There's much weirder things than you, Carter. When I was at the circus—I was raised in a circus," he explained to Fen. "An elephant shifter told me that her mom told her that once an elephant shifter who wanted to be a snake instead asked his friend the cobra shifter to bite him, and he turned into a regular-sized cobra with a regular-sized elephant head, which if you don't know the respective sizes is like a regular-sized mouse with the head of a regular-sized cat. And then he got stuck that way."

Merlin paused for a moment, thinking it over, then added, "She might have made it up to discourage me from trying to get my shifter friends to bite me and make me a shifter. But, you know, that's my mental high mark for grotesque. And even that poor elephant-headed cobra who probably doesn't actually exist isn't a monster, just a person with a very difficult life."

"It's one thing to hear some cautionary tale about an elephant-cobra, and another to see a giant writhing heap of hideous body parts right there in front of you," Carter snapped.

"Not really," said Merlin, unperturbed. "I have a very vivid imagination."

Ransom fixed Carter with a cool stare that reminded him that Ransom had been a sniper in the Marines. "Do you seriously think a strange shift form is going to shock and horrify *me?*"

"Well..." Once Carter was forced to discuss it aloud, rather than just thinking about it in a haze of panic, it did seem unlikely. "It's so gross, though."

"Gross is spending days covered in mud with only swamp water to bathe in," put in Fen.

Pete gave an exasperated snort. "Carter, are you telling us you've been hiding and refusing to tell us about this because your shift form isn't pretty enough for you?"

"It's not about being *pretty*." Now he felt defensive. "I didn't want you to see something hideous and disgusting."

"What about shifters who turn into animals lots of people think are hideous and disgusting?" Natalie put in. "Spider shifters and vulture shifters and rat shifters. Should they hide themselves away?"

"There's nothing wrong with spiders and vultures and rats," Carter retorted. "Nobody should hide their true nature because of bigots. But I'm not a perfectly fine animal that some people have a stupid prejudice against. I'm damaged. I'm *wrong*."

Roland gazed at him with his deep brown eyes. "Carter, we're all damaged here."

Carter couldn't argue with that. All the men had been kidnapped and experimented on, just like he had, forcibly given beasts they couldn't control and powers they didn't understand. Roland was still grieving the death of a woman whose name he'd never known, who'd given her life saving his. Natalie hadn't been victimized in the same way, but she'd endured enough to break most people.

Maybe he'd been a little self-centered, obsessing over his own problems and blowing them up to be bigger than anyone else's. Just a little.

Fen slipped her hand into his. "Remember how you talked to me about having ADHD? You didn't say 'I'm damaged and wrong and so are you and we should never ever tell anyone.' You said it was how we were and no one should call us names about it, and there were things we could do about it. You weren't ashamed, and that made me think maybe I shouldn't be either."

"Of course you shouldn't!" Carter exclaimed automatically.

"Then neither should you," she said. "About anything."

He searched her face, but could see nothing but acceptance and sympathy. There was no disgust. No horror. No rejection.

And when he examined all of the Defenders in turn, he saw none of that in their eyes too.

"I think maybe I made a bigger deal of this than I should have," Carter mumbled at last.

Merlin laughed, sprang forward, and clapped him on the back. "It's okay. I refused to tell anyone about my power for ages."

"So did I," said Ransom.

"Me too," said Pete.

"I ditched everyone I knew and ran away because of something I was too scared to tell them," Natalie pointed out. "So you're in good company."

From the ground, Roland said, "Let's continue this conversation on the boat. I'm sure we'd all like to get back home as soon as we can. And we need to talk about what Balin and Eunice said as a team. I mean, as a team and Carter."

Carter looked at the Defenders. These were the people who'd come to his defense, accepted him exactly as he was, invited him to join them, and kept on welcoming him no matter how many times he refused to admit that he was one of them. He'd thought he couldn't bear to join a team that would reject him in horror if they ever saw the monster that lurked beneath his skin. But they had seen it, and they hadn't rejected him.

"As a team, period," Carter said. "If the invitation to join is still open."

"Of course it is," said Roland.

"Not full-time," he added hastily. "I still have a company to run. But part-time… If you'll take me on part-time…"

"Part-time counts," said Roland. "Welcome to the Defenders, Carter."

The irrepressible Merlin added, "Hope you survive!"

To Carter's astonishment, the Defenders applauded. They were joined by vigorous splashing. Norris, still a Dunkleosteus, had his head poking out of the swamp and was slapping his fins against the water's surface.

"Thanks, Norris. Have you been there the whole time?" Carter asked.

Norris flapped a fin.

"He's been watching and munching popcorn," Natalie said with a grin. "Well, not literal popcorn. But he's been tossing fish and shrimp into his mouth with his fins."

Fen approached him. "Norris, can you change back?"

Norris gave a shake of his head. Since he didn't exactly have a neck, that required him to shake his entire body. She jumped back from the wave of swamp water that washed the beach.

"Uh-oh," muttered Carter. "I was hoping Eunice was bluffing, and her control over our shift forms stopped when she left—she *is* gone, isn't she?"

"She's gone," said Ransom. Carter didn't ask him if he was sure. That was the thing about Ransom: he *knew.*

A surge of panic welled up in him at the thought of slowly turning into a monster, but he squelched it. That had to have been a bluff, even if Norris being stuck as a fish wasn't. How would that even work? It was probably impossible.

But either way, he owed Norris. The man had come all the way to the swamp to warn him about Balin—correctly, as it had turned out. Norris had protected him and Fen, and had gotten stuck as a fish for his pains.

"I'll—*we'll* figure out a way to get you out of this," Carter promised. "Will you be okay in the swamp till then?"

Norris flapped his fins.

"Was that a yes?" Carter asked.

Norris flapped his fins.

Fen rolled her eyes. "Norris, let's set flap for yes, no flap for no. Will you hate it in the swamp?"

Norris didn't flap.

"Will you starve to death?"

Norris didn't flap.

"Will you be fine?"

Norris flapped.

Fen grinned. "Want to go terrorize the hunters and make sure they stay on their island till the police collect them?"

Norris flapped hard enough to splatter Carter's clean clothes with swamp water. He heaved a sigh.

"Okay, Norris," Carter said. "As soon as I figure out how to change you back, I'll come to the swamp and send up a flare. If I can't figure it out, I'll fetch you and take you to Eunice."

Norris flapped, did a barrel roll, and swam away.

Carter was left standing on the island with Fen and the Defen—his team. He reeked of swamp water. Everyone knew his terrible secret. And he might be slowly turning into a monster.

He didn't think he'd ever been happier.

CHAPTER 16

A familiar squeak caught Fen's attention. Sugar glided in, landed on her shoulder, and dropped something cold and wet into her cleavage.

She let out a yelp and yanked it out. It proved to be a Leatherman multi-tool, dripping with swamp water.

"Thanks, Sugar." Turning to Carter, she asked, "Is this yours?"

"I think it must've belonged to one of the hunters." Carter flipped out one of the tools, a large knife. "Sugar probably thought you needed a weapon."

"Aww. How sweet. Though a bit late." Fen popped the Leatherman into her purse. "It's mine now."

Precious flew in, her usually fast and elegant flight jerky and slow. She was clutching something black in her taloned paws, which she dropped into Carter's waiting hands.

"My gun! You're the best, Precious." He examined it. Like the Leatherman, it was dripping with swamp water. So was Precious. "She must've dived into the swamp to get it back for me. And the Leatherman, too, since Sugar's not wet. What a sacrifice. I know she doesn't like getting dirty."

Carter lovingly dried her off with the least swampy parts of his own shirt.

"I never thought I'd see the day that Carter Howe voluntarily messes up his own clothes," remarked Pete.

Carter gave him a sardonic smile. "You still won't. These aren't mine."

"All aboard," Roland called.

Fen sat beside Carter as they took the boat out of the swamp. After all that agony, both physical and emotional, it was wonderful to see him so lighthearted. It was as if a weight he'd been carrying the entire time she'd known him had been lifted off his back. As they recounted the story of their adventures in the swamp, his hazel eyes sparkled, he teased his teammates, and he joked with Fen.

Though Balin and Eunice's threats still hung over their heads, they now seemed distant and unlikely. Making someone switch from human to animal or keeping someone stuck in a single form seemed quite different from making a person slowly transform into a monster. Fen agreed with Carter: that had to be a scare tactic to make him show up at the end of the month, in case he didn't care enough about Norris to do so for Norris's sake. Considering how upset he'd been about revealing his shift form, she was relieved that he wasn't taking the threat too seriously.

"So how did you find us?" Fen asked.

"Ransom, I assume," said Carter. "That's his power—he knows things."

"It's not that simple," said Ransom. "Some things just come to me, but others I have to look for."

Natalie jumped in. "It can be difficult and painful for him to look. He'd have to have a reason, and we had no idea you were even missing."

"That's what happens when you're not on the team and have a habit of vanishing for months on end," Pete put in.

"All right, all right," said Carter. "So how *did* you find us, then?"

Merlin leaned over and petted Precious, who rubbed her gleaming head against his hand. "This little cutie here showed up at our office and dropped a pawpaw on the carpet."

"What, really?" Carter said.

Merlin nodded. "Splat."

Carter rolled his eyes at Precious, who trilled proudly. "I gave you a note!"

Roland took up the story. "We had no idea what she was doing there. I thought at first… Never mind."

Fen realized that Roland was the only Defender who had never mentioned having a magical pet. Carter had said the magical animals chose their owners, and she wondered if Roland had briefly thought Precious was his. No wonder he'd sounded so regretful.

"Then she flew off," Roland went on. "I called our west coast branch, but they didn't know anything about her. So I asked Ransom if he could figure out what was up with her."

"And I got a glimpse of you, Carter, and a location," said Ransom. "That was it. But it was enough."

Pete gave Carter a sardonic glance that made Fen bristle. "We knew there was no way you'd be in a swamp voluntarily."

"Oh, I don't know." Carter nudged her. "I've almost gotten to like it here. The food's a bit monotonous, though."

"And that was that," said Roland, spreading his big hands.

That was that, thought Fen. Carter hadn't even officially been a member of their team, but they'd dropped everything to come rescue him, even when they didn't have any idea of what sort of danger they might be walking into.

The motorboat pulled up at a wooden dock, and they all climbed out. Finally, they were out of the swamp. Fen felt a huge wave of relief. They could eat food they hadn't foraged themselves. They could *shower.*

They could have hot shower sex.

They could have hot shower sex followed by hot bath sex.

They could…

"I can't tell you how much I hate to say this," Carter said. "But I think the police will take us more seriously if we show up as we are."

Fen looked ruefully down at her own mud-covered body, then at Carter in his swamp-stained clothes and hair that was still covered in mud and paint, and gave a reluctant nod. "I guess."

The Defenders had flown in, then rented a van. They drove it into the city and to the police station, where they parked it.

"I'll keep Precious and Sugar for you," Merlin volunteered.

Fen extracted the little sugar glider from her cleavage. It took some doing, as he hung on with his tiny sharp claws, chittering and squeaking in protest. She finally unpicked the last claw and handed him to Merlin. "Be good, Sugar. I'll be back soon."

Sugar squeaked again, then dove into Merlin's cupped hands. Carter whistled and pointed, and Precious flew to Merlin's shoulder.

While the rest of the Defenders waited in the van, Roland accompanied Carter and Fen into the police station. He needed to lean on Carter's shoulder, but he pointed out that as the head of Protection, Inc: Defenders, he'd have the most credibility. Fen had dreaded having to tell the police their story, which was bizarre even when you left out the magical animals, the shifters, the wizard-scientists, and the Dunkleosteus, but it was much less intimidating when she knew she had Carter and Roland to back her up.

But when they arrived, it turned out that Fen was the key person. Unlike Carter, she was not in the habit of randomly vanishing without notice, so she'd been reported missing within hours of not showing up for work. Also unlike Carter, she had no history of disappearing and then returning with some implausible explanation. When she told them she'd been kidnapped, they believed her. Carter and Roland, in the guise of a security consultant who worked with Carter, were just the icing on the cake.

There were so many interviews done and reports made that all three of them were still at the station when a squad of officers came in with the mighty hunters, all of them drenched in swamp water and babbling about swamp sharks. Fen stared as hard as she could at Bill, trying to telepathically convey, *Confess or I'll feed you to the swamp shark.*

"Eldon McManus told us to do it!" Bill said, avoiding Fen's gaze. "I can prove it! I have emails!"

"He led us on!" Horace babbled. His eyes were haunted; she could practically see Norris's reflected teeth in them. "It was all Eldon!"

"Step this way and tell us all about it," said a detective.

Carter, Fen, and Roland took the opportunity to flee to the van.

"Do you want to find some place to clean up, then drive straight back to New York?" Roland asked.

Fen and Carter looked at each other. She was certain he was thinking the same thing that she was.

"Actually," Fen said, "Why don't you all go ahead, and we'll meet up with you later? We have some things we should probably discuss. We're in quite a complex situation here when it comes to business."

"And financial matters," Carter added.

"Legal matters too," said Fen.

"Not to mention law enforcement," said Carter.

"And publicity," said Fen.

"Right." Roland seemed to be repressing a mischievous smile. "Business and finance. Of course."

"And legal matters." Merlin winked at them.

"There's some kinds of publicity you definitely don't want. So here." Ransom presented them with a small suitcase. "For Precious."

Fen and Carter stepped out of the van, waved, and watched it drive away. They had Precious in the suitcase, and Sugar down the front of Fen's blouse.

"You know what I really, really want to do?" Carter asked.

"Probably the same thing as me," said Fen.

"But I want to have sex afterward," he assured her.

She laughed. "I was going to say, but I want to shower first."

They caught a cab—they had to bribe the driver with double the fare to get him to agree to let them in, as muddy as they were—and directed him to take them to the fanciest hotel in the city.

He looked deeply dubious. "They won't let you in smell—uh, looking like that."

"That's our problem," said Fen.

The driver shrugged and drove them to a hotel that, she was pleased to see, looked more than fancy enough to turn away muddy, swampy people without reservations...

...unless those muddy, swampy, reservation-less people happened to be Carter Howe and Fenella Kim.

Together they swept into the lobby. The doorman stared at them. The guests side-eyed them. The receptionist glared at them, pointed to the door out, and said, "There's a motel right around the corner. It has showers."

Carter slapped his drivers license down on the counter. When the receptionist looked at it, then at him, he said, "Yes. *That* Carter Howe."

Fen followed it with her own. "Yes. I'm back. The police are aware. And if you'd like this to continue to be a five-star hotel with a good reputation, you'll give us a suite and not tip off the paparazzi."

The receptionist's eyes bugged like a bullfrog's. "Oh! Yes. Of course." Lowering her voice, she said, "We quite often get celebrities in here. I assure you, we are *very* discreet."

In short order, they were escorted to a private elevator—something which made Fen feel better about the possibility of remaining undiscovered—and shown to a suite. They tipped the bellboy, shut and locked the door, and released Precious from her suitcase. She hissed at them as she emerged, and flew to the top of an exquisitely carved antique wardrobe. Sugar joined her.

Carter grinned and grabbed her hand. "Let's go!"

Like a pair of teenagers running to skinny dip in a lake, they clasped hands and rushed to the bathroom. She barely took in the luxurious surroundings. All she could think of was that she and Carter were alone at last, with nothing standing between them. And nothing was standing between them and hot water, either.

Fen stripped down faster than Carter. Once she'd hurled her clothes into a laundry basket so nice that she hated to pollute it with swampiness, she caught sight of herself in the mirrors. One thing the swamp had lacked was bright artificial lighting and full-length mirrors. With those aids to show exactly how much of a disaster you were, she noted that she had smears of mud and paint everywhere except in her cleavage, but that one area of clean skin was covered with sugar glider hairs. Bruises and scrapes showed through some of the mud. Her hair was tangled, there were scratches on her face, and her nail polish existed only in patches that made her nails look worse than if she hadn't had any polish to begin with.

"I look like I got kidnapped, dumped in a swamp for days, and knocked down repeatedly," she remarked.

Carter laughed as he tossed his boxers into the laundry basket. "What do you think? Who's more of a mess, you or me?"

His hair was no longer black, but a mix of mud-brown and paintball-rainbow. That color scheme continued for most of his body, occasionally interspersed with bruise-black and blood-red. He was as far from the polished, stylish, put-together, magazine cover Carter Howe as it was possible to get.

She'd never wanted a man more. And when she looked into his eyes, she saw the same hungry passion there.

Fen caught his hand in hers. As one, they scrambled into the shower. The first cascade of hot water was the most luxurious sensation she'd ever felt. She lifted her face to it, letting it wash away mud and paint and sweat and swamp. The water was so soft that it felt silken on her skin. She turned around, stretching as it beat down on her back like the best rain ever.

The luxury shower head was big enough to cover two people at once. Carter too stood beneath the flow. Water cascaded over him, washing away the paint and grime. It turned his hair into black satin. Water ran over his broad shoulders and strong forearms, and dripped off his clever fingers. It sheeted over the muscles of his chest, making them shine as if they been oiled. Tiny water drops clung and fell from his long eyelashes. The expression on his face was one of sheer ecstasy.

"You sure clean up nice," remarked Fen.

Carter eyed her appreciatively, his gaze lingering on her body like a caress. "I could say the same for you."

He reached for the selection of soaps and body washes. "Want me to give you a hand? What's your favorite?"

"I like soap better than body wash," she said.

"Me too," he replied. "There's something much more luxurious about real soap. Pick one and I'll give you a massage."

There was a good selection, from a Bulgarian soap shaped and scented like a red rose to a brown rectangle with a woodsy masculine aroma. She picked up a handmade cake with a subtle pattern of white and green, sniffed it and inhaled a complex modern perfume, then put it back down. That was pleasant and sophisticated, but she was in the mood for something more cozy. At last she selected a smooth oval with sunset colors, scented with peaches and honey.

She handed it to Carter. "Here you go."

"Good choice."

Carter rubbed the soap between his hands, lathering it up, and cupped her cheeks in his hands. She gave an involuntary shiver at his touch. It was so gentle and yet so sensual. He gently massaged her cheeks, stroking and caressing them, touching them with the hands of a lover. She swallowed, as shivery warmth running through her entire body that had nothing to do with the warm water.

He rubbed the peach scented lather all over her face, shielding her eyes with his hands, before rinsing it off. She had never had a man take such care with her before. She touched her both as if she was made of glass and might break if you did it wrong, and as if she was a living woman who appreciated all the care he took.

"That's marvelous," she sighed. "Have you ever considered a new career as a facial masseuse?"

"Oh, Fen," Carter said, his voice husky. "Just wait till you see what I can do with the rest of your body."

He worked up more lather with the peach and honey soap, and then pulled her back so she was leaning against his chest. He gave the same treatment to her neck and shoulders and arms and hands and fingers. He even rubbed gently around her fingernails, removing the dirt from beneath each one. When he was done and they were rinsed clean, he lifted her hand to his lips and kissed each fingertip.

"Careful." Her voice wavered as her breath caught. "You promised me a full body massage. I'm starting to get distracted."

"You have no idea how distracted I can make you."

His clever hands slid down to her breasts. Her nipples instantly hardened under his fingers, and she rubbed herself against his hands like a cat. He caressed her breasts until she dazedly began to wonder if she could come from that alone. By the time he let the water rinse them clean, she was in a dreamy haze of desire. She sagged back against him, and gave a little wriggle against his rock hard shaft for the pleasure of feeling him jerk and gasp.

"Now you know how I feel," she murmured.

He too was having trouble catching his breath; she could feel it as well as hear it. "I think I saw…"

"Yeah, me too…"

"By the sink."

"Right, the little brass bowl."

Carter, who had longer arms, leaned out of the shower and secured a condom. He ripped it open, and Fen snatched it from him and rolled it on. She meant to take her time with it and tease him, but she only managed a little bit of that before she got impatient. Teasing was all well and good, but she wanted him inside her *right now.*

He lifted her up, holding her easily in his arms. His strength was an astonishing turn-on, and so was the feeling of his entire length and width against her, hard as steel for her. She wrapped her legs around his waist, and he slid himself inside her.

"Fen…" Her name came out halfway between a gasp and a growl.

She couldn't reply. Her face was buried in his shoulder, her fingers clenching on the bulging muscles of his upper arms. She too was gasping, her heart hammering. Little shocks of pleasure went through her at every thrust, increasing and increasing until they became a wave of sheer bliss that took her apart. A moment later, he was crying out her name, his head thrown back, his chest heaving. Then they both went still, slipping from ecstasy into the afterglow.

She leaned against him, breathing hard and letting her heart rate slow, as he held her tight and the hot water cascaded over them both. She had never felt so meltingly relaxed. He bent down and kissed her, and she turned her face up to his and kissed him as if under a tropical waterfall.

"So," Carter said, nudging her hand between his thighs. "Before I build the prototype, how do rate the product?"

"Eleven," Fen said promptly.

"The scale only goes to ten."

"Exactly. Eleven."

"Hmm. Could be hard for the prototype to live up to the original."

"Yep. Especially if the owner of the original also does shampoos."

"Subtle," Carter remarked as he reached for the little bottles, offering her each to sniff in turn.

She chose a honey-colored concoction that smelled like cinnamon and apples. "This one."

"You're making me hungry. Hungrier. You're sweet as honey."

"Not sweet as a pawpaw?" she teased.

"Thankfully, no. Close your eyes."

She closed her eyes and let him shampoo her hair. He rubbed the scented shampoo into her scalp, massaging every inch of it with his fingers. It was an incredibly sensual experience, and one she didn't want to have end. After he rinsed the shampoo out, holding his hand to her forehead so none of the suds would get in her eyes, he repeated the massage, this time with the matching conditioner.

Fen opened her eyes. "It stays in for a while. Let me do you now. Kneel down so I can get your hair."

He knelt on the shower floor, head tilted back, throat exposed. It was an incredibly trusting posture, especially since he was nude. She wondered if he was trying to make it up to her for having kept so much from her earlier.

Like he had done for her, she offered him sniffs of the shampoo bottles. He vigorously rejected one with a classically masculine "green" scent. "Smells like a swamp."

"I wouldn't go that far," she said, though she grinned as she replaced it on the shelf. "But I'll also be staying away from green and grassy and watery scents for the foreseeable future. How about this one?"

He tried out the bottle she offered him, breathing in the notes of bay leaf, amber, and orange peel, then nodded. "Yes, I like that. No swampiness at all."

As she applied the shampoo to his hair, she remarked, "We should start a shampoo line. We can call it Dry Land."

"'Sick of the swamp?' Dry Land will waft you away to a world where absolutely nothing squishes, squelches, or croaks!'" His advertiser's voice broke into a sigh of sheer pleasure as she ran her fingers through his hair, making little circles on his scalp with her fingertips. "That feels incredibly good."

"To me too." His hair felt like liquid silk. She gave him a good long massage, then applied conditioner. "Stand up."

He stood up, and she had him select a soap. He chose a rich brown cake with notes of whiskey, black leather, and nutmeg. "This is definitely a Dry Land soap."

"An excellent choice." She rubbed it against her hands, then caressed him from head to toe. It was an enormous pleasure for her to get to touch him like that, feeling the swells of his muscle and the angularity of bone, discovering all the parts of his body. It was both sensual and very intimate. When she was done, she tugged him under the showerhead and let the water rinse him clean, conditioner and soap and all.

They put their arms around each other, reveling in the warmth and closeness, his head bent to touch hers. Fen could feel their hair mingling and flowing together under the falling water. When they kissed again, a few drops of hot water slipped into her mouth.

They finally, reluctantly got out and dried each other off with marvelously fluffy towels.

"I never before appreciated the wonder that is bath rugs," she said, happily wriggling her toes in the cloudlike softness.

"Or soap," said Carter, heartfelt. "I'll never take it for granted again."

She hung up her towel and reached for the bathrobe. He did the same. But both of them stopped, naked and with the robes hanging from their hands, and stared at each other. In the shower, Fen had been more engaged with her sense of touch than with sight, and soap and water had obscured the details. But now, with both of them dry and under bright lights, she could see Carter clearly.

His wet black hair covered most of the healing wound on his temple, but a purple bruise spread out from it. There were more bruises on his hips and shoulders, the points you hit on a fall, and assorted scrapes and scratches. But what stood out the most, and what really infuriated her, were the round black bruises scattered across his strong and beautiful body. Those were where the paintballs had hit him as he'd shielded her.

"We're getting new phones immediately," she said. "I want to take photos of this so we can present them in court."

"Yes, definitely." He stabbed a finger, not at himself, but at her. Following his gaze, she saw that she too was bruised around her hips and shoulders and elbows. "I wish I'd shifted around the cavemen. They deserved to be attacked by that... that *thing*."

Fen winced internally. She hated hearing him talk like that. That *thing* was him. But she didn't want to pester him about a deeply sensitive topic. "I don't know, from their perspective Norris might've been worse."

Carter relaxed, chuckling at the memory, and put on his bathrobe. She followed suit.

"I just realized something," she said. "We don't have anything to change into."

He made a dismissive gesture. "Not a problem. What do you think of calling the front desk and having clothes delivered, eating an absolutely luxurious dinner in bed while we wait for our clothes to arrive, then putting them on and going shopping for something better?"

"You're a man after my own heart," said Fen fervently.

In their velvety hotel bathrobes, they returned to the bedroom. The thick carpet was wonderfully soft beneath her feet. She remarked, "It's so reassuring not to have to wonder whether the ground is going to wobble when you step on it."

"I was just thinking how great it is to get wet in water that's clear and definitely won't have a bullfrog in it," Carter replied.

Sugar had made himself at home on a pillow on the bed, while Precious was initially invisible until Carter spotted her blending into a chandelier. Fen scooped up Sugar's pillow and placed it by her side, got another pillow to lean against, and then she and Carter got in bed.

She stretched out, wiggling her toes and delighting in the firm yet yielding mattress and being clean between clean sheets. "Glorious."

"I don't think I've ever appreciated civilization quite so much," said Carter.

"Pop quiz: which is the greatest accomplishment, indoor plumbing or beds?"

After some thought, he said, "I'm going to go with indoor plumbing. I could sleep on that carpet and be pretty comfortable."

She snuggled up against him, breathing in his scent of the whiskey-and-leather soap and his own clean body. He put an arm around her, pulling her in even closer, and picked up the hotel phone. Carter dialed the front desk and explained their clothing situation, emphasizing that they had literally nothing to wear. A few minutes later, he handed the phone to Fen. "Ladies first."

She gave an unladylike snort, but took the phone and requested a set of casual clothes and shoes in her size. After her, Carter did the same. Then he picked up the room service menu from the table beside the phone and opened it. They gazed at it rapturously.

"Food that an actual chef cooked in an actual kitchen," she murmured.

"Food that isn't pawpaws," said Carter. "Look, it even has suggestions for wine pairings."

"Too bad it doesn't have suggestions for other pairings. Will you kick me out of bed if I confess that I don't like wine?"

"Not at all. Wine is fine but liquor is quicker."

"And also tastes better," said Fen. "I think so, anyway."

They made their selections and called it in, then relaxed in each other's arms. Fen couldn't think when she'd last been so blissfully happy. She was considering suggesting a second round of lovemaking when there was a knock at the door.

Carter waved her back as she started to sit up. "I'll get it."

She flipped a section of blanket over Sugar's pillow where he was still snoozing, but realized that Carter had forgotten about Precious when he opened the door with the golden dragonette still perched on the chandelier. He got back in bed as a pair of waiters set up dinner in bed trays and began explaining what everything was.

"For madame, an appetizer of burrata and salmon caviar on toast," said the waiter. Fen stared very hard at the toast with its jewels of red caviar atop the creamy mozzarella, determinedly not looking up.

"For monsieur, an appetizer of a miniature Gruyère souffle with Dijon mustard." The souffle looked very temptingly fluffy, with steam rising from it. It had obviously just come out of the oven.

A tiny clink came from above. Fen promptly knocked over a container of pens on the side table. "Oops!"

"Never mind, madame," said the waiter who'd introduced the souffle. He jerked his head at the waiter who had pushed in the cart, who immediately started picking them up. "For madam's entree, duck confit with fingerling potatoes and roast peach compote. For monsieur, filet mignon with sauteed mushrooms and a baked potato."

"That looks amazing," said Carter. "Yours too, Fen."

Another clink. Also a furry squirming sensation against her side. She dropped a hopefully casual-looking hand down on the blanket, pinning the struggling Sugar to the mattress.

"And for dessert—"

She cut the waiter off. "Thank you very much! We, um, like to guess our desserts, don't tell us what they are. The sides and drinks too. Thank you!"

The waiters both gave her odd looks, but took off. As the door was closing behind them, Precious swooped down from the chandelier and attempted to dive-bomb Carter's steak. He flung out his hands, protecting it. Precious veered off, shrieking angrily.

"My God," Carter muttered. "What a disaster that would have been."

Precious screeched.

"All right, all right." He hastily cut into his steak, chopping off a good third of it and slicing it into dragonette-sized bits, then scraping them off onto a bread plate. He placed it on the side table, where Precious pounced on it and began to devour her chopped filet.

"Thanks for getting rid of the waiters, Fen."

"Good thing people mostly don't look up."

"And that it wasn't on their mind to do a visual sweep of the suite for dragonettes," said Carter. "I wonder what she ate when she was in the swamp."

"Not pawpaws, that's for sure," said Fen.

Sugar wriggled out from under the blankets, sniffed at her plate, and chittered angrily.

"Don't worry, I thought of you," she said soothingly, and uncovered the side dishes. She'd ordered a salad, dressing on the side, just for him. Fen wasn't a big salad fan. She put some of the salad on a plate, put the plate on the other side table, and watched him pounce.

Carter took a spoonful of his cheese souffle and closed his eyes in ecstasy. "You have got to try this… Here."

He scooped up a spoonful and held it to her mouth. She closed her lips around it. The souffle was light as a cloud, saved from being too rich by the sharpness of the mustard. "Delicious."

They ended up splitting all their dishes, eating Carter's souffle first before it collapsed, then turning to Fen's toast. The caviar popped in her mouth, the burrata was deliciously creamy, and the toast was perfectly golden. After that they turned to her duck and his steak, both of which were excellent. The duck was savory and crispy, with the tangy peach compote cutting the richness, and the steak was seared to perfection.

"I notice a distinct absence of fish," he remarked. "I'm not surprised."

"Well, the caviar comes from a fish. But I had to make an exception for caviar."

"Of course." He laughed. "Did you see that their signature dessert is pawpaw pudding?"

She shuddered. "I saw. Horrible."

"To think I thought they were so delicious when I first ate one."

"Me too," said Fen. "I suppose if I lived on nothing but caviar I'd get to hate it eventually. But I think it would take more than a couple days."

Carter had an Old Fashioned to accompany his meal, and Fen had Glenmorangie neat. They tried each other's drinks, but only once. He said her whiskey would overpower his steak, and she thought his cocktail was good for what it was, but would have been better without the non-whiskey ingredients.

With a flourish, he uncovered the desserts. All things considered, they'd decided it was a three-dessert night. They had chocolate mousse with sea salt and whipped cream, a chocolate-pistachio tart, and a very pink confection of two big raspberry macarons sandwiching a filling of fresh lychees and rose cream. It looked like a lot, especially after all they'd eaten already, but they had no trouble tackling them.

"Which is your favorite?" Carter asked, when they were down to just one bite of each.

"The chocolate mousse, I think," said Fen. "Which is yours?"

He pushed the mousse to her. "You finish it, then."

She scraped up the last bite, then looked up. "Which is your favorite?"

He gave her a wry grin. "The chocolate mousse."

Fen gave him a mock glare. "Okay, which is your second-favorite?"

Carter helped himself to the macaron. "The incredibly girly dessert."

They split the last bit of chocolate-pistachio tart into two tiny slivers. He fed her one, and she fed him one.

Fen felt very well-fed and content. They kissed lazily, and then less lazily, and then there was a knock at the door. They broke apart, Carter leaping to grab Precious in one hand and Sugar in the other. He deposited them both in the bathroom and opened the door. It was a person from the hotel with two shopping bags full of clothes. Carter thanked and tipped and ushered her out, and released Sugar and Precious from the bathroom. Then he and Fen pounced on the bags like a pair of ravening swamp sharks.

They'd both gone for inexpensive, easy-fit, off-the-rack clothing that wouldn't look too bad or be much of a loss even if it didn't fit quite right. In other words, nothing that normally would have warranted excitement. But Fen felt an enormous thrill as she ripped open the packet of plain white cotton panties and shimmied into a pair, followed by a white bra with no underwires. Glorious, glorious fresh clean underwear!

Carter had chosen a pair of white boxers. Despite his bruised and battered condition, he looked truly fine in them.

"You should be an underwear model," she suggested. "Can I get a runway strut?"

He grinned. "Only if you do one too. If I was a modeling agent, I'd snap you up in a hot second."

Under normal circumstances, she would never have dreamed of doing such a thing, even for a lover. It was far too undignified. She might get laughed at in the wrong way. That kind of foolery required a level of trust that she'd always thought just wasn't in her.

But this was Carter, who had not only thrown himself in front of a hail of bullets (he'd thought) for her, but had revealed a form that he found shameful and humiliating for her. He'd never mock her or use her vulnerability against her. And the thought of getting to watch him do a model catwalk in his boxers was too tempting to resist.

"Okay. You asked for it." She walked to the door and spoke in a voice that was more sports announcer than haute couture. "Presenting! The Latest Hanes For Her Model! Fenella KIIIIIM!"

Fen struck a pose at the door, head held high, breasts thrust forward.

Then she strutted across the carpet, trying to catch the rhythm of the model walk, posed in front of Carter with her hands on her hips, then turned and strutted back. On the return trip, she made sure to put some extra swing in her hips, the better to showcase how the plain white panties stretched across her butt.

"Bravo!" Carter shouted. "I'm going to place a call to buy some Hanes stock right now."

She returned to the bed, laughing. "Okay, I did it. Now you have to."

"You asked for it," he muttered as he headed for the door. But once he got there, he straightened up, giving Fen a good look at his masculine silhouette. Broad shoulders, narrow hips, long legs, muscular arms… Carter actually could have been a model if the most important qualification was being incredibly hot. But from what she understood of the industry, it was more important for them to conform to bizarrely persnickety body measurements. And, of course, to look bored and arrogant.

Carter began to walk. He had the bored and arrogant look down, which cracked her up. Once upon a time, she'd thought that was really him—well, not the bored part, but definitely the arrogant part. He strutted across the hotel room, looking lofty and full of himself. (The boxers were certainly full of himself, she noticed appreciatively.) He reached her, paused, and struck a very model-like pose with one arm flung up, highlighting his lean muscle. Then he dropped his arm and strutted back.

When he turned around, his face was a bit flushed. "Well?"

"Bravo!" Fen shouted. "A plus plus! I'd buy those boxers! And the 'smelling your armpit' pose was perfect."

He returned to the bed and said with dignity, "I was not smelling my armpit. I see models doing that pose all the time."

"So do I. And it always looks like they're checking to make sure their new deodorant is actually working."

"Or to make sure they washed off all of the swamp."

Fen ostentatiously sniffed the air. "Oh, I think you're all right."

She put on her own outfit. She'd chosen a light blue cotton sundress—not her usual style, but women's clothing was so hard to fit without trying it on first that she'd been forced to pick something very forgiving—and ballerina slippers in darker blue.

"Gorgeous," remarked Carter.

She pulled a face at him. "It's baggy and the color washes me out."

"I didn't mean the dress. I meant you."

Carter put on the rest of his clothes. He'd selected casual black pants, a white button-down shirt, and black shoes. Nothing special, but he looked good in them.

"Want to buy a coat tonight?" Fen asked.

"Hmm. Maybe. Normally I get them specially tailored, with pockets and so forth to my specifications, but I would like one, even ready-made. I don't feel quite dressed without one."

"Oh, but you must have a couple spares at home." Fen always got at least one extra of any item of clothing she particularly loved. You never knew when it would stop being made.

"I did, but not anymore," he replied glumly. "They all got destroyed. That was my last one."

"How do you destroy a coat? Other than falling into a swamp."

"Helping out the Defenders." He seemed wary, then took a deep breath, calmed himself, and went on, "Now that you've met them, not to mention Balin and Eunice, you can guess the kinds of situations they'd get into. I wouldn't shift in front of the Defenders—I was too ashamed—but if I could catch an enemy alone, I didn't much care if they saw me. I'd try to take off my coat first, but sometimes there wasn't time."

"I'm going to make you tell me all your Defenders stories. They sound amazing." She nudged him. "I'll even tell you how brave and heroic you were, how's that for incentive?"

"Excellent. You tell me how brave and heroic I am, and I'll tell you what a good listener you are."

She tossed a pillow at him. "Hey, how come no one else's clothes ripped off when they shifted? Is it because of your, uh, problem?"

He shook his head. "No, that used to happen even when I was a snow leopard. I'd have to undress before I shifted if I didn't want to destroy everything I was wearing. Most shifters can't take their clothes with them. The only ones who can are the ones who turn into mythical or extinct animals."

"The ones who can turn into mythical or extinct animals," she repeated, marveling. "What a month I'm having. So why is that?"

Carter shrugged. "I don't think anyone knows, really. The theory is that mythical beasts are inherently magical, so there's enough magic left over to take care of their clothes. It might be similar for extinct animal shifters—maybe it takes magic to recreate an animal that no longer exists."

"It must have been amazing to grow up like you did," she said wistfully. "Surrounded by magic. Knowing you're special."

His face darkened. "You should have grown up knowing you were special."

Fen didn't know how to reply to that. She did believe that he believed she was special. But it was a long way from that to believing it herself. Her parents' voices echoed in the back of her mind.

"Do you ever think, *Fenella?"*

"Why don't you just try harder?"

Uncomfortable with the topic, she stood up. "Come on. Let's go shopping."

CHAPTER 17

As they left their hotel room to go on a shopping spree, they swung their clasped hands between them like a pair of high school sweethearts. It made Carter realize how long it had been since he had done anything purely for fun. Usually he was either busy with Howe Enterprises, or busy with the Defenders, or busy vainly researching wild leads off strange internet boards about how to get rid of unwanted inner monsters.

Who would have thought that getting kidnapped would be the best way to go on a vacation?

As they approached the elevator, he said, "Hey, I just remembered. Do you care if the press finds out about us?"

Fen's beautiful dark eyes widened in surprise. "I can't believe I didn't think about that. I guess even a couple days safely away from the paparazzi got me relaxed. What do you think?"

Don't hide, howled a monster.

Be honest, hissed a monster.

Tell, tell, tell, gibbered a monster.

For once, he agreed with them. He adored Fen. He wanted everyone to see that she was with him. He wanted to shout it from the rooftops. The brilliant and brave Fen Kim, drinker of fine whiskey and thrower of soda cans, who could scream fit to wake the dead and find food in the wilderness, and was absolutely, positively, no doubt about it the sexiest woman alive had chosen *him.*

"It's up to you, of course," he said. "But personally, I'd like to go public. The only reason I see for keeping it a secret is that Eldon McManus might claim we made everything up and conspired together to frame him, but he'll probably say that anyway. Besides, once we get back to Refuge City, the only way to keep it a secret would be to sneak around like a pair of burglars. I'm picturing the kind from old comic strips, where they wear striped suits and flat caps."

She snickered. "The flat cap might look good on you, but I draw the line at striped suits. And if we sneak around, it'll only make us look guilty once the paparazzi catch us—and they will eventually. So let's not hide."

Let's not hide. Her words struck him with their unintended double meaning. He'd stopped hiding his monstrous shift form, even though it hadn't exactly been completely by his own choice. Fen had stopped hiding her insecurities from him. It was terrifying, but freeing, too.

"You're right," he said. "Let's stop hiding. I want to let the whole world see we're in love."

YES! His monsters set up a chorus of noisy agreement.

[happy aqua]

Bing!

The elevator arrived. They stepped in and the doors slid shut, leaving them alone together in the box.

"Did you say in love?" Fen asked.

Carter swallowed, abruptly nervous. It had just slipped out. He hadn't even realized it himself, at least not consciously. But now that he thought about it, he knew that it was true.

But that's impossible, he thought. *I'm a shifter. For me to be in love—really in love—Fen and I would have to be mates.*

Shifters knew their mates at first sight. Their inner animals had the power to recognize their true loves. And Carter's inner animals had said nothing. But of course, they weren't his real inner animals. They were monsters that had been forced upon him against his will. The death of his snow leopard must have left him unable to recognize his true mate even when she was right there next to him.

A pang of grief for his lost snow leopard squeezed his heart, but it was followed by a flash of pure joy. Fen *was* his mate. She had to be. He loved her like he'd never loved any other woman.

All of that flashed through his mind in an instant. The elevator was still moving down. Fen was still looking at him, her beautiful face upturned, waiting for his response.

"Yes," Carter said. The elevator doors slid open, but he barely noticed. His heart was pounding like a hammer. "Yes, Fen, I'm in love with you. I hope—I hope—"

"Of course I'm in love with you," she interrupted. "Can't you tell?"

She grabbed him by the collar, pulled him down, and kissed him. The passion of that kiss left him in absolutely no doubt that she was telling the truth, the whole truth, and nothing but the truth.

Lights flashed. Bulbs popped. Fen and Carter jumped. They were still inside the elevator, which was stopped at the lobby, and a mob of reporters were rushing them like a stampeding herd of buffalo.

"Hey!" Fen yelled in the general direction of the front desk. "I thought you said you didn't let the paparazzi in here!"

From the front desk, a beleaguered voice yelled, "I'm so sorry! They pretended they were guests. Security!"

The gathered paparazzi took one glance at the approaching security guards and began madly hurling questions at Carter and Fen as their cameras flashed and popped and flashed again.

"Fenella! How long have you been together?"

"Carter! Was the kidnapping a hoax?"

"Fenella! Were you secretly on a honeymoon?"

"Carter! Did you fall in love while you were kidnapped together?"

"Fenella! Is Little Bit going to cancel the hostile takeover?"

"Carter! Was your rivalry always fake?"

"Fenella! What's your favorite perfume?"

"Carter! Do you manicure your eyebrows!"

They were still yelling questions and taking photos as the security guards dragged them out. A particularly determined reporter shrieked, "Fenella! Is it true that you secretly prefer Howe phones?" as the front door slammed in her face.

Fen whispered in Carter's ear, "They know about the eyebrow manicuring. You can run but you can't hide."

Carter whispered back, "Search my bathroom. You'll find nothing."

Flash! Pop! A paparazzi lunged out from behind a large potted plant, and was promptly dragged away.

Fen snickered. "She got a nice shot. Bet your eyebrows show up well. What do you think? Should we promise them a press conference later?"

Carter nodded. "I think they'll lay off if we offer to put it together ASAP."

"I'm up for it." She gave him a mischievous yet tender smile that made him melt inside. "So we're in love."

He touched her hair, marveling that this was a thing he could do now. He could touch Fenella Kim's beautiful, silky hair. "We are. It's pretty great, isn't it?"

She slipped her hand into his. "It's the best."

CHAPTER 18

Carter was an old hand at press conferences. Before he'd been kidnapped and turned into a monster, he'd enjoyed them. As he stood side by side with Fen before a mob of both paparazzi and reporters for respectable news outlets, he reflected that this was the first press conference he'd actually had a good time at since then.

It was the delightful culmination of a wonderful weekend. He and Fen had enjoyed shopping together in Georgia, where they'd slipped into each other's dressing rooms and admired each other naked and clothed. They'd spent the night at the hotel, which had been even better, and then had the treat of waking up to headlines like **ELDON MCMANUS ARRESTED IN KIDNAPPING AND FRAUD PLOT** and **RIVAL CEOS ESCAPE KIDNAPPING BY OTHER RIVAL**, and they'd laughed at **FENELLA KIM AND CARTER HOWE STAGE SWAMP SEX SCANDAL.**

They'd flown back to Refuge City, where they'd been forced to separate to deal with a whole lot of company business, not to mention police business, but they'd sent each other texts during meetings. At last everything had been sorted enough that once they were done with the press conference, they'd have the rest of the day off. They'd spend it together, of course.

He glanced at Fen, and caught her glancing at him. They smiled at each other. Bulbs flashed, and he knew that whatever goofy look of lovestruck adoration had been on his face would be plastered all over magazines tomorrow. He didn't care. He did adore her, and there was no reason to hide it.

The photos of Fen wouldn't be goofy. They'd be gorgeous. She looked incredible in one of the new outfits she'd picked out in Georgia. It was another one of her iconic black-and-white business suits, but he especially liked the short, slightly steampunk-styled jacket. Her hair had been professionally styled, her makeup was perfect, and her nails had been manicured in a startling, eye-catching copper. She looked like she could take over a company and kill a man before breakfast. Only he knew that she could forage in the wilderness and made dad jokes and swore like a British sailor.

He hoped she was enjoying the press conference as much as he was. She'd done her part beautifully, but her public persona was more buttoned-down than his so it was hard to tell. Fen had been crisp, cool, and collected as they had alternated telling the story of how they'd been kidnapped, dumped in a swamp, and hunted, how they'd been attacked by men with paint guns, how a fortuitous alligator attack had allowed them to turn the tables on the hunters and question them until they'd learned of Eldon McManus's plot against them, and how they'd then been rescued by the security agency Protection, Inc: Defenders, whose team Carter had recently joined as a technical consultant.

And also, that they were now dating, and they would appreciate some privacy in this challenging yet happy time.

"Thirty minutes for questions," said the press manager.

The room exploded with shouting and waving hands. Carter had always thought of this part as like a cartoon of a boy fishing: you throw out your line and pull it back in, and sometimes you get a fish and sometimes you get an old boot.

Fen pointed. "The reporter from *Refuge City Times,* in the pink shirt."

The *Refuge City Times* journalist asked, "Can you tell us a bit about how your relationship developed while you were in the swamp?"

Carter relaxed. That question was definitely a fish. Fen smiled and told the story of the pawpaws and how they'd built a compass together. The reporters laughed appreciatively.

"We realized how much we had in common," she concluded. "Eldon McManus meant to destroy us, but he accidentally did us a favor. Maybe I'll send him a box of chocolates in jail. Next!"

Carter indicated a baby-faced reporter who had determinedly shoved his way into the front row. He had a soft spot for ambitious young people. "The gentleman from *Nexus News*, in the brown jacket."

The Nexus News reporter asked, "Did you invent your own contact lenses?"

That question was so out of left field that it wasn't even a boot. It was more like a banana. "I don't wear contact lenses."

"Then how are you making your eyes change color?" the reporter asked.

Carter's entire body went ice cold with horror.

"See, there they go again," said the reporter. "They're black now. They've been aqua for most of the conference, but when Fenella Kim talked about how she was kidnapped, they turned red for a while. Are the colors random or a pre-set pattern, or are you manually changing them with your cell phone?"

Carter's stomach felt like it was filled with concrete. He knew what those colors meant. His color-communication monster used aqua for happy and shades of red for angry. Black was terror.

Eunice hadn't been bluffing. He really was turning into a monster.

He had to get out of sight before he sprouted tentacles.

"Yes, you got me." He forced a chuckle, amazed at how smooth and calm his voice sounded. Inside his mind, sirens were wailing and emergency lights were flashing and all his monsters were shrieking and gibbering. His head felt like it was exploding. If he didn't get out of there soon, his head might literally explode, and then reform as some monstrosity that would send everyone screaming and running.

"I meant to save the reveal for the end of the conference, but I just got a message that I have urgent business to attend to, so this is the end for me anyway. Yes, I'm wearing my latest invention, Howe Enterprises color-shift contacts. They're a prototype, so no details yet—I was just so thrilled with how well they worked that I had to show them off. And that's it for me, good-bye!"

He did his best to stride confidently offstage rather than bolt in suspicion-inducing panic, but he wasn't sure how well he did with that. The instant he was off the stage, his own people mobbed him, asking him questions he couldn't hear over the roaring in his ears.

"Sorry, I think I have food poisoning," he said. "I have to get to a bathroom. And I'll probably lock myself in it for a while."

That sent them backing off, looking apologetic and slightly grossed out. With any luck, a reporter or ten overheard, which meant they wouldn't attach any importance to his ignominious exit. With that shred of reassurance, he bolted for his car. The red Ferrari convertible was thankfully easy to spot, because he had zero recollection of where he had parked it.

When he grabbed for the door handle, a dainty hand with polished copper nails came down over his. "I'll drive."

Carter started to shake his head—he was so panicked that he wasn't even sure whether he meant that she shouldn't come or she shouldn't drive—and then realized the likely consequences if he turned into a monster while he was driving. He shoved the keys into her hand, hit the button to roll down the roof, and scrambled into the back seat so he wouldn't destroy the car or accidentally hurt her with a stray claw or fang if he did transform all the way.

Fen got in, adjusted the seat and mirrors, and glanced at him in the rear-view mirror. "Where are we going?"

"Let's start with 'away.'" He half-expected his words to come out in a screech or hiss, and was relieved that he still had a human voice.

"Sounds good." She started the car, glanced at a freeway entrance, and passed it rather than getting on, explaining, "I'm thinking high speeds are a bad idea."

Even in the midst of his panic, he was impressed with how calm, collected, and practical she was. He could barely think straight, but she was already planning ahead.

"Um..." Fen began cautiously. "How do you feel?"

"You mean, am I going to grow twelve eyes and a bunch of tentacles at any second?"

"Well... Yeah."

"Got me. I couldn't even tell that my eyes were changing color." He peered over her shoulder into the rear-view mirror. His eyes were still panic-black. But his inner monsters were subsiding, no longer an incomprehensible shrieking mob. As he watched, his irises lightened to anxious eggplant-purple.

Are you taking over? Carter demanded of his inner monsters.

Not on purpose, growled a monster.

I'm not trying to, chattered a monster.

[apologetic apricot]

Desperately, he sent them a question. *Can you stop it?*

[apologetic apricot]

Carter sighed. "I just checked with the monsters. They're not doing it on purpose and they don't know how to stop it. Fucking Eunice!"

In the rear-view mirror, Fen's eyebrows rose. "You *checked with the monsters?*"

"Oh. Right. I forgot to tell you about that. Remember how I said that a shifter's inner animal is the most primal part of our self, almost like our soul? It has a personality, too. You can talk to it inside your head. My snow leopard was... me, basically, if I was a snow leopard. I can talk to the monsters, too. Sort of. There's one that communicates in color, and that's the one that's making my eyes change. It says... well, it doesn't *say* anything. But it's showing me an apologetic light orange."

Fen, sounding fascinated, said, "How can you tell that light orange is apologetic?"

"I get a sense of an emotion along with it."

"So what does..." She glanced over her shoulder. "...rose pink mean?"

Praying that she was joking, he looked at his reflection in the rear view mirror. She was not joking. He looked like a white rabbit.

"Worried and embarrassed." But his eyes had already changed the instant he'd seen his reflection. Now they were a weird orange-pink-purple, like a night sky when there's a lot of light pollution. "That's horrified, anxious, and embarrassed."

"Oh, Carter." She reached back through the divider between passenger and driver's seats, feeling around until she caught his hand. She squeezed it tight. "How awful. We have to do something about this. Your teammates have dealt with the wizard-scientists before. Why don't we go talk to them?"

A week ago he'd have refused vehemently, starting with "They're not my teammates!" Now, with Fen squeezing his hand, he could not only see the sense in her suggestion, but he actually wanted to talk to them. Not only was she right that they might have some ideas, but they'd be sympathetic. They'd all had problems with their powers and shift forms too. At this point, Carter felt like he could use all the sympathy he could get.

CHAPTER 19

It wasn't the most nerve-wracking car ride Fen had ever taken. She'd gone on a number of supposedly educational road trips with her parents when she'd been a kid. But the drive to the Defenders office with Carter in the back seat trying not to have a panic attack and possibly turning into a monster was definitely up there.

She wished he'd at least sit in the front seat so she could comfort him more easily, but having seen his shift form, she understood why he wouldn't. Even so, if he did completely transform while they were driving, she had no idea how she could possibly explain some strange creature suddenly bulging out from the open roof of the convertible.

So she drove with one hand on the wheel and one around his. He gripped it like he'd fallen into a swamp and didn't know how to swim.

"You know, Carter, Eunice said you'd slowly turn into a monster," she said. "Slowly being the operative word. I don't think you'll suddenly have a complete transformation right now."

He didn't seem to find that very comforting, and she couldn't blame him. Watching him in the rearview mirror, she saw his eyes turn an apocalyptic gray-orange as he said glumly, "Great. So today my eyes start changing color, and tomorrow, tentacles."

She squeezed his hand. "Hopefully it's tomorrow, nothing. Don't count the Defenders out."

"As a last resort, there's always Ransom. I hate to ask it of him because using his powers can be really rough on him, but if all else fails, he might be able to figure something out." His eyes went from that eerie gray-orange to an attractive, piercing light blue.

"What emotion is Cillian Murphy?" Fen asked.

Carter chuckled wryly. "Hope."

A little green faded into the blue as he said, "All else aside, I did want to bring you to the office. I was even going to ask if you wanted to come today. Everyone will be there. You haven't met all the Defenders yet. There's Tirzah, Pete's fiancée. She's a genius hacker, and she takes care of their computers and internet research. And Dali, Merlin's mate, is the office manager."

Fen wondered what he meant by mate. Was Dali Australian?

Before she had a chance to ask, he added, "It's too bad we had to leave Precious and Sugar to go to the press conference. I was looking forward to introducing them to everyone else's pets. Sort of. Sometimes they don't get along at first."

"Oh, right, they have magical pets too!" Fen had totally forgotten about that.

"Forgetful Fenella."

"Fenella would forget her head if it wasn't tied on."

I've had a lot on my mind, she told her imaginary parents. *Having the love of your life in the back seat worrying that he'll turn into a monster at any second could distract anyone.*

"I can't wait to meet them," she said. "Flying kittens! Teleporting puppies!"

"They're flying cats by now." He frowned, his eyes flickering reddish brown. "There's also Merlin's—oh, turn here, this is a shortcut."

Fen parked in an underground lot beneath the Defenders headquarters. She was glad they'd finally get to see looking properly dressed and professional, rather than at the end of her tether and drenched in swamp water, mud, and paint.

They took the elevator up to the office. Just before the doors opened,

Carter muttered, "What color are my eyes now?"

"Purple. Just like Elizabeth Taylor." She squeezed his hand. "Nervous, huh?"

"Not exactly. If it's the shade I'm thinking of, it's more like…"

The elevator doors opened. A living mop the size of a large dog but with bright blue fur leaped at Fen. She attempted to jerk backwards and collided with Carter. The blue mop plonked a pair of huge paws on her shoulders, and a giant pink tongue swiped across her face. She recoiled and banged the back of her head into Carter's chest.

"Ugh!" Fen exclaimed, vainly trying to fend off the blue creature. She regretted opening her mouth when she got a lick right across the lips.

The blue creature's tongue was everywhere, licking off her carefully applied mascara, eyeshadow, eyebrow pencil, blush, foundation, and lipstick. When she finally managed to shove its paws off her shoulders, it banged itself hard into her legs, sneezed on her shoes, and collapsed in an ungainly heap halfway in the elevator and halfway in the lobby, blocking the elevator doors.

Fen stared down at the creature. It was something like a large dog and something like a small bear, extremely hairy, and extremely blue. A pair of absurdly tiny dragonfly wings grew from its back, buzzing madly and sending blue hairs everywhere. They floated in the air and stuck to her black platform pumps, her narrow black pants, her black silk blouse with its asymmetrical pattern of white Battenberg lace, her short black steampunk inspired jacket, and no doubt her black hair as well. When she glanced at Carter, she saw that he too was completely covered in bright blue fur.

"What is that thing?" Fen inquired.

"It's blue." Merlin, the cheerful blond Defender, was hurrying up to the elevator.

"I know it's blue," she said icily. So much for making a more dignified and less literally colorful second impression. "It's blue and it's all over. But what is it?"

"Every time," said Carter wearily, offering her a hand to step over the blue creature. "Every. Single. Time. Fen, remember how I had blue hairs on me when we were first kidnapped and you asked me if I had a blue cat?"

"Oh, right," she said, remembering. "It's a magical pet. But what is it?"

"He's a bugbear," Merlin said proudly. "He's my magical pet, and his name is Blue."

"Are my eyes still purple?" Carter whispered to Fen. She nodded. He went on, "Like I was saying, I'm pretty sure that shade is 'resigned anticipation of total chaos.'"

She glanced around the lobby. A handmade paper banner caught her eye:

WELCOME TO THE DEFENDERS, CARTER FINALLY!

The letters were neatly stenciled until halfway through **DEFENDERS.** After that they became wobbly and hand-drawn. The **C** in **CARTER** was smeared, making it look more like **OARTER**.

"Aww, that's sweet." Fen glanced at Carter to see if he appreciated it too. His eyes—now a very deep blue-green—were suspiciously shiny.

"Yeah." His voice was thick, and he sniffed hard and said no more.

"Sorry about the Oarter," said Merlin. "Guess who stepped on the banner when we were making it? Bad bugbear, Blue!"

At the sound of his name, Blue gave a snort, leaped up, and squeezed between Fen and Carter, leaving wide swathes of bright blue hair on their pants. He shambled over to Merlin and rolled over at his feet. Merlin scratched his belly with the toe of his shoe, and Blue ecstatically kicked his legs, sending up a cloud of sky-colored fur.

"I know it's hard to believe, but Merlin brushed him last night," came a woman's crisp voice from behind the front desk. She had dramatically arched eyebrows and black hair pinned up in a coil of braids atop her head. The woman offered Fen her right hand; her left was a prosthetic.

"Welcome. I'm Dali Batiste, the office manager. Also Merlin's mate."

"I'm Fen Kim. Pleased to meet you." Fen shook her hand, a little puzzled. There was that mate thing again. Dali didn't have an Australian accent. It had to be some kind of slang for significant other. She and Merlin were definitely that; they'd exchanged giddily adoring glances.

"Dali does an amazing job of keeping things organized around her," said Carter. "You wouldn't believe what a disaster it was before she came. Of course, there's only so much she can do, given that Merlin works here."

"Hey!" Merlin said. Fen thought he was annoyed at Carter's implication that he was a disaster, but he went on, "Dali can organize even worse chaos machines than me and Blue. In the circus—I was raised in a circus," he added, turning to Fen. "—she once helped stage manage a show that included unplanned appearances by a flying kitten, a pegasus, and Blue, and the audience—which included government inspectors—didn't notice a thing!"

Fen, who didn't believe a word of it, glanced at Carter. To her surprise, he was nodding. He said, "Okay, point taken. Dali can overcome anything."

"Merlin!" Dali said sharply.

Blue had moseyed over to a large, unhappy-looking potted plant. Merlin grabbed the plant just as it tipped over. Several leaves broke off and fluttered to the ground. Blue started to eat them, and Merlin's attempts to keep them out of his weird pet's mouth broke off more leaves.

"That plant is doomed in an office with Blue in it," Fen remarked.

"It's doomed anyway," said Carter. "Roland brought it in."

"He's not good with plants," Merlin explained, dragging Blue away from the leaves. "It's odd. He seems to take very good care of them. But they always die."

"I can't imagine why," said Fen, eyeing Blue.

"Mostly he keeps them in his own office, and Blue doesn't get in there," said Dali. "He put this one out here because he thought there might be something bad for plants in his own office, but…"

Three small creatures flew into the lobby and began chasing each other around in mid-air, flapping and buzzing and… meowing?

A grin cracked Fen's face as she gazed upward. A tiny and very fluffy black cat with black wings and enormous yellow eyes was chasing a spiky green cat with spiky green wings and a gray cat with dragonfly wings. The cats flapped around below the ceiling, tails lashing, meowing fiercely.

Enchanted, Fen held up her hand. "Here, kitty, kitty!"

Dali whistled, then called, "Cloud, go to the nice lady."

The gray cat swooped down and landed on Fen's shoulder. Fen scritched the dragonfly-winged cat behind her ears. Cloud purred and nuzzled her as the other two winged cats continued their game. When the little black cat dove lower to avoid a light fixture, Blue abruptly leaped at it, his absurdly tiny dragonfly wings buzzing as if he really expected to take off. He came nowhere near the cat, but he did knock over a table with magazines on it.

Merlin went to pick up the table and the magazines. The green cat swooped low and the wind from its wings blew papers off Dali's desk. She crouched to pick them up.

Carter turned to Fen. "Never leave anything unattended around here unless it's in a locked room."

A pair of husky puppies materialized in the middle of the room, barking. Fen almost jumped out of her skin, accidentally dislodging Cloud from her shoulder. The gray cat fell off, her wings buzzing, hit the newly upright table, skidded claws-out on its polished wood surface and sent all the magazines flying, then launched herself into the air again.

"I take that back," said Carter. "That pair of noisy menaces can get into locked rooms too. Nowhere is safe."

Natalie ran into the lobby, her rainbow hair shining under the light. "Wally! Heidi! Knock it off!"

The husky puppies instantly stopped barking, as if she'd hit a switch.

The green cat caught the black one, and they wrestled in mid-air. Roland came through the door, holding something. "Hello, Carter. I made you a welcome to the team—"

The cats smacked into his hands, knocking a misshapen green thing to the floor. It bounced twice, then rolled off into a corner.

"Well, it *was* a cake," Roland said.

Fen, who didn't think cake was supposed to bounce, said with some relief, "That was very kind of you. What a shame it got ruined."

"But it's the thought that counts," said Carter. "Thanks, Roland."

Roland brightened. "Maybe the inside could be salvaged if we sawed off the outside."

"I don't think so," said Dali. She pointed at Blue, who was nosing the green object toward the chewed-up leaves.

Roland looked from his dusty cake to his battered houseplant and sighed. More to himself than anyone else, he muttered, "I am *not* giving up."

A woman came in, rolling herself in a manual wheelchair with a laptop sitting on a built-in lap shelf. She was curvy and cheerful-looking, with curly brown hair. She whistled, looking upward, and called, "Batcat! Shoulder!"

The black cat plummeted downward, landing hard on her shoulder with her claws out.

"Ow," the woman muttered, then offered her hand to Fen. "Hi! I'm Tirzah Lowenstein, the Defenders IT person. Pleased to meet you!"

Pete followed her, holding up his arm to the green cat. It landed on his wrist, much more gently and with claws in, and perched there like a falcon. "Tirzah's my fiancée. And this is my cactus cat, Spike."

"Cactus cat," Fen murmured delightedly. "I wish we'd been able to bring our pets. I'd love to have introduced them to yours. But we came straight here. Carter…" She trailed off, uncertain whether he'd rather explain himself or have her do it for him. From the look on his face, he'd rather do neither.

"My eyes," he muttered, staring at the floor. "They've started changing color."

Everyone immediately clustered around, trying to get a look at him. He looked deeply pained, and his eyes went cloudy-day gray.

"They're normally sort of greenish-brown, aren't they?" Pete asked, putting his face much too close to Carter's.

Tirzah stood up from her wheelchair, balancing on one leg and holding the back of it for support. "I always thought more of a brownish-green."

"They're hazel," Carter said shortly. "It's the color between brown and green."

"They were gray a second ago," said Dali. "Now they're kind of... dark pink."

"Like a medium-rare steak," Merlin added helpfully.

Carter jerked backward. "You don't need to get this close!"

"Oh, now they've gone redder," Merlin said with interest. "Like a rare steak."

"What makes them change color?" Natalie asked. "Is it camouflage? Or—wait—they get more red the more pissed off you get, right? Like a mood ring?"

"Like a mood ring from hell," Carter muttered. Then, as everyone leaned in closer to hear him, he said loudly, "Eunice wasn't bluffing. I'm turning into a monster!"

"You're not a *monster*," Merlin said immediately. "You're a man with an involuntary transformation problem."

"Whatever you call it, I need help," said Carter.

A shocked silence fell. At first Fen thought everyone was having a delayed reaction to him telling them that he was turning into a monster. Then she realized they must have never heard him ask for help before.

"We're all shifters," Carter went on. "And we've all dealt with the wizard-scientists before. I thought maybe if we brainstormed and pooled our ideas, we might think of a better solution than me procrastinating on summoning Balin while I grow tentacles and extra legs and—"

He was interrupted by a trill. Precious flew in the window, with Sugar gliding behind her.

"Oh!" Fen exclaimed, delighted. "They came on their own! Now they can meet—"

She was interrupted by an ominous yowl. Batcat's fur was puffed out until she was twice her normal size, which brought her from tiny up to small. Tail lashing, hissing and spitting, she sprang into the air and zoomed straight at the newcomers.

Sugar dove into Fen's cleavage with a squeak of alarm. Precious let out an ear-splitting shriek and dive-bombed Batcat. Carter leaped on to a chair and snatched his dragonette out of the air, while Pete grabbed the flying cat. Batcat howled and hissed and thrashed, and Precious shrieked and squirmed, and Sugar chittered angrily, and the husky pups set up an excited barking, and the other flying cats yowled, and Blue flopped down on the floor and snored.

"Somebody, make them stop." The voice was Ransom's. He was leaning in the doorway, his face very pale and tense with pain. "My head is splitting."

The pet owners leaped into action. Pete rounded up all three cats, stuffed them in an office, and threw in a catnip mouse. Fen cuddled Sugar until he stopped chittering, and Carter stroked Precious until she fell silent. Merlin prodded Blue until he woke up with a snort.

Natalie hushed the puppies, then ran to Ransom's side. So did Roland. Together they helped him to the sofa, where he leaned back and rubbed at his forehead. The husky puppies jumped up on to the sofa, one sitting beside him and one crawling into his lap.

"I'll get you some coffee," said Dali, and went out.

Ransom looked up at Carter. "I have a lead for you."

Carter scowled at Ransom. "You were supposed to be the last resort, not the first!"

Ransom shrugged, then winced. "Too late. Do you want to know what I found?"

"I *guess*," Carter said grumpily. "Like you said, it's too late to stop you."

Fen was touched by the bond between them, which their cranky talk didn't obscure in the slightest. Without being asked, Ransom had decided to help Carter at what looked like a considerable cost to himself. For his part, Carter had decided not to ask Ransom to use his powers even though he was desperate for help.

Dali returned with a cup of coffee, which she pressed into Ransom's hand. He drank it like it was medicine. Apparently it was in a way, because his pained stiffness eased and a little color came back to his face. He set down the empty cup on a coaster, took a paper out of his pocket, and handed it to Carter.

Fen peered over Carter's shoulder, expecting a magic spell to remove a curse or a chemical formula for an antidote. Instead, it had the enigmatic words KERENZA COUCH, followed by a phone number.

Carter's eyebrows rose as he looked at Ransom. "I know this isn't a prank no matter how much it looks like one. So what is it?"

"It's what I got when I looked for something that might help you. Otherwise..." Ransom shrugged. "No idea."

"The area code's for Iowa," said Tirzah, who had tugged Carter's hand down so she could read the paper.

"That's the solution?" Fen said incredulously. "A furniture store in Iowa?"

"It's not a furniture store," Merlin put in. "That is, it could be. But it's also a name. It's from Cornwall. 'Couch' comes from 'C-O-U-G-H,' which means the color red. It's pronounced 'cooch.'"

"I'd be very surprised if the current holder of the name uses that pronunciation," remarked Roland.

Everyone looked at Carter expectantly. He took out his phone with apparent calm, but Fen didn't miss the tense way he was holding his shoulders.

"How are you going to find out if Kerenza Couch—" Fen began.

"Cooch," Merlin put in.

Fen glared at him and went on, "If a person is safe to discuss the reason for the call?"

"It's tricky," said Carter. "This comes up with shifters a fair amount. You have to feel it out."

"I thought Ransom might be a shifter when we were Marines together," Merlin put in. "But he wasn't yet, so when I tried to sound him out, he got the impression that I was trying to come out to him—I mean as gay, not as a shifter—and he was very nice and matter-of-fact about it. If I *had* been gay, I'd have felt completely accepted and—"

Carter glared at Merlin. "Will you please go eat some cookies or put a pillow over your mouth or something? I'm trying to make a phone call that's going to determine my entire life!"

Merlin made a lip-zipping gesture. As Carter dialed, Blue spotted a stray leaf on the table and lunged for it, sending Ransom's coffee mug flying. With astonishing speed, Merlin caught it in mid-air.

Carter strode to the corner, followed by Fen, and turned his back on everyone else. She squeezed his free hand. He squeezed back hard.

"Hello?" It was an elderly lady.

"Hello, is this Kerenza Couch?" Carter asked. He pronounced it like the sofa.

"If you knew me, you'd know it's pronounced Coach," snapped the lady. "If you're a telemarketer, take me off your list or I'll put a curse on you. If you're a scammer, you're already cursed. I have my phone set up to do it automatically."

With a grin at Fen, Carter said, "Neither. I want to get a curse reversed."

"Oh, that's more like it," said Kerenza Couch. "What sort of curse?"

"Well... Do you feel a special kinship with wild animals?"

"No need to beat around the bush, young man. I'm a porcupine shifter."

Very appropriate, Fen thought. *She's prickly.*

"Okay then." Carter proceeded to tell her a short version of the story. She didn't seem particularly surprised at any of it. He concluded, "So I need to get Norris de-fished, and I need to stop myself from turning into a monster. Do you think you can help?"

"Hmph," said Kerenza Coach. Fen didn't think she'd ever actually heard a human being say that before, though she'd read it in novels. "I can't make any guarantees over the phone. I'll have to examine you both in person."

"But it is the sort of thing you theoretically could do?"

That seemed to annoy her. "Young man, my great-great grandmother only escaped getting burned at the stake because she turned into a porcupine and waddled off into the woods. I come from a long line of porcupines with power. I'm a Couch!"

Carter determinedly didn't look at Fen, which was just as well. She had the same urge to throw herself on the floor and howl that she'd had when Norris had been going on and on about the Dunkleosteus.

In a somewhat strangled voice, Carter said, "Yes. Excellent. Thank you."

Slightly more graciously, Kerenza Couch said, "Come on over and I'll see what I can do."

"I'll fly you to Georgia," he said. "In my private plane. Or I can get you a ticket on a commercial plane if you prefer. Business class."

"I said 'come on over' and I meant come on over. I'm eighty-nine years old. I don't fly."

Fen didn't think she'd ever seen Carter look so flummoxed. His eyes turned from aqua, which she figured meant "pleased and relieved," to an unflattering shade of bubblegum pink. "I don't think I quite explained what a Dunkleosteus is. It's not a goldfish I can carry in a bowl on my lap. It's a prehistoric armored fish the size of a bus."

"Transporting your fishy friend is your problem, young man," snapped Kerenza Couch. "Transforming him is mine."

She gave him her address and hung up. Carter leaned against the wall and groaned. "How do I get a Dunkleosteus in a swamp in Georgia to a witchy old lady's house in Iowa?"

Fen squeezed his hand. "On the plus side, she did think she could help."

"It's simple," Merlin said brightly. "Rent an aquarium truck and drive him. My circus had an aquarium truck for a while. It was when we had a shark shifter underwater dance act. My mom said just driving it around was the best advertising we ever did. Unfortunately, one of the shark shifters got in a fight with one of the flying squirrel shifters, and the sharks left in a huff. It all began when a very pretty lady shark—"

Carter gave him a withering look, his eyes flaring gold. "I am not driving an aquarium truck containing a giant prehistoric fish from Georgia to Iowa."

"Why not?" Merlin inquired.

"Because! It's dangerous and it's absurd."

"Do you have a better way to transport him?" Pete inquired.

Carter scowled and didn't reply.

"I guess you could fly him," said Natalie. "But there'd be a lot of questions if you did it commercially. And I don't think your own plane is big enough."

"It's not," Carter muttered. "Nowhere near. I could rent a transport plane…"

"But you'd still need an aquarium truck to get him from the swamp to the airport," Roland pointed out, his eyes glittering with mischief. "And then from the Iowa airport to Kerenza Couch. In which case you may as well take him all the way."

Coldly, Carter inquired, "Roland, is there some reason you want me to take a giant marine dinosaur on a road trip?"

"Yes." Roland smiled. "It's funny."

"You're such a troll, Roland," said Tirzah admiringly.

"Here's a tank that's less conspicuous." Merlin held up his phone. It showed a video of a container truck with a window in its side where a shark could be glimpsed swimming back and forth. The video was tagged **VIRAL SHARK TRUCK VIDEO!**

"That's a viral video with ten million views." Carter's eyes flared crimson. "You can't get more conspicuous than that!"

"Yes, you can," said Merlin. "Our shark truck was completely transparent."

"Merlin has a point," said Ransom, somewhat reluctantly. "You could tape over one window."

"That'll make people wonder what we're hiding," muttered Carter.

Fen intervened. "They can wonder all they want, but it's not as if they can do anything about it if they only see us for thirty seconds on the freeway."

Carter flung up his hands. "Fine! I give up. We'll go on a road trip with a Dunkleosteus while I'm turning into a monster. At least nothing's going to get *more* stressful than that."

Fen's phone rang. She glanced at the caller ID, and her stomach sank like an aquarium truck crashing into a swamp. Fen considered not answering it, but she knew what happened if she did that. They'd keep on calling, and then accuse her of dodging their calls when she did pick up.

She stepped out of the lobby and into the corridor, took a deep breath to gather strength, and took the call. "Hi, Mom. Hi, Dad. What's going on?"

Her father got right to the point. "We saw your press conference on the news."

Right, Fen thought. *That.* She'd been so distracted by Carter's... everything... and then by the prospect of driving a mobile dinosaur aquarium to a witch in Iowa that she'd completely forgotten about it.

What her parents had to say about the press conference was anyone's guess. It could be anything from congratulating her on a fine performance to demanding to know why she was dating an obviously erratic man who rushed away from his own press conference to criticizing her for holding a press conference at all when she was a witness in a criminal case and ought to go into hiding until it was over.

Cautiously, testing the waters, she said, "Uh-huh?"

"Whyever didn't you tell us you're dating Carter Howe?" her mother asked. "How wonderful! Darling, I'm so happy for you."

That ought to have relaxed Fen, but instead it made her more nervous. She didn't trust it when her parents were being nice, because she never knew when they'd stop. "Thank you. It's very new."

"It sounded serious," said her mother.

"It is, yes."

"Then we ought to meet him."

The thought of Carter and her parents in the same room filled her with irrational horror. She didn't even know why. They'd definitely be nice to Carter. They were charming to everyone but her. "Sure, some day—"

"Tomorrow night." Her father's voice, which had brokered agreements between nations, brooked no argument. "At our house. 7:00 PM."

"Dad, he's going to be busy. You know what my schedule is like. His is worse. I'm sure he already has plans."

"If he really cares about you, he'll make time for what's important for you," said her father.

"But…" Fen tried to figure out how to answer that without implying either that Carter didn't care about her or that meeting her parents wasn't important to her.

"We'll see you both then." Her father hung up.

Fen resisted the urge to hurl her phone against the wall. It was hardly the phone's fault. She stood staring down at the blank screen. She was an adult woman. A businesswoman. A very, very successful businesswoman. So why couldn't she figure out how to get her parents to treat her like an adult rather than a child they could boss around?

She returned to the lobby and nudged Carter. "Remember when you said things couldn't get any more stressful?"

His eyes turned orange-purple. "Oh God, what now?"

CHAPTER 20

Carter had regretted agreeing to have dinner with Fen's parents ever since he'd done so. Under normal circumstances, he enjoyed meet-the-parents. Without exception, they liked him, were impressed by him, and came away thinking he was a fine match. But in this case, he not only already disliked them and didn't care what they thought of him, but he might sprout tentacles at the dinner table.

"I don't care if you do," Fen had said when he brought that up.

"I care," he'd pointed out.

"Then say no. If you don't want to do it, I'll go by myself and tell them you couldn't make it." Her voice had been confident, but her eyes had been unhappy. She obviously didn't want to show up by herself, and just as obviously felt like she'd have to.

He'd agreed, then immediately bought a set of colored contact lenses. He was absolutely not going to have dinner with Fen's parents with steak-colored eyes. But now that he was pulling up beside the house, he regretted everything. Fen had been tense for the entire drive, responding only in monosyllables.

"Let's get it over with," she said, and reached for the car door handle.

He reached across and caught her wrist. "Hey. We don't have to do this, you know."

She looked at him as if he was out of his mind. "We're already here."

"We can leave now, have a fantastic evening by ourselves, and call them and say we got food poisoning. Just say the word." He wished she would, but he knew she wouldn't.

Sure enough, she said crossly, "I can't do that. They're my parents."

Carter held his tongue. It was obviously not the time to argue with her over the importance of family. Besides, he didn't have a leg to stand on. His family was important to him too.

Right, he thought. *My family that I've barely seen since I was turned into a monster. I don't have a leg to stand on.*

They walked up to the house. It was tasteful and expensive, but not showy or unique. It reminded him of something, but it wasn't until they reached the door and she raised her hand to knock, showing her dark red nails, that he realized what it was. When he'd picked Fen up, he'd been surprised to see how she was dressed. She was beautifully put together, but in a much more conservative way than usual. Tonight she'd dressed like a generic businesswoman, not an unusual, exceptional, Fen Kim kind of businesswoman. Even her nails were a conservative color. Her outfit and her entire look was tasteful and expensive, but not showy or unique. Like her parents' house.

Carter wore a suit and his trademark long black coat. He only hoped he wouldn't grow a tail. But he and Fen had a plan for what to do in case of sudden monstering. His cell phone was set to ring at the touch of a button. He could set it off at any point and go outside, and Fen would follow him. Then she'd go back in and claim he had an emergency.

Fen's parents answered the door and greeted them. Both of them looked distinguished and slightly formal.

Tasteful and expensive, but not showy or unique, he couldn't help thinking.

"Fenella, how lovely to see you," said her mother. Turning to Carter, she said, "And Carter Howe. So nice to meet you. I'm Edwina Ashdown Kim. Please call me Edwina."

"Hello, Fenella," said her father. To Carter, he said, "I'm Sang Kim.

You may call me Sang. Pleased to meet you, Carter. I always use your phones."

That was the first time Carter had ever not been happy to hear that someone liked his phones. Shouldn't Fen's own father use a Little Bit phone, even if a Howe phone was the one that actually was a little bit better?

Her parents led them into the living room. Remembering how Fen hadn't been allowed to read the Babysitter's Club, he glanced at the bookcases. They were full of exactly the sort of books she'd described: classics, critically acclaimed works of literature, and serious nonfiction on politics, world affairs, and history. There was absolutely nothing anyone could possibly describe as fun.

In addition to tasteful and expensive art, there were framed photographs on the walls. Carter spotted family photographs of Sang with his family and Edwina with hers, plus a few of Sang and Edwina as a couple. There were photos of Edwina riding horses and cutting ribbons, and photos of Sang shaking hands with politicians. But Carter had to look closely to find any that included Fen, and all of those were family photos from when she was a child. Where were the framed photos of her in magazine articles or on the cover of *Wired?*

Edwina opened the liquor cabinet. "I'll get us some drinks. What would you all like? We have some excellent whiskey—Sang is quite a connoisseur. And we have wine, of course. Or I could make you a martini. Or a Pimm's Cup—have you ever had one? It takes an Englishwoman to make them right."

"Whiskey on the rocks, please," said Sang.

Edwina poured a glass of Chardonnay and handed it to Fen, then began making Sang his drink. Fen took the wine without a word.

Carter, surprised, said, "I thought you didn't like wine."

Before Fen could say a word, Edwina said, "Carter? Have you made your decision?"

"Whiskey on the rocks, please." But he was still puzzled by the Chardonnay. Turning to Fen, he said, "Or is this Chardonnay your one exception? Maybe I should try it."

"Oh, our Fenella has never appreciated spirits," her father said with a light chuckle. "She couldn't tell the difference between a fine whiskey and bathtub gin."

Carter glanced at Fen. She was grimly sipping the Chardonnay as if a white wine fanatic was holding a gun to her head.

"You're joking, right?" Carter addressed her father. "Fen can take one sip of a mystery whiskey and identify it. I've seen her do it."

"It's true. I can. And I'll have a whiskey too." Fen spoke abruptly and loudly. She set down the Chardonnay glass so hard that wine slopped over the rim and splashed on the table.

"Oh, Fenella." Her mother shook her head. "You're always so careless."

Her father looked at Carter in a man to man way and chuckled, inviting him in on the joke. "She's always been like this. Even when she was a little girl. You couldn't give her anything, because she'd break it."

"Or spill it," said her mother.

"Or lose it," said her father.

"Or forget about it," said her mother.

Her parents laughed as if this was a cute family joke. Fen stared down at the table like she was trying to set it on fire with her mind. She obviously didn't find the joke funny or cute in the slightest. How could her parents not notice that they were upsetting her?

Or did they notice but not care?

"Can we change the subject?" Fen snapped. "How about discussing anything but how incompetent I am?"

"Oh, for goodness sake, Fenella," said her mother. "Don't be so sensitive."

"It's a joke, Fenella," said her father. "Can't you take a joke?"

Carter was incredibly thankful for his contact lenses, because he was sure that beneath them, his eyes were flaming red. "It's not funny. Fen isn't a little girl. She's a Fortune 500 business woman. She's capable, competent, and brilliant."

Lightly, her mother said, "Oh, yes, Fenella can do great things when she sets her mind to it. But she only works at things she cares about, like her little business. If it's something she doesn't care about, like someone else's heirloom wineglass, she pays it no mind."

Carter could hardly believe his ears. Her *little* business? He again looked to Fen, to see if he was somehow misinterpreting everything and her mother was only making a pun on the name of Little Bit. But Fen was still staring straight down, her face set, her cheeks bright red. He couldn't see her eyes, but he thought she was trying not to cry.

He had a sudden vision of what it had been like for her growing up in this tasteful, expensive house with its tasteful, expensive owners. She'd told him about it, but he hadn't realized quite how awful it must have been. In his mind's eye, he could see her as a little girl retreating into angry silence, believing what they told her about herself.

He wasn't going to let that happen again. Not while he was there.

Bite them, bite them, growled a monster.

Fly them to a height and drop them, screeched a monster.

Roast them to a crisp, hissed a monster.

Toss them across the room, gibbered a monster.

[furious crimson]

[bloodthirsty scarlet]

[protective amber]

All excellent ideas, Carter informed his monsters. But he didn't think Fen would appreciate him murdering her parents. Probably.

"Are you aware that Fen has ADHD?" he demanded.

"That's a very fashionable diagnosis," said her father. "Everyone seems to have it nowadays. It's such a handy excuse for being forgetful and lazy. When I was a boy, people knew the value of hard work."

"Do you have a diagnosis, Fenella?" her mother asked.

"Not yet," said Fen. "But—"

Her father interrupted her to address Carter. "Did Fenella tell you she has ADHD?"

"No, she didn't." Carter heard his own voice rise, but he didn't try to modulate it. He was too angry. "She told me what you told her: that she was careless and lazy. That's what you made her believe. Who treats their child like that?"

Her father glared at him, and his voice rose as well. "Who are you to tell me how I can talk to my own daughter?"

"I'm the man who loves her," said Carter.

CHAPTER 21

Fen had been using all the self-control she could muster to not burst into childish tears in front of her parents and Carter. She couldn't even speak for fear that her voice would reveal how upset she was—how weak she was—how her parents still had the power to make her feel like a child again.

But her biggest fear of all was that once Carter saw her in this environment, he'd see her the way her parents saw her; the way she really was, down deep. Lazy. Careless. An imposter pretending to be a competent businesswoman when she depended on an excellent assistant and an enormous amount of workarounds to cover for her absent-mindedness and lack of interest.

But he hadn't. He'd defended her. He'd gotten angry on her behalf. He hadn't despised her for failing to stand up to her parents, let alone agreed with them. He'd stood up for her.

Right now, he was holding her hand tight.

Carter turned to her. "Fen, do you want to leave?"

It had never occurred to her that she could get up and walk out. They were her parents. Family was important. She'd always believed that.

But family wasn't only about genetic relationship. Family was supposed to mean love. And the only person in this room who loved her was the man holding her hand.

"Yes," said Fen. Carter squeezed her hand, and his rock-steady support lent her strength. "I don't need to spend a dinner getting sneered at, and neither do you. Let's go."

Her father gave her a scornful look. "Let me tell you something about the world, Fenella. People will say things you don't like hearing. You can't just run away every time that happens."

"What is *wrong* with you?" Carter burst out, rounding on her father like he wanted to punch him in the face. "Both of you! Where are your photos of Fen? Why aren't you proud of her?"

"Of course we're proud of her," her father said stiffly.

"You have a funny way of showing it," said Carter.

Fen was so full of love for him that she could hardly bear it. There he was, squaring off against her parents for her. There he was, making a socially unacceptable scene for her. There he was, declaring his love and trust in her.

If he could stand up for her, she could stand up for herself.

She took a deep breath and addressed her parents. "Remember when Carter said I had ADHD and you asked me if I had a diagnosis? You know what? The diagnosis doesn't matter. Even if I was careless and lazy, you still shouldn't have treated me like that. I was a little girl! You should have encouraged me, not called me names. And you shouldn't call me names now. Are you going to stop talking to me like this, or should I stop talking to you at all?"

Fen had never before threatened to stop talking to them. She expected a shocked silence. But her parents didn't miss a beat.

"I just call it like I see it," said her father.

"You can't dictate how I speak," said her mother.

Once again, Carter squeezed her hand hard. His love and encouragement flowed from him to her, just through their skin to skin contact. He was going to support her, no matter what, and that gave her confidence.

"Don't you threaten us, Fenella," said her father. "If you're not going to speak to us unless we do what you say, then we'll have to think hard about your inheritance. Right, Edwina?"

To her own astonishment, Fen laughed. "My inheritance? I make more money than you do! Lazy, careless Fen Kim and her *little* company can support herself. Go ahead and disinherit me. You can leave your money to the Foundation for Truly Terrible People."

She knew a good closing line when she heard one. Fen stood up. "Come on, Carter. Let's go."

Her parents were shouting behind them, but Fen wasn't listening to the words they said. All she needed to hear was the tone, and it was a tone she never wanted to hear again.

Carter slowed, subtly nudging her with his elbow. He gave a jerk of his chin toward the expensive sound system, then casually brushed his fingers against it as they passed by. There was a soft pop from the speakers, and a tiny wisp of smoke rose up.

Her parents kept on yelling. They obviously hadn't noticed a thing, but Fen was certain that system would never play again. True love was using your weird curse to get revenge on your girlfriend's mean parents.

As they opened the front door, her mother shrieked, "Fenella Kim, don't you dare slam that door!"

Poised in the doorway, Fen looked at Carter. Very softly, she said, "I hadn't planned to, and I know it's childish, but..."

He grinned at her. Even with his colored contact lenses, she could see the light of mischief in his eyes. "Like frying their sound system was mature. Go for it."

Fen slammed the door as hard as she could.

They got in the car, but Carter didn't start it immediately. Instead, he stroked her hair and said, "How are you doing?"

She leaned back in her seat, exhausted. "I should have done this years ago. How embarrassing is it that I waited this long?"

"Not embarrassing at all. Family stuff is hard. Honestly, now that I've met them, it's even more amazing to me how brave and strong and sweet you ended up. They spent years and years crushing your self-esteem. You could have been crushed and never tried to do anything with your life, or you could have ended up just like them. But you didn't. You created yourself, Fen Kim. And what you created is wonderful."

Tears stung at her eyes. It was strange how hearing all those hurtful things didn't make her cry, but hearing positive things from a man who loved her did. Tears trickled down her face. But they felt cleansing, like the water that had washed away the mud of the swamp.

Not caring whether her voice cracked or not, she said, "I love you, Carter."

"I love you, Fen." He reached out a gentle hand to brush the tears from her cheeks. "You're my mate."

"My what?"

"My mate. My one true love."

"Oh, right. Dali called Merlin her mate too." Fen had to smile. "Love your office slang. It's a bit caveman, but…"

"Mate isn't office slang. It's a shifter thing." Carter's expression was a bittersweet mix of sorrow and love. "People who are born shifters, like me, normally know our true love at first sight. Our inner animals can recognize the person we're completely compatible with—the person we'll love our entire life—the person we can never fall out of love with. I don't have my original animal anymore, so I lost that ability. But I love you so much, I know you have to be my mate. I don't need my snow leopard to tell me so."

Fen was both astonished and deeply touched. She wanted to stay with that moment, but her mind couldn't help leaping to the equally incredible thing he'd told her, that there was an entire society of people for whom love at first sight was a completely real thing.

"So if we'd met earlier, when you had your snow leopard, he'd have said, 'That woman you think you hate is actually your true love?'"

"Yeah, he would've. It has to be first sight in person, though. It doesn't work over video or telephone."

"And you'd have walked up to me and said, 'Hi, I love you?'"

"I would hope I'd have had more sense than that," he said with dignity. "Given that you're not a shifter and wouldn't have felt the same way about me. And also, sorry I didn't mention this before. I didn't because… Because my snow leopard should have told me. And he was gone."

It was always so difficult for him to talk about the snow leopard he'd lost, but he was doing it for her. She leaned into him, pressing their bodies together. Side to side, shoulder to shoulder, cheek to cheek. That was how she always wanted to stay.

"You're my everything," she whispered. "I don't have to be a shifter to know I'll never fall out of love with you."

"And I don't have to have my snow leopard to know I'll love you forever." He hesitated. "I know I shouldn't make any commitments now. I'm still a hot mess."

"No, you're not. At least, not any more than I am." Fen caught his hands in hers. She had a feeling she knew where this was going, and she wanted it. She wanted him, forever. There would never be anyone who was more right for her, and she knew she was right for him. What more did they need? "Commitments aren't about things being easy. They're about sticking together whether they are or not. For better or for worse, right? Not 'for when everything is perfect.'"

He frowned slightly. "This is not how I pictured doing this. I was thinking of a custom-made ring, your favorite restaurant, me going down on my knees, and…"

"You can do all that later." Her cheeks were still wet, but she no longer felt sad. She felt joyous. "Go on. Sit there in the driver's seat and ask me to marry you."

To her amusement, he pushed the seat back and knelt on top of it. "Fen Kim, will you marry me?"

"Yes." Her smile felt like it might crack her face. "Yes, I will."

He leaned down and kissed her. She put her arms around him and held him close, shedding all her sadness in the passion and love of their embrace. He held her just as tight, his mouth hot as fire, his hands stroking and gently rubbing her back.

A sharp pain pricked her back. She jumped. "Ow!"

Carter jerked back, releasing her. He hit the overhead light and stared at his hands. Little dents had appeared in his fingertips, just below his nails. He flexed his fingers, and a set of catlike claws emerged.

Looking upward, he demanded of the car ceiling or, more likely, the universe, "Really?!"

CHAPTER 22

Carter had never experienced such a mix of emotions in his entire life. He'd asked the most wonderful woman in the world to marry him, and she'd said yes. And also, he had mood ring eyes and a brand new set of claws, and he was about to take a road trip with a swimming dinosaur.

"Think of the bright side," Fen advised him. "We did find an aquarium truck—in Georgia, even!"

Carter was not reassured. It had been a long, tiring drive from Refuge City to Georgia—too long for Fen to have done all the driving. They'd had to take turns, which was nerve-wracking. He'd rather have flown, but if they'd taken a commercial flight, they wouldn't have been able to bring Precious, and he didn't trust himself to fly his own plane. At least with a car, if his hands suddenly turned into tentacles or his feet into paws, he could pull over. If worst came to worst, Fen could grab the wheel. But she didn't know how to fly, so his own plane was out of the question. He'd really wanted to take her flying, too.

By the time they arrived, they'd been so exhausted that they'd booked a hotel and collapsed into bed. The next morning, they returned their rental car and took a taxi to the business that would rent them the aquarium truck, which came complete with a hoist to lift Norris out of the swamp. Fen had Sugar hidden in her cleavage, and Carter carried Precious in her little suitcase/carrying cage. They'd gotten her a small raw steak to keep her happy.

Carter tried to stay hopeful, but it was hard given how self-conscious he was about his eyes and hands. Sure, he could wear contact lenses to hide his eyes turning steak-colored and gloves to hide the weird dents in his fingers. But who wore gloves on a hot Georgia day? The checker at the supermarket where they'd bought the steak had stared at him.

As if Fen had read his mind, she said softly, "The checker stared because she recognized you. You're famous, remember?"

"I'm hoping not to become famous for being a lunatic. I feel like Howard Hughes in these gloves."

"Relax." Fen squeezed his gloved hand. *She* certainly seemed relaxed. It made him happy to see that after the stress and tension of the horrible evening with her parents. Once she'd told them off, it was as if she'd shed a lifetime of second-guessing herself, and could just *be* herself.

They knocked at the door. A harried-looking man with rumpled sandy hair ushered them inside, barely glancing at them. Carter had expected a normal business office, maybe with lots of aquariums, but the place looked more like a technical workshop. It did have a few aquariums, but it had many more machines, robots, and computers.

Oh goodie. Please don't let anything explode or short out. He sent the thought up to a universe that seemed to have it in for him.

Two women crouched in the middle of the floor, gazing intently at something blocked by their bodies. All Carter could see was that one of them had long locs tied back into a ponytail, and the other had a pixie cut dyed bright blue.

Pixie Cut exclaimed, "She's doing it! She's doing it! She's turning left!"

The sandy-haired man rushed to their side, crouched down, and shouted, "Yes! She's avoiding the obstacle!"

All three of them cheered.

The trio seemed to have forgotten that their customers existed. Carter peered over them to see what was going on. A miniature pickup truck loaded with a goldfish bowl containing a single goldfish was slowly trundling across the floor through an improvised obstacle course of coffeemakers, shoes, purses, and a six-pack of artisan hard cider.

"What," said Fen.

The trio continued cheering as the goldfish truck moved around a coffeemaker. It was, Carter noticed, a Little Bit Smoother. He cleared his throat. "Excuse me. We're here to rent an aquarium truck."

Locs glanced up and cheerfully remarked, "What perfect timing! This here is Goldie Twelve, and she's driving her own aquarium truck."

"Your goldfish is driving?" Fen sounded incredulous.

"Yes!" Sandy replied. "Goldie Twelve is in control. It's such a coincidence that you want to rent our truck."

For the second time in two days, Carter's heart sank and sank until it was resting somewhere near his toes. He had a horrible feeling that he already knew the answer, but he asked, "Exactly why is that a coincidence?"

The three goldfish watchers laughed merrily. Beaming, Pixie said, "Because the aquarium truck is also rigged so its inhabitants can drive it!"

"What the actual fuck," said Fen. Carter understood exactly how she felt.

Sandy explained earnestly, "We were going to use it to raise money for our workshop by doing a demonstration with a shark driving the aquarium truck. But then you called and wanted to rent it, so we decided to put that off and rent it to you instead."

"You see," explained Locs, "We don't yet have a shark."

Fen nudged Carter and said, "So what I'm hearing is that if we get tired on the road, we could let Norris spell us."

He knew she was joking. It was still the most horrifying idea he had ever heard. Hoping against hope that he was somehow misunderstanding what was going on, he said, "Let me get this straight. Are you saying that if we put a large fish in this truck, it can take over and drive it?"

"No, no," Sandy assured him. "We'll disable those controls. You'll drive it yourself."

With a gleam in her eyes, Pixie said, "Unless you want the fish to drive!"

"We absolutely do not want the fish to drive," said Carter.

Fen, her voice wavering in a way that he knew meant she was stifling hysterical laughter, said, "Let's take a look at the truck."

"I'll take you to it," said Pixie.

As they walked out, Carter brushed against a robot. It made a sad popping noise and fell on its face.

He hurried past, ignoring the exclamations of dismay behind him. But the sight Pixie led him to was no improvement. Carter had been very clear over the phone about what kind of aquarium truck he wanted. He'd specifically said he did not want whatever was in the tank to be visible from the outside. Whoever he'd spoken to had assured him that it wasn't. And yet the enormous tank mounted on the truck was completely made of glass.

He wheeled accusingly on Pixie. "I was told that the aquarium wasn't visible from the outside."

Pixie blinked a pair of innocent blue eyes at him. "Why would anyone want an aquarium tank if they don't mean to drive on the freeway and have everyone see the sharks swimming around and video it and post it on Instagram?"

"Never mind why," Fen said icily. "The point is that we were promised that the aquarium would be hidden. Why were told that it would be if it isn't?"

Fen's dark eyes met Pixie's blue ones, and Pixie quailed. "Oh, um, I'm sure whoever you talked to meant that it *can* be hidden. We can put a tarp around the tank if you like."

"Yes," said Carter. "We would like."

While Locs and Sandy wrestled a huge canvas tarp around the tank and tied it down, Pixie showed Carter and Fen the fish driving controls and how to disable them. Carter checked three times to make sure they were disabled.

As they paid, Locs appeared to register his name for the first time.

"Hey… You're Carter Howe!"

"I am." He waited for her to say something nice about his phones.

"You're Carter Howe, and you're not going to let the fish drive the truck?" She heaved a disappointed sigh. "I thought you'd be cooler."

He was so irritated that he had to stop himself from deliberately touching another robot as he left. But Fen, seething beside him, deliberately bumped him so his hand brushed up against a robot. Nothing happened.

Outside, she said disappointedly, "I thought you'd blow up the robot if you touched it."

"Sometimes I do, sometimes I don't. There doesn't seem to be any pattern to it." He bent and kissed the top of her head. "But I love that you tried to get revenge on my behalf."

"She called you uncool." Fen shot a glare over her shoulder fit to blow up a robot. "Coming from a woman who thinks we should let Norris drive…"

"To be fair, she didn't know what we'd have in the aquarium."

"That makes it even worse."

Fen was only soothed by the distraction of trying out the aquarium truck. It wasn't the easiest vehicle in the world to handle, but they could manage it. They took turns driving it around quiet streets until they felt comfortable enough to take it to the swamp. They parked it at the secluded dock they had used before, and Carter released Precious from her cage. She launched into the air, swooping and chirruping. Clearly she had fond memories of the swamp. Sugar popped out of Fen's cleavage and joined Precious, gliding from branch to branch.

"Little darlings," remarked Fen, watching their pets play.

Aren't you glad you listened to us about our small sister? a monster hissed.

You should listen more often, growled a monster.

[smug ochre]

Yeah, yeah, Carter muttered inwardly.

He walked to the edge of the dock and took out a flare gun. He was about to fire it when he remembered what had happened when he'd touched the robot, and handed it to Fen.

"Yes," she said, delighted. "Give the girl the gun."

She fired it into the air. It went off in a brilliant orange burst. Carter was beginning to wonder if Norris was asleep when they heard a noisy splashing. He watched glumly as the enormous armored fish swam up to the dock and poked his vast head out of the water.

"Somehow, I'd forgotten quite how big he was," remarked Fen.

Norris couldn't grin in fish form, but he seemed pleased by that comment. He flapped his fins, making both of them jump back to avoid being splashed.

"Stop that," Carter said crossly.

Norris stopped flapping and floated, his eyes and toothy jaws above the water. Without changing his expression—fish didn't really have expressions—he managed to convey, *I'll be good.*

Carter returned to the edge of the dock, crouched down, and explained to Norris what was going on and what they planned to do. As he did so, he thought, *I'm squatting on a dock talking to a fish. This is my life now.*

Halfway through he realized what was going to happen and backed up. Sure enough, when he got to the part about taking Norris on a road trip to Iowa in an aquarium truck, the immense fish not only flapped his fins, he did a barrel roll.

"I'm glad someone is happy," said Carter bitterly.

He and Fen had decided not to tell Norris that the truck had fish controls. Better safe than sorry, they had agreed. She had pointed out that it would also spare him the disappointment of knowing he had the capability of driving but wasn't allowed to. But when they removed the tarp to laboriously get him onto the hoist, and then hoisted him into the aquarium, it became immediately obvious that he recognized the set up. Norris immediately swam to the fish driving controls and hopefully nudged them.

Carter wasn't sure if Norris could hear outside noises from within the tank, so he shook his head emphatically. Beside him, Fen was rapidly typing on her phone. She held it up to the tank. The entire screen was covered with the words, FISH DRIVE IS DISABLED.

Norris swam to the bottom of the tank and sulked.

CHAPTER 23

Fen was having a surprising amount of fun on the road trip. Once they'd gotten more accustomed to driving the giant truck and she at least had stopped worrying that Norris would somehow be able to seize control of it, she could relax and enjoy taking a trip with Carter. In a world where shape shifters and giant prehistoric fish existed, it seemed completely possible that a porcupine witch in Iowa could undo a gargoyle's curse.

"I've never really done a road trip before," she said. "We should do some fun road trip things. It's too long to drive in one day anyway, and the last thing we want is to get so exhausted that one of us falls asleep at the wheel."

"Now there's a viral video waiting to happen," said Carter, instinctively glancing over his shoulder at the tank. "I did some road trips when I was a kid, but I haven't as an adult. I fell in love with flying when I was pretty young, so for long trips, I mostly flew my own plane."

"You have to take me flying someday."

"Oh, I will," he assured her. "After I get… everything… figured out."

"So what did you do on road trips when you're a kid?"

"Asked 'Are we there yet?' about a million times. Stopped at skeevy gas stations with bathrooms I've tried to block from my memory. Stopped at little roadside diners and weird roadside attractions."

"Now that part sounds good," said Fen. "Let's keep an eye out for roadside diners and attractions."

"Absolutely. Half the fun of a road trip is seeing how the food changes at diners between wherever you're going and wherever you arrive at."

"Georgia definitely has its own food," said Fen. "But does Iowa?"

Carter shrugged. "Guess we'll find out."

They had loaded Norris's tank with live trout they'd bought at a wholesaler, claiming they were stocking a pond, so he didn't need to stop for food. With a slight pang of guilt, Fen hoped he wasn't too bored. At least he could watch the traffic along with them via the camera feed projected into his tank that had been intended to allow him to drive the truck.

While they were still in Georgia, they stopped at a diner called the Peach Pit. Fen took advantage of their breakfast all day and got biscuits hot from the oven, golden on top and soft inside, along with country sausage and scrambled eggs. Carter had fried chicken and turnip greens. For dessert they split a peach cobbler with homemade peach ice cream melting into it.

Fen took Sugar into the diner inside her blouse, then transferred him into her lap. If he was spotted, nothing worse would happen that being told to take her pet outside. Carter brought Precious in her suitcase carrier and slipped bits of chicken and sausage to her through the discreet air holes. Fen got fresh fruit on the side for Sugar, and set it down for him on the napkin in her lap. She was relieved to note the lack of pawpaw.

Apparently she wasn't the only one who felt slightly guilty about Norris, because Carter ordered three servings of fried fish to go. They drove the truck until they reached a wide shoulder of the highway, then they pulled over. Using flashlights, they wriggled underneath the tarp, as there was no way they were going to untie it, climbed up the tank on the built-in ladder, and opened the hatch.

Norris still seemed to be sulking. But when Carter held the fried fish over the hatch, he came to the surface and opened his jaws. Carter tossed the three full dinners into the dinosaur's gaping mouth, where they were swallowed in a single gulp. Norris flapped his fins, so Fen supposed he was pleased.

"We're going to stop for the night and do the rest of the driving tomorrow," she said. "It's too long to do in a single shift."

Norris flapped his fins. She presumed he understood.

They found a reasonably decent looking hotel to stop at, which they selected primarily on the basis of it being in a brightly lit and busy area. The last thing they wanted was for someone to try to steal the truck.

The bed wasn't the most comfortable, but it had Carter in it, and that made up for a lot. They lay together and kissed, but when she began to move against him, he pulled away.

"I can't," he said gloomily. "I'm worried that if I get too excited, those damn claws might come out."

"So put your gloves back on," said Fen.

That got his attention. "And be naked except for my gloves? A bit kinky, don't you think?"

Smiling, she said, "If you like."

He liked.

The next morning she was still suffused with the glow of great sex with her fiancé.

My fiancé, she thought, marveling at it. She'd never been one to dream about marriage in the abstract, but the thought of marrying *Carter* was glorious. They'd go to bed together at night and wake up together in the morning, every day for the rest of their lives. Even her distractible, novelty-seeking, possibly ADHD brain would never ever get tired of that.

She nudged him awake, kissed him, and said, "After all this is fixed, you should still wear the gloves sometimes. There's something so hot about being naked except for a single article of clothing. Being ninety-five percent naked makes the rest of you seem even more naked than if you were one hundred percent naked."

"Well, that definitely makes me want to see you one hundred and ten percent naked." He was smiling too. "Sometime I'll have you wear nothing but gloves too. Black silk. Elbow length."

"Hot," said Fen. "I presume you're buying?"

"Absolutely. I can't wait for that shopping trip."

"Me neither."

They went to the hotel's café to have breakfast before they left. Guiltily, Fen said, "Let's make it quick. I feel bad for Norris. He must be bored to death, floating there in a dark tank watching a video feed of a parking lot."

"It'll just be half an hour," said Carter. "He's probably having his own breakfast anyway. There's plenty of trout left."

The waitress came around to take their order. Fen requested coffee and shrimp and grits with a side of fruit for Sugar, and Carter ordered coffee and Georgia Eggs Benedict (on a biscuit instead of an English muffin) with a side of sausage for Precious.

As the waitress left, he said, "I see the horror of the swamp is wearing off. You got shrimp."

"You'll know I'm fully recovered from the batrachian trauma when I get the pawpaw pancakes."

A family with an excitedly chattering small boy took the table beside them. Fen had just taken the first exquisite bite of spicy shrimp over buttery grits when she overheard the little boy say, "It's a great big shark tank! And it has a great big shark! I saw it!"

She froze. Carter almost choked on his coffee.

The small boy's mother said, "On YouTube?"

Fen held her breath.

"No, in the parking lot," said the small boy. "It's all wrapped up, but there's a rip in the wrapping and I saw it! It has a giant eye and a giant mouth and giant teeth and—"

In perfect synch, Fen and Carter cast regretful glances at their almost-untouched meals, threw money down on the table, and fled. Sugar and Precious let out simultaneous angry screeches at being snatched away from their meals. Fen rushed back, dumped the fruit in one paper napkin and the sausages in another, and fled with them, praying that no paparazzi lurked in corners.

There was indeed a rip in the tarp over the truck. As she watched in horror, a toothy mouth came into view and sucked up several trout.

"There's the culprit," she said, pointing. A beat-up truck parked way too close beside them had shreds of tarp dangling from a sharp piece of metal where someone had hit its side mirror.

Swearing, Carter whipped out a screwdriver and some twine, hurriedly punched holes in the tarp along the rip, and tied it shut. Just as he was finishing, Fen heard the clear voice of the small boy. "Look! There's the tank with the great big—"

She jumped into the driver's seat, Carter took the passenger seat, and they peeled out of the parking lot as if a great big shark was pursing them.

They didn't stop again, except briefly to refuel and get coffee, until they crossed the Iowa border. But despite eating granola bars and beef jerky instead of shrimp and grits, they were happy. Carter plugged his phone into the truck and they played each other their favorite songs and podcasts as they watched the scenery change from green and swampy to flat fields of corn.

They were playing Twenty Questions when a T-rex loomed up from a corn field.

Fen let out a startled shriek. Carter stomped on the brakes. The truck lurched forward, water sloshing, before she realized that the T-rex was a statue clutching a soda bottle and a hamburger in its tiny hands. It stood beside a faded billboard.

t

"Not sure they thought through the implications of 'dinosaur buffet.'

It sounds like we're the food." But Carter was already pulling toward the exit.

"It could mean that it's a buffet of dinosaurs," Fen pointed out.

The Dinosaur Play Park consisted of life-size statues of a T-rex, a Triceratops, a Stegosaurus, and, rather inexplicably, a knight in armor. Fen was not all that impressed with the statues, but she took a few photos for Norris's benefit before they headed into the buffet. She was slightly relieved to see that it did not appear to be dinosaur-themed.

A hostess greeted them pleasantly. "Welcome to the Dinosaur Park and Buffet. Got any questions?"

"Yes," said Carter. "The main one being 'why?'"

"Why what, hon?"

"Why dinosaurs?"

"You stopped, didn't you?" the hostess asked.

Carter smiled. "I see your point."

"What can I eat here that I can't get anywhere but Iowa?" Fen asked.

The hostess pointed. "You want the salad bar."

Fen was disappointed. Salads were nothing to get excited about. If the best Iowa food was salad, she hated to think what the rest of it was like.

Carter also did not look thrilled about salad. As they headed for the salad bar, he said in an undertone, "There better be bacon bits."

"Ugh. Seriously?"

"The fake stuff is ugh. Chopped real bacon is delicious."

"You don't call chopped real bacon 'bacon bits,'" Fen pointed out. "And if Iowa's specialty is any kind of bacon over lettuce, I'm never coming back."

But when she reached the salad bar, she realized that she had underestimated the art of the Iowa salad. She'd been thinking of the standard American salad type of "leafy greens plus something else." But these salads had no leaves anywhere in sight, and the only green was the spooky neon of lime Jell-O.

The bar had an entire section devoted solely to Jell-O salads. Some were transparent, with grapes or marshmallows suspended in them like a mad scientist lab where mysterious things floated in jars. Some were beautifully molded. Some were chopped into cubes of all the colors of the rainbow, so long as the rainbow was made of neon or food coloring. Some were opaque with whipped cream or mayonnaise—alarmingly, it was hard to tell which.

There were non-Jell-O salads as well, like a concoction of kidney beans, cheese chunks, and mayonnaise—at least, Fen hoped it was mayonnaise. And that wasn't the only bean salad, by far. There were six different types of coleslaw. There were marinated vegetables – every type of vegetable. There were relishes. There were pickles. There were pasta salads. It was a gigantic feast of dishes that Fen had never seen in her entire life, let alone tried. And all of it was much, much more interesting than what she had previously thought of as salad. She could feel her horizons expanding.

"I don't know about this," Carter muttered, eyeing an amber Jell-O salad with olives and shredded carrots floating in it.

"Expand your horizons," said Fen, piling her plate with seven-layer salad, macaroni salad, and Snickers salad. "Think of them as side dishes, like Korean banchan, not typical salads."

"When you put it that way..." He helped himself to a scoop of warm German potato salad. Poking a bit of bacon with his fork, he said, "Real bacon."

She enjoyed the potato salads and coleslaw, but they both ended up leaving most of the Jell-O on their plates. Carter was openly and she was secretly glad that another Iowa specialty turned out to be hamburger and corn on the cob. There was a limit to how much she could enjoy a meal consisting entirely of side dishes. Precious had bits of their hamburgers, and Sugar had assorted fruits and vegetables with the Jell-O scraped off.

Fen got a family-sized tub of herring salad to go for Norris. He gulped it down and flapped his fins enthusiastically.

"We're pretty close to Kerenza, right?" Fen asked.

"Less than an hour, if we make good time," said Carter.

It occurred to her that Carter hadn't acquired any more strange attributes, they hadn't had any serious problems with Norris, and they were almost at their goal. TicTech stock had tanked while Little Bit and Howe Enterprises stock had surged. Eldon McManus was in jail awaiting trial for kidnapping, assault, and stock market manipulation. She'd walked out on her parents and had an appointment for ADHD testing. She and Carter were engaged.

If the Iowa porcupine witch could de-curse Carter and Norris, all their troubles could be over within the next couple hours, and they'd have nothing pressing to attend to but planning their wedding and following Eldon McManus's trial.

But she said nothing. It wasn't over yet, and in a world with magic, she didn't want to risk a jinx.

CHAPTER 24

Carter didn't want to admit that he was starting to relax, even to himself, in case that would jinx things. But he was. Maybe Kerenza Couch could help him, and he'd never have to deal with Balin and Eunice at all. He'd spent most of the trip braced to grow tentacles or a tail, but nothing had happened. And with his Fen by his side—as his fiancée!—every moment was a little piece of heaven.

Maybe, just maybe, for the first time in years, everything would turn out all right.

He took the driver's seat and pulled out of the Dinosaur Park & Buffet. As he merged onto the freeway, the dashboard gave a sudden pop. The truck began to slow. He instinctively stepped on the gas, but nothing happened.

"What was that?" Fen asked sharply.

Carter looked down at the dashboard. He was horrified to see that the control marked FISH DRIVE had been activated.

"Pull over!" Fen yelped.

He frantically twisted the wheel. Nothing happened. He had no control over the car. It was drifting toward a stop in the fast lane, with cars and trucks honking all around it.

Carter wrestled with the controls, trying to disable the fish drive and enable normal driving. Fen twisted around and banged her fist sharply against the back of the cabin, screaming, "Norris!"

With a sudden lurch, the truck began to speed up. It zoomed forward, drifted into the next lane, over-corrected and almost hit the concrete median, then over-corrected again and barreled across three lanes, barely avoiding a collision with a fruit truck. The fruit truck slammed on its brakes, and oranges flew out and bounced across the freeway. Every car and truck and bus and motorcycle on the freeway honked at them as they wobbled uncertainly along. From her carrying cage, Precious let out a piercing shriek.

Carter took his hands off the steering wheel, since that was completely useless anyway, and leaned his head in them, moaning, "Norris took the wheel."

"I should have let us stop," said Fen. "We could have gotten towed."

"The last thing we want is a cop taking a look at what's under the tarp," said Carter grimly.

"But if the alternative is Norris driving…"

The truck steadied, keeping within its lane, though it continued to weave within it. Norris steered by watching the video feed and moving his head. It seemed like he was getting the hang of it.

"Does he know where we're going?" Fen asked.

"Yes, our GPS map is superimposed on the video footage," said Carter absently. He was trying to figure out how to get Norris to pull over and stop. "He seemed to hear you, or at least feel the vibration of you banging your fist. I wonder if he knows Morse code."

She shrugged. "Worth a try."

Fen began banging the rear wall with her fist for dots and her elbow for dashes in a pattern that spelled out PULL OVER AND STOP AT NEXT SHOULDER. Carter watched, impressed. Of course Fen knew Morse code. She'd probably learned it in the Girl Scouts and remembered it twenty years later. That was his brilliant, capable, clear-headed Fen.

Unfortunately, Norris either didn't know Morse code or did know it but was ignoring it so he could keep driving. He kept on going. Carter had the distinct feeling of being trapped on a runaway train.

"Now I know exactly how Keanu Reeves and Sandra Bullock felt in *Speed*," Fen muttered. "If it was a crossover with *Jurassic Park*."

Norris barely avoided a collision with a SUV as he merged the truck onto the next freeway. The SUV driver honked angrily.

At that point Carter felt fatalistic. Norris hadn't crashed them immediately. Maybe he wouldn't. Maybe they would just arrive at the home of the porcupine witch in a truck driven by a prehistoric fish, and that would be that.

Norris exited the freeway, knocking over a stop sign as he did so, and began driving with unwarranted confidence along surface streets. Fen was biting her perfect manicure. Carter gave up on watching the road and devoted himself entirely to trying to fix the controls.

"We're almost there—" Fen began, then let out a yelp. "Norris! No! Stop!"

Carter jerked up his head as she pounded on the back wall. They were barreling toward a low bridge with a big sign:

11' 8" CLEARANCE

Below that, someone had graffitied **THE CAN-OPENER.** Someone else had graffitied **THIS BRIDGE EATS TRUCKS.**

Norris steered the truck straight for the bridge.

There was a brief moment when Carter thought it would be all right. The truck was just below the maximum clearance. They could get under it with a couple inches to spare, though it would be tight enough that he wouldn't have risked it himself.

The tank, however, was slightly higher than the truck.

The bottom of the bridge caught the canvas tarp and yanked it off. There was an enormous ripping sound like the removal of the world's biggest Band-aid.

Precious screeched angrily, and Sugar launched out of Fen's blouse and began gliding around the truck like the world's slowest, cutest ping-pong ball. She snatched him out of the air, stuffed him back down her blouse, and held him in with an arm over her cleavage.

They emerged at the other end of the bridge with a pile of canvas creating a traffic hazard behind them, driving an aquarium that was now completely visible. And so was Norris.

Carter could see everything in the rear-view and side mirrors. Norris had polished off the last of the trout, so there was absolutely nothing to obstruct the view of the massive prehistoric armored fish with a gaping maw full of teeth driving a truck through a small, picturesque Iowa town.

Cars and trucks swerved in alarm or made unsafe swings around to follow them. People ran after them, cell phones aloft. When they stopped at red lights, children rushed out of houses to gawk, followed by their parents. Sudsy-haired women and gloved hair stylists rushed out of a salon to get a better look.

Norris loved the attention. He flapped his fins, swished his tail, and opened and closed his mouth. Every time he did, people squealed and screamed with terror or delight.

"I bet your eyes are 'resigned anticipation of total chaos,'' said Fen.

"I bet your mind is a giant screen flashing WHAT THE ABSOLUTE FUCK," said Carter.

A police siren started up with a yelp behind them. Carter didn't know what color was 'resigned anticipation of inevitable doom,' but he was sure his eyes had it beneath the lenses.

"If Norris doesn't pull over, we're jumping out," he said. "I'll hold you."

"If Norris doesn't pull over, I'll take a sledge hammer to his tank," said Fen.

To Carter's immense relief, Norris pulled over.

A pair of cops got out of their police car, stared at Norris for a long time, then stalked up to the truck. Fen and Carter rolled down their windows.

"Er," said Carter. "What can I do for you, officer?"

The first cop gave him an understandably incredulous stare. "You can tell us what that… that *thing* is."

The second cop gave him a different sort of incredulous stare. "Are you Carter Howe?"

The first cop gave him a second glance, then stared at Fen. "Are you Fenella Kim?"

"Yes!" Fen smiled brightly. She still had one arm holding Sugar inside her blouse, and now casually dropped her other arm to conceal the tiny moving bulge. "Hello. We're so sorry to cause a disruption—we had a tarp over the tank, but it got caught on a bridge and pulled off. So you two are getting a sneak peek at the very first Little Bit-Howe Enterprises collaborative project, a hyper-realistic marine robot!"

I'm engaged to a genius, Carter thought.

The cops stared at the enormous armored fish. Norris flapped his fins.

"That's a robot?" asked the first cop.

Carter managed a smile. "Well, it's certainly not an actual prehistoric fish!"

The cops laughed. Fen laughed. Carter forced a laugh, though inside he was screaming. He had a sudden, irrational conviction that he was about to grow tentacles.

"Is it actually driving the truck?" asked the second cop.

Fen shook her head with a convincing look of astonished horror. "Of course not! We're just transporting it for testing. We needed a remote area."

The first cop plastered on a stern look. "You should have stopped at the bridge when the tarp got pulled off."

"Yes," Fen said humbly. "We're sorry. We were worried so many people would gawk at the robot that it'd cause a traffic pile-up."

"It's so realistic," said the second cop. "It's incredible."

Both cops stared at Norris. Carter tried not to look at Fen as she took the opportunity to remove Sugar from her blouse and hide him in the glove compartment.

"What are you going to use it for?" asked the second cop.

"I'm afraid we can't say," Carter replied, hoping the cops would assume he meant it was some kind of military project.

He was relieved that they did exactly that, glancing at each other and nodding. The first cop said, "I'll radio someone to fetch that tarp."

Carter shot a desperate glance at Fen, hoping she would pick up his unspoken cue. She promptly began chatting with the second cop, holding his attention while Carter made another attempt to turn off the fish drive. This time it responded normally. He turned it off, then disabled it.

Of course, he thought. *Of course my electronic curse happens at the worst possible time.*

It stopped happening at the best possible time, a monster growled.

Carter grudgingly conceded the monster's point.

What seemed like the entire police force of the town arrived along with the tarp, ostensibly to help put it back on but actually to gawk at the hyper-realistic marine robot.

"I'll drive the last leg," said Fen.

He was happy to switch with her. With her hands on the controls, he was confident that the fish drive would stay off.

"Do you need an escort?" asked a cop hopefully.

Carter firmly shook his head. "I'm afraid it's to an undisclosed location."

The cops held off the looky-loos while Fen took the wheel and drove off. As soon as they were out of sight of everyone, Carter opened the glove compartment. Sugar leaped out, chittering angrily, and glided down to sulk atop Precious's carrying cage.

"I'm going to murder Norris," said Carter.

"I'll help," said Fen. "To think we gave him all those treats, too!"

"If the witch can't help us, he can drive himself back to the swamp."

"I totally agree."

Kerenza Couch lived on the outskirts of town, in a small forest of oak, white pine, and hickory. Fen maneuvered the truck along a dirt road and came to a stop at a little log cabin that looked like it had been there since the American Revolution. Given what the porcupine witch had said about her ancestors, maybe it had.

He'd expected a skinny old lady with straggly gray hair, wearing a black dress and a pointed hat, but the woman who emerged from the cabin was comfortably plump and wore a bright pink velour pantsuit. She did have gray hair, but it was clipped short and topped with a sun visor. Her scowl, however, was exactly as expected.

She marched up to the truck and snapped her fingers. "Let's have a look at your fishy friend."

They hauled off the tarp and revealed Norris. Kerenza and Norris gaped at each other. She recovered first. "This is his natural shift form?"

Carter nodded. "That is, he wasn't born a shifter. He was made into one by a wizard-scientist."

"Oh." Kerenza wrinkled her nose like she'd spotted a cockroach in her Jell-O salad. "*Them.*"

"You know about them?" Fen asked. "Can you tell us about them?"

The porcupine witch gave a disgusted snort. "They've been around forever. Since King Arthur's time, though they were wizard-alchemists then. They have more power than wisdom—more power than they ought to have."

Carter, intrigued, said, "Do you know where it comes from?"

"No, but I do know some tricks to counter theirs." Kerenza gave a satisfied snort. "They stay away from me, let me tell you! One of them tried their silly freezing trick on me, and I sent him home with a backside full of quills."

"They took out my entire team by freezing us," said Carter. "Is that something you can stop?"

She nodded. "I can make you some charms for that."

"And a gargoyle with the power to control our inner animals used that on us. That's how Norris got stuck. And I'm turning into a monster." Even now, with more time to get used to it, Carter had to force the words out.

He took off his gloves, feeling like he was stripping in public. Fen put a comforting hand on his back, but he still felt a hot wash of shame as he flexed his hand, showing the witch his claws.

They're masterworks of deadly elegance, hissed a monster.

"Hmph." Kerenza peered at the claws. "You seem complicated. Let's de-fish your friend first."

"I'm not sure he qualifies as a friend," Carter muttered, but Kerenza was already marching toward the aquarium. She climbed up the ladder, opened the top hatch, and peered down at Norris. He rose to greet her, flapping his fins and twitching his tail.

Carter was expecting a long ritual, complete with sigils drawn on the ground around the tank, mystic hand gestures, and hours of chanting. Probably a bubbling cauldron. Maybe some eye of newt.

With a total lack of ceremony, Kerenza reached into a pocket of her pink velour pants, took out a zip-lock sandwich bag half-full of green powder, and emptied its contents into the tank.

The next moment, a fully-clothed and very human Norris was thrashing around in the water. With a satisfied nod, Kerenza dusted off her hands and descended the ladder. Norris spluttered, then grabbed the ladder, hauled himself out, and followed after her.

"That was amazing," breathed Fen. Then, turning on Norris, she demanded, "What were you thinking, driving the truck? You could have gotten us all killed!"

With an injured look, Norris protested, "I had to take over. The regular controls were locked out."

Carter, who had been about to pile on Norris, realized that he was right. Sort of. He *had* been turning the steering wheel and stepping on the gas and brake pedals, with no effect whatsoever.

"You should've pulled over and stopped," grumbled Fen.

"You told me to keep going. In Morse code!" Norris gazed at her admiringly. "I learned it in seventh grade, when I was thinking of enlisting in the Navy and trying to get on a submarine crew. When did you learn it?"

"Girl Scouts," she replied. "But I told you to pull over and stop."

He banged on the tank with his fist. "Was that supposed to be a dash? I thought it was a dot."

She banged on the tank with her fist. "That was a dot." She banged on it with her elbow. "This was a dash."

Kerenza intervened. "Stop squabbling. I'm already missing *The Bold and the Beautiful*, and I don't want to miss *The Young and the Restless*." She stabbed a plump finger at Norris. "You! Fish Boy. I've fixed it so you can't lose control of your shift form again. But I advise you to stay away from wizard-scientists anyway. They're bad news."

"I will. Thank you so much." Earnestly, Norris said, "What do I owe you? Money? A favor? A ride in a Dunkleosteus-driven truck?"

"No!" Fen, Carter, and Kerenza all spoke at once.

"You can owe me a favor," said Kerenza. "You never know when you might need to summon a big fish."

Carter eyed her suspiciously, but she seemed completely serious.

"I owe you both a favor, too," said Norris, turning to Carter and Fen. "Anything. Any time. Er… Could I start by returning the truck? Or do you want to drive it back yourselves? Either way, I'll cover the rental fee."

Carter and Fen exchanged resigned glances. Without speaking, they knew exactly how he intended to return it. Carter felt so punch-drunk at that point that he no longer cared if Norris drove the truck back to Georgia as a fish, so long as he didn't have to be present for it.

"I'd rather rent a car here for the drive back," said Fen. Giving Carter a smile that made him go weak at the knees, she said, "Get a little alone time."

"Sounds good to me," he replied.

They took out their luggage, plus Sugar and Precious. Fen tossed Norris the keys. "Knock yourself out."

Norris seized them, thanked all three of them again, and eagerly climbed into the truck. Carter opened the carrying suitcase. Precious flew out, and she and Sugar began zooming around the forest.

Kerenza eyed them. "Pesky critters, dragonettes. Never wanted one myself." She caught Carter's expression at her criticism of his darling, and added, "Don't give me that hoity-toity look. I have my own familiar, the same kind my mother had and her mother before her. *Much* less trouble."

Before he or Fen could inquire, Norris distracted them by backing the truck into an oak. Acorns showered down. As he carefully corrected his course, Fen said, "I wonder how long he'll wait before he gets out of the cab and into the tank."

"Probably the instant he's out of sight," Carter predicted. "Well—he's not our problem anymore."

"No," said Kerenza, eyeing him. "You are. Let me get a good look at you, young man."

She marched up to him and peered at him intently.

"I'm wearing colored contact lenses," he said. "Should I take them out?"

"No need. I know what they're hiding."

Kerenza circled him several times, prodding him occasionally in uncomfortable spots like the small of his back, right below his ribs, and the hollow of his throat. After what felt like an excruciatingly long time, she pointed to a patch of grass. "Lie down."

He lay down on his back, feeling deeply awkward in his suit and long coat.

"Stay there." Kerenza went off into the cabin, leaving the door ajar.

Fen sat down beside him and whispered, "What do you think?"

He tried to summon hopefulness, like Kerenza summoning a big fish. "She fixed Norris. And she sure seems to know what she's doing."

"You don't sound like you mean it," Fen pointed out.

"You don't miss a trick," he returned. "I guess I don't want to get my hopes up."

"Disappointment is the worst," she agreed. "But don't give up, okay?"

She took his hand. Her small, strong, clever fingers pressed into his, giving him strength and hope.

A plump porcupine waddled out of the cabin. As Carter watched in excruciating suspense, she slowly made her way to him and proceeded to repeat the examination she'd made in her human form, only with sniffing instead of poking. When she was finished, she slowly waddled back into the cabin.

He sat up and released the exasperated sigh he'd been holding back until the porcupine was out of sight. "Something better come of this."

Fen gave him an attempt at an encouraging look. But he could see that she had not found the slo-mo porcupine very inspiring.

The cabin door opened and Kerenza came back out in her human form, carrying a shopping bag. She marched up to Carter and said, "Sonny, you're a mess."

A faint snort came from Fen's direction. He tried hard not to look at her.

"That gargoyle locked the fish boy in fish form, so all I had to do was unlock him. But she didn't lock you up—she *unlocked* you," Kerenza said. "You're afraid of your animals—"

"I am not!" Carter said indignantly.

She continued over him, ignoring his interruption. "—so you're used to holding them back. That only frustrates them. The gargoyle knocked some holes in your control, so they can get out a little at a time. Once a bit of them is out, they won't get back in because they're afraid if they do, you'll never let them out again."

"Of course I will. I do still shift. They know that."

Kerenza eyed him. "Would you rather stay as you are, or get rid of them entirely and never shift again?"

His monsters screeched and howled and gibbered and color-flashed and snarled and shrieked their angry protests.

No!

No!

Don't kill us!

We won't let you!

How dare you!

We deserve to live!

[angry scarlet]

For the first time, Carter felt a pang of guilt at the idea of getting rid of his monsters. They hadn't chosen him any more than he'd chosen them. It was hard to be angry with someone who only wanted to live.

He pushed it away. They were parts of himself, and he had the right to decide which parts to keep and which to discard. It was his life.

It's our lives! A monster snarled that so loudly that he had to clench his fists to stop himself from clapping his hands over his ears.

"*Can* you get rid of them?" Carter asked Kerenza.

She gave a disgusted snort. "See, that's what I mean. Your animals know you don't want them, so they're not cooperating."

He wanted to bang his head against the nearest tree. "What am I supposed to do about that? I can't change how I feel."

The witch shrugged, then took a zip-lock bag out of her pocket. This one was entirely full of green powder with streaks of silver. She opened it and dumped it over his head.

It smelled like hot metal and the back of an old spice cupboard. He sneezed, and a wild hope filled his heart. "Is this going to fix me?"

She shrugged. "Maybe. You'll have to see what happens. If you get more animal attributes, it didn't work."

"No shit," Fen muttered.

Kerenza put her plump hands on her plumper hips. "No swearing on my property, young lady."

With uncharacteristic meekness, Fen said, "I'm sorry. We really appreciate your efforts."

"We do," Carter added. He had to physically stop himself from brushing off the green-silver powder in his hair and all over his suit and coat. Some of it had gone down the back of his neck. It itched. "Thank you so much. I appreciate the try, whether it works or not. You mentioned charms to stop the wizard-scientists from freezing us…?"

"Yes, yes." Heaving a put-upon sigh, Kerenza said, "I suppose you may as well come in."

They followed the porcupine witch into her cabin. It was clean and bright, dominated by an enormous wall-mounted TV blaring commercials. She shooed them to a comfortable couch in front of the TV, then began rummaging around in a cupboard.

A creature padded into the living room. It was the size of a large cat, hairless, with a scorpion's tail and enormous, protruding fangs like a saber-tooth tiger. Its yellow eyes had goat-like slotted pupils. It caught sight of the strangers in the house and hissed, showing a forked tongue. Fen let out a faint shriek, and Carter started up from the sofa.

Kerenza clicked her tongue at the weird creature. "Friends, Blossom!"

Blossom hissed again, but grudgingly avoided the sofa and went into the kitchen. It sat up on its hind legs, begging. Kerenza tossed it a doggie bone treat from a glass jar, which it caught and crunched up.

"What is that?" Fen asked. Carter was certain she'd just barely stopped herself from completing the question with *thing.*

"Blossom is a purebred miniature manticore," Kerenza replied proudly. "Delightful creatures. So intelligent. Marvelous watchdogs. They are a bit subject to cold, on account of being hairless, so I knit little sweaters for her to wear in winter."

The image of Blossom in a knit sweater made Carter feel like his mind had just bluescreened.

"How many of you want amulets?" Kerenza called over her shoulder as she resumed her cupboard rummaging.

"Six who are shifters," Carter said. "And four more who are mates and family members and might be around."

"Irrelevant," Kerenza said. "The freeze spell works the same whether you're a shifter or not."

"Great. How about some powder to fix anyone whose inner animal gets controlled by the gargoyle?"

She shook her head. "That doesn't work by itself, young man. It works because I sprinkle it. I can give you antifreeze amulets, but that's it. Do you want them?"

Trying to stifle his disappointment—having someone else control one's inner animal was far worse than being paralyzed—he said, "Yes, please."

Kerenza fixed him with a stare. "You'll all owe me a favor."

"Done," said Carter. He couldn't imagine what favors she'd want, but he felt confident that no one would object.

She dumped a handful of little charms into what he was beginning to think of as the inevitable zip-lock bag and thrust it at him. "Keep them on your person. They've got little holes drilled in case you want to wear them as a necklace or bracelet. Good-bye! *The Bold and the Beautiful* is about to start."

Kerenza scooped up Blossom and hustled them outside. The door slammed, cutting off the opening notes of the soap opera's theme song.

Fen took the zip-lock bag from him, inspecting the charms more closely. "These are Lego bricks. With tiny zip-lock bags full of purple powder glued on them on one side, and bits of twigs on the other."

"I think the twiggy things are actually bits of porcupine spines," said Carter. "And… glitter? Fish scales?"

She held up a particularly hideous blue brick. "I'm not wearing this as jewelry. It can live in my purse."

Carter tucked an equally tacky yellow brick into an inner pocket of his coat. "Same. Good thing they don't have to actually touch your skin."

"Or worse, have to be visible. Imagine trying to explain wearing *that* at a press conference!"

They both shuddered.

CHAPTER 25

Fen stretched her legs contentedly, watching the fields of corn pass by. They could have flown back, but since they'd have had to rent a car and drive to the city that had the airport, they'd decided to instead re-do their road trip in style.

"So much more relaxing when you're in a Porsche instead a giant truck," she said.

"So much more relaxing when you don't have a giant prehistoric fish backseat driving," said Carter.

"Backtank driving," she said with a grin, settling her hand on his thigh. They'd been on the road for four hours, and she was starting to get hungry. "What do you think about looking for a nice diner once we get out of the corn fields?"

"You mean if we ever get out of the corn fields. They're starting to feel eternal. But yeah, sounds good. I could definitely go for some—" He broke off with a gasp.

"What? What is it?"

"My back." The words were forced out through gritted teeth.

A knife of icy fear went straight through her heart. Carter swung the car to the shoulder, slammed on the brakes hard enough to throw her against her seat belt, flung open the door, and fell as much as jumped out. He didn't even turn off the ignition; she had to take the key.

The silence once the engine stopped felt deeply ominous. Precious broke it with a high keen that was even more unsettling.

Fen tried to open her door, but he'd stopped partially off the shoulder and it was blocked by tall stalks of corn. She crawled over the driver's seat and scrambled out, then turned back to grab Precious's carrying cage; she couldn't leave the dragonette alone in the car. But when she looked back, she saw that the golden dragonette had escaped the cage on her own. Still keening, Precious arrowed into the corn field after Carter.

Fen ran after her and caught sight of him. He was staggering, almost doubled over as he stumbled deeper into the field. There was obviously something terribly wrong with him, but the green stalks blocked most of her view.

"Carter! Carter!"

He didn't seem to hear her. She bolted forward before she could lose sight of him, pushing the corn aside. Her high heels sank into the soft dirt. Sugar jumped out of her blouse and glided ahead of her, chittering urgently.

She caught up with Carter as he fell heavily to his knees. Precious landed in front of him, rubbing her face against his legs and crooning. Even in the midst of Fen's confusion and worry, she was puzzled by why Precious wasn't on his shoulder. That was where the little dragonette always loved to perch.

Fen knelt beside him. "What's wrong?"

His face was white and set with pain, his jaw clenched, but she couldn't see anything visibly wrong. He managed to get out, "Help me get my coat off."

She helped him pull off his long black coat, then sucked in a horrified breath. The entire back of his white shirt was soaked through with blood.

Fen couldn't imagine what had happened—a silenced gunshot?—but there was no time to waste on questions. She had to stop the bleeding, immediately. She snatched up his coat and started to fold it to create a makeshift dressing.

Carter cried out in pain. His bloody shirt seemed to explode off his body. The remnants fell to the ground in scarlet tatters.

A pair of wings unfurled from his back. They were shaped like a dragonette's, with translucent membranes stretched between a bony structure, but they were black and huge. The corn was pushed aside all around them.

Bare-chested and kneeling, his skin very pale where it wasn't streaked with blood and with those magnificent wings outstretched, Carter had the look of a fallen angel.

But this was no time to admire him. Fen leaned in close, trying to see if he was still bleeding from where the wings had emerged, the folded coat ready in case he still needed it.

He recoiled from her. "Get away from me!"

"What? I need to check—"

He jumped to his feet and tried to back away, but the outspread wings caught in the corn stalks and held him in place.

"It's all right—" Fen began, but he didn't let her finish.

"It's not all right!" he shouted. "Look at me!"

"Carter..."

"Look!" He ripped off his gloves and flung them to the ground. Carter bent his head, carefully touching his eyes. When he straightened, the contact lenses were gone. His eyes were wild, the irises flaring black and gray in stuttering flashes. He flexed his hands, displaying his claws.

"I'll never be able to go out in public again."

"Carter..."

His voice rose over hers. "I'll have to hide inside so no one has to look at me, in a room without mirrors so I don't have to look at myself!"

He sat down hard in the dirt and buried his face in his hands. His shoulders were shaking, and the delicate membranes of his batlike wings trembled. Precious nuzzled him and crooned, and Sugar jumped up on his knee and squeaked, but Carter didn't even look at them.

Fen sat down beside him. She wanted to hold him, but in the state he was in, she knew he'd flinch away. She wanted to comfort him, but she wasn't sure her reassuring words would sink in. And she worried that at any moment, someone might see a Porsche crashed in a corn field with its door open and come to investigate.

So she spoke in the voice she used to command a board meeting. "What's more important to you, Carter? Looking pretty in a mirror, or me?"

That caught his attention. His head jerked up, and he stared at her with eyes that had shifted from the panic and despair and self-hatred of black and gray and orange to the brilliant yellow of surprise shading into the maroon of annoyance. He snapped, "Of course I care more about you."

"Then we're on the same page. I care more about you than about your reflection, too. So get up, put your coat back on, and get back into the car before someone shows up and sees your wings."

His fists clenched. He took a deep breath, then another, forcing on self-control like a suit of armor. His eyes went gray, then a cool green. "Hand me my coat."

He struggled for a minute, his wings flapping and fluttering, before he managed to fold them tightly to his back. With Fen's help, he got his coat back on, though it bulged as if he was wearing a huge backpack under it.

Precious launched off the ground and landed on his shoulder. She rubbed her little head against his cheek and crooned. Automatically, Carter reached up and scratched her neck.

"See?" Fen said. "She cares about *you*, not what you look like."

Sugar scrambled straight up a corn stalk and leaped off the top of the ear. He skimmed lightly over the corn and landed on Fen's shoulder. The sugar glider cocked his head and squeaked.

"Sugar thinks we should get out of here," said Fen, deadpan. She grabbed Carter's hand. "Come on."

His hand was cold and shaking, but steadied as she held it tight.

"Did you let Precious out?" Carter asked.

Fen shook her head. "I think she knew you needed her, so she just… came."

Carter stroked her. "Best dragonette."

Fen took the driver's seat and started the car up. Carter got into the passenger seat, pushed it all the way back, and leaned forward with his elbows on the dashboard.

"So much for Kerenza Couch and her magic itching powder," he said glumly. "And I'd meant Ransom to be my last resort. I think Eunice is the only person who can fix me."

Alarmed, Fen said, "Not necessarily. Ransom was your last resort—that means you haven't tried any of your first ideas. At least get a good night's sleep before you make any decisions."

"Where? We can't get a motel. They'll think I'm concealing a weapon. A real hotel would be even worse. We could run into paparazzi. And a plane is out of the question."

"An AirBnB with a no-contact check-in?"

"I guess," he began, then snapped his fingers. His claws clicked together on the pop. "I know! If we keep driving toward Refuge City, there's a place we can stay while we figure things out. It does have some… er… risk factors, but we'd be guaranteed not to be disturbed."

"What risk factors?" Fen asked nervously.

"Me," said Carter glumly. "It's a prototype for a fully automated house I designed. So everything will probably short out as soon as I walk in. But the beds will still be sleepable even if the massage function doesn't work."

"Is there more than one bed?" Fen asked.

"Yes, it's designed as a family home."

"Excellent. Don't come near one of them, and I'll get a massage."

For the first time, his gloomy expression lightened. "You've earned it."

He was silent and depressed as she drove, and there was nothing to distract her from her worries. They bounced around her head like ping pong balls, skittering from one to the next.

Was there anything Balin and Eunice would accept to fix Carter other than him becoming a Dark Knight? What did a Dark Knight have to do, exactly? Was Precious still in the case, or was she escaping *right now?* What if none of Kerenza's charms worked, and even her spell on Norris was only temporary? Would Norris care if he was now permanently a fish? Was Carter wrong about her having ADHD, and she really was just lazy and absent-minded and not trying hard enough? If she was really brilliant like he thought, wouldn't she have figured out how to fix this?

She barely noticed as the road began to climb upward and the air got colder until Carter touched her arm. "You're shivering."

"I am?" She barely got the words out. Her teeth were chattering. "I guess I am."

He closed the sunroof and turned on the heat. She glanced around in surprise. "Your automated house is on top of a mountain?"

He nodded. "It's full of experiments and prototypes, so I wanted to put it somewhere remote. I haven't been here in a while, but it's fully maintained. And it has an alarm system, of course. I told the caretaker to take off for the weekend."

"You did?"

"I texted him while you were driving. You seemed pretty focused on the road."

"I was the opposite of focused," she admitted. "Except on everything I'm worried about."

"Join the club."

It lifted her spirits marginally to know that at least she wasn't alone in spending the entire time obsessing about depressing things. Marginally.

From the outside, the experimental house looked like a beautifully designed vacation home, not like something out of a science fiction novel. She parked and got out. Carter struggled out, wincing as his wings caught on the roof. Fen came around and helped him disentangle them.

"Do they hurt?"

"Not exactly. They're sensitive. They feel new. Strange."

"Do you think you can fly?"

Carter shrugged. He didn't seem to care, which surprised her. He was a pilot, after all. He'd said he loved to fly. She'd have thought he'd have been eager to try out the wings. It saddened her to realize that having them was so depressing for him that he didn't even care if they meant he could fly.

"Let's go inside," he said. "It's freezing out here."

They grabbed their luggage and went to the door.

Carter eyed it and groaned, his eyes flashing a frustrated pink. "It's supposed to respond to a retina check, but obviously that won't work."

"Got any alternate ways of getting in? After all, you don't want to be trapped outside your house if there's a power outage."

Loftily, he said, "This house can't ever have a power outage. It's got solar panels and redundant generators."

"What if you'd just had cataract surgery or something and you couldn't take off your dark glasses?"

"There's also fingerprint recognition. But the way things have been going, I'm worried it'll explode and completely lock us out if I try it."

"A key?" Fen suggested, her eyebrows raised. "Please tell me you have a key."

He gave a sigh as if the suggestion physically pained him, but said, "Yes, fine, I do have a key."

He took out a key ring in and unlocked the front door with an ordinary metal house key.

"Bravo!" Fen said, grinning. "Sometimes no tech is the best tech."

He managed a faint smile. "Sometimes a leaf is the best compass."

From within the carrier, Precious let out an indignant squeak.

They went inside. Carter commanded, "Jeeves, turn on the lights and raise the temperature to 73°."

Golden light flooded the house. Fen instantly felt warmer. "Jeeves?"

"He's a valet in this book series—"

"—by P. G. Wodehouse," she finished. "Bertie Wooster's

omnicompetent valet. I read those books too. One of the very few works of classic literature my parents owned that's actually fun to read."

"I could have gone with a woman's name, like Alexa," he said with a shrug. "But I felt weird ordering a woman to do things for me around the house, even if it's not a real woman."

She patted his shoulder. "And this is why I'm willing to put up with you."

He gave her such a hurt look that she was both startled and dismayed. "I was kidding. I meant, this is why I love you."

But that didn't seem to reassure him. His eyes darkened to deep gray, like a cold mist.

They released Precious, who flew to a window and trilled until they opened it. She flew out and vanished into the trees. Sugar glided up to a ceiling lamp and curled up in its bowl, lounging in the warmth.

Carter showed Fen around in a perfunctory way. The house was beautifully designed, which didn't surprise her. He didn't show her the automated functions, but only explained that everything could be voice commanded. Voice commands were nothing new, so she was sure this home had many more tricks up its sleeve. But he was so depressed about the wings that she supposed there was no room in his mind for anything else.

She stopped him in the middle of showing her the guest bathroom. "Carter. I don't really care about the house. I mean, I'm sure it's great, but you obviously don't care about it either, so let's cut to the chase. I know you're really upset about the wings. I get it. Anyone would be. But we're going to fix this. Why don't we sit down and talk about our next moves instead of pretending either of us is dying to see the color scheme in the main bedroom?"

Carter gazed at her with eyes the dull gray of despair. "Okay. Fine. No point delaying the inevitable. I appreciate you driving me here. You can go now."

"Go?" Fen echoed blankly. "Go where?"

"Home. Little Bit. Anywhere, so long as it's away from me."

She felt punched in the gut. Was he dumping her? Had she been an idiot to think he loved her?

Fen forced herself to stop jumping to the worst possible conclusions. She *knew* he loved her. She could feel it. So why…?

Then she realized. "Are you planning to summon Balin?"

He looked so startled and furtive that she knew she'd been right. So that was it. Love and annoyance swelled in her as she realized that he was making a misguided but well-meaning attempt to protect her.

Firmly, she said, "Forget about it. I'm not leaving you here to deal with Balin all by yourself. I get that you want to protect me. I get that I'm not a shifter and I don't have any special powers, but I can throw a mean can of soda, and things don't explode when I touch them, and I don't have an inner animal that can be commandeered and used against you. So in fact, I'm in less danger than you are. I'm staying."

She folded her arms. When he had nothing to say of up in response, she added, "So that's settled."

But his eyes stayed gray, a dull lusterless shade like depression itself. "This isn't about Balin. It's about me. I'm a monster. You're a brilliant, sexy, beautiful, kind, funny, brave, absolutely wonderful woman. You deserve someone like you. I've been stringing you along because I wanted to be with you so much, but I can't do it anymore. You need to go."

Frustrated, she made a sudden dart at him and yanked the coat off his shoulders. His folded wings spread out in an instinctive startle reflex, framing him within their span. His skin looked very white against that stark black, as if he was a statue carved from marble and onyx. Blood was smeared across the strong muscles of his bare chest like a warrior angel returned from battle. His eyes shone copper with surprise.

"Carter, you idiot, you're hot," said Fen. "You're not a monster, so stop saying that. I know you don't want the wings and obviously you have to get rid of them, but you are every bit as sexy and gorgeous like this as you are in your normal body. You're like some hot dark angel. And if you don't believe me, let's go to bed right now and I'll prove it to you."

"It's not about how I look!" His shout seemed to shake even the sturdy walls of the house. The despairing gray of his eyes was shot through with streaks of self-loathing orange and angry scarlet. "It's about who I am. I turned into a monster because I *am* a monster. This isn't something that randomly happened to me. It's my punishment. I did something terrible and now I'm getting what I deserve."

"What are you talking about? Don't tell me you're still hung up on the hostile takeover of Little Bit! Sure, I was mad at the time, but –"

"It's not about that!"

"Well, what is it then?"

Carter hunched his shoulders, gazing down at the floor. His eyes turned a color she'd never seen before, a muddy gray–brown. She thought it might be shame. "You don't want to know."

"You mean, you don't want to tell me."

"No. I don't." He sat down heavily on the sofa, clumsily folding his wings across his back. "But I guess this is the only way to make you leave. Because you won't want to be in the same room with me once you find out what sort of monster I really am."

CHAPTER 26
CARTER'S STORY

This story starts three years ago. I'm sure you remember the year, because it's when I tried to take over Little Bit. It was a good year for me, up to a point. Everything I touched seemed to turn to gold. I didn't succeed in taking over Little Bit, but that was all right. Mostly, I'd wanted to get under your skin and I was pretty sure I'd done that.

I had a place in Las Vegas then, living the high life. The only thing that bothered me was that I was lonely. I dated lots of women, but I always knew they weren't my mate. It really puts a damper on first dates when you already know they're not the love of your life and never will be. But not every shifter ever finds their mate. I was starting to think it just wasn't going to happen for me.

Then I met a woman. Her name was Fiona, and she wasn't my mate either. But I liked her. I liked her a lot. She was beautiful and smart and sophisticated, which as you know is my type. We were taking it slow, but I started thinking we might get serious someday.

I'd broken up with women before because I got the feeling that they liked my money and fame and persona more than they liked me as a person. They didn't want to date me, they wanted to date the famous Carter Howe. I never got that feeling with Fiona.

Until I did. I don't remember exactly what made me start to wonder. Maybe it was something she said or something she did. Maybe it was nothing but me being paranoid because I'd gotten burned in the past. But whatever the reason was, I got suspicious enough that I looked into her background. And I don't mean checking her Instagram. I did a full-on, hacker-style investigation. I'd never done that before and I felt like a real jerk.

But in retrospect, I think I must have gone that far because I was sensing something real. It turned out that her entire identity was completely fake. It was a good fake, but not good enough.

She wasn't dating me because she loved me or even liked me. And she wasn't dating me because she liked getting her picture taken with me and going to fancy restaurants and ski resorts. She was a con artist. She dated rich men, she hacked into their bank accounts, and she drained them dry.

I was furious and I was hurt, and I felt like an idiot for having been taken in. Then I thought maybe I misunderstood the situation somehow. Maybe someone had framed her. Or maybe she really was a scammer, but she wasn't targeting me. Even con artists have to have real relationships with somebody, right?

So I set a trap for her. She came over to my house one night. We were supposed to go to the opera. I told her I had to make a business call and it'd take about fifteen minutes, and I went into my bedroom and closed the door. And I left her alone with my laptop.

I'd set up hidden cameras in the living room with monitors in the bedroom. I sat on my bed and watched while Fiona hacked into my laptop, set up remote access on it so she could get into it from her own computer, then wiped off her fingerprints, sat down on the sofa, and pretended to read a book.

It wasn't my actual laptop with my actual accounts on it, of course. It was a spare that I'd set up so it looked like my real one, and I'd given it protections that were easy to break. I'd just wanted to see what she'd do.

I came back in and showed her the videos I taken. I didn't have any real plan beyond finding out what she was up to. I probably wouldn't have called the police—I was too embarrassed that she'd fooled me. I think I just wanted to have her stop lying to me for one second.

But she didn't. First she claimed she was an FBI agent investigating me, then she made a grab for her purse. I thought she might have a gun in it, so I got to it first and threw it across the room. At the time, I thought I was just trying to make sure she couldn't get to her weapon. But I was angry, too. I think I scared her more than I'd realized. She tried to leave, and I stood in front of the door and demanded that she stop lying to me.

She panicked and bolted into my kitchen, I assume trying to get out the back door. But she was wearing high heels and a floor-length gown. Fiona tripped in the kitchen, hit her head on a marble countertop, and knocked herself out cold.

It all happened so fast. One moment I was confronting her, and the next moment she was unconscious on the floor with what looked like a serious head injury. That was when I panicked. I thought of taking her to the emergency room, but I wasn't sure how much they could even do for her. Shifters recover from injuries much better than humans do. Remember how those Most Dangerous Game guys hit me over the head and knocked me out? If I hadn't been a shifter, they easily could have killed me by accident.

The thing was, part of me still liked her. I didn't want her to die or have headaches for the rest of her life or anything like that. And also, I was afraid of what she might say if I did take her in. What if she said I'd hit her over the head or pushed her? After all, she was a professional liar, and I'd already confronted her. What if she thought the only way she could stay out of jail was to accuse me instead?

Then I got an idea. If I bit her and made her into a snow leopard, it would give her shifter healing and make sure she recovered from the concussion. It would also make sure that she never accused me of anything, because then she'd be the one with a story no one would ever believe. And it'd give me the chance to get revenge on her in a way that wouldn't do her any permanent damage, but would really teach her a lesson.

I thought.

I turned into a snow leopard and bit her hand. Then I scooped her up, high heels and fancy jewelry she probably stole from someone else and scarlet evening gown and all, and I dumped her in my plane. I flew out to the coldest, snowiest mountain I could find that had a place to land on. I picked her up again, hiked out far enough that she couldn't see the plane, and dumped her in a snowfield. Then I shifted so I could blend in with the landscape, and I watched her until she woke up.

I'm not going to lie, the first few minutes of watching her stumble around in her high heels and fancy jewelry felt pretty good. That's how long revenge is sweet: about three minutes. After that, I started feeling guilty. I'd wanted to scare the hell out of her, but as she got more and more scared, the less fun it got. After about fifteen minutes, I felt like a real asshole.

I was trying to decide whether I felt guilty enough to go out there and fly her back when she turned into a snow leopard. I'd known that her new instincts would make her shift, and a snow leopard would have no trouble with the cold or the wilderness. My plan all along had been to wait until she shifted, then leave and let her find her own way down. I'd figured she'd lose all her jewelry in the snow, not to mention her high heels, and have to deal with being in another state with nothing but a scary mystery. I thought it might make her think twice before doing the 'love 'em and drain their bank accounts' routine again.

So I left. I can tell you, I didn't feel good about myself. But at the time, I told myself that I haven't done her any real harm and anyway she deserved it.

It never occurred to me that anything could happen other than her leaving the mountain as a snow leopard, turning back into a woman, and getting on with her life. But I'd also never bitten anyone before.

I don't know for certain exactly what went wrong. But—and I found this out long after it was too late for me to do anything about it—Fiona couldn't turn back into a woman. She was stuck as a snow leopard for months and months. Finally, another shifter heard there was a snow leopard on the mountain where no snow leopard belongs, guessed what was going on, and rescued her. He helped her get her real human form back.

I should have done that. I changed her in the first place. She was my responsibility.

I don't know if you can understand exactly how wrong it was, what I did. It wasn't only vengeful and mean and careless with another person's life. It's absolutely forbidden in shifter culture to bite a human except to save their life, or if you're very close and they ask you to. Even then, you have to really think about it. It's true that Fiona was injured, and maybe could have died if I hadn't bitten her. So that part was maybe okay, though I hadn't exactly done it because I was such a great guy.

But regardless, whatever my motives were, once I'd bitten her, it was my responsibility to look after her. I violated that by dumping her on the mountain, and then I violated it again by not following up and making sure she was okay. I was embarrassed that she'd tricked me and ashamed of what I'd done to her, and I wanted to forget about the whole thing and pretend it had never happened.

Six months later, I got kidnapped. It was a much more sophisticated job than what the man hunters did to us. I went flying, I landed in an isolated area where I was planning to spend some time as a snow leopard, and I got shot with a tranquilizer dart. I woke up in a lab.

It wasn't run by the wizard scientists. I only found out about them later. This lab was run by a black ops agency called Apex. They were experimenting with humans and shifters, trying to make super soldiers they could control and blackmail.

I was so arrogant. I told them who I was, like they didn't know. I told them I was rich and famous and they'd never get away with kidnapping me. I even tried bribing them. They didn't care about any of it, which was a bit of a blow to my ego. All they cared about was that I was a shifter, and they could use me to try out something they'd been planning for a long time.

They didn't kill my snow leopard on purpose. That wasn't what they wanted at all. They wanted to give me the ability to shift into a lot of different animals, my original one included. But something went wrong. The very first time they strapped me down and put another animal inside me, it killed my snow leopard.

I knew it had happened, but they didn't believe me. And they didn't stop. They put more and more animals into me, and then they put me in a room and told me to shift. I would have refused, but at first I couldn't even control whether I shifted or not.

I came out as this hideous mess of body parts, twitching in a pile on the floor. It was disgusting and horrible. I think it even freaked out some of the Apex scientists.

It was six months before I could even stop myself from shifting, and a year before I could force myself into a shape like the one you saw, a horrifying, painful jigsaw puzzle that at least could move in some kind of coordinated way. But still, a monster.

There's something else I haven't told you. It's about my snow leopard.

Remember how I said that a shifter's inner animal has a voice and can talk to you? My snow leopard didn't want me to bite Fiona. He wanted me to take her to a hospital. When I ignored him and bit her anyway, he was fighting me all the way. I think that's what went wrong with her—why she couldn't change back to human for so long. My snow leopard didn't want to change her, and that may have interfered with the process.

After I bit her, he wanted me to stay with her. He didn't want me to dump her on some mountainside. And when I left, he wanted me to go back and check on her. We fought and fought over it. He was angry at her too, but I was the one whose pride had been hurt. She'd fooled me and I was set on making her pay for it. He was the better part of me, and I overruled him every step of the way.

I hadn't known you could have that level of conflict with your inner animal. I didn't know your inner animal could get that angry with you. But mine did. By the time I got kidnapped, my snow leopard had stopped speaking to me. He was still there. I could feel him. But I already hadn't heard his voice in months.

I think that's why he died. I think that's what went wrong with everything. He was the part of me that was so disgusted with what I'd done that he didn't want to be a part of me anymore. And those monsters inside me weren't monsters originally, they were ordinary animals. If I was a better person, I bet they wouldn't be monsters. I think I'm the reason why their experiments didn't work the way it was supposed. I'm a monster, and all they did at Apex was make it visible.

I know I should have told you earlier. But you saw me as the person I was before, that golden boy who had everything and could do anything. I wanted to be that man again. I wanted to be the man who deserved a woman like you. But I'm not. Eunice didn't do anything to me that I didn't deserve.

CHAPTER 27

Carter fell silent. Despite the heat, he felt cold. But that too was what he deserved. He'd left Fiona in the cold because she'd hurt his feelings, and in return he'd ruined her life. He'd alienated his own snow leopard, and he'd lost him. He'd behaved like a monster, and he'd become a monster.

Now that Fen knew what sort of person he really was, she'd turn her back on him and walk out, leaving the monster alone in an empty house full of his own useless inventions.

Carter fixed his gaze on the floor. He didn't want his last sight of Fen to be her look of horror, betrayal, and disgust.

A warm body hurled itself at him. Startled, his arms instinctively closed around her. Fen's arms locked around him, holding him tight. Her hands were clasped behind his back, her arms right up at the base of his hideous wings. She scooted into his lap and nestled her head into his shoulder, rubbing her silky hair against his skin.

She rested her legs atop his and put her feet over his. As much as was physically possible, every part of her was touching him. Her touch said, *acceptance.* Her touch said, *intimacy.* Her touch said, *unconditional love.*

Carter was stunned. "What are you *doing?*"

"I'm hugging you." Her voice was a muffled as she spoke against his throat. He could feel her warm breath and the vibration of her lips. "You idiot."

"But I'm—"

"Don't say it!" She twisted around, glaring up at him. "You know what word I'm sick of? 'Monster.'"

"But I am a—"

"No, you're not!" Her glare intensified. She had a shine in her dark eyes, the brilliance of a strong-willed woman who is really and truly pissed off. "You're a man who was lied to and had your feelings manipulated and your trust taken advantage of by a thief who pretended to like you, and you were angry and hurt and you hit back. That doesn't make you a monster. It makes you human."

That makes you human. Those words reverberated inside his head. When she said it about him, it felt true.

It is true. The voice was inside his mind, from one of his monsters or maybe several of them at once. *You* are *human.*

"I did something terrible." Carter wasn't sure whether he was talking to Fen or to his inner monsters or to himself. "I did something so bad, my own inner animal—the best part of myself—abandoned me!"

He did not. It was the voice of a monster or several monsters, more firm and less frantic than usual.

"He did not," said Fen, almost at the same time. "You got in a fight and he sulked—just like you do, which makes sense because he was you—and he died before you could make up. It was an awful, tragic thing to happen, but it doesn't prove anything about you."

"It proves everything about me."

"That you did something impulsive and mean that you regretted afterward? That you were kidnapped and harmed and traumatized by a bunch of sociopaths?" Her eyes burned like black flame. "*They're* the monsters, not you!"

There was something so comforting about her anger on his behalf. She'd been angry about what Fiona had done to him, too. It felt good to know that Fen would take his side; that his enemies were her enemies.

He recalled them toasting the downfall of the manhunters, and he almost smiled.

"Did you ever see Fiona again, by the way?" Fen asked.

Carter nodded. "A couple times, actually. She's on the west coast branch of Protection, Inc. team."

"Awkward," Fen remarked. "At least she's not on your team. Did either of you apologize?"

"Yeah. Yeah, we both did."

"Didn't that make you feel better?"

He shook his head. "I know it's supposed to. But I still did what I did, you know?"

"Look, Carter," she said, snuggling in closer. "We've all done things we regret. I haven't done anything as dramatic as turning someone into a snow leopard and dumping them on a mountaintop, but I've done a lot of things I'm not proud of. I was a mean girl in high school. In retrospect I was trying to build up my non-existent self-esteem by putting other people down, but my motives didn't matter to the girls I bullied. I've been more ruthless than I've had to be. And I can still be mean. Once I made a paparazzi cry."

"What's wrong with that?" Carter couldn't help joking.

She gave him a wry glance. "I'm not saying I feel all that guilty about that one. But my point is, we're all flawed. We've all made selfish choices and lost our tempers and hurt people. That doesn't make us monsters."

He wanted to believe her. But even as she spoke, he could feel his wings trembling against the back of the sofa, and he knew his eyes were probably changing color. If he flexed his fingers, claws would emerge. And that was only the beginning. A whole host of hideous, malformed beasts lurked inside of him, and he was becoming one of them.

"There are monsters in me, though. Very literal ones. You've seen them."

"Yes, I have," she replied crisply. "So has your entire team. And not one of them thought you were a monster. They explicitly said otherwise."

"What else would you call them?" Carter burst out. "A horrible collection of body parts all thrown together! Wings and claws and tails and paws and tentacles! You don't know what it's like."

"And you don't know what it's like to suddenly start bleeding once a month," Fen retorted. "You're not the only person who's had to deal with a body that changed in a way you didn't like. How do you think Dali and Tirzah felt getting a new disability as an adult?"

"Disabilities are normal, though."

"How about your teammates getting shift forms when they didn't even know shifters existed? You don't catch them calling themselves monsters!"

"I think some of them did, actually," Carter admitted. "Pete, probably. Ransom, for sure."

"Do you think they're monsters?" Fen demanded.

"No, but—"

"Do your inner animals think they're monsters?"

That was a question that had never occurred to him before. "I don't know. I don't know what they think they are."

"Why don't you ask them?"

"Hang on. I will."

What do you *think you are?* Carter asked.

I don't know, hissed one.

I can't tell, chittered another. *Who knows?*

[baffled fuchsia]

If you'd stop shoving us away, maybe we could figure it out, growled another.

That caught Carter's attention. *What do you mean?*

You keep pushing us down, screeched another.

Squashing us into the tiniest corner of your mind, snarled another.

Stop it, shrieked another.

He repeated this exchange to Fen, adding, "I don't know what to do about it, though. If I don't push them away, they yell so loud I can't hear myself think. I'll work on it, though. It was a good idea of yours. Maybe if they feel like I'm giving them more space, they can sort themselves out a bit better."

"You've gotten better at controlling them, right? Maybe eventually you really will be able to shift into a bunch of different animals."

He didn't believe it, but he shrugged. "Maybe. In the meantime, I'm stuck with all this." He waved a clawed hand at his eyes and wings.

Fen looked up at him with an odd expression. "You still don't believe I think you're hot like this."

He didn't want to outright accuse her of lying to spare his feelings. And she *had* had sex with him when he was partially monstered. But he'd had his gloves on. And that was before the wings. "Well..."

"You don't," she said. "Okay. I'll prove it."

CHAPTER 28

"Carter, do you know what women read?" Fen asked.

He blinked confusedly. "That's an interesting change of topic."

"It's not, and I'm serious."

He clearly seemed to think it was a trick question. Cautiously, he said, "Different women read different things. Your mother reads anything that wins a prestigious award. You read P. G. Wodehouse."

Grinning, Fen said, "I appreciate your attempt to not stereotype, but for the purposes of this discussion, I'm talking about romance. Erotica. *Porn.*"

"*Fifty Shades of Gray?*"

She took out her phone, opened it to Amazon, and, using voice commands, said, "Wing romance."

Triumphantly, she tapped the screen with a fingernail, forcing Carter to look at all the book covers with sexy shirtless winged men. "Angel romance. Dark angel romance. Fallen angel romance. See? Wings are hot!"

"Those are feathered wings."

"Demon romance," she said to the phone.

"That's a thing?"

She tipped the screen so he could see *Falling for the Demon* and *Dealing with the Demon* and *Demon Barista.*

"Huh," he said, eyeing the sexy shirtless men with bat wings and demon wings.

"Yours are hotter, of course," she said.

"Okay, point taken," he said, though she could tell he still didn't believe her. "But neither of us knows what I might get next. This time it was wings. Next time it could be tentacles."

"Tentacle romance," Fen told the phone.

"That's not a real—" Carter began, then broke off as the screen filled up with *Craved by the Kraken* and *The Billionaire's Tentacles.* She made sure he got a good look, then began paging down. She was on book twelve of *Ensnared by Tentacles (Ensnared by Tentacles: The Tentacle Sea Captain's Blushing Bride)* when he finally said, "Okay, okay. But everything you've showed me is fiction. It's fantasy."

"Yes," said Fen. She took the phone and put it down on the side table, then stood up and pulled Carter to his feet. "And now I'm going to show you something real."

She knelt down and took off his shoes and socks.

"I always thought feet were a bit gross," she said. "Dirty, you know. Not sexy-dirty, literal dirty. Prone to toenail fungus."

"Hey!"

"That was before I got acquainted with *your* feet. Yours are surprisingly sexy. Strong."

"Yours are unsurprisingly sexy," he returned. "Do I get to take off your shoes, if you're taking off mine?"

"If you like."

He pulled her up, then knelt in turn and removed her high heels, cupping her feet as he did so. He had big hands and she had smallish feet, so he could almost envelop them, doing an all-over foot massage in a single hand. "Yours are beautiful. Kind of sculptural, with those high arches. And I like your tiny toes. They're cute."

"My toes are proportional," she said with dignity.

"Tiny and cute. Can I take off your stockings?"

"Stockings and underwear, please." She extended her legs to him, one by one, pointing her feet like a ballerina. His touch along her legs made her shiver with pleasure.

"I like your legs," he said. "They're so graceful. Like a dancer's. Did you ever dance?"

"Not formally. My parents enrolled me in ballet lessons when I was a little girl, but I was a disaster. I didn't like it so I stomped around like Godzilla until the teacher suggested that I might do better with something with fewer rules, like hip-hop. That was the end of dance lessons."

"I hate your parents," said Carter. "I hope they didn't ruin all dancing for you."

Gratified, she said, "No, I do dance sometimes. At clubs. At parties. I'd dance with *you*. Stand up."

He stood, and she took off his pants, then his boxers. "Your legs are excellent. Nice and lean, but still muscular. Like a runner's. Do you run?"

"Sometimes. Not seriously." His breath was hitching, as if her gaze was a physical caress. "Can I take off your blouse?"

"Blouse and bra, please."

He lifted off her blouse, put it on the sofa with the other discarded clothing, and reached around her back and undid her bra by feel. Of course Carter, with his clever fingers, would never fumble with a bra.

"Your breasts are beautiful. I can't see them without wanting to touch them. They're like pink pearls. And your nipples are like buds in spring." His gaze traveled lower, but not as low as she'd expected. "I love your belly."

"Really? It's so poochy."

"I love that it's poochy. It means you're a real person, Fen Kim, not an airbrushed picture in a magazine."

She could see in his eyes and hear in his voice how sincere he was. He loved every bit of her, even the parts that the world said were flawed.

"I love your hips," she said. "Men's hips are a very underrated part. I like the way the bones curve. And your shoulders. It all works together, the big shoulders tapering down to the hips. And the wings—"

He didn't move, but she could feel his withdrawal trembling in the air. "I love your wings, Carter. They're beautiful and strange. They make your skin look whiter and your hair look blacker. You really do look like a dark angel, but you still look like you. I love *you,* Carter, claws and eyes and wings and all. Just like you love me, poochy belly and all."

He didn't reply, but his expression now held doubt rather than outright disbelief.

She reached up to his shoulders and pressed him down so he again knelt on the floor, black wings outstretched.

"I love your hands," she said. One by one, she lifted them to her lips and kissed them. Fen flexed his hands to make the claws come out, and one by one, she kissed them too.

"Careful," Carter said, but he didn't stop her.

They were hard and cool on her lips. She was careful to avoid the sharp tips, but having to take that care gave her a delicious thrill.

"Danger is sexy," she said. "The right kind of danger. I'm not afraid of *you*, Carter. I could never be afraid of you. But being careful with your claws… Well, that's hot."

"It is?"

"It is and I'll show you," she said. "I'm going to go behind you, and I'm going to do some things to you, and maybe sometimes I'll use *my* claws. Watch out for it."

He swallowed. His voice was thick as he said, "All right."

Fen circled behind him. Her bare feet were silent on the floor. His wings stretched out before her, very black against his light skin. She knelt and began kissing up his spine. His muscles shuddered and jumped beneath her lips, and his wings trembled.

She kissed and nibbled and licked between the wings, then she turned her attention to the wings themselves. They had a different texture from the rest of his skin, thicker and slightly velvety. He trembled and gasped as she kissed and stroked them, and that made it harder for her to stay in control of herself. She felt like a living flame of desire.

Her mouth was on his shoulder, her hands on his wings, her naked body pressed into his. She wanted him so much, all of him. Her sharp teeth nipped his shoulder, and he jumped and gasped.

"The right kind of danger." His voice was very low, almost a growl. "You're right. Come around to the front."

"Only if you believe I want you exactly as you are." Her voice was shaking, jittery. She too was trembling.

"I believe you."

She slipped around to the front. His eyes were back to their usual hazel. It was a beautiful shade. But she had little time to admire it, because he caught her by the shoulders and stood, pulling her to her feet. Then they were kissing with a passion so fierce it struck her like a tidal wave. She couldn't believe she'd managed to draw it out so long before. Where had that patience come from? She had absolutely none now.

He ran one hand down her side in a possessive gesture, then lifted her off her feet. She wrapped her legs around his hips and sank into his welcome hardness. His wings wrapped around her as he thrust, a living robe of black velvet.

"Fen," he growled. "You're mine."

"Always," she managed to gasp. "Always, Carter."

And then she was lifted again by a rush of ecstasy. She was weightless. She was flying. She was loved.

CHAPTER 29

Carter held Fen close, marveling. For the first time in a while, he felt lucky—eyes and claws and wings and all. He still wanted his body back the way it had been. All else aside, the wings were almost impossible to hide in public. But against all odds, he had the love and acceptance of the most amazing woman in the world. Nothing could damp down that joy.

They showered and got dressed, enjoying every moment of each other's company, then returned to the living room. He lay on the sofa, his wings draping down to the floor, and Fen snuggled up beside him.

"So," he said. "About Balin. After you left, I was going to summon him and agree to be his Dark Knight so Eunice would fix me, then go back on it later. But there's a couple problems with that. One is that it's just kicking the can down the road. The other is that some of my teammates tried that too, but the wizard-scientist told them to prove their commitment by killing someone."

"What about a different sort of trick?" Fen suggested. "Kerenza told us you were a special case and her powder might not work on you. But it worked on Norris. I bet her antifreeze charm will work on the Defenders—and their non-shifter mates. Could you give everyone their charms, summon Balin, have the non-shifters jump Eunice so she's distracted, have the shifters jump Balin, tie them up or something so they can't mess with us, and threaten Eunice till she fixes you?"

He bit his lip. "Were you including yourself in the non-shifters who attack a gargoyle?"

She rolled her eyes. "Yes, of course. I could bean her with a rock if I didn't have to worry about Balin. Dali's a Navy vet, so she can fight, and Tirzah could operate an attack drone. We could take her."

Carter's chest was hot and tight with pride. His Fen was planning to take on a gargoyle with a rock! And, admittedly, some very formidable backup. Much as he hated to imagine her charging into danger, he loved how brave and smart she was.

"It's a good plan. Balin kicked our asses last time without breaking a sweat, so it should take him by surprise when he can't do it again. And Roland and Natalie can fly. If Balin's surprised and Eunice is distracted, they can go straight for her and take her out."

"You might be able to fly, too," Fen pointed out.

That hadn't occurred to him until she mentioned it. Slowly, he said, "You're right, I might. Actually, I've sometimes managed to get monst—animal forms that can fly. Though not very well."

She stretched like a cat, rubbing against him in a way that made him want to replay the last hour or so, immediately. "Shall we go back, then?"

Reluctantly, he nodded. "Yeah. The sooner we do this, the better. God knows what sort of animal parts I could get next."

"Maybe you'll get the ability to change color all over," she suggested with a wicked smirk. "I could have myself a dick of many colors."

"For you, I'd do it. What color do you want? A nice bright blue?"

"Good for the times when we want to role-play abducted human and sexy alien," she said, her grin widening. "Or silver, for human scientist and the sexy robot she built."

"I can see you've devoted a lot of thought to this."

Unabashed, she went on, "Green, for elf maiden and sexy orc. Bronze, for virgin sacrifice and sexy dragon. Red, for repressed woman and sexy demon. White, for naïve nun and sexy angel."

"This could replace the Pantone color scale," Carter remarked. "Sexy alien blue, sexy robot silver, sexy orc green, sexy dragon bronze, sexy demon red, sexy angel white… How about gold?"

"Priestess and sexy sun god," Fen said immediately.

"Gray?"

"Human hiker and sexy werewolf."

"Orange?"

There was a long silence.

Carter suggested, "Sexy traffic cone?"

"Okay, we're leaving now," said Fen, sitting up.

He followed suit, absently reaching out to turn off the lamp on a side table. He'd designed it to change colors and brightness with a touch. But the instant his fingers connected with it, the bulb flared up in a brilliant white flash, then began pulsing through its entire range of colors set at their maximum brightness, like a disco club run by Lisa Frank.

"I can't believe you were thinking of summoning Balin here," Fen remarked. "I know you weren't planning on a fight, but can you think of a worse place for you if it came to that? The whole place would explode around your ears!"

"Yeah, yeah, I know. Not one of my brighter moments."

She caught his hand and kissed it. As always, her touch sent sparks dancing up and down his spine. "You weren't in the best frame of mind."

"True." He paused at the door, reaching for his phone. "I'll call the office and tell them what's going on. Roland can help us flesh out our plan. He's the strategy guy."

His coat pocket sagged, suddenly heavy. Carter knew what had happened even before his fingers touched a cell phone that was colder and rougher than it ought to be. He instinctively stepped in front of Fen, trying to shield her.

Useless, he thought bitterly. *I don't even know whether Balin and Eunice are at the front door or the back door or flapping around the roof.*

"Carter?"

He held up the stone rectangle that his cell phone had become. "They're here."

"What?" Fen said indignantly. "They were supposed to wait till you summoned them." She looked up at the ceiling and screamed at the top of her lungs. "LIAAAAAAAAAAARS!!!!"

Though his heart was racing, Carter couldn't help smiling. "I love you so much."

"Same." She held out her hand. "Give me that."

"The phone? It's a rock—oh." He handed it to her. "Knock yourself out."

Fen pocketed it, then glanced around, looking for something else to throw. Catching his eye, she jerked her chin in the direction of the kitchen, held up her hand to indicate that he should stay where he was, and took a step toward it. He wondered if the Girl Scouts had taught her to throw knives. At this point he wouldn't put it past them.

"Welcome, guests," announced Jeeves.

"Goddammit," Carter muttered, and once again stepped in front of Fen.

The front door swung open. To his utter lack of surprise, Balin and Eunice came in.

"Nice place you got here," said Eunice with a smirk. "Very friendly."

"Greetings, Dark Knight," said Balin. "Are you ready to hear my offer?"

"What happened to him summoning you?" Fen demanded.

Carter, desperate to get her out of the line of fire, gave her a shove toward the kitchen. "Go make some coffee. We have guests!"

Her eyebrows shot up, then she nodded. "Yeah. Sure. I'll go do that."

"The female stays here," said Balin. "She is a crucial part of the negotiations."

A hostage, you mean. Carter's chest felt like a solid block of ice.

"How do you like your new body parts?" Eunice inquired.

"I don't," Carter said through gritted teeth. "I was going to summon you anyway. I want you to fix me, and I'm willing to pay."

Balin smiled. "Excellent. I see you're ready now to hear my complete offer. If I'd told you what it was earlier, you wouldn't have believed me."

"I believe you now." Carter tried as hard as he could not to sound sarcastic. He *did* believe Balin. "You can restore me to my original body and you can get rid of my monsters. Great. I'll take it."

"Oh, but that's not all." Balin's smile widened. "Here's the part you don't already know. Your snow leopard isn't dead."

Carter's heart seemed to stop, then re-started with a jolt. "What?"

As if Balin was talking to a slow child, he repeated, "Your snow leopard isn't dead. He is still within you. Crowded out. Damaged. Traumatized. But still living. If you join with me, he can be restored to you."

"I don't believe you. My snow leopard is dead."

Eunice spoke up. "You know he isn't, or you'd have destroyed your monsters yourself. You know it can be done."

"What, by drinking enough tincture of shiftsilver to kill them? That much would kill me too!"

"You know that's not true," said Eunice placidly. "You're strong enough to survive it. You're afraid that if you did that, it would kill your snow leopard along with them, if he's still alive deep down."

Carter's ears rang. His hands felt numb. Everything felt unreal, as if he'd stepped into a nightmare. Nothing they said was new to him. They were all ideas he'd had, but found so disturbing that he'd tried his best to never think of them again. If he let himself hope that his snow leopard was alive and it turned out that he'd been dead all along, it would destroy him. And if he tried to kill his monsters and murdered his snow leopard along with them, he'd rather be dead.

"It's not true." He didn't even recognize his own voice.

"It is," Balin said calmly. "You know it is."

Carter didn't know what to think. Desperately, he grasped at his original plan of playing along, of accepting Balin's offer and betraying him later. "Yes. All right. Fix me, kill the monsters, and bring back my snow leopard, and I'll be your Dark Knight."

The wizard-scientist tut-tutted. With a condescending air that made Carter want to punch him in the face, he said, "You haven't even asked what being my Dark Knight means."

Carter couldn't stop his eyes from rolling or keep the sarcasm out of his voice. "So what does it mean? Other than working for you."

"It means that my enemies become your enemies." Balin's demeanor was abruptly chilly, so much so that it felt like the air in the room dropped several degrees. "Such as the failed Dark Knights, their mates, and their leader. I will require proof. What kind of fool do you take me for? Eunice can restore you and your snow leopard, and I can heal the other damage Apex caused you. I can fix everything. But at a cost."

"I'll pay any—"

Balin cut him off. "No. I want you to think about it. I will give you one hour. Spend it imagining what it would be like to have your body back, to have your snow leopard back, to have your self-confidence and pride back. To shift without pain. To be a beautiful, agile creature. To touch your beloved machinery without having it explode in your hands—yes, I can change that too. I can turn back time for you, Carter Howe. I can make you be what you were if you had never encountered Apex. How much do you want that?"

More than anything, Carter thought, his throat tightening. He wanted it so much that even thinking of it was unbearable. But as Balin had spoken, he hadn't been able to help imagining it all.

The front door swung open.

As the wizard-scientists began to step out, Balin glanced over his shoulder. "One more thing. I have no intention of asking you to harm the female, as my idiotic colleagues demanded. She has no part in this battle, so she's not part of the price."

The door closed behind them.

Carter sat down heavily on the sofa. He was immediately forced to lean forward, because of his wings.

Those could go away. I could have my body back.

He tried to push that thought away.

If I say no, it'll get even worse. There's a limit to how much even Fen will think is hot. Wonder what her breaking point will be…

He felt like a terrible person for even thinking that. Fiercely, he tried to squelch that thought too.

My snow leopard. I could get him back. The friend who was with me for my entire life. The joy and freedom of leaping in the snow. I'm only half myself without him.

"No!" Carter said aloud. "I can't. I can't."

Fen put her arms around him. He hadn't even realized she'd sat down beside him. "Oh, Carter. This is so hard."

Balin won't hurt Fen. He doesn't care about her. I could have her and *my snow leopard* and *my real body* and *peace in my own mind…*

"Original plan," said Carter, whispering in her ear in case they were listening. His voice sounded tinny and false. "I'll say yes. The Defenders aren't here, so Balin will have to send me out to attack them. We'll team up to attack him instead. That's all."

"Um." Fen was also whispering. "Don't you think he's thought of that?"

"Probably, but what else can I do?" Carter whispered back. "At least it'll get him off my back for now."

And then I turn into a monster, bit by bit. Can I really let that happen to me?

"Will it, though?" Fen whispered. "He's obviously put a lot of thought into it. I don't think he'll do anything for you until he sees you do something for him."

"What if I said yes, and I did attack the Defenders? I could let them hurt me some, and maybe scratch them up a bit, just to make it convincing."

He felt Fen go still beside him.

"What?" he said defensively. "I'm not saying I'd really hurt them. You don't think I would… Do you?"

"I think Balin's setting you up to think exactly like this," she whispered.

"I think he's led you to a slippery slope and given you a nice big push."

Anger flared up in him. After all she'd said, she still didn't trust him. She still thought he was a monster—

No! The inner chorus of beasts was unified, for once. *Fen loves you. She trusts you. She's looking out for you.*

That was the one thing his beasts had always agreed on: they liked Fen.

We love *Fen,* they corrected. *We trust Fen. Listen to her.*

How bad could they really be, if they loved Fen? Sure, they were frustrating and difficult and annoying, but…

I'm frustrating and difficult and annoying, he thought. *And Fen loves me anyway.*

"You're right," said Carter. "It's a set-up. I'd go in intending to pretend to attack them, and Balin would cast some spell to throw off my aim or make me bite down a little too hard. I can't risk it."

She gave a sharp nod, her dark eyes intent on him. "So, what next?"

"Welcome, guests," said Jeeves.

The front door opened, and Eunice and Balin came back in.

"Time's up," said Balin.

"That was not even close to an hour," said Fen, aggravated. "You two are the worst!"

"Silence, female," snapped Balin. "What do you say, Dark Knight? Join with me and gain your heart's desire? Or be a monster in the company of monsters?"

"They're not monsters." Carter could hardly believe those words were coming out of his mouth. "They're a part of me. I didn't choose them, but I didn't choose my snow leopard either. And they love Fen, so I guess I love them too. A bit."

"Are you telling me you're turning me down?" Balin sounded so outraged that it was almost comical.

"That's right," Carter said with satisfaction. "I'm telling you to take your Dark Knighthood and shove it up your scrawny ass."

Balin's jaw dropped, making his scraggly gray beard waggle. Then, enraged, he raised his hands.

Carter didn't wait around to find out what spell he was going to cast. He grabbed Fen's hand and bolted into the kitchen. Slamming the door behind him, he shouted, "Jeeves! Lock the door!"

He'd finished speaking before he realized what a horrible mistake he'd made. He waited for the door to explode or the lights to go out or—

"It's already locked," replied Jeeves.

Carter's hand was still on the door. He hadn't needed Jeeves to tell him it was locked; he could feel it, the same way he could feel Fen pulling out of his grip. When she ran to the knife block and started taking knives out of it, discarding the bread knife and selecting the chef's knife and the filleting knife, he could feel that, too.

He'd modified the knife block to make it childproof, putting in a locking function that made him and the caretaker the only ones who could remove the knives. But when he'd seen Fen go for it, he'd wanted her to get all the knives she wanted. That intention had traveled from his mind to his hands to the door to the floor to the counter to the knife block, quick as thought. It had happened so naturally that, like the door locking, he'd only realized he'd done it in retrospect.

His senses spread throughout the house. Wherever there were cameras, he could see. Wherever there were microphones, he could hear. He felt Balin and Eunice's feet on the temperature-controlled floor, and heard their shrieks as he heated the part beneath their feet until their shoes began to melt.

"GET OUT!" His voice boomed through the speakers.

They ran for the door. It swung open before them. His teeth bared in a fierce grin as he made it hit their asses on the way out.

Through the lenses of the security cameras, he watched Eunice shift into her gargoyle form, grab Balin under the armpits, and flap off with him. A moment later, they vanished into the clouds.

"Carter?"

It was Fen's voice, echoing strangely as he heard it with both his own ears and the microphones in the room. When he turned to look at her, he saw her with the double vision of his own eyes and the kitchen cameras. She stood fierce and fearless, gripping a chef's knife in her right hand and a filleting knife in her left, ready to defend him. Sugar was perched on her shoulder, his tiny teeth bared.

The doubled sensory inputs made his head ache. He took his hand off the wall. With the loss of contact of his bare palm to the house, his control and sense of it instantly cut off. The next thing he knew, he'd sat down hard on the floor, disoriented and dizzy.

Fen put down the knives, grabbed his shoulders, and peered into his eyes. "Carter! What happened? Are you okay?"

Her touch restored his strength and cleared his head. "Yeah. I'm fine. I'm better than fine. Look."

He got to his feet, swaying slightly, and touched the wall with his index finger. This time he tried to limit his sphere of influence to the one thing he wanted to do. The machinery and electronics of the house obeyed him like his own hands obeyed him. A hidden panel slid aside, revealing a bank of monitors.

"Is that safe?" Fen asked. "They're not going to explode?"

"Nope." He still had the doubled vision, so he tried mentally cutting himself off from it, imagining his finger as a closed eye. It worked. Now he had control, but only saw with his human eyes. "This isn't a touch-pad control panel you could use. Well—I could build it for you, if you liked. But I'm doing it myself. It's like the house is part of my body. I can see through the cameras. I can hear through the microphones. I can feel the people inside it. And it does what I want. All I have to do is touch it."

"Whoa."

"Whoa, indeed." He began to laugh, giddy with happiness and relief. "Watch this. I did this!"

He made the monitors replay exactly what he'd done to Balin and Eunice. When the door hit them on the ass on their way out, Fen burst out laughing. He could hear the giddy note in her laugh too, but also her delight and amusement and relief.

"Amazing! How did it happen?"

"I think it's the power I was always supposed to have," Carter said slowly, thinking it through as he spoke. "Except for Roland, the other Defenders have two special powers, apart from shapeshifting. So do the other shifters who were created by Apex. I always assumed I didn't have any powers because they'd screwed up with me in general. But in retrospect, I think electronic and mechanical things exploding around me or when I touched them was my power trying to work. I just didn't get the hang of it until now."

"Why now, I wonder," mused Fen.

He began to shrug, but his inner beasts spoke up in that strange choral voice they'd been using lately.

Because of us.

Because you accepted us.

Because you love us.

He repeated that to Fen, adding aloud, "Were you stopping me before because you were mad at me?"

You were stopping us *before.*

Once again, he repeated their words, adding, "They sound really different now. More unified. They're all talking at the same time, but they're saying the same thing. Like a chorus instead of a howling mob."

"I wonder what would happen now if you shifted," she mused. "Think it'd go better?"

Despite everything, he still flinched at the idea. "Maybe. I can't say I'm dying to try. Anyway, we have to get out of here. There's no communications—Eunice turned every single thing we could use to get a message out into stone. I could feel it when I was in touch with the whole house."

"Right." She gave a brisk nod. "Let's go straight to the Defenders. Our original plan is still viable—in fact, it's even better now that you have a new power!"

He took her hand, then caught her in his arms and kissed her. "There is no one like you for distilling an impossible, hopeless disaster into a solvable problem. It's what makes you such a genius businesswoman. And battle strategist, apparently."

She grinned up at him, light dancing in her eyes. "Need to market a coffeemaker or defeat a magical enemy? Call Fen Kim!"

He couldn't resist trailing his hand against the walls as they left, making the doors open for them and the lights go out behind them without saying a word.

"You're loving this," she said as the front door closed behind them.

"I am," he admitted. "What I'd really like to do is fly a plane like this. I bet it'd be amazing."

"You should do it. Take me."

"I will," he promised, then eyed the car speculatively. "I could push the driver's seat way back and still drive it. I wouldn't even need to touch the steering wheel."

"You should though, just in case we pass a cop. But do it! It'll be fun."

"Just a little way," he said, but his fingers were practically itching at the idea. "It was pretty tiring to do all that stuff in the house. I don't know how a long drive would go."

"I expect you have to work up to it," she said, circling around to the passenger seat. "Everything gets easier when you practice."

"Where's Precious? I thought she was flying around out here." He whistled. "Precious! We're taking off!"

The golden dragonette arrowed out of the cloud cover, shrilling an urgent warning. As he raised his forearm for her to land on, a gargoyle followed her. It was Eunice, carrying Balin. She set him down and gave a harsh laugh like gravel grinding. The car turned to stone.

Carter grabbed Fen's wrist and turned to bolt back into the house. A wall of stone rose up around it, blocking their way. They were forced to skid to a halt before they collided with it.

Eunice laughed again, then rose up, her black wings flapping. She soared up into the clouds and was gone.

Fen turned to Carter. "Can you, I don't know, dissolve it or something?"

He doubted it, but he touched the wall, just in case. It was only stone, cold and rough beneath his hand. He shook his head. "Seems like it only works on electronic and mechanical things."

"So your power flows freely," mused Balin. "You are all the more precious now, Dark Knight."

Carter turned to Balin. "Give it up. I already said no. I'm not going to change my mind."

"Yes, you are," the wizard-scientist snapped. "No more games. You can join me as the Dark Knight Pride, or else. Choose now!"

"Or else what?" Carter asked warily.

There was a crack like a gunshot as the wall of stone cracked. A piece of rock the size of a television fell off right above Fen. Carter instantly shoved her aside.

As the rock smashed into the ground where Fen had stood, Eunice swooped down. She seized Fen around the chest, clamping her arms against her sides. Carter lunged at them, but he'd pushed Fen too far away from him and Eunice was very quick. His reaching fingers closed on air as Eunice flew up into the sky, holding Fen tight. Fen kicked and struggled, but the gargoyle was far bigger and stronger than her, and had tough and leathery skin.

"Or else your treasured female takes a fall from a height," said Balin, with relish. "If you want her to live, you must pledge yourself to my service. And by the way, I can tell if you're lying. If you make the pledge meaning to go back on it later, I'll have Eunice drop her."

Carter had never in his life been filled with such a mixture of fear and rage, not even in his year at Apex. But another emotion rose up to swamp it, and that was love. He loved Fen too much to let her die, and too much to do anything that would make her unhappy. She'd be furious if he joined the dark side, even to save her life. And she'd be furious if he didn't have the faith in himself that she had in him.

She believed he was fine exactly the way he was. If he couldn't believe that too, then he wasn't worthy of her.

Carter flung off his coat. His black wings opened, and he leaped into the air.

He moved so quickly that he took both Balin and Eunice by surprise. He took himself by surprise, too. He'd had no idea if his wings were strong enough to lift him. They were not only strong, but quick and agile. Before either of his enemies could react, he was upon Eunice, slashing at her with his claws. Her skin was tough, but not enough to withstand the sharpness of his claws.

With a shriek of pain, the gargoyle loosened her grip on Fen and swiped at him with her talons. Fen instantly took advantage of that, wrenching one arm free and bashing the gargoyle across the face with the stone cell phone. Eunice let out another yell of pain.

Carter caught Fen around the waist and wrested her free. Eunice made a grab at her, but Carter kicked the leathery creature hard in the solar plexus. The gargoyle began to spiral downward, the breath knocked out of her.

His batlike wings beating the air, Carter began to fly down from the mountain. Fen was warm in his arms. Sugar clung to Fen's blouse, chittering excitedly. Precious had again disappeared, but Carter figured she was probably spying on their enemies.

"Still hate the wings?" Fen asked when she'd gotten her breath back.

"Not so much now," he admitted. "The claws, too. They did come in handy."

"I wish I'd taken the knives with me," Fen said. "I totally forgot about them."

"You didn't need them. The rock was plenty."

Her dark eyes gleamed. "I still have it."

"Good," he said grimly. "Because I don't think we're done yet."

A familiar shriek sounded. It was Precious, angry and frightened. Carter looked up and saw her flying faster than she ever had before. She was pursued by a beast so weird and huge that he could barely comprehend what he was seeing.

The creature was like a pterodactyl but far bigger, with disturbingly human-like hands at the joints of its immense leathery wings. Its beak was long as a car and needle-sharp, and both the hands and the hind feet had cruel hooked talons. It screeched as it flew, and it was coming fast. The weird beast would overtake them in a moment.

Carter veered off, flying back toward the mountain. If he could reach the woods, he could at least drop Fen off there, where the thing would have trouble getting to her due to its sheer size.

"Is that Balin's shift form?" Fen gasped.

"Must be," said Carter.

"What the hell is it?"

"Got me."

The Balin-beast whipped a wing forward, striking at them. Carter folded his wings and dropped like a stone, evading the blow, then unfolded them and darted into the woods.

He landed hard, stumbling against a big oak, and hurriedly put Fen down. "Run."

"No!" She was clearly ready to stand up to that immense and vicious creature with nothing but a rock that had once been a cell phone.

But Balin was already crashing through the woods, breaking small trees and shaking big ones.

Carter snatched the bag of amulets from his pocket, thrust them into her hands, and gave her a push. "Do it! Get to the road, flag down a car, and call the Defenders. It's our only chance. I'll hold him off."

"Don't you dare get yourself killed," she ordered. Then she turned and dashed through the trees.

Carter turned to face Balin. He had no real hope that Fen would find the road any time soon, let alone see a car on it. And even if she did, the Defenders were at least an hour away. He'd kill Balin or he'd be killed by him. There was no other way this could go.

If he does kill me, though, Carter thought, *I'm taking him with me.*

It was the only way to protect Fen. And that was the only thing he cared about.

We'll protect Fen, his inner animals agreed. *Let us at him!*

Carter was comforted by their love for her and their eagerness to do battle to protect her. It really did make him love them. Maybe they were monsters, but they were *his* monsters. And it would take a monster to fight something like Balin.

Be big and fierce and winged, he thought. *I don't care what you look like, and I don't care how much it hurts. Just be something that can fight Balin and win.*

Carter shifted.

CHAPTER 30

Fen ran through the woods. Not for the first time, she vowed that the next time she went anywhere with Carter, she'd bring along a pair of practical running shoes. Her high heels kept catching up on lumps and hollows and fallen branches. Behind her, she could hear the horrible beast that was Balin crashing and screeching.

What Carter had said had been logical. There really was nothing she could do to help him fight that beast. They really did need help. But she also knew perfectly well that he was sending her out of danger so he could put his own body between her and the real monster.

She didn't even know if she was running in the right direction, or how far she was from the road. She gripped the stone cell phone as she ran, wishing Balin was in front of her. She'd like to bash him over the head with it. If she could even reach his head.

"Hey!"

Instinctively, she hurled the cell phone. Even as it left her hand, she wished she could take the action back. The person who had burst out from behind the tree wasn't Balin or Eunice, but Merlin. And she'd just flung a rock at his head.

He vanished a split second before the rock would have hit his forehead. The rock slammed into a tree, knocking off a shower of bark.

"Sorry!" Fen gasped.

The hamster-sized velociraptor that Merlin had become grew to a Merlin-sized velociraptor, then became Merlin again.

"Good aim," he said admiringly. "Where's Carter?"

"Back that way. How do you know he was in trouble?" She cut herself off. "Never mind. He needs help."

Other people were dashing through the forest. Natalie arrived first, her rainbow hair bright even in the shade, followed by Ransom with his lean runner's frame. The more muscular and heavier Pete and Roland came behind them. To Fen's surprise, a gasping, sweaty Norris was trailing behind them.

"What are you doing—" Fen began, then again stopped herself. She could get explanations later. Hurriedly, she said, "Balin turned into some gigantic I don't even know what, but it has wings and a beak and hands and it's huge. Eunice is somewhere around here too." She shoved the zip-lock bag at Roland. "All of you, take one of these. It'll stop Balin from freezing you. But it won't stop Eunice from taking over your inner animal, so watch out for her!"

She didn't wait for questions. Beckoning, she turned and bolted back the way she'd come. The Defenders and Norris followed. Soon they emerged from the woods and stood on the side of the mountain, with a perfect view of the aerial battle in progress.

At first all she could see was the weird beast that was Balin. He was so huge that he blocked the view of his opponent. Balin flapped and screeched, stabbing at something with his enormous sharp beak.

A winged form darted upward into the sky, escaping his attack. It was Carter. Fen knew that instantly. But it was a Carter like none she had ever seen before.

He was beautiful, a lithe winged beast that turned and twisted in the air with astonishing grace.

His snow leopard is back, Fen thought. *And it has wings!*

At first glimpse, Carter's new shift form did look like a snow leopard with white feathered wings. But as she looked at him longer, she realized that there was more to him than that. His paws and tail didn't look quite catlike, and there was something else strange about him that she could sense but not identify.

Balin twisted to attack him, and the beautiful beast that Carter had become opened his jaws wide and breathed out flame.

The huge beaked creature shrieked in pain and dove downward. Carter pursued him, sending bursts of flame after him.

Fen watched the fight, her heart pounding. As much as she was afraid for Carter, she was filled with joy watching him in his new form. He moved with astonishing grace, agility, and power, as at home in this new body as in his own. His every movement seem to rejoice in it.

"Is that Carter?" Pete asked.

"Yes," said Ransom, before Fen could reply.

The two Defenders who could fly were already transforming. Natalie's slim frame shifted to that of a great white hound with white wings and eyes like pieces of sky. Roland spread out his arms as if in invocation. Fire blossomed from his palms, sheathed his forearms like gauntlets, and clothed his body like living armor. The next moment, he was a bird made of pure flame. The Gabriel hound and the phoenix launched off the side of the mountain and joined the fray.

But Balin was so big that he rapidly outdistanced them all. He left them behind, then drove back upward, toward the side of the mountain where Fen stood. Merlin and Pete instantly moved to protect her, Pete becoming a great shaggy cave bear and Merlin becoming a twelve-foot velociraptor. Norris gave them a doubtful glance, then became a Dunkleosteus.

Fen hurriedly stepped back to avoid getting squashed. Balin screeched and dove to the side, knocking over a tree with a swipe of his vast wing. Everyone jumped aside.

Balin transformed back into a man, landing lightly on the mountainside.

"Piscine fool," he sneered at Norris. "You'll drown on dry land."

Norris shifted back human form. "No, I won't."

Balin stared at him. "How—"

Before he could finish his sentence, Merlin and Pete charged him. The wizard-scientist made a quick gesture, then looked alarmed when nothing happened. He hurriedly shifted and leaped back into the air. The aerial battle between Balin and the three Defenders resumed.

From the corner of her eye, Fen caught a movement above. A shadow with a familiar shape was amongst the clouds.

"EUNICE!" Fen screamed at the top of her lungs. "DEFENDERS, RUN!"

Pete swung around and rushed back into the forest, his bare paws thudding as they hit the ground. Merlin leapt after him, flying through the air like an acrobat. Norris fled after them. Roland and Natalie also broke off the fight, flying away as fast as they could. They vanished into the cloud cover.

Fen stood alone on the mountainside, as Carter was alone in the air.

It had to be that way. If they'd stayed, Eunice would seize control of them and force them to attack her and Carter. But now the odds had turned against them.

Eunice dove down from the clouds with an angry screech, flying to join Balin.

Carter was once again alone in the air, facing off against two foes. His tail lashed, and the claws of his great paws flexed. They were very big, like the talons of a bird of prey. His tail too seemed unusually long. But none of him looked disproportionate or malformed. He was perfect. He was just different.

He and Eunice flew straight at Carter, coming from opposite directions. He couldn't breathe fire at both of them at once.

"Carter!" Fen yelled. "You're beautiful! Get them! You can do it!"

Carter's jaws opened, and he gave a cry like a crystal bugle.

But he made no move to evade the attack. He waited, his wings flapping hard, hovering. Fen watched in an agony of anticipation. Balin and Eunice were almost upon him.

And then he vanished.

Balin and Eunice collided in mid-air.

There was a tremendous crash. The gargoyle shattered into a million little pieces of black rock, and fell from the sky like hail. Balin shrieked, thrashing as if he'd forgotten how to fly, turning this way and that in surprise and confusion.

Fen spotted something above him. It was very hard to see because it was the exact color of the sky, all the way down to the clouds, but it had the shape of a great winged cat. The sky-colored beast that Carter had become dropped down, fire exploding from his jaws at point blank range.

Balin was engulfed in a gigantic fireball. He didn't even have time to scream. A cloud of smoke filled the place where he had been. A moment later, ash began to gently drift down from the sky.

CHAPTER 31

Carter flew away from the cloud of smoke and ash that was all that was left of Balin.

His keen eagle's eyes could see Fen, alone and brave on the mountainside, in as much detail as if she was close enough to touch. Her hair was rumpled, her makeup was smeared, her clothes were torn, and one of her shoes had a heel broken off. But her imperfections and messiness and flaws were what made her beautiful. His Fen could scream like a banshee and murmur like a femme fatale. She could slam the door on her own parents and open her heart to a man like himself, flawed and messy and imperfect.

Imperfect but whole, said his inner chimera. A lovely shade of blue, the color of a cloudless summer sky, accompanied the voice. It was the color of happiness.

That inner voice was no longer a chorus. Like his inner animal, it had united as an imperfect but beautiful whole. His shifted body no longer felt wrong. It was different, but it had a feeling of rightness to it. And it was wonderful to be able to fly.

Carter spiraled downward out of the sky, glorying in every flap of his powerful wings. He landed by Fen with the lightness and precision of a leaping snow leopard, and lifted his head to nuzzle her.

Delighted, she stretched out her hand and stroked his fur. "It's so soft!"

She scratched behind his ears until his chest began to vibrate. It was a feeling he'd always loved and had thought he'd never experience again. He was purring.

Fen walked all around him, admiring and exclaiming at his chimera form. She stroked his wing feathers, complimented his talons for their sharpness, and praised his eagle eyes.

"Guess you won't be getting any less vain," remarked Pete, emerging from the forest in his human form.

Carter spread his vast wings in an admire-me gesture, accidentally-on-purpose whacking Pete in the face with his primary feathers.

Natalie landed neatly in her Gabriel hound form, then shifted back to being a rainbow-haired woman. "His wings *are* very pretty, Pete. Almost as pretty as mine."

"I don't know if I'd go that far," said Ransom, walking out of the forest. "But they're definitely an improvement over the cryodrakon's."

"The what?" Pete asked.

"Balin," said Merlin as he came out from behind a tree. "His shift form was a cryodrakon boreas. It's one of the largest flying dinosaurs."

"You *would* know that," remarked Pete. "I suppose you had one at the circus."

"No, but once I realized that dinosaur shifters existed, I started reading up on them," Merlin explained. "I mean on dinosaurs. Not on dinosaur shifters. I *wish* I could read up on dinosaur shifters. Someone should write a book."

Norris emerged from the woods. "Wow. That is an extremely, extremely cool shift form. Not quite as cool as a Dunkleosteus, but…"

Fire streaked across the sky as the phoenix returned. Roland landed away from everyone else, but the heat of his passage still struck Carter like a blow. He was a bird of fire, too bright to look at directly; he was a man haloed in flame, like a fiery angel; he was Roland, their leader, who had always believed in him no matter how hard Carter had made it.

"Welcome back, Carter," said Roland. "Welcome, chimera."

"Chimera?" Pete said. "He's a griffin, right? Half eagle, half snow leopard?"

"A sniffin," Natalie suggested.

Carter was so indignant that he shifted on the spot. Another benefit of now being a mythic shifter was that his clothes shifted with him, so he could launch right into the argument without having to get dressed first. "Roland's right. I'm a chimera—a beast made of many animals joined together. My chimera has the head and body of a snow leopard, the eyes and wings of an eagle, the talons and ability to breathe fire of a dragon, the sense of smell and hearing of a wolf, the prehensile tail of a monkey, and the camouflage ability of an octopus."

"Very impressive," remarked Roland.

"Poor monkey," said Natalie. "It only got the tail."

"A prehensile tail is very useful," said Merlin. "And fun! I assume. I can't dangle from my tail. I've tried."

"Of course you have," said Pete.

"Carter's chimera is magnificent. And deadly. And beautiful," said Fen. "And he purrs when you scratch behind his ears."

Carter gave a jerk of his hand, trying to cut her off, but it was too late. The other Defenders instantly seized upon it.

"Just like Batcat," remarked Pete.

"Awww," said Merlin. "It's so cute when big cats purr."

"Did you try skritching his floofy belly?" Natalie inquired. "The circus tigers all loved that."

"I was going to make over a room so Carter could have his own office," said Roland, his expression completely deadpan. "I could add some carpet to the wall. I don't think they make scratching posts big enough."

Fen was starting to glare at them, so Carter gave her a little head-shake. They were only teasing him because they knew it was longer a real sore spot. But he had to maintain his image, so he said, "You're all just jealous because you can't fly."

"I can fly," Natalie said.

"You're jealous because you can't breathe fire," said Fen.

"I can fly, and I *am* fire," said Roland.

"You're just jealous because you can't change colors," said Carter.

Roland raised his eyebrows, stepped back, and stretched out his arms. The flames that burst from his palms burned red, then orange, then white, and finally blue before they winked out.

"I didn't know you could do that," Carter said, intrigued.

Roland shrugged. "There's not much call for it. I don't normally need to make a fire hot enough to melt metal."

There was a brief silence. Carter wondered exactly how hot Roland's phoenix fire could burn.

Hotter than ours, said his inner chimera. *Much hotter. Hot enough to burn the world.*

Roland's expression was unassuming, but he had to know that himself. Even in his new body that was part dragon, Carter couldn't imagine what it must be like to have that kind of power contained within himself.

"How did you all know to come here, anyway?" Fen asked. "I was running to try to flag down a car and call the office, and I ran straight into Merlin."

"This is going to sound odd," said Roland. "But back at the office, things started falling out of thin air. Literally. A stone cell phone materialized in mid-air, fell on the coffee pot, and smashed it. Then Fen's driver's license."

"My driver's license?" Fen repeated, baffled. "But I have that with me. And I still had the stone cell phone when you got here—I threw it at Merlin."

Carter laughed. "Of course you did."

"Very accurately, too," Merlin put in. "Lucky thing I shrink fast."

Natalie snickered. "Not many men feel that way."

"But what about your own cell phone, Fen?" Carter asked. "Did that turn to stone too?"

"It must have. My purse suddenly weighed more. But I don't think it does now." Fen opened her purse and felt around. "It's gone." She took out her wallet. "My driver's license is gone too."

"It was obvious that someone was trying to tell us that Fen was under attack by a gargoyle," Merlin put in. "Carter put tracking devices on our phones and cars a while back, so we could look up where his phone was when it had stopped signaling. Then we came straight here."

"Almost straight here." Pete glowered at Norris. "We had an unscheduled stop."

"You didn't have to," Norris said defensively. "I was doing fine."

"No, you weren't," chorused the team.

"He was driving as a fish with a store mannequin sitting in the driver's seat," said Pete, glaring. "The first cop who wasn't literally sleeping on the job would've pulled him over."

"You tried," said Fen consolingly to Norris. "It was a clever idea... sort of."

It was one of the worst ideas Carter had ever heard, but he supposed it was clever compared to driving as a fish with nothing in the driver's seat.

"So we stopped him and suggested that he come with us," said Merlin smoothly. "Since he was very concerned about you both."

"And since we all knew if we didn't, he'd jump back in the tank the instant we left," grumbled Pete.

Norris ducked his head guiltily.

"Here you go." Roland handed Fen's her driver's license.

As she replaced it in her wallet, Sugar jumped out of her purse. He scuttled up her arm and clung to her shoulder, chittering softly.

"Sugar?" Fen asked. "Did you do that?"

Sugar gave a self-satisfied squeak and bumped her earring with his nose. It vanished, and in the same instant Carter felt a small, cool weight in his hand. He gave Fen her earring.

She put it back on and stroked Sugar. "Clever, clever boy. So *that's* what you do."

Precious gave an indignant trill. Carter hastily petted her. "You're clever too. Funny how that turned out. Precious can fetch things, and Sugar can send them away. They're a perfect match."

"Like us." Fen pulled him down for a kiss.

He wanted it to go on forever, and it more-or-less did. It was a very long moment of sheer heaven. Carter was barely aware of anything but Fen, the sweetness of his mouth, the softness of her skin, and the love that bound them. He only vaguely registered the Defenders and Norris fidgeting, glancing at their cell phones, and finally giving them a wave or a wink as they left.

Eventually, Fen glanced around. "Where'd everybody go?"

"Home, I assume. I think they felt like third wheels." Glancing around, he saw that someone had left a cheap burner phone under a tree. "Oh, that's considerate. I guess they left it in case we needed to call for a ride. But there's no need for that."

"No?" Fen arched an eyebrow. "Our car's a big rock."

"We don't need a car. I can fly."

"Oh, right! Carter, I'm so, so happy for you. How did you do it?"

"I did it because of you," he said simply. "Because everything you said to me finally got through my thick skull. My beasts always loved you, and that made me love them. All they ever needed to become the chimera was for me to accept them."

Not quite, said his chimera.

"Oh?" Carter said, adding to Fen, "He says, 'not quite.'"

We needed acceptance, said his chimera. *We needed love. And we needed our mate.*

"I knew it!" Carter exclaimed.

"Knew what?"

"That you're my mate."

She kissed him. "Of course I am. We don't need your chimera to tell us so."

"No, but it's nice. I kept wanting my snow leopard to tell me you were my mate. Not having that happen was a constant reminder that he was gone."

"Is he still? Or is he back now?"

"It's complicated," he replied, thinking it through as he spoke. "My chimera is what my snow leopard became—what all my beasts became."

"Like the way you're not who you were as a teenager, but you're still Carter?"

"A lot like that, actually. He's not gone. He's just different." He couldn't wait to see Fen's face when he told her the next part. "There's something else that's different, too. Remember when I said the rest of the Defenders have two powers—well, except for Roland?"

"Yeah, I do. What about him?"

"He only has one: his phoenix fire. No idea why. I used to think I didn't have any, but of course all those exploding microwaves and burnt-out robots and so forth were actually a misfiring power. So…"

"Oh!" Fen's face lit up. "Do you think you might have a second power, too?"

He smiled. "I know I do. I haven't tried it yet, but my chimera says I can do it. You're going to be the first person to see it. And I think you're going to like it."

"Ooh," she sang out, her tone half teasing and half genuinely excited. "Let's see!"

With a deliberately dramatic gesture, he took off his long black coat and draped it over a tree branch. Precious flew to the branch and perched on it, her delicate golden head cocked, her sapphire eyes bright with interest. Sugar leaped off Fen's shoulder and glided to the branch to perch beside the dragonette.

"You've got an audience," she remarked. "This better meet expectations."

"It will." He slowly unbuttoned his shirt, stretching out the drama.

"Is this a power demonstration or a strip-tease?" Fen inquired. "No complaints either way, mind."

He gave her an enigmatic smile as he draped his shirt over his coat, then turned so she could see his back.

Like shifting, his chimera coached him. *But more focused.*

Wings unfolded from his back. They were his white eagle's wings, but slightly smaller than they were in his chimera form, sized to lift his human body. He stepped away from the tree and beat them, lifting into the air. Fen gave a delighted gasp as he flew to her and landed lightly in front of her.

"Wings," she breathed. "Your power is wings!"

"Oh, it's more than that." He concentrated, and the white feathers darkened and then vanished. He stretched out his black dragon wings, letting her get a good look at them before he made them go away. Then he focused on his eyes, changing them to Cillian Murphy ice blue, then Elizabeth Taylor purple, and finally wolf yellow before he shifted back to his usual Carter hazel.

Fen laughed in delight. "And the color changing eyes!"

"And claws." He flexed his hands, extending dragon talons before making them vanish. "My only full shift form is the chimera you saw, but as a man, I have the power to get any animal feature that belongs to any of my original animals. Only one at a time, though."

"Does the color shifting work everywhere, or just your eyes?"

Carter grinned. He knew exactly what she was thinking. He concentrated, and watched his bare hands turn a deep, almost burnished gold.

She gave him a slow smile hot as dragonfire. "So bored housewife and sexy sun god is still a possibility. Excellent."

"I see we've started mixing and matching now."

Generously, she said, "Feel free to contribute your own ideas."

"If you don't mind going on pure imagination, no actual wings involved, I'm going to put in a vote for bored business executive and sexy demoness who offers him a deal."

"Deal," Fen purred.

CHAPTER 32

Carter returned his skin to its usual color. "Ready to fly?"

She was about to agree when it occurred to her that even in Refuge City, where it wasn't entirely unusual to see, say, a man dressed as a tree buying a double latte at Starbucks, the sight of a man flying with his own wings would attract unwanted attention. "How are you planning to stop paparazzi from filing stories about Carter Howe's new mechanical wings, and everyone complaining when they never appear in stores?"

He chuckled. "Good point. You can ride me—"

"Oh, I will," she put in.

"—in my chimera form. It has camouflage."

"I don't," Fen pointed out.

"We'll have to get you some flying outfits. Black for night flying. Blue for day flying. Mist gray for cloudy days."

She glanced down at her sadly torn outfit, which was mostly black. "Wait till nightfall, then?"

Carter looked thoughtful. "There's a place we could go right now where the only people who'll see us come in for a landing are shifters. It's a place I'd like to go to. And I think you'd like it too."

"Where?"

He didn't reply immediately, his expression both hopeful and wistful.

"My family home."

"Oh! Did you ever call and tell them what was going on with you?"

He shook his head. "I never got up the nerve. They left me some messages after our press conference, but I made sure to call them back when I knew they'd be asleep, so I could avoid having an actual conversation with them. But it's about time that I did."

"And you want to show off your chimera, right?"

Carter shot her a wry glance. "Actually, I want to show *you* off."

"And your chimera."

"And my chimera," he admitted.

Fen knew how much this had to mean to him. She wanted to support him, but the idea of visiting his family was a little nerve-wracking, considering how fabulously well it had gone when he'd visited hers. But that was her family. He'd said his was different. If he wasn't going to let himself be caught up in old fears, neither was she.

"Okay. Let's go meet your family."

His smile could have lit up the sky. "Oh, good. They're going to love you. I can't wait to introduce you. Just so you're prepared, they can be a bit overwhelming. But if you don't mind going to kind of a messy house and being swarmed by a whole lot of people who really do mean well…"

"As opposed to going to a house straight out of a magazine and not being swarmed by two very proper people who are also absolute assholes?" Fen inquired with some bitterness. "I think I can cope with some swarming."

"You deserve so much better than that. I hope someday you'll feel like my family is your family. If nothing else, I have a grandma who's a fantastic cook."

She abruptly realized that she was starving. "Sold."

Carter kissed her. "I can't wait to fly with you."

He took a step back and transformed into his beautiful chimera form. Fen had to take a moment to admire it anew. It was extraordinary. Magnificent. Unique. His snow-white wings made her understand why the eagle was America's national symbol, and his black-spotted coat was an irresistible temptation to touch. He stretched like a cat, his wings flaring, then turned and nuzzled her.

Fen settled herself on his back in front of those enormous wings. His body was slimmer than that of a horse, easier to grip with her thighs and knees. She leaned forward and locked her arms around his neck. His fur was so soft and velvety, and his body was warm.

His prehensile tail curled around her waist, holding her safely in place. It was covered with the same fur as his body, but unlike a cat's tail, it could grasp and hold.

"Excellent use of the tail," she told him. "I feel completely safe."

He made a soft sound of feline smugness, and his wings and fur turned to a beautiful sky-blue. His muscles tensed beneath her as he leaped into the air. She let out a gasp of excitement and delight.

Fen felt like she was in the world's greatest fairytale. She had a magnificent flying steed who was also her true love—her Prince Charming. Well, she amended with a smile, sometimes Carter could be Prince Cranky. But she didn't want him any other way.

They flew high in the sky, the world stretching out beneath them. His eagle's wings beat steadily, and sometimes he caught an updraft and glided. For the first time, she understood why people were obsessed with flying. She knew now why Carter had become a pilot. In the air, it felt as if you were in a beautiful dream, free from all worries and cares, high above it all.

And now they were sharing this wonderful thing together, as they would share everything together from now on. Fen bent down and pressed a kiss onto the top of Carter's velvety head. She felt the vibration as he began to purr.

After several hours of sheer glory, they reached a big ranch house nestled in a forest of cedar and pine. As the chimera began to spiral downward, his color changed from sky-blue back to his usual snow leopard's coat. Once he was low enough to be heard, he let out a distinctive rasping roar.

People began to run out of the house, and animals emerged from the woods. Carter took his time circling down, letting them get a good look at him. Fen waved at them all. By the time he landed, the gathered crowd consisted of six people (one holding a baby hedgehog), two snow leopards, and a baby elephant.

Once Fen climbed off his back, Carter folded his wings and shifted back into his human form.

"Hi, Mom! Hi, Dad! Hi, Grandma!" Carter raised his voice to be heard over the hubbub. "I'll explain everything! But for now, I want to introduce Fen Kim. She's my mate!"

The hubbub hit deafening levels. Everyone flung themselves on Carter and hugged him, then flung themselves on Fen and hugged her too. Even with Carter's warning, it *was* a little overwhelming. Especially since the snow leopards stood on their hind legs and flung their paws around her shoulders, nearly knocking her down

"Easy, easy," said Carter, steadying her. "Fen's not a shifter."

No one went easy. Carter finally grabbed one of the snow leopards by the scruff of its neck and said, "Emma! Take Fen inside and get her out of this madhouse and into some new clothes, will you?"

The snow leopard promptly transformed into a woman with black hair like Carter's, but tied back into a messy ponytail. Emma was stark naked, but neither she nor anyone else took any notice of that. She grabbed Fen's hand and hustled her inside. The living room had multiple coatracks scattered about, and Emma grabbed a bathrobe from one and tossed it on.

"Hi! I'm one of Carter's sisters," said Emma. She eyed Fen. "I don't know what Carter's done with you, but you obviously need new clothes. You look about my size, so I'll get you something of mine. It won't be as nice as yours. Sorry."

Before Fen could protest that she was sure Emma's clothes were just fine, she was getting hauled off at high speed. Emma kicked things out of the way as she went. Fen caught brief glimpses of flying toys, clothes, and pillows.

Next thing she knew, she was in a bedroom. It was furnished in a pleasant rustic style, and had a number of tools scattered randomly about, including a hammer on a pillow.

"What's your shoe size?" Emma asked.

"Seven."

Emma stuck her head out the door. "Riley! Fen needs shoes! High heels! Your nicest ones!"

"It's really not—" Fen began.

A woman's voice yelled, "What's her favorite color?"

"Honestly, anything—" Fen started to say.

"What's your favorite color?" Emma demanded.

Resigning herself, Fen said, "For shoes, black or red."

"Black or red!" Emma shrieked, then slammed the door. "Right! Let's get you some clothes. Normally we'd just offer you something from the stash—we have a stash of clothes in all sizes, in case anyone shifts unexpectedly and needs something—but they're all pretty basic, you know? And you should have something *elegant*. You obviously like elegant things. Riley's at least two sizes bigger than you, and I don't have your sense of style which is *awesome* by the way, loved the steampunk jacket at the press conference, but I can at least get you something that's not ripped to bits."

Before Fen could reply, Emma flung open her closet door, then began pulling out all her dresser drawers. "Take anything! Try it on!"

Emma's taste overall ran more to the practical than the pretty, but Fen found a nice black linen skirt and a cream-colored sweater. As she tried them on, Emma confided, "I'm not even going to ask what's up with Carter's shift form because I'm sure he'll want to tell all of us at once, but I just want to thank you for looking out for him. He looks so happy! He hasn't looked happy in years, since that awful thing happened to him. He can be so proud and annoying and closed-mouthed, so don't take any bullshit from him, but he is my brother and I love him. Does the skirt fit? I could try taking it in with safety pins."

Fen, slightly dazed, said, "No, the skirt's fine."

The door opened without knocking and another woman barged in. She was plump and very curvy, with her black hair in tumbling curls, and held a pair of high-heeled shoes in each hand. "Here you go! I have more if you don't mind them not being in your favorite colors. Hi, I'm Riley. Carter's sister."

"Pleased to meet you," said Fen, taking the shoes. "How many sisters does he have?"

"Four," said Riley. "All older. He's the baby. Zinnia and Ashley aren't here right now, but we've called them. They'll be here by dinner time."

"Four older sisters," said Fen thoughtfully. "You know, that explains a lot."

Riley and Emma laughed. Fen selected the red satin heels, and they praised her when she modeled them.

"I always knew Carter's mate would be something," said Riley. "You know how he is about never settling for anything less than the best. And here you are!"

"Well, I—" Fen began.

"Absolutely gorgeous," said Riley, looking her over.

"And brilliant," said Emma.

"A *very* successful businesswoman," put in Riley.

"And tough. Very tough," said Emma.

"She needs to be, to stand up to him," said Riley.

"And to think all the times he ranted about you at the dinner table!" Emma exclaimed. "Fenella Kim this and Fenella Kim that!"

"Fenella Kim is ruining my vacation!" Riley's voice was a hilariously apt imitation of Carter's.

"And here she is—his mate!"

His sisters burst out laughing.

"Well, come on," said Emma, wiping tears from her eyes. "You have to meet the rest of the family."

The next thing Fen knew, she was hauled out of the bedroom and back to the living room. Carter was sitting on the sofa, glass in hand, surrounded by the family. He was in the middle of a story, but as soon as Fen came out, everyone jumped up and introduced themselves. She met his mother, father, grandmother, two aunts, and a nephew, plus two foster kids (the elephant and the hedgehog.)

Every single one of them seemed absolutely thrilled to meet her, and kept promising that the rest of the family had been summoned and would be there soon. It was true. New family members kept arriving until the house was bursting at the seams, and then they were all settled down for a lavish and delicious dinner.

"Made with Little Bit appliances," said Carter's grandma, with a wink at Fen.

Carter heaved a long-suffering sigh for the benefit of his family, then winked at her too.

Dinner was a long and noisy affair, with multiple conversations going on at once. Everyone kept piling food on Fen's plate, congratulating her for putting up with Carter, and asking her questions about herself. Chatty as they were, they all seemed very interested in her, too. But she noticed they were carefully avoiding the topic of what exactly had happened to Carter to change his shift form. From the pointed looks, they weren't going to get into that until the younger kids were asleep.

Fen took the opportunity to keep up her end of the conversation by asking about Carter's childhood. He looked increasingly pained as his family recounted a number of hilarious and embarrassing stories. But they also told stories about how smart he was, how he'd stood up for bullied kids, and how impressed they were with his piloting, inventing, and business skills. They teased each other and pushed each other's buttons, but there was no malice in it. Whenever anyone looked like they might be on the verge of anger or hurt, they backed off.

As the parents went off to put their kids to bed, Fen thought, *This is what a family that loves each other looks like.*

Once the kids were tucked in, Carter began telling his story. It turned out that the Howes could be quiet when they wanted, and they let him talk with very few interruptions. Fen sat beside him and held his hand under the table. But he got through the story much more easily than he had when he'd told it to her, and she could see that he was no longer afraid of being shamed or rejected.

His mother cried, and Emma shouted at him for not telling her what was going on so she could help, and his grandmother scolded him for not bringing Fiona home after he'd bitten her. But no one shamed him. No one rejected him. And everyone told him they loved him. After a while, Fen could see that they were getting into some deep family stuff, and she excused herself and went up to his old bedroom in the attic.

Carter joined her about an hour later. He looked tired and his eyes were reddened, but he was smiling.

"Everything all right?" she asked.

He nodded. "A bit intense, but I guess that's what I get for dodging them for two years."

She beckoned him into bed. Fen was already in it, wearing a pair of Emma's pajamas. "Emma left these for me on the bed. Also a water bottle, a saucer of cookies, and clothes for next morning."

"She's sweet like that."

"They're all sweet. You're lucky to have them."

"I am." He grinned. "They do drive me crazy if I have to interact with them for more than about three days at a time. But in three-day installments, they're great."

"I'm jealous," Fen confessed.

He pulled her close. "Don't be. They're dying to be your family too, you know. All you have to do is let them."

If he'd said that before she met them, she wouldn't have believed it. But now that she had, she knew it was true. They loved her for Carter's sake, but they liked her for her own. His sisters admired her as a strong female entrepreneur, and his grandmother thought her appliances were brilliant, and his mother had an enormous heart and was delighted to acquire another daughter, and his father shared her taste in movies, and the foster elephant kid had been utterly charmed by her willingness to sit on the floor and play *Jumanji.*

Her eyes stung with tears. Blinking hard, she said, "Of course I'll let them."

"They'll be thrilled," he promised her. "Honestly, they're lucky to have you. And they know it."

"I'm the lucky one," said Fen.

"No." Carter kissed her. "I am."

CHAPTER 33

Fen sat with Sugar nestled in her lap as Carter typed up their wedding guest list. They'd already filled in the obvious—family, friends, the Defenders, the women entrepreneur's softball league, and a number of Little Bit and Howe Enterprises employees—and were now getting into the questionable cases.

"I want Norris," said Fen.

Carter rolled his eyes, but typed him in. "If he turns into a giant fish when they ask if anyone has any objections, it's on you."

"I think he'll manage to hold out till the shifters' reception." The wedding was for all the guests, but they were holding two receptions. Like the wedding itself, both were on a tiny, privately owned island, but on different days. One was for the guests who didn't know about shifters, and the other was for shifters and their friends and family. "He can swim all he likes at that one. Anyway, he has to come. I owe him a very special wedding favor."

"That signed copy of *Wired?*"

"You got it." She peered over his shoulder. To her amusement, Precious, who was perched on his shoulder, also peered down at the screen. "Who's next?"

"I want Fiona," said Carter. He shot her a glance as if he expected her to object, but it didn't surprise her. She was part of the Protection,

Inc. west coast team, so either they invited her or they disinvited the rest of the team.

"She can come." Fen supposed it would be healing for him to have her there, though she did hope that would be it as far as his exes were concerned. She certainly didn't plan to invite any of hers. "But I'll tell you who I *don't* want: my parents."

"Good. I don't want them either. They don't deserve a daughter like you, and they don't deserve to attend the wedding of the century."

Fen grinned. The phrasing was from the article in *Vanity Fair*, but she liked to think that it really would be. It was certainly lavish enough.

She glanced around the room. It was their shared home office; she had one for Little Bit and he had one for Howe Enterprises, but they used a third for joint projects. It was currently devoted to wedding planning, with idea boards and wedding dress design proposals and sample menus. Even with the boost in her ability to focus that she'd gotten from her ADHD diagnosis and medication, it was somewhat overwhelming. But she enjoyed big complicated projects with big payoffs, and it was fun to collaborate with Carter.

So many changes, she thought. *A new shift form for him. A new diagnosis for me. Getting pets. Getting married. Joining a team. Leaving a family. Finding a new family.*

New perspectives. New love. A new future, together.

"It's a beautiful night," said Carter. "Want to go for a flight?"

"You bet!" She jumped up, and they took the elevator up to the roof.

The air was a little chilly, but she'd thrown on a warm angora sweater. It was black, of course. She didn't need to change anything else, as she was already wearing black pants. She'd be invisible against the night sky.

Fen caught his hand. "Hey… After we get back, want to be a sexy genius inventor?"

"If you'll be a sexy genius businesswoman."

"Deal."

They kissed for a long moment, and then Carter stepped back. He shifted into his beautiful chimera form, using his color-changing ability so he'd blend in with the night sky. He stretched like a cat, the muscles rippling under his velvety midnight pelt, and stretched out his black wings. Fen settled herself on his back, gripped with her knees, and locked her arms around his neck.

Carter sprang aloft, his magnificent wings beating. Together they soared beneath the stars.

CHAPTER 34

Burn it. The words came in the crackling roar of a forest fire. *Burn it all.*

Roland ignored the voice of his phoenix. This wasn't a time for fire and fighting, but for happiness and love. Everywhere he looked, he saw proof of that.

Fen was radiant in her wedding gown, and Carter was so happy he bordered on unrecognizable. His dragonette perched on his shoulder like a sleek golden accessory, while her sugar glider peeped incongruously from her cleavage as they waltzed together.

Pete and Tirzah were also dancing, improvising to make it work with her wheelchair. Batcat clung to Tirzah's shoulder, her furry wings outstretched for balance and her yellow eyes enormous.

If I could get a magical pet, what would I want? Roland wondered. He liked animals, which was just as well considering the zoo the Defenders office had become—and that wasn't even counting the magical pets, he thought with an inner grin. But his career in the Army had made it impossible to have a pet, and no magical animal had chosen him.

He supposed he could get an ordinary pet now. A nice big dog, maybe. He could take it for runs in the morning, and it would get along with Merlin's Blue. But if he had a pet already, would that drive away that hypothetical magical animal that might otherwise choose him?

"Cake bite?" A waiter offered a tray of bite-sized miniature wedding cakes, copies of the actual one down to the smallest detail.

"Thank you." Roland took one, trying to remember where he'd seen the man before. Then he recalled the Defenders' first case, and a very small alligator shifter in a pink princess dress. "You're Angelica's dad, right? Sorry, I've forgotten your name."

"Sam," he said, smiling. "Carter put out a call in the shifter community for waiters, or people who at least had some waiter experience. I haven't been one since college, but I owed him one. Also, Angelica really wanted to come."

Roland followed Sam's gaze to the window. Out on the beach, a number of little animals were playing at the waterline. He spotted a hamster, several tiger cubs, three seal pups, and a very small alligator. They were supervised by two dads, a mom, and a sea lion.

Out in the water, an enormous prehistoric fish swam with a pair of delighted teenage girls on his back. Pete's daughter Caro and her friend Raelynn rode hands-free, showing off their skills like they were on a bucking bronco. Raelynn's step-mother stood on the shore videoing them on her cell phone. The last time Roland had spotted Norris out the window, he'd been giving rides to the younger kids. Much like Merlin, the Dunkleosteus shifter was clearly in his element entertaining youngsters.

A pang went through Roland as he watched the young folk play. He'd never intended to stay single all his life. He'd always thought some day he'd meet a woman, marry, have kids, and settle down. But time had passed, and he'd never met the right woman, and...

"Angelica looks like she's having a great time," said Roland. He turned away from the window and popped the cake bite in his mouth.

Sam moved on with his tray, leaving Roland alone with the cake bite. It was fluffy and delicious, completely unlike his own attempts at baking. All the desserts at the reception were wonderful. He noticed that Natalie and Ransom had commandeered an entire platter of assorted pastries, and were steadily making their way through them. In between bites, they were having an earnest discussion with Merlin's mother Janet, Carter's grandmother, and Kerenza Couch.

Roland still couldn't believe that the porcupine witch had actually showed up to the wedding. Carter had been positive she wouldn't, but she not only had, she'd brought her familiar. The fat little manticore sat in her lap, incongruously dressed in a fuzzy sweater with a pattern of pink roses. Roland noticed that all the other magical pets were giving it an extremely wide berth.

A burst of laughter rose up. Merlin was entertaining a rapturous audience of small children by juggling ping-pong balls—in his velociraptor form. His mate Dali was holding back his bugbear Blue, who clearly wanted to get in on the action, and laughing until she cried.

Happiness and joy surrounded Roland, everywhere he looked, but he kept coming back to his team. They'd all changed so much since he'd first met them. Carter had forever been hurrying out the door, running from his team and from himself. Ransom had been deeply depressed and self-destructive. Merlin had hidden a desperate loneliness behind a bright exterior. Pete had been full of rage he was afraid to face. They hadn't been a team, they'd been a bunch of angry, unhappy, traumatized misfits with shift forms they hated or powers they couldn't control.

But they weren't just happier now. They were a team. The most rewarding part of being in the Army had been the moment when a bunch of men and women who had nothing much in common transformed into a smoothly functioning unit. The Defenders had been his hardest task yet, but now he saw it achieved. He was proud of them all.

Ashes. The voice of his phoenix was the whispering hiss of flames. *It's all ashes.*

Roland knew what the phoenix meant. Love for others, but never for him. They all had their mates. His had died.

Could he even say he'd had a mate when he'd only met her for a few minutes before he'd become a shifter? But it felt true. Every instant he'd seen her was burned into his memory like a brand.

He could see her now, so vivid in his mind's eye that she seemed to float before it, a ghost at the wedding. She'd been tall and slim, her hands long-fingered, her nails clipped very short. A working woman's hands. Full lips, broad nose, brown eyes brimming with warmth and intelligence and courage. Her skin was a couple shades lighter than his, her silver-streaked hair falling in loose curls around her face. She was the most beautiful woman he'd ever seen—and the bravest.

She hadn't even known him, but she'd fought for his life. She'd *given* her life for him, and she'd died alone. He hadn't been able to fight for her as she'd fought for him, and he hadn't been there to comfort her and hold her hand.

He'd never even know her name.

Burn it all. The voice of his phoenix was the all-consuming roar of a firestorm. *Burn down the world.*

EPILOGUE

Hazel was so exhausted that it took her several tries to unlock her own front door. It had been a satisfying day at the ER, but also a long and tiring one. She figured she had about fifteen minutes left before she'd collapse, and she'd better spend them wisely.

The houseplants were a priority. It had been a hot day, not that she'd had a chance to enjoy the sun, and several were drooping.

You could change that, whispered a voice in her mind like cracking ice. *You could freeze the world.*

Hazel ignored the voice. It subsided, leaving behind a lingering chill.

With the quick, efficient movements that were her hallmark as a nurse, she put the watering pot in the sink, turned on the water, opened a cupboard, unwrapped a granola bar, and ate it with one hand while she watered her plants with the other.

She liked to think they welcomed the attention. The song of India, with its sharp-tipped leaves edged in bright lime-green, seemed to brighten, while the succulent leaves on the trailing vines of the string of pearls seemed to plump up as she watched. Hazel chatted with them as watered them, her words muffled by granola, telling them about her day at the ER and how pretty they were and how happy she was to be back home with them.

One of the benefits of being middle-aged and single, she thought. *You can be as eccentric as you like.*

As always, she saved the prayer plant for last. It had always been a favorite of hers—its red-veined oval leaves were spectacular—but this particular one had a special meaning. It was the only one of her plants that hadn't died from lack of watering when she'd been kidnapped.

"My beautiful survivor," Hazel murmured to it.

As water fell from the pot, tears welled up in her eyes. She'd saved lives that day at the ER. She saved lives every day. So why hadn't she been able to save the life she'd most wanted to preserve? He'd given his life for her, and all her efforts to return the favor had been in vain. She hoped he'd at least known she'd tried.

She could see him now, his face as clear in her mind's eye as if he'd been one of her patients that day. A handsome black man with silvering hair and beard, and humor and courage and passion in his eyes.

I could have loved him, she thought.

Hazel wiped away her tears. She understood trauma, but not why she felt such a desperate longing for a man she'd met for a few minutes years ago. Intellectually, she knew he was long since dead and she'd never meet him in this life again. Emotionally, she felt like she'd loved him her entire life and was always waiting for him to knock on her door.

He's gone, she told herself. *You have to accept that.*

She'd never even know his name.

A NOTE FROM ZOE CHANT

Want to know how Protection, Inc. began? Keep reading for a sneak preview of the first two chapters of the book that started it all, *Bodyguard Bear*. It's the first in the Protection, Inc. series, which contains the first appearances of Carter and the other Defenders characters.

Thank you for reading Defender Chimera! I hope you enjoyed it. The final book in the series will be Roland's book, Defender *Phoenix*.

Shifter Vets is a related series about veterinarians for magical creatures. It has guest appearances by the Defenders and Protection, Inc. characters.

If you enjoy *Protection, Inc.* and *Defenders,* I also write the *Werewolf Marines* series under the pen name of Lia Silver. Both series have hot romances, exciting action, emotional healing, brave heroines who stand up for their men, and strong heroes who protect their mates with their lives.

Please review this book on Amazon, even if you only write a line or two. Hearing from readers like you is what keeps me writing!

THE PROTECTION, INC. SERIES

Bodyguard Bear
Defender Dragon
Protector Panther
Warrior Wolf
Leader Lion
Soldier Snow Leopard
Top Gun Tiger

THE PROTECTION, INC: DEFENDERS SERIES

Defender Cave Bear
Defender Raptor
Defender Hellhound
Defender Chimera

SHIFTER VETS

Unicorn Vet
Bear Vet
Winged Wolf Vet

BODYGUARD BEAR: SNEAK PREVIEW

PROTECTION, INC: # 1
CHAPTER 1

Ellie McNeil was not having the best night of her life.

It was 3:49 AM, and she felt every second of the sleep she hadn't gotten. Her eyes burned, her feet hurt, her head throbbed, and her muscles ached with weariness.

Remind me why I volunteered for the overnight shift, again? Ellie asked herself. *Oh, right. Because I really, really need the money.*

And also, she had to admit, because sometimes there was nothing more exciting than being the paramedic on call in the middle of the night.

This wasn't one of those times.

Ellie and her partner, Catalina Mendez, had taken call after call since their shift had begun at midnight. Every time, they'd sped out in the ambulance with sirens screaming. And not a single call had been for an actual emergency. In between calls, Ellie and Catalina debated over which was more ridiculous, the drunken frat boy who thought his sleeping roommate was dead because he'd stopped snoring or the elderly man who thought he had a fever because he'd forgotten to turn off his electric blanket.

As the ambulance raced through increasingly sketchy neighborhoods, Ellie decided that it wouldn't hurt to close her eyes. Just for a second…

Catalina brought the ambulance to a stop with a screech of brakes, nearly flinging Ellie into the dashboard.

"Wakey, wakey!" Catalina sang out, her voice bright with sadistic cheer. She was a night owl by nature, and volunteered for overnight shifts because she actually preferred them.

"I was *not* asleep," Ellie retorted. "I was just… resting my eyes."

"That's what sleep *is*," Catalina pointed out. "Up and at 'em, Ellie. Just two more hours till we can go home and cuddle up with... Uh, cuddle up."

Ellie repressed a sigh as she grabbed her medical bag. At 6:00 AM, Catalina got to go home and cuddle with her beloved cats. Ellie had nothing to cuddle with but her pillow.

One year, eight months, and two weeks since I last had sex, Ellie thought glumly. Not that she was counting.

It could easily be another year—or two, or five, or ten—till she found a man willing to put up with a woman who spent half her nights saving lives away from home. Catalina made do with short-term flings, but Ellie didn't want to settle for anything less than a committed relationship. Which meant that she'd settled on nothing at all.

When she scrambled out of the ambulance, the icy night air chilled her lungs and face, shocking her to full awareness. She forgot about her weariness and lack of romantic prospects, and focused on her job.

"Review call," she said automatically.

Equally automatically, Catalina recited, "Male, age eighteen, awoke disoriented and combative. Call placed by mother."

"Bet you a pizza he snuck out and partied too hard," Ellie suggested.

Catalina elbowed her in the ribs. "I'm not taking your sucker bets."

The apartment building faced a dark alley too narrow for the ambulance to park in, so they left it on the wider street that the alley intersected. Side by side, they walked down the dark, garbage-strewn alley toward the apartment belonging to the disoriented, combative male and his mom.

Ellie's smile vanished as they hurried up the stairs. She and Catalina might privately joke about their jobs—they had to have a sense of humor, or they'd lose their minds—but once they were in the presence of their patients, the paramedics were completely focused on doing the best they could for them. Even if the teenage boy was just drunk or high, Ellie and Catalina would examine him, make sure he was all right, and reassure his worried mother.

The woman who opened the door was tiny and white-haired, ninety if she was a day. "Oh, thank God you're here! My poor baby Ricky!"

Ellie frowned in confusion as she followed the woman, who seemed way too old to have an eighteen-year-old son. Maybe the 911 operator had misheard "grandmother" as "mother."

The old woman pointed dramatically. "Here he is!"

Ellie bit down on her lower lip to stop herself from bursting out laughing.

Ricky was a fat, fluffy, contented-looking Angora cat. He blinked big blue eyes and yawned at them from his perch on the back of the sofa.

"Ricky is a cat," Catalina said, her voice quivering slightly.

"He's my baby," the old woman corrected them. "I woke up and went to get a drink of water, and I reached out to pet him as I passed by. He always purrs when I pet him, but tonight he meowed and twitched his head like he was going to bite me. My poor baby!"

"I think you just startled him," Ellie said soothingly.

The old woman shot her a doubtful look. "I guess that could be it. He does look better now. Don't you, baby?" She bent her head and nuzzled her cat, who purred loudly. "But better safe than sorry! Aren't you going to examine him, just to be sure?"

Fighting to keep a straight face, Ellie said, "Catalina, why don't you do the exam? I'll go radio the hospital with our estimated time of return."

As she walked past her partner, Catalina whispered, "You owe me a pizza."

"Come on, you love cats," Ellie whispered back, and made her escape.

Once she was safely out the door, she gave in to laughter. Poor baby Ricky, the world's most pampered cat!

She was still smiling as she walked down the stairs. It was calls like these that reminded her of why she loved being a paramedic, despite the crazy hours and the lonely nights at home. Whatever else you could say about the job, it was never boring.

Ellie entered the alley. Blinking down the dark strip of asphalt, lined with garbage cans and buildings with darkened windows, she tried to remember which end of the alley led to the street where they'd left the ambulance. One dented trash can looked vaguely familiar. Yawning, she turned right.

The alley stretched on for longer than she remembered walking when they'd first come to the apartment. There were no street lights, and everything was dim and shadowy. The still air smelled strongly of mold, oil, and rotting garbage. There was no sound but the occasional rumble of a car driving by several streets away.

Uneasy, Ellie wondered if she'd gone the wrong way. One step later, and she came to a dead end at a brick wall. It was a T-shaped intersection, with even darker and narrower alleys leading to the left and right.

Definitely the wrong way, she thought. She turned around to go back.

"Are you sure he's dead?" The question, in a man's low voice, came from the alley to her left.

Ellie froze in her tracks. Obviously, someone was in desperate need of medical help. Normally she'd have run forward to offer her assistance. But the speaker's tone chilled her blood. She felt certain that he *wanted* someone to be dead.

"I'm pretty sure, Mr. Nagle," said a different man, sounding slightly nervous. "I shot him three times."

Ellie knew that the best thing for her to do was to walk away quietly and call the police. But she hadn't become a paramedic because she liked to play it safe. She stepped behind a dumpster, careful to place her feet away from anything that might snap or squish or crunch. Her heart pounding, she cautiously peered out into the alley. Though the light was dim, her eyes had adjusted to it. She could see perfectly.

Two men stood in the alley, looking down at the limp body of a third man. One of the standing men was in his fifties, tall and gray-haired, dressed in a black suit that looked out of place in the filthy surroundings. The other was in his late twenties, a big bruiser in jeans and a blood-spattered T-shirt, holding a gun. But it was the sight of the man down on the ground that made Ellie stifle a gasp.

She wasn't shocked because he was bleeding, or because he might be dead. Ellie had cared for lots of injured people, and seen her share of dead-on-arrival bodies. What shocked her was that she recognized the man.

She didn't know him personally, but she was familiar with his face. She'd voted for him at the last election, barely three months ago. He was Bill Whitfield, the new district attorney of Santa Martina. He'd run on the promise to fight organized crime.

He was dead. She'd been a paramedic long enough to know that, even from a distance. There was nothing she could do for him.

"Shoot him again," the tall man ordered. "In the head. Execution-style. Just to send a message."

"Okay, Mr. Nagle," the younger man— the hit man— replied.

He adjusted his aim, then shot the dead man in the head. The gun must have been silenced; it made a soft popping sound, not a loud bang.

Ellie flinched. Her heart was beating so hard, she felt like it would smash through her ribs. She had to get out of there and call the police, before these men saw her and killed her too. She took one last look, memorizing their faces, then turned to tiptoe away.

A rat emerged from beneath the dumpster and scurried over her foot. She jerked backward, barely managing to stop herself from letting out a yelp. But the rat was as surprised as she was. It bolted madly into a nearby heap of beer bottles and soda cans, producing a tremendous clatter.

"What's that?" demanded Mr. Nagle.

"Someone's there!" the hit man shouted.

Ellie flung herself forward. She was still moving when she heard another soft pop. The bullet barely missed her head, hitting the brick wall beside her. Chips and dust exploded out, and a sharp pain stung her cheek.

She ran like she'd never run in her life. Sheer terror lent her speed. She heard the men shouting behind her, and then another soft pop. Her lungs burned as she forced herself to go faster, expecting any second to feel the impact of a bullet in her back. Or to feel a brief explosion of pain in her head, and then nothing ever again.

Ellie burst out of the alley, looked around wildly, and spotted the ambulance. She yanked out her keys, dove for the rear door, wrenched it open, and scrambled into the rear compartment. She heard another soft pop as she slammed the heavy metal door. Ellie flinched, but she felt no pain. She hadn't been hit.

She scrambled forward and slammed her hand into the button that turned on the lights and siren. Bright lights flashed, and the siren screamed.

Ellie hoped that would be enough to scare the murderers away, but she had one more way to make sure. She hit the button that projected her voice outside of the ambulance. Usually she and Catalina used it to order careless drivers to get out of their way.

"GET AWAY FROM THE AMBULANCE." Ellie's voice boomed out, amplified and deepened. "I'VE HIT THE EMERGENCY ALERT. THE SWAT TEAM IS ON ITS WAY."

There was no emergency alert, unfortunately. But she bet the murderers didn't know that.

Black spots suddenly danced before her eyes, and she felt her knees give way. She sank down to the floor, dazedly thinking, *So this is what it feels like to be so scared that you pass out.*

Then she remembered that when she saw patients on the verge of collapsing from shock, she told them to put their head between their knees. Ellie put her head between her knees. Slowly, her vision cleared, though she still felt shaky. She fumbled for the radio button, and finally got it turned on.

"Ellie McNeil here," she said. "Paramedic on duty at Ambulance Forty-Nine. I've just witnessed a murder."

Ellie sucked down the dregs of her fifth cup of black coffee and glanced at her watch. 1:00 PM. If she'd had a normal night at work, she'd be at home now, fast asleep. If she was a normal person with a normal job, she'd be eating lunch.

Instead, she'd spent the last eight hours at a police station, telling and re-telling her story to multiple sets of detectives, and identifying photos of the men she'd seen. Whoever the murderers were, the police knew about them; the hit man had his photo in one of the books of mug shots, and Mr. Nagle had appeared in an envelope of photos a detective had shown her.

Ellie yawned again, wishing the police had allowed Catalina to stay and keep her company. Catalina had offered, but the police had sent her home. Now Ellie was exhausted *and* bored. The cops had given her coffee and sandwiches, but she'd been awake for twenty-four hours now, with no sign of being allowed to leave. And they'd been crappy sandwiches and worse coffee.

Worst of all, the last cop who'd spoken to her, Detective Kramer, had confiscated her purse to "take it into evidence." Then she'd been left alone in a tiny room without even her cell phone to distract her. There were a few magazines on a side table, but one was *Popular Mechanics*—a subject she had less than zero interest in—and the others were news magazine that were nearly old enough to vote.

Just when she'd gotten desperate enough to dip into ancient news, Detective Kramer returned with her purse. "Sorry about that. Just procedure."

Ellie gratefully took her purse. "Thanks. Can I go home now? You've got my number. You can call me whenever you arrest those guys, and I can come in and ID them."

Detective Kramer rolled his eyes. Sarcastically, he said, "Sure you will."

"Why wouldn't I?" she asked.

The detective gave her a startled look, then slowly whistled. "I thought you were putting me on. But you really have no idea who Mr. Nagle is, do you?"

Frustrated, Ellie snapped, "No! Now will you please tell me what's going on?"

Detective Kramer sat down across from her. "Have you ever seen a movie called *The Godfather*? Nah, you're probably too young..."

"Of course I've seen it."

"Nice to know people still watch the classics," the detective remarked. "Well, Wallace Nagle is the Godfather. He's the head of organized crime in Santa Martina. No one testifies against him, because—"

"They'd wake up with a horse head in their bed," Ellie said. She'd thought the night couldn't get any worse, but her stomach lurched at the memory of that gory scene.

Detective Kramer raised his eyebrows. "They wouldn't wake up at all. As you saw. Now, I can offer you Witness Protection..."

"You mean, I change my name, leave Santa Martina, move to some tiny town no one's ever heard of, get a different job, and never have any contact with any of my friends or family for the rest of my life?"

"That's right."

"No way," Ellie said. Imagine never seeing her brother Ethan again! Or Catalina. "Absolutely not. Who'd do that?"

"No one." With a sigh, the detective stood up. "Well, thank you for your time. Pity you won't testify, but that's the way it goes. You can go home now."

He turned and headed for the door.

Ellie jumped up, raising her voice to halt him. "Wait a second. I never said I wouldn't testify. I just won't go into Witness Protection."

Detective Kramer froze, then slowly turned to face her. "Let me make sure I heard you right. You're not willing to do Witness Protection, but you *are* willing to testify against Wallace Nagle."

"That's right."

"You realize that he's going to try to kill you. And that he can. Easily. I appreciate your courage, Ms. McNeil, but unless you go into Witness Protection, you won't live to testify."

The detective's words made Ellie's entire body tingle with anxiety. But she'd seen an innocent man ruthlessly murdered. How could she *not* testify, no matter how dangerous it was?

But she wasn't willing to give up her entire life, either. How could she agree to abandon her family and friends, and never see or speak to any of them again? She didn't want to give up her job— she loved being a paramedic in the big city. And on the off-chance that she found a man who loved *her*, job and all, how could she have a real relationship when she could never even tell him her real name?

On the other hand, she'd never have a relationship with anyone if she got shot by one of Mr. Nagle's hit men.

Ellie bit her lip, trying to think of alternatives to ruining her life, ending her life, or letting a vicious murderer get away with it. Catalina wasn't just her partner, she was her best friend. But good as she was at emergency medicine and pedal-to-the-metal driving, she couldn't fight off a hit man. Ellie's twin brother Ethan was completely capable of protecting her, but he was on some secret Marine mission. He wouldn't be able to leave it even if she had any way of contacting him, which she didn't.

"Can't the police protect me?" Ellie asked. "You want to put Nagle away, right? Then keep me alive so I can do it."

"We don't have a budget for round-the-clock protection," Detective Kramer replied.

At that point, Ellie's stress hit maximum. She wasn't hot-tempered normally, but hearing that the cops couldn't afford to save her life made anger burn through her body. "I bet your boss could find some money for getting rid of the Godfather! If you can't help me, I want to talk to the watch commander."

"That won't be necessary," Detective Kramer began.

"I want to talk to the watch commander," Ellie repeated.

"He's busy."

She folded her arms across her chest. "Fine. He can see me when he's ready. But I'm not leaving till I've talked to him."

The detective seemed taken aback. "Hold on. I'll see what I can do."

He hurried out. The door shut behind him, leaving her alone and feeling like she'd just made the worst mistake of her life. She couldn't bring herself to deny what she'd seen, but the idea of being hunted like an animal made her heart start pounding again.

I'll be safe, she told herself. *The watch commander will find the money, and then I'll have a police officer to protect me.*

The thought didn't make her feel much better. Detective Kramer might be good at solving crimes, but he looked like he spent more time eating donuts than chasing down criminals. And while the detectives she'd spoken to had been nice, several of the patrol officers had openly ogled her curves when she'd walked through the station.

With the luck she was having that night, she'd probably get Officer Creeper, one step up from a mall cop. He'd stare at her generous breasts and big ass, get in her way as she tried to work, lurk creepily in his car outside her apartment at night, and shed a trail of donut crumbs wherever he went. He'd breathe heavily and stand way too close to her. And if anyone attacked her, he'd be so out of shape that *she'd* have to protect *him.*

Worst night of my life, Ellie thought.

CHAPTER 2

Hal Brennan was exercising alone in the gym of Protection, Inc., when he got the call.

Stinging sweat dripped into his eyes, and even his powerful muscles felt the burn as he lifted the bench press bar high. But one of the advantages of owning your own private security company was having your own private gym. He and the other shifters on his team could lift weights heavier than any normal human could manage without having to worry that some outsider would see them and contact the Guinness Book of World Records.

Weight-lifting wasn't his favorite form of exercise. That honor went to hiking in the woods, preferably as a grizzly bear. But as far as gym-based exercise went, lifting was the best. Living in a city—hell, being human—was so damn complicated. It made him appreciate things that were simple. And lifting was as simple as it got. No rules to tie him down. Just Hal vs. the iron. It was as close as he could get while human to feeling like a bear, with a bear's straightforward desires.

The shrill tone of his cell phone broke his concentration. It was his private phone, with a number he gave out only to a select few. Which meant that the call was from his parents or a member of his team, or some kind of emergency. Whatever it was, he couldn't ignore it.

Hal replaced the bar on its rest and reached down from the bench to pluck his phone from his gym bag. He glanced at the screen. Yep. Parents.

"Hi, Dad," Hal said. "How's it going?"

His father's deep, gravelly voice, which everyone said sounded just like Hal's, rumbled out from the phone. "How's your search for a mate going?"

Hal grimaced. "It's not."

"Why not?" Dad demanded, as if they hadn't had this conversation a hundred times already. "Get out there and look for her! Your mother wants grand-cubs."

"You mean, *you* want grand-cubs."

Unruffled, Dad replied, "The entire clan wants grand-cubs."

There was a scuffling noise, and then he heard his mother's voice. "It makes us so sad to think of you all alone in the big city." She gave a melodramatic sigh. "Aaaaall aloooooone."

Hal was torn between the desire to laugh and the urge to throw the phone across the room. "I'm hardly alone. I have my team. You know how close we are. We're like brothers and sisters."

As if she hadn't even heard him, Mom repeated, "Aaaaall aloooooone. The city is no place for a bear. It's full of violence and loud noises and electric things. Bears need a peaceful, quiet life, fishing and eating honey and sleeping in the sun. Drop this silly city thing and come back to the woods."

"Mom," Hal said, trying to keep a grip on his patience. "Dad. We've had this talk. I'm not like you. I need excitement. I need danger. I need to make a difference to people. And I'm not going to find any of that in the woods. There is absolutely nothing in the forest that can threaten a bear."

"Who wants to be threatened?" Dad asked.

At the same time, Mom exclaimed, "I want cute, furry grand-cubs to love and spoil! Go find a mate and settle down!"

"Mom..." Hal sighed. "I don't *want* a mate. And I don't want to settle down. I like my life exactly the way it is. I do my own thing, and no one tells me what to do. My job is dangerous and unpredictable. I have to run off to deal with emergencies on a moment's notice. No woman is going to want a man who lives like that. And I don't want to make some nice woman miserable trying to change me into something I'm not."

"You'll think differently once you actually meet your mate," said Dad. "You'll be willing to make any sacrifice."

"You *need* a mate," Mom said earnestly.

"I don't need anyone," Hal argued, frustrated. "I can handle anything the world can throw at me. By myself!"

"All bears need a mate," Dad replied.

Hal gave up. "I have to get back to work. Talk to you later!"

He hung up, dropped his phone back in his back, and settled back on the weightlifting bench. Hal loved his parents and his clan, but he'd lose his mind if he had to live with them. The forest was great for a vacation, but he wasn't made for a peaceful life. And he had absolutely no desire to settle down.

My mate, he thought, unable to help himself. *I wonder what she's like? I don't need her, but does* she *need* me? *Am I screwing up* her *life by not looking for her?*

He hoped not. With any luck, she'd find someone else she could be happy with.

An unexpected pang of loneliness stabbed right through his heart at the thought of his mate with another man, followed by a surge of possessiveness.

No one but us gets our mate, Hal's bear growled.

"I don't need anyone!" Hal's voice rang out, startling himself. He hadn't meant to speak aloud.

He took a deep breath, trying to regain the sense of peace he'd felt when he'd been lifting. Eventually it returned, washing over him like a cool shower.

He'd just reached for the bar to do another set when his phone rang *again.*

"Goddammit," he muttered to himself, then picked it up. This time it was his main police contact in Santa Martina, Watch Commander Carl Gutierrez.

"Brennan," Hal said. "What's the emergency?"

Hal listened to the watch commander's story with growing amazement. "She's going to testify against *Nagle?* Seriously?"

"She is. And that's not all," Gutierrez said grimly. "She's refused to go into Witness Protection. So I need your help. I've found a grant to pay for her to be protected around the clock. I want the best person you have."

Hal opened his mouth to say that he didn't hire anyone who wouldn't be the best person at any other security company, and anyone on his team could protect the witness. Instead, he heard himself saying, "I'll guard her myself."

He headed to the locker room to shower, wondering all the while why he felt so compelled to take on the assignment. He rarely did straightforward bodyguard work. Maybe he was drawn to the challenge of protecting someone the Godfather of Santa Martina was gunning for.

As he was getting dressed, two of his team members came in. Of all his team, Nick and Lucas probably had the least in common, which was why Hal had assigned them to work together. He'd hoped it would break the ice.

Nick entered first, slamming the door open like he wanted to knock some sense into it.

"Hold the door." Lucas's hard-to-place accent made even those simple words sound like a line from some very classy play.

"Don't fucking order me around." Nick gave the door a shove back, apparently hoping to slam it in Lucas's face.

A hand adorned with several gold rings caught the door, then gave it a matching shove that threatened to knock it off the hinges.

If Hal didn't move fast, ice wouldn't be the only thing that got broken. He cleared his throat.

Nick whipped around to look at him. His surprise was briefly replaced with a "who're you looking at" challenge that Hal hadn't seen directed at him in a while. Then the challenge vanished. It had been a long time since Nick had been the alpha of a criminal werewolf pack, fighting ferociously to maintain his power.

"Hey, Hal." Nick stripped off his shirt and armored vest, then tossed them aside, exposing a muscular torso covered in an elaborate tattoo of wolves hunting deer in a deep, dark forest. They were shifter tats, so they were less obviously criminal than if he'd belonged to a human gang. But Hal knew what they meant. One drop of blood on a deer for each fight won, one drop of blood on a wolf for each fight lost, and one dead deer for each kill.

"Hi, Nick," Hal said.

Lucas strolled in, radiating unconcern. "Good day, Hal."

"Hi, Lucas."

Lucas removed his shirt and bullet-proof vest, then set them neatly down on the bench. His angular chest was marked by an intricate pattern, glittering gold. It looked like a tattoo, but Hal knew he'd been born with it.

Hal made sure he was looking at both of them as he asked, "How's the job going?"

"Fine," Nick said shortly.

"It goes well," Lucas replied.

Hal stared at them until they both dropped their gaze. He didn't believe in micro-managing his team, but he also didn't believe in letting problems simmer till they exploded.

"Is there an actual problem, or do you two just wish you had a different partner?" Hal inquired.

The men glanced at each other, Nick's green eyes meeting Lucas's golden ones, and seemed to come to a truce.

"No problem," said Nick. "Guess I'm just used to working with someone I can have a beer with after work."

"There is no problem. I am not used to working with…" Lucas

paused just long enough to make it sound like he was about to say something stunningly insulting, then concluded, "…others."

Hal addressed both of them as he said, "Well, get used to it. I'm about to take a bodyguard assignment myself, so I won't be around to babysit."

As he'd intended, the men stopped shooting pissed-off glances at each other, and turned their pissed-off glances on Hal.

"Yeah, whatever, man," Nick said. "We're cool."

"Babysitting is not required," Lucas replied icily.

They went into the gym together, leaving Hal alone. He caught a snatch of their conversation just before the door closed. It didn't sound friendly, but at least it didn't sound hostile. It seemed like his ploy had worked.

Lucas was his newest hire, and it was always hard to join a team that had already bonded with each other. Hal had assembled his team one by one, so everyone on it had been the new guy once. But even on a team of shifters, Lucas stood out. Hal hadn't even known his kind of shifter existed until they'd met.

Hal set aside thoughts of his team as he left the locker room and went to the parking garage. He had his own job to focus on now.

As he drove to the police station, he couldn't stop wondering about his new client, Eleanor McNeil. What sort of woman was brave or crazy enough to agree to testify against Nagle? That man practically ruled the city.

Hal would have understood it if she'd been a criminal herself, desperate to cut a deal to escape prison. But according to Gutierrez, she was an ordinary citizen: a working woman, a paramedic on the late shift. She must be terrified. She was probably regretting her decision already.

He pulled into the police parking lot and went into the station, half-convinced that he'd find that she had changed her mind about testifying and gone home.

Watch Commander Gutierrez indicated a room. "She's in there."

Mildly surprised, Hal headed for the door. He had to duck his head to go in. Most places weren't built for men his size.

Eleanor McNeil sat with an empty paper coffee cup in her lap, her head lowered, her hair hanging forward to hide her face. She seemed to have dozed off in her chair. Everything about her posture spoke of utter exhaustion, which didn't surprise him. She'd worked a full shift, then witnessed a murder and nearly gotten killed herself, and then had been questioned at a police station for eight hours, with no time to sleep in between any of it. Talk about a rough night!

He couldn't see her face behind a tumble of curling dark blonde hair. It was a pretty color; it reminded him of clover honey. Her practical paramedic uniform didn't conceal her generous curves. Though her shirt and pants were cut loosely, Hal could see the shape of her wide hips, her plump thighs, and her lush breasts. She had exactly the sort of body he liked: soft and curvy.

Hal forced himself to stop that train of thought. He'd come to protect her, not to hit on her. The fact that she was incredibly hot was completely irrelevant. Unfortunately.

He cleared his throat. "Excuse me."

"Wha—" She jumped, her head jerking up. So she *had* been dozing.

Hal stepped forward, holding out his hand. "Hi. I'm Hal Brennan, your bodyguard."

"I'm Ellie McNeil," she said sleepily. "Oh. I guess you know that already."

She pushed her hair out of her face and looked up. Their eyes met.

The force of the contact nearly knocked Hal backwards. It was an earthshaking, heart-stopping jolt of recognition.

Mine!

The roar of Hal's bear was so loud that he half-expected her to have heard it. But of course, she hadn't. She just sat there, her head tilted quizzically, her kissable pink lips parted in a smothered yawn.

Everything about her was perfect, from her snub nose to her blue-green eyes to the sprinkling of freckles on her upper arms. He knew nothing about her other than that she was a paramedic and beautiful and sexy and incredibly brave, but he loved her already.

Holy shit, Hal thought. *She's my mate.*

He was nearly overwhelmed with joy. There was the other half of his heart and soul, sitting right there in front of him. If he took a single step forward, he could sweep her into his arms, kiss her and caress her, and never let her go. They'd be together forever.

If Nagle didn't kill her first.

Hal was jerked from happiness to a protective fury in the blink of an eye. He'd finally found his mate, and the most powerful crime lord in the city was trying to murder her.

He knew then that he'd give his life to protect her.

"Mr. Brennan?" she asked. "Are you feeling all right?"

Hal was jerked back into reality. Ellie was peering at him, looking concerned. God knew what sort of weird impression he'd just made on her.

"Yeah," Hal said shortly. He couldn't think of anything but getting her away from Nagle, immediately. "Come on, let's go."

"Oh, good." She stood up, then swayed wearily.

He caught her elbow, steadying her. Her arm was warm and soft in his hand. "Easy. I know you're tired. You can sleep in my car."

Ellie straightened, rubbing her eyes. "I'm not *that* tired. My apartment is only about ten minutes from the station."

He shook his head as he began to lead her to the door. "We're not going to your apartment. You have to get out of the city."

She stopped abruptly, pulling her arm out of his grasp. "I'm not leaving the city. Didn't Watch Commander Gutierrez explain that to you? He said he was assigning me someone to protect me here, in Santa Martina."

Hal turned to look her in the eyes, trying to convey how serious he was. "First of all, I'm not a police officer. I'm private security."

She looked dismayed rather than relieved at that. "You're a *security guard?*"

"I'm not a mall cop," Hal replied. "I run an elite private security company. We provide bodyguards for politicians and celebrities—and private citizens like you. Nobody's ever been hurt under our protection."

"Oh. Well, great. Then you can protect me right here."

"No!" Hal exclaimed. "I have to get you out of the city!"

Ellie's ocean-colored eyes narrowed, reminding him that she was one tough woman. "Mr. Brennan, can you protect me or not?"

Hal gritted his teeth. Of course he could protect her—he'd showed up expecting to guard her right there in Santa Martina. But that was before he'd known that she was his mate. His instincts, not to mention his bear, were roaring at him to not merely stand between her and any possible threat, but to get her far away from anyone who might try to harm her.

"Because if you can't," she went on, "I'll talk to the watch commander again and ask him to assign a police officer."

"I can protect you," Hal said immediately. "But you'd be a lot safer if you left Santa Martina."

"I already had this conversation," Ellie replied. "I'm not going anywhere. I already ran through my sick leave this year. If I take off for more than a couple days, I lose my job. Anyway, I thought no one ever got hurt under your protection."

Take her home and keep her safe, Hal's bear demanded. *Grab her and carry her away to the forest!*

I can't do that, Hal replied. *But I will take her home. To* my *home.*

"All right," Hal told her. "I'll guard you here. But you can't go straight to your apartment. I need to have my team check it first."

"Check it for what?"

"Hit men. Bombs."

"Oh." The delicate skin of her throat bobbed as she swallowed. He could see the fear under her cool exterior, and it made him want to kill the men who had frightened her.

He laid his hand on her shoulder. Touching her, even through cloth, gave him a surge of desire. It was hard to do nothing but keep his palm there, comforting and still, when he wanted to scoop her into his arms, kiss her, and hold her safe and tight.

He still couldn't believe how completely right everything about her felt. With thinner women, Hal always worried he'd hurt them by accident. They seemed so fragile, especially given how big and strong he was. But with a woman like Ellie, plump and voluptuous, he wouldn't have to worry about anything but whether she was enjoying herself as much as he was. Besides, he liked the way curvy women felt. He imagined running his hands over the gentle swell of her belly, the delicious weight of her breasts, the silky softness of her thighs…

Hal forced his mind away from those fantasies. She'd shown no sign of responding to him the way he had to her. She wasn't a shifter—she knew nothing of mates. He had to give her time to get to know him. In the meantime, he had to be professional.

"I swear, I'll keep you safe," Hal said, willing her to believe it.

Ellie let out a sigh and leaned into his hand, as if she liked having it there. Then, to his disappointment, she pulled away. "So, do we go to a hotel?"

"No. We're going to my place. I have a guest bedroom."

"Why not a hotel? Security, again?"

Because I want to welcome you into my home, Hal thought. *Because it'll make* me *feel safe knowing that you're in my lair, where I can protect you.*

Fishing for a reason that would make sense to her, he said, "Yeah, security. And…" His gaze fell on the empty coffee cup. "It's got a cappuccino machine."

For the first time, Ellie smiled. It was like the first bright burst of sunlight on a cloudy day. Sure, it was at the promise of coffee rather than at him, but he'd take it. "Cappuccino, huh? Lead on."

Made in the USA
Monee, IL
01 June 2023